* * *

Shuffle an Impulse

*** Survival Instinct ***

The most powerful emotion a human brain exhibits

Dedicated to Shawn Paul Delorey

[1989 - 2013]

***

Published in the United States of America

WordWizard Publications

**411 Walnut Street Suite 6317
Green Cove Springs, Florida 32043**

Shuffle an Impulse
A work of fiction

ISBN: 978-0-9970410-2-6

www.billdelorey.com

Shuffle an Impulse

By William Delorey
(c) 2015

Cover Design: J Lacy Coughlan
Copy Editor: J Lacy Coughlan
Content Editor: Susan Carr
Cover Images: Bill Delorey

Special thanks always to Genie
for her support and encouragement over the years

Thanks to Susan Carr for her excellent editorial contributions

Thanks to Professor Luke Wallin and Writer Michael Lee
A little piece of both of you resides in everything I write

Thanks to my colleagues
Dr. Fred Bercovitch and Dr. Marc Whaley
Their professional contributions in the fields of behavior, biology, and
psychiatry bring realism to these characters and the biological triggers that
rule all life.

And to athlete and trainer Mike Decker for all you did when it mattered -
Thanks Mike ...

www.billdelorey.com

*** Emotion ***

Fundamental human consciousness embraces equally the magic of delight and the torment of rage whilst the brain alone remains pungent but reposed amidst the angst of choosing

Shuffle an Impulse

Aging gracefully, superbly maintained, the regal structure resembles a medieval castle spread across a grassy knoll. A newly paved driveway cuts between a pair of black wrought-iron gates and leads uphill to its sculptured stone and masonry fascia. Dark slate walls absorb bright autumn sunlight, defeating temporarily in its own quiet way the rage that burns within. Short stout maple trees shade the grounds during hot summer months but now stand naked in an early November freeze.

Deceivingly docile at first glance, chilling upon a second, the medical research center spreads across two acres covered with neatly trimmed plantings and red cedar chips, and confines the most disruptive and sadistic mental patients in the country.

Haunting and unapproachable, its silent grandeur preens in the breeze as if its keepers embrace the brutality and fierceness it conceals. Violence rolls over this facility like a continuous nasty fog.

A Beauty and her Beasts...

*

A bell rings twice, the call to dinner. A security officer toggles a switch. Six cell doors in each residential unit remotely unlock and remain unlocked for exactly five minutes before and after each meal. Twenty-four doors swing open simultaneously and thirty-nine men step out, some alone, some in pairs.

Inside his cell, a short, wiry inmate opens his eyes and flips back a gray cotton sheet. Walter Ferguson stares at his clock. A white face and black numerals document the hours and minutes, a thin red arrow ticks off the seconds. Obsession and compulsion rule his life. He lifts one finger each time the red spike cycles past twelve, and counts four minutes aloud.

"One ... Two ... Three ... Four." He hops off his bunk, quickly wiggles into orange coveralls, and wraps a blue scarf around his neck. Less than a minute remains.

Ferguson peeks out his door, cocks an ear in each direction, listens carefully. Silence. He glances left and right along the hallway, checking for demons or spooks. As always, he finds the corridor empty and hurries toward the dining hall, continuously glancing over one shoulder then the other. He exits the corridor through an open steel gate and enters the common space. Six cell doors and the steel gate bang shut and lock.

A security officer barks, "Forty," steps out and locks the gate behind him. "Full tally." The officer glances at the clock and marks a chart. "Seventeen-oh-six."

In its main residential wing, a fat green stripe defines a no-walk boundary bordering the food counter.

Inmates shuffle along the lane. Each one lifts his tray and watches a server fill the slots – corn, mashed potatoes, brown gravy, a chicken chunk, a frosted cake square, and a milk carton or juice box. Each man sits and wraps his arms around his portion, glances over a shoulder, watching his back and guarding his grub. The eyes dart everywhere. No trust amongst felons, a world filled with fear and suspicion.

Ferguson picks up a tray, and pokes the last man in line. The inmate looks back once and steps aside. Ferguson takes his place, and taps the next man. The man turns, looks into two cold dark eyes glaring directly back at his own, and steps aside. Ferguson edges up another notch and pokes again, three more times he moves up, filling his tray as he goes. He suddenly stops and hops backward one quick step.

Walter Ferguson frequently envisions demonic hallucinations that arc around in his brain and scream orders at him, demanding violence. Unable to resist its spell eleven years ago, Ferguson received four consecutive life sentences for killing his housemates, a very nasty and bloody mess, a butcher knife and a fireplace poker helped. Now, he stands wide-eyed and points a finger at the next man in line, a red-haired convict.

He sets his tray on the counter. "Hold still Harry, I'll knock it off." He slaps Harry Parker from behind, a left then a right palm pop on each ear.

Parker drops his tray and raises his arms as the assault continues. The tray bounces off the concrete floor and food splatters both men. Fear and anger redden his face as Parker ducks sideways and begs, "No Fergie, please, not again!"

Ferguson snaps a quick fist, opens a cut over one eye, a second blow splits his lip. Parker covers up and jerks away. Ferguson swings again, another punch drops his victim to the floor, both nostrils leaking blood.

Parker curls into a fetal ball. Bright red fluid drips off his chin and stains his coveralls. Ferguson grabs the shirtfront, muscles his victim up off the concrete and punches again, his knuckle cuts a cheek this time.

"Got it Harry, gonna save your life even if it hurts, just lie still a minute and let me kill it." His fist lands once more, aimed at an imaginary demon hiding behind Parker's left ear, a demon only Ferguson can see. He frequently imagines a similar demon on other friends as well, always eager to rip it off and protect his pals.

Ferguson cocks a fist. Two security officers tackle him, wrap zip-straps around his wrists and ankles, then jerk him to his feet and shuffle him out into the corridor. "Wait, wait, gotta get my tray," Ferguson howls, squirming back toward the chow line. The burly guards ignore his squawk and hustle him along the hall and into an isolation cell. No food tray, a major penalty, much worse than lockdown or a beating.

An inmate assists the injured man and sits him at a table. Parker grabs a napkin, wipes the blood and sweat off his face, dabs gingerly at the cuts. A vivid red bruise begins swelling beneath each eye. A food server offers ice wrapped in a towel. Harry Parker hunches over and leans his face into the cool cloth, pain spilling down his cheeks.

"Gonna miss dinner now I bet," Parker grumbles into the wet red towel.

1

A young athlete pushes his mountain bike through the brush, lays it down beside a tent centered in a small clearing, and drops a blue tarp over it, protecting it from dew and pine pitch. The tarp catches maple leaves and dead needles that began falling this month, too. Be chilling up soon.

He sits on a stump, ignites his Coleman, drops a teabag into a cup, and hides from the rangers, most of them anyway. One girl ranger he met and befriended sneaks him food two, three times a week at least. She brings him soap occasionally, so he can clean himself and his clothes.

He chops his hair short with a razor blade wrapped in tape, keeps the sweat from sticking it to his head and neck when he runs. He slips over and uses the washroom late at night so no park officials see him, a two-week maximum stay in this park and if a ranger finds his home, he'll lose it. He hides his tent in the woods, no marked site and off the trails. That helps.

He sips his tea, worries about his future, hopes his work picks up. Been a bit slow lately, no wind, no storms, no down trees. Sonny likes storms. Bothers his living space - the wind does - but it gets his chainsaw working.

A low scratchy voice whines a few words back in a corner of his mind, scares him a little, getting louder lately, making demands. *That ranger wants to lock you up. Better give her a flat tire, poke your knife in it. It's easy.* The voice comes more often lately, a little louder, a little meaner. Sonny ignores it.

His eyes circle the camp, pause beside each thicket, each bush, watching for a spook spying on him. Finds nothing but trees, brush, and rocks. Finally, he sneaks in under a shrub growing a few yards behind his tent, flips over a stone, spends a few seconds and twists up a bud then rolls the stone back quickly. He crawls back out and squats beside the stump, touches a match to its tip and soaks up its relief.

"Never inhaled, Clinton once claimed." He whispers the words aloud, inhales a second time, grinning. "What a mistake."

An imaginary spook engages his mind now and again, mostly at night, never lets him rest easy, keeps his mind tight and twitchy. The alien entity sits in his brain, a figment of dysfunctional brain chemistry.

Started a year or so ago when hormones began pushing into his bio-system. It arcs across his mind as if it somehow belongs, barks at him, orders him around like a supervisor, like the boss of his life. Smoke helps push the voice away, allows him sleep.

Running and heavy sweat beats it down too, a lesson he learned accidentally. One day he realized when he sweats he never hears it, so he hit the trails harder and proved it. Wears himself out some days just pushing out the anger, pulling in the silence, outrunning that nasty voice.

He checks inside the tent, his bag and pillow lie beside two clothing piles, one stack clean, one stack worn a day or two, sometimes three. His saw sits on a flat brick, chained to a tree limb through a small hole he cut in the tent wall for that purpose, keeps the saw dry inside, and safe. If a thief wants it, he has to earn it not just grab it.

He owns one power saw, a Stihl 290 he babies and carries in a crossbar saddle while he knocks on doors. Two round files and a few miscellaneous wrenches complete his tool kit. An axe and a splitter maul lie beside it. He earns his pay clearing brush and cutting broken tree limbs all over town, keeps himself fed. People pay him to cut broken trees he packs out and sells to others that need firewood. Smart thinking.

Cooler weather slipping in now and winter gets much tougher in these woods.

Last few months though, a haunting voice been gabbing at him even during the daylight hours, growing stronger, and pushing harder, not so easy now, sending it off somewhere else. Getting a bit more demanding, it no longer just lies up there in his brain, spying on his life. No longer accepts his choices, it tells him what to do now, raises its tone, insisting instead of simply advising like the early days when the demonic noise first emerged in the back of his mind.

Sounds a bit altered too, this newer voice, like a different entity entirely than earlier in his life, two separate voices. The loud and mean bossy voice gains dominance and rules the meek spiritual voice lately. The words order him to punch space aliens that live in human forms, but Sonny runs miles and breaks things instead, the sweat releases his frustration because down deep inside he never wants to hurt anyone he knows, or even a stranger. But the demon pushes harder, demands violence, louder and louder it rages at him. He ignores it as best he can. Gets more difficult as it gains power.

The meek spirit voice he remembers as a child mostly hides in the background, not saying much anymore but then it never pushed hard anyway even early in his life, just offered a little advice once in a while when he asked it, when he bounced a question off it about a thing that puzzled him. He calls the nice one his spirit brother because it sounds like a young boy the same age as himself, but it reveals no face and hides its gender, its slim body hovers like a wispy shadow at the edge of his mind, more often then but now only occasionally as the malicious demon grows stronger.

The loud, mean voice emerges only during his time awake and overwhelms the friendly spirit so any help it may offer disappears into a piercing vacuum. He likes the meek guiding tone, but hates the shrill demanding alternate. It makes him angry and provokes uncontrollable rage.

A nasty voice barks. *Find something alive. Punch it. Kill it.*

"Shut up!" He yells and jumps up, grabs a branch, and swings hard, breaks it against the tree trunk at the edge of his camp. He grabs another, breaks it, and another, and another. He drops the chunks on his firewood pile and takes off running down the trail, circles through the forest, and arrives back at the camp twenty minutes later. Heavy sweat streaks his body.

Sonny drops down and counts fifty push-ups aloud, then

sits on his stump and holds his head in both hands. Alone and afraid. A tear leaks out one eye and dribbles down his cheek.

He begins a worry, not much a one though, not yet anyway. His mind plays rough, like the rest of him, but the rage forces longer runs and more biking. Exercise kicks the spook out, the heavy sweat and the smoke, but he needs a gym. Cold weather coming soon, harder to run or bike outdoors when the snow falls, though he can do it, he knows that right here in his heart. A gym allows him to push weights and run a treadmill without weather interfering. A nice option.

Hope sits in there too, like comfort, and he feels good about it. "I can ask," he tells himself. "I will ask." The gym at this time of year means no cold air chilling his bones. He hopes the owner agrees. A great word, hope. He likes that word just fine, cradles it down into his word basket until he needs it again. "Hope." He says it aloud, just once. No one else hears.

2

The windowless conference room contains two old wooden chairs painted red, one gray metal table bolted to the concrete floor, and a convicted felon chained to the table. Bleached nearly transparent and worn thin from years of washing, an orange jail-suit and a dark blue neck-rag tucked into his collar tops off his felony wardrobe.

Walter Ferguson ripped off the sleeves above his elbows years ago and prison inks color his once muscular forearms, the red and blue artwork faded with age and wear. Half an inch of oily brown fringe speckled with gray circles his balding head, and tasteless jailhouse grub leaves his body a bit leaner than he likes. He last scraped whiskers off his face more than a week ago, and no-shower days fill his routine more often than not in a lockdown cellblock where he awakens each day to life without parole and at least one green demon sitting in his brain yapping at him. His mornings really suck.

A short stout security officer opens the steel entry door, steps aside, and admires a shapely figure as the psychiatrist enters the room. The escort locks the door behind her then slouches against the wall outside, his brown staff uniform and a silver badge pinned on its pocket hint at his official capacity – observe and manage inmates at Stark Medical Facility. The escort monitors Walter Ferguson and the doctor through a glass peep window, and yawns.

"Hello Cat." Surprisingly soft spoken, Ferguson reveals stained broken teeth in a friendly pretense masquerading as a grin. A rusty steel ring anchors his handcuffs to the table, a nylon braid links the cuffs to a cable wrapped around his bare ankles, and worn leather sandals protect his feet. Hardcore convict, a very dangerous character. He would probably break her neck if he could reach it, or give her his only coat and hat and freeze himself if a snowstorm catches her outside one day - depends on the time of day and his mood at that particular moment.

Cat sits and plants a genuine smile on her face. "I miss our chats Fergie."

The ghostly Russian tickle still haunts her English and becomes more noticeable whenever she gets excited. A touch of accent Cat tries hard but fails to hide reveals her childhood homeland despite the fact she's lived in the United States almost half her thirty-one years.

An odd pairing early in her medical career, the four-time convicted murderer and the bright rising star at Harvard Medical Center once spent uncountable hours swapping stories right in this building. Elusive and unpredictable, his mood swings dump peaceful, or solemn, or boisterous, or violent into the mix on the spur of a moment and at the whim of his choice with no warning.

Cat grew quite fond of Ferguson despite his disconcerting anti-social behavior and violent tendencies. Neither regret nor reservation blunts his words and he reveals the torturous truths that live in his brain to no one but Cat. A refreshing honesty bridges two contrary characters in a world where most commercial and social values today reflect at least one false component everyone accepts no matter how misleading.

Walter Ferguson lives an extremely brutal lifestyle but never once told Cat a lie.

Ferguson stretches his fingers as far as he can reach through the steel cuffs and bindings.

Gently and briefly, Cat touches his fingertips, a mini-handshake between two old friends, but no hug. "Nice suit Cat," Ferguson observes, eyeing her mint green jogging sweats. "Been a while."

"Easy to run in, and machine washable," she quips. "And yes it has, almost two years." She checks the back of his hands. Knobby scar tissue and a few fresh scratches across his knuckles give it away.

Cat nods her chin at his hands. "You still punching walls Fergie?"

Cat grins across the table, always upbeat even at the state mental facility. Her relationship with Ferguson dates back more than six years to when he volunteered in a two-year study she led during medical school. Ferguson tops her list as one of six intensely psychotic and violent subjects she counseled and treated during a psychiatric internship she and Doctor Aaron Clark administered through Harvard Medical Center after she earned her medical degree. She turns toward the window and wiggles a Snickers bar at the guard. Cat peels down the wrapper and pushes it across the table.

Ferguson eyeballs his favorite snack. Cat eases the bar closer and centers it on the table, pulls her hand away.

"Didn't forget, did you?" His infatuation obvious, he stares at the bar for a few seconds then picks it up, bends his head down and bites off the end. His eyes caress the nuts, the chocolate, the smooth caramel topping. That nasty smile spreads impossibly wider, but slicker now, and more content. He takes a bigger bite and chews, moaning its sweetness.

"Yeah, punching walls," he grumbles. "Turned forty-three two days ago and it pissed me off, one more birthday stuck in this fuckin' rat-hole. Got a little blood on the concrete, but not too bad this time, couple cuts and scrapes. Warden Brooks hung up some thick wall pads last year, but I can still punch between 'em in a few thin spots." Ferguson chuckles briefly at his own stupidity, examines his swollen knuckles.

"The demons still piss you off too?"

Yeah, you know how it is Cat, can't stop myself sometimes. Damn spooks holler at me, and the guards never help. They just ignore 'em, let 'em yell at me. Keeps me awake sometimes, don't know how the rest of those guys sleep through it, so fuckin' loud."

"Your demons Fergie, they live inside your head. No one else hears them."

"Yeah, maybe you think so, but I hear 'em even if you can't. Just gotta pay more attention, listen with both ears." The convict chuckles again, admires her ears.

Ferguson pulls lightly at the cuffs, testing. No luck, the steel digs into his wrists so he settles for another nibble instead, a single bite remains. The convict stares at the solitary chunk as if watching his best friend melt away right before his eyes. Ferguson gobbles the last piece then sneaks a peek at Cat, a silent query, as if afraid to ask outright if she brought a second treat because she might tell him no, and that would truly bum him out. So he rides out the torture, uncertain but hoping she brought two.

Cat reads the question on his face but offers no answer. Lets him wait, testing.

"I hear you're getting angry. That you're getting lockdown most of the time."

"Yup, keeps me safer. Demons gettin' into the yard now too, sittin' on guards, make 'em push me around and search me all the time, stealin' back the food I smuggle out the mess hall after I done all that work. So, gotta whack at 'em to keep 'em away. Damn spooks even snuck into some lifters out in the weight yard too, so I can't buff iron anymore or they'll git me."

"You're losing a little tone Fergie, you should exercise more," Cat declares. "You're too thin." A mother hen scolds an offspring much older than herself, but he loses weight without his workouts and extra food he steals, plus the stress and worry plaguing his brain.

Ferguson ignores her health advice, wipes off his grin, installs a serious look on his face.

"Got worse after that, demons came into my room again, almost every night. Pads hung on the walls so the spooks hid in the gates and made me punch the bars instead. Got 'em both, but it cut me up pretty bad. Chased 'em away that day, not for long though. Always creep back in. Fuckers!"

"Fightin' still works sometimes but when the demons hide inside them walls it ain't so easy on my fists. Getting good scar tissue on 'em again so it don't hurt as much, just bleeds a little."

"I thought we stopped all that Fergie, you hurting yourself."

"Not hurting myself, just hurt the demons. Punch it out no matter where it hides." He runs his eyes up and down, checks out Cat the woman not Cat the doctor after two years of separation.

"Lookin' good Cat. Still runnin', workin' out I see, trim and fit. Little fuller up top where it counts since I seen you last." Ferguson sneaks out a giggle after that observation, fills his mind with her features, and turns his lips up at each end. "Green always a good color on you, matches those eyes."

Cat ignores his flattery. Once he starts in on her appearance, he keeps at it, the OCD kicking in. Gets his mind stuck in a loop and continues that line of thinking no matter it never goes anywhere. She evades it best she can, and changes the subject, distracts his thought pattern each time he starts. Most of the time, it works.

"So, what about your meds, do you still take them?"

"Not the good ones you gave us, something different."

"Oh no!" Her eyes flash, a note of concern. "When did it change? Why? Who did it?"

"Pretty soon after you left us, a year or so, maybe less - went back to the blue med and two brown capsules, then that small whitey for sleep. Warden changed everyone back you treated once you and Aaron left us. Once in a while when we act out, me and the demons, we get the fat red capsule that makes us drowsy all day so we don't cause no trouble."

"Why do that? Why change it? I thought it kept the demons away."

"Well, they never was gone Cat, just quiet. Still bossin' me around, but was less pushy. Voices talked softer, and faces hung around like smoke. Could see 'em, but spooks just couldn't control me. Could ignore what it said if I don't agree with it."

"Was just with those meds you gave I could blow it off, didn't have to follow its orders, but the demons still laughed at me, and pissed me off. Not all the time and it couldn't make me punch the wall then. It still makes me punch walls with brown and blue stuff. Warden took away the ones you gave us and the demon snuck right back in, powered itself up, and got me."

"Like when I hit Harry Parker during dinner last month, guards locked me down again. Harry was standin' there looking innocent but that damn spook kept yellin' at me right out the top of his head, wigglin' its ears and flappin' its gums. Tried to beat that sucker outta Harry and save his life. Wasn't too happy about it though, didn't even tell me thanks after."

"You put him in the hospital Fergie. Why should he thank you?"

Ferguson shrugs, pulls at the cuffs again, a little harder this time, his eyes dart around the room. His feet sway back and forth under the table, bang rhythmically between the chair and table legs, chains clink each time he swings his feet.

"Tried to tell Harry, but he don't believe me. Says he don't see or hear no demons, but he don't listen hard enough. I can hear 'em just fine. Got mad at me for those cuts over his eyes and two nasty shiners he got when I hit his spook for him. No wonder he can't see 'em though, eyelids swollen half shut like that." Ferguson grins as the image flits across his mind then floats away, the damage he did, believing he hit a demon.

"I thought Harry was your friend? Roomies last time I was here, right?"

"Yeah sure, cellmates, not roomies." His grin transforms itself into a snarl, "This ain't no college, Cat." Just as quickly, his smile reappears.

"But when Harry got a demon too I had to kick him out. He moved upstairs with Tommy Jenkins after that chow hall fight. Told me I was nuts, but Harry got away before I could help him. Was gonna kill his demon for him. His own damn fault if that nasty green spook finishes him off someday. Harry's the nuts one, not me."

"Want to talk about your own demons for a minute? Exactly what they look like now and what they tell you."

Ferguson squirms around a little. His body agitates, his eyes flick from Cat to the window, watching the guard watch him. He stretches his hands up as high as the chains allow and wiggles his fingers at the window, a mini-wave. The guard smiles and tips his cap. Ferguson elevates both middle fingers then giggles with sick humor only he appreciates at the moment, then turns his attention back to Cat, looks her right in the eyes.

"Just told, that's enough, gets me antsy." He ponders his spooks a few seconds longer, reconsidering, shakes his head. "Nope, don't want to talk about 'em. What about you, you got demons Doc. You talk about 'em, I'll listen, Doctor Walter J. Ferguson, my new pay number." The convict cackles again, basking briefly in his new title.

"Maybe can get your old job Cat. You punch any walls lately? Come on, lie down on this table, and tell me all about it?" Ferguson laughs aloud.

Cat laughs with him, "Sorry, job's not open Fergie, I still

have it. That's why I'm here."

Cat remains in her seat, motionless, predicting exactly what will happen next. A repeat behavior every time she interviews Ferguson, he always jumps at her right after his eyes dart and he licks his lips, an absolute and undeniable compulsion anchored in his psychotic brain. She sits and waits, makes no attempt to escape it. It never works but he never learns from his repeated failures. The chain anchors him halfway and flops him face down on the table each time he tries. Cat knows it and expects it. Patient as her namesake, she waits.

His agitation elevates, his eyes dart around the room, and Ferguson licks his lips. Suddenly, he lunges toward Cat but the cuffs stop him short and dig into his skin. He grunts and grits his teeth, flops back down in the chair.

Cat remains rock still, never flinches.

"Missed again Fergie, when are you going to learn?" Her eyes never leave his.

The same event happens nearly every time, and numerous times during earlier sessions, so she expects it each visit. She watches Ferguson settle back. The felon glares at her for ten silent seconds, then blinks and shows his crooked yellow teeth again.

"Told me what you give us is too expensive, he feeds us different meds now, something else. 'Gotta meet the budget,' Brooks said after you and Aaron left. New pills don't work so good. Can still see demons, see 'em inside you too Cat, same ones yakked at me before, pissing me off again. Starting now, right here again!"

Ferguson grunts, his anxiety more apparent, sweat pops out on his forehead. He suddenly lunges across the table a second time but the cuffs and chains pull him up short once more. He slumps forward this time and his head hits the table. His chair slides sideways and Ferguson thumps his head on the metal top three times intentionally. He squirms backwards and scoots sideways, half on the table and half under it. He lies still a moment then suddenly screams and rages at the demons, kicking his feet and struggling with the chains, losing control.

The door swings in and the guard enters. Ferguson shouts at him. "Get away! Get the fuck away! Get out! You're just like the rest!" He thumps his fists on the table, jerks at the restraints.

Cat holds up her hand, shakes her head, and flips her fingers toward the escort twice, indicating he should step out and close the door. She brought a document stamped and signed by the governor authorizing Doctor Catherine Morgantholavich full access to the facility and its inmates. The officer reviewed it earlier when Warden Brooks assigned him as her escort. Reluctantly, the guard backs out and locks the door again, but pays much closer attention through the window, his eyes wide open. No yawns this time.

Ferguson pulls at the cuffs, trying to wrestle his hands free, and suddenly kicks up and out of his chair, sends the chair flying against the wall behind him. He loses his footing and his legs slide farther under the table, his chin bangs on its edge. Trapped, hanging on the chains, laid out and swaying just off the floor, his feet splayed apart, his wrists leak a little blood, the cuffs bite deeper.

Cat studies him a full minute. His sandals lose traction and his fists remain clenched in the cuffs, his arms lying flat across the table. Tangled in the restraints, he just hangs there breathing hard.

"You see 'em Cat? You hear 'em? Yelling at me inside your head, just like Harry. Gotta rip 'em out Cat, only way I can save you."

Cat circles behind him and grabs Ferguson beneath the shoulders, and lifts him.

He drops as if falling but regains his balance exactly as he planned it. Neatly, he fakes a slip sideways and Cat makes a huge error, she grabs him around the waist.

Ferguson quickly slides a knee on either side of her hips then squeezes his legs together and traps her, then twists an elbow over her head and forces the chain around her neck, eases her gently back against the table and presses the chain tighter across her throat.

"Gotcha, you sweet little kitten." His lips flat-line, as if deciding her fate, and his eyes bug out then glaze over and for an instant Walter Ferguson envisions a distorted world no one ever sees but Walter Ferguson. The chain rattles beneath her chin and Ferguson tightens his chokehold.

Sweat runs down his checks and drips off his chin, he growls directly into her ear. "Gonna kill it for you Cat, gonna save your life."

Cat struggles and twists, unable to break the hold. A week-old no shower stink rises off Ferguson and fills the stagnant air, forcing Cat into a gag reflex and a cough. Twice more she coughs – the chokehold and nasty odor takes her breath away. "You need a bath Fergie," she grunts, hoping to draw his attention away from the violence.

Ferguson twists and pins her in place, licks his lips and whispers directly into her ear again, a hoarse rumble. "You made a mistake Cat, got too close. Should know better after all this time, my demon told your demon, twice, but it don't listen. Just like Harry." The horrid grin returns and Ferguson licks his lips repeatedly, a continuous action now.

The door bursts open and the guard rushes in, unarmed, with no stun gun, unsure how he should respond, young and untrained. Torn between grabbing Ferguson and running for help, he stands motionless, undecided, finally blinks then fingers a radio button on his shirt collar, yells a code into it and his location then moves toward the table.

"Stop right there, or one little twist gets you a dead Cat for Christmas."

Accustomed to obeying orders, the escort stops immediately, his eyes skip back and forth between Cat and Ferguson.

In a very soft and patient tone, Cat speaks. "Stop Fergie, it's me, it's Doctor Cat. Let me loose. You forgot about your second Snickers bar." Cat coughs again then holds her breath and turns her face away, evading his offensive stench.

Walter Ferguson remains motionless for what seems an hour but in reality freezes three lives for a mere five seconds. Ferguson blinks, moisture rolls down his cheeks, and he quiets immediately. His rage and anger release as quickly as it arrived, leaving tears in its wake and docile reactions.

Wet-eyed, Ferguson relaxes his grip, releases the chain, and begs. "Where is it Cat?"

"Not until we're done Fergie."

3

The small brown speed bag earns its name. A blur rebounds off its backboard faster than an eye can track. An athlete swats the leather sack one final time and peels off his gloves, finishing a fifteen-minute punch-out. He grabs a jump rope, begins bounces, doubles, and crossovers. Sweat rolls off his sleek muscular body.

Gym rats call him K.O. Has nothing to do with his fight record though, Kenny Olsen never won a boxing match in his life, in fact, fought just four times as an amateur before giving it up for good – zero and four lifetime. Course no one counts street fights, that's just part a growing up, otherwise his record could read a thousand and four instead. One very tough teen K.O. was, got him in trouble more than once.

Six teenage trainees skip the ropes, each one working to hold his pace, all trying hard but K.O. spins faster, easily. No give-up allowed, a thing K.O. demands in every athlete he trains. The youngsters never see that soft spot he hides inside himself. If he shows it, kids might just laugh and ease off when he pushes this hard, so K.O. masks that spot most times, keeps it right here in his heart where no one sees it. Better if these young athletes think he's a mean old tiger, at least close enough that it keeps everyone in line and improving fitness skills instead of jerking around, causing trouble.

K.O. winds down and hangs the rope on a hook, tells the kids, "Okay guys take ten. Shake it out." K.O. grabs a towel, wanders over and stands inside the window, wipes sweat of his face and neck. A half inch of sandy brown hair and two ice gray eyes reflect off the glass. An old razor scar runs along his right cheek from ear to chin, and a few knots he earned on the streets while growing up add character to his face.

Born thirty-seven years ago as of last week, K.O. spends enough time at the gym teaching a fit and healthy lifestyle that an extra large t-shirt looks small on his frame, but he won't wear double large or triple large because the waists fit fat men, and K.O. ain't fat. He talks about ripping one off above the navel like some do, but figures it looks stupid, not stylish. Stupid like the raggedy-ass low-pants patchy-underwear hanging out style some kids wear and K.O. despises. So he scares folks with how he looks, that scar, them eyes, and a too tight t-shirt with muscle busting all out of it, even though he don't mean it most of the time, the scaring folks part.

*

The kid had zipped up his tent and hopped on his bike, cruised across town and into the parking lot, and now jumps off and chain-locks the black Novara hardtail to a rack outside the gym. He hooks his helmet on the seat, ruffles sweat out of his short blonde hair, and wipes his palms across his pants. A sign above the door reads KNOCKOUT in bold capitals. The kid crunches across the gravel, opens the door, and steps inside. He walks directly up to K.O. as if they already met.

"Eleven-mile ride here and I got no job. Work hard, never late, and need a trade for gym time." The words roll off his tongue.

"Just do like this, makes it easy." The kid nods his head up and down a few times. "See, don't even need words." He sticks a big smile on his face, offers K.O. no signal for declining, finds little room in his life for a negative answer.

Kid rode his mountain bike across town just to ask if he can exchange a little cleaning and sweeping for workout time. Could have phoned instead and saved all that pedal work, but figured a face-sized meeting with a big grin hung on it might make it more difficult to say no. Not too tall but definitely stout, a bit of muscle in his arms and thighs, the kid shuffles his feet, vibrating in place, a ton of energy with no way to release it standing still.

"Long way to ride on a maybe." K.O. sticks out his paw. "Kenny Olson but everyone calls me K.O."

"Sonny Bones and you better not laugh." Sonny grins

sideways and wiggles his tongue out the corner of his mouth.

High pitched and clear, a giggle escapes, even though K.O. tightens his lips and tries hard to hold it back.

"See, knew you'd laugh, but it's my real name, like it or not." Sonny straightens his face and gets serious. "It's all right though, the ride. Most days I ride twice that far just keeping busy, unless I run instead, depends on the weather."

"So, you run a lot?" A couple miles two or three days a week for kids his size and age might impress some folks, takes five or more miles every day rain, shine, or snow to impress K.O. though, and more than that for fighters he trains. Running builds stamina and wind, proves dedication.

"Nope, not a lot, just run until it feels good, ten miles most days, less some days if I ride the bike. Skip a day or two if the weather sucks. Only ran five this morning, but then rode here after. That counts."

K.O.'s eyebrows raise just a touch, impressed a little bit maybe, but the rest of his face stays still as a stone. He treats kids special once they earn it, not before.

Sonny Bones locks eyes with Kenny Olsen, no fear in his clear blue eyes, just confidence and the grim knowledge he can meet any challenge head on. He shows folks that anyway, as most kids will even if deep down they lack true belief in it. Sonny believes in himself, has been on his own more than half a year, survives, works, and fights a demon that lives in his brain, an imaginary spook few folks ever meet.

"Well, can I trade work for gym time, or not? Getting dark and I got a long ride home. Can't waste my time if you're just gonna say no, got important stuff to do." Still vibrating, Sonny dances one foot to the other, always ready to sprint hard if he needs it.

Right then, a little fright appears in his eyes, proving hurt comes often in his life. Sonny glances at the wall, at the ring, at the floor and the door, lifting up his word. Hope.

K.O.never denies a kid that needs him, especially if a kid asks the right way, and in his mind, ain't no wrong way of asking if a kid needs his help. Kids ask and K.O. steps up every time, no denials. Everyone gets a chance to prove worth.

"Let's see if you can work a broom and a window rag well

as you ride that bike."

"Start now? Will be dark and that bike got no light." A little worry flashes across his face, and Sonny looks over his shoulder as if dusk and shadow might sneak up on him.

"Well, I'm heading that way after we close up. Toss that no-light bike in the back of my pick-up and that truck will give it a lift home. You can ride along too."

"How'd you think that? You don't know where that bike lives."

"Don't matter, truck heads down that road anyways, wherever. Pretty small town here, no way you get lost without trying."

After a couple hours proving his worth and sneaking half a pizza K.O. bought, Sonny pops his bike in the back, hauls himself up in the front seat, and slams the door. He looks around, runs his fingertips across the smooth leather seats, admires the old style reconditioned interior. Sonny grins and says, "Too sweet."

K.O. aims scare-eyes at Sonny and growls, "Gently. How you shut that door, gently. Got it?"

Unafraid, Sonny ignores the scare-eyes. He knows already how soft K.O. hits on kids he meets, heard all about K.O. before he rode over. Sonny opens the door then shuts it gently. "Sorry."

K.O.'s twists the key and, like all great GMC engines do when its owner babies it, and tunes it often, and fills it with whatever it needs whenever it needs it, the grand old small-block burbles to life.

"Whoa! Way too sweet." His eyes pop and awe rings in his voice, beyond his control. Then he lifts up his chin and laughs. "Bike still beat you out the hole, though."

K.O. hides his grin but not his pride and straightens up behind the wheel, pushes his chest out against his too tight t-shirt, a thing he never denies when folks admire his truck, even if it's kids. Half the time kids know more than adults, more about trucks and more about life too, sometimes. Kids growing up fast nowadays.

"Okay with me, K.O., those hours you said. But I need ten bucks a week for gas money."

"What you mean gas money? You got a bike."

"So? You think a bike runs on air? Nope, runs on groceries and juice. Need a stop at Quik Mart and pump in some calories or this kid be dead and worthless when he gets here to work." Sonny drops that wiggle-tongue sideways grin on K.O. once more.

"Alexander Hamilton slides neat and clean under the table too. Can't be paying taxes on that slim-ass salary, that's for sure," Sonny says.

"Once you get rich stealing that ten bucks a week, you owe me five for half that pizza you ate."

"What you mean? Owe you. OWE you? Saw that little sign set on it saying 'eat me or toss me in the trash.' You didn't see it?" Sonny grins at his fabrication. He knows K.O. knows it too, both know both know it, and both grin at it.

"Was right there, big old red letters, and you already ate the biggest half. Eat more than half you get fat, bust out that t-shirt altogether. New shirt cost more than five bucks – saved you money. You should pay me for eating it instead of crabbing." His backwards logic puts another grin on K.O.'s face.

"Besides, hate to waste good food. Hard to come by nowadays," Sonny admits, accidently giving away a secret he hides from most folks he meets.

*

K.O. eases up along the curb outside an apartment complex on the north side, the streetlights dim, one lamp unlit and one broken. Once a high-end residential area, the north side houses more rentals than owners now, the area has begun deteriorating but remains reasonably maintained, a few apartments and condo conversions spread around the neighborhood.

"So, how old are you anyways?"

"Sixteen in a week." Sonny lies almost a year, afraid of the rules. At least one state law says a kid under sixteen needs a special work permit. He turned fifteen less than a month ago, and it ain't a real job, he decides, just a trade except the ten bucks. He once read somewhere that Feds counts trade as work too, and wants a tax even from kids. Not positive, but smart enough to take no chances in the grab-not-give world where he lives. Sonny learns his lessons well, often the hard way. A true survivor.

A locked gate only residents can key into protects the parking lot in the building where Sonny lived almost seven years with his mom. Some drunk speeder stuck her on his bumper then up over his hood as she crossed the street walking home from work late one night eight months ago - dumped her lifeless in the dirt. Cops found the driver passed out six blocks away, nose of his Buick punched into a power pole, broke his wrist and an ankle.

The drunk got a year and free medical care. Single mom rests in a grave. Don't seem fair to Sonny, but nothing he can do about it. Left him an orphan.

He climbs out, grabs his Novara, opens the pedestrian gate, pushes the bike inside and waves K.O. away, pretending he's safe at home. Sonny sneaks a peek around an edge, watches the light blue truck blink left and swing the corner then hops back on his bike, aims it toward the state park, and his tent home.

4

Sonny eases into the clearing and drops his backpack, hangs his hat on a nail stuck in a tree trunk. Starving, even after he ate the pizza, he opens a cooler sitting beside his tent and grabs a sandwich. A young male athlete needs plenty of groceries.

A nasty voice in the back of his mind barks at him. *Don't eat that. It's poison.*

He shakes his head, ignores the order, takes a large bite, and twists the cap off a water bottle. He drains half and takes another bite.

Sonny met a woman ranger a few weeks ago while he was picking up trash to build a small fire at his campsite one evening when a chill carried into the night. A true environmentalist at heart, she spent all her teen and college years loving nature, and now spends her work years protecting the wilderness and its wildlife. She thanked Sonny for collecting the trash that reckless and inconsiderate people dump in the woods.

She told him, 'Keeps nature clean, and saves critters from choking'. At the time, she had no idea he built illegal campfires with it. He explained a week later - after she gained a little trust - that he lives in a hidden tent site, at least temporarily, until he finds a real job.

By that time, a new friendship ruled and she stayed stuck, too late to tell on him. Besides, she enjoys the evenings, sitting alone with him, inspecting his innocence. Not quite as innocent as she believes though, Sonny keeps some secrets.

A bare nine years separate the two in age, probably more like a hundred in life experience. Sonny wins that second category easily. His struggles just this year alone add experience most folks never get. Both found common ground immediately when he laughed at her name – Willow Parks – and explained that everyone laughed at his name too, grew an alliance right off.

*

Willow steps into the clearing, drops down on the stump. "Hey, Sonny."

Sonny pops his cooler, offers her ice tea in a bottle. Both sip and watch the fire burn, talk when it needs it, but comfortable just staring at the flames too, friends hanging out, passing time. Willow drops the bottle in a recycle bag Sonny returns and claims the nickels.

"Can't stay, a duty night," Willow says. "Talked to Janice Merchant again today, she says you can come in and sign up with social services any time."

Her words put a little scare on his face. "You didn't tell her about me? You promised you won't tell. Already told you no. They'll take my saw, my bike, stick me in a cell."

"Nope. Didn't tell your name or where you stay, and it's not a cell, just a room. So think about it again. Okay? See you tomorrow."

Willow heads toward the trail, sadness etched on her face. She keeps her word, and leaves the sheriff out of it, temporarily, but watches out for Sonny in secret. Truth of it, she respects his independence, but she worries about his age and his ability to care for himself. She hopes he finds his own way soon, and accepts help in town before he gets hurt.

She pushes the law a little, maybe, unsure of it exactly, but his size and maturity easily passes for eighteen and she did not ask his age for that very reason, so she can deny it if anyone questions her. She engages a bit of mental turmoil with it but keeps her promise, wants Sonny to choose for himself and balance an unspoken pact between them. Winter on its way though, and she worries about her new friend. She has no way to protect him that he will allow, and she wants to maintain his trust.

*

The voice emerges again, barks at his peaceful evening. *She wants you in town. Don't trust her. She wants you in a cell, her prisoner. Punch her next time, she deserves it.*

Sonny covers his ears, tells it, "Leave her alone. Leave me alone. Get away!"

He sticks a branch in the campfire. Willow always tries to talk him into town and getting help, but each time it comes up he refuses, annoyed a little that she just met him and wants to change his life so quick. Sonny figures she will never turn him in, just on principle. Believes she will counsel him instead, make him choose. He allows that chatter whenever she visits but never really falls for it exactly. He just sits, talks, and dreams a little, admires her perfection.

Sonny liked her right away, the first meeting. He enjoys time with her whenever she appears. Nice and friendly, she smiles and laughs a lot. Hair the color of rust curls below her ears, curious dark eyes shine beneath the billed cap all state park people wear. A dark green ranger uniform wraps itself around a bit of chunky she works hard keeping off but rounds her out like a real woman, definitely not a girl. Still too young to judge that characteristic with any real truth in it, but his eyes work fine and she makes him laugh. Nope, definitely not a girl.

Hope. Sonny mouths the word. Wishing hard, he hides a secret smile inside Willow never sees, and a hushed thump in his chest she never hears. He has little control of a bumped up bio-rhythm in a too young fifteen, no match for an already ancient twenty-four that can never be his. Sonny knows it but dreams it anyway. What harm in that? His first crush.

The demon stays gone when he sleeps. Willow fills him up at night even when she skips a visit. Courtship and pairing hormones beginning to boil, beyond his control as Mother Nature defines his maturing male world. Gut feelings and wishes but more a simple chemical force than anything else.

No exact understanding yet about women, but someday maybe, once Sonny fills up a few more years of his life he might meet the right one. One he can share his truths without fear or failure, and share his physical self as well. Hope fits in his life always, that perfect word.

5

Kenny Olsen, one hell of a trainer. Grew up tough, but these young gym rats know nothing about his early life, at least until he feels the right time and tells it. A little older than most kids when he boxed due to his past, his gutter upbringing, and all that time crime stole off his youth, K.O. tested his fists at the local gym soon as he hit parole. Keeping active and in shape for whatever his future throws at him.

K.O. hauls out that passion and pushes it down hard on the youngsters he trains until they all get it right, accepts no excuses, and no slack. Slack gets you lazy and K.O. may be many things but lazy ain't one of them. He teaches kids heart and pride in themselves, an experience all kids need even more than physical skills.

Any athlete can learn physical skills if he works a little muscle, finds a little balance, gains a bit of speed in his hands and has good eyes, but if he ain't got heart, a win remains elusive in the real world. K.O. embeds that passion into every teen he touches, even if some just bounce around his gym, get fit and healthy, and never box at all. That gift carries over into life later. Many of his gym rats ride that passion into different but equally successful lives in a larger world that aims a different kind of punch at them.

"If I'd never done time, I'd never straightened myself out and probably be looking ahead at a life full of trouble later anyways. Right!" K.O. repeats those words often in a too soft voice that fools some folks, least at first, until folks get to know him better. He squeaks that last word out, making it like a statement not a question each time he shares that history, not really wanting an answer because K.O. already knows its truth right here in his heart.

"Glad I did my time early. Knew it was coming and got it over with, can spend my days and evenings helping kids stay straight and away from that kind a life." All his athletes get that same lecture, on the very first day.

Interesting maybe, a little curious mostly, people think that about K.O. when they meet him and hear him speak for the first time. Many never take him serious at the first. Sure do later though, once they figure him out and realize that tough as a nail fits him, and that too soft voice slides out so smooth and deceives most kids unless he needs it sharp for a youngster that steps over a line. Folks then get curious about why he quit boxing so young.

Years ago, that fight bell rang, launching each match. As soon as he saw what skills his opponent had that first time they met, K.O. just kept weaving sideways and dancing backward, batting those fists away instead of simply taking the guy out immediately, like he could have done easy enough. Was afraid he might actually hurt an opponent, which he never wanted to do, and the reason why he lost his amateur bouts all on points without getting hit solid even once in the ring.

Then K.O. just quit boxing rather than damage some youngster full a talent and on his way up the ranks. Surprised everyone that knew him, including his trainer. A few age years and a lot of street years older than most of the young fighters, and much wiser because of it, K.O. decided he would rather teach kids the right way instead of stopping a potentially good career before it began, and keep the young athletes out of trouble too as best he can.

He packed up his gloves and started training kids instead, eventually bought the gym. He lives in the small apartment above it. His wife divorced him a few years back, wanting the high life and the big sports payroll. Pushed K.O. after it until she finally gave up and moved on. K.O. just wants to teach youngsters how to stay clean and fit, and launch a career if a kid has quick hands and a heart big enough to win.

Three regional championships in sixteen years and one Golden Gloves favorite out of his gym won Olympic silver nine years ago. Jake Archer, long gone but not forgotten, K.O. was proud that day, prouder than ever, just like a dad, like the dad-mentor he offers all kids he meets, even if they already have good parents. Jake Archer has one each, George and Ellie, but still treats K.O. like a dad too, whenever he sees him, which ain't often enough anymore. K.O. never competes. He just sits and waits, and steps up when a kid needs him.

6

Willow in her ranger uniform and Sonny in his workout sweats sit cross-legged beside a very small trash fire in the clearing, building a habit over the weeks. "You know about animals, Willow. You work with wildlife. Right? So, are gorillas pretty smart?"

"Gorillas?" Willow lifts her eyebrows, wonders where this comes from, no gorillas around here.

"Yeah, you know. Big, strong, hairy things from Africa or maybe other places, like Panama."

"I know what they are, Sonny. Yes, they're pretty smart. Not quite as smart as chimps, but pretty smart. Not in Panama though, Gorillas live only in Africa. Why'd you ask?"

"No reason. Playing video games with Randy couple nights ago, listening to news, keeping up on stuff, just watching how the world works."

K.O. steps around a bush and flops himself down on the stump, sidelines the current events chat before Sonny gets all his answers. "Followed you in."

Fright dots his mind for a few seconds then flees into the firelight and burns out. Sonny always feels its jolt when something unexpected breaks into his space, a little twinge in his chest that makes him feel like jumping up and running away.

"What you mean, 'Followed you in?' When?" Sonny barks the words, more upset that K.O. interrupted his time with Willow than with his arrival at the campsite unannounced.

Sonny shrugs it off. "Might as well sit then."

"Already sat," K.O observes. "State campground, anyone

can sit here.

Sonny says nothing, a bit annoyed now once his fright fled, that K.O. pushed in through the trees without asking, like an ambush, but mostly because he feels a little embarrassed caught in an untruth about his home after K.O. helped him out last month trading work for gym time. Sonny protects himself first, even at the cost of lying when it matters and as long as the lie hurts no one but himself.

"Getting cold though. No place for a kid over the winter, even in this nice fabric castle you got here."

"My home, like it or take off." Sonny fits a challenge on his face and watches K.O. sit and say nothing for a few seconds.

"Warm enough here anyway, never snows deep and melts quick, mostly rains instead. Besides, I like sleeping in puddles. Add a little soap and splash around, keeps my sheets clean."

"Hell of a vision," K.O. says, as that scene hits them all at once, Sonny splashing in a puddle, kicking his feet and hands like a toddler in a backyard pool. Suddenly, all three bust out with laughter and it kills the tension.

"Tried to catch you the other night when you split. You're too quick on that bike, skip lights, short-cut alleys, and speeding." K.O. glances at Sonny and grins. "Had a couple free movie tickets, wanted to share but you never went to the apartment, rode straight here. Don't mean to pry, just happened, accidental like."

Sonny says nothing, thinking about it, forgives K.O. already as he has become a good friend this month. "Told you before, bike beat you out the hole so bad you never catch it." Sonny sticks on a grin, then shuts it off and laughs alone, a short choked-off chuckle that drops a touchy issue back on the table.

Willow says, "You feel like talking about your family yet? Why you live here with no home? We don't want to hurt you Sonny, just help if you let us."

A demon voice shouts. An order echoes in his mind. *Don't tell it. They're not friends. Keep your past secret, it's not their business.*

Sonny stands, wraps his arms around his body, and shakes his head once. "Shut up," he whispers quietly, almost to himself.

Willow and K.O. look at one another, then at Sonny.

Sonny studies both faces. A minute slips past. Finally, he

makes up his mind. He sits, tells it, about growing up nearby, about hanging out with local friends, about shooting baskets some evenings at Town Center, about quitting school because he has no home. About his mom and the drunk that killed her, same mom that adopted him as a baby then lost her husband a year later.

"He just took off, disappeared one night, decided kid-raising wasn't for him, left me and mom alone. Never saw him again, never heard nothing."

"Found her savings, eight Ben Franklins and four little Georges rolled up in a sandwich bag and tucked inside the sugar tin, nothing in the bank. Bought the saw with it, the tent, chain and lock, sleeping bag and pillow, the rest kept me going, bought food until the saw got work."

"Mom bought the bike last year, my ride to school."

*

She never heard from or cared about the husband after he left her alone. The spirit of her life, a baby she could never conceive herself but a gift from one woman to another, filled a void she was unable to fill herself.

Eight hundred and four dollars in a can, the complete savings a single mom earned working two part-time jobs with a few benefits, and raising one child. That very small inheritance launched a teenager into his life.

Sonny has no memory of his traitor father and never saw a photo. Knows nothing about his birth parents either, neither one in his life beyond a single day his biological mother gave him birth and a life, sent him down a road she hoped would be good to him.

Neighbors and friends asked after him at first, where he was staying, and how he was doing. School officials sent letters to the apartment, but Sonny was long gone that first month after the rent expired, living in the tent. He never got letters and sent no answers. School stopped mail after a couple months, might have sent someone around to look for him but new tenants knew nothing. Everyone getting on with life, not much room in folks' busy days to find a kid unrelated to any of them.

Even now, a mom or a dad asks when he visits a friend but he mumbles around it and that query disappears into general conversations. He mostly hangs out with friends around town anyway, typical mid-teen behavior for all of them, skirting parents most of the time at this age. Kids drop in, fill the belly and fatten the wallet, sleep only when required. His secret life remains safe and undiscovered.

Sonny tells it all with a straight face and no tears, gave up on crying a long time ago. He huffs out a breath, stares into the fire, raises his eyes, looks at K.O. than Willow, then drops his eyes back at the flames again. One tear finally spills out and trickles down his cheek, a single salty memorial for the mom he misses every day.

"Got a storage room at the gym. We can move some stuff out and you can set up camp there for the winter." K.O. knows the answer, but asks anyway. "You interested?"

K.O. already talked this out with Willow. She accidentally saw K.O. the same day he followed Sonny home. She's been watch-dogging his safety since that first day she met him although Sonny never knew it. Not a secret anymore once K.O. knows it too. Willow showed up at the gym one day while Sonny was out running the trails, introduced herself, and they hatched a plan together.

"Cheap rent, two bucks a week." K.O. never gives anything away, makes all his trainees earn it. "You can afford it. We just deduct it."

"What you mean two dollars a week? Bedroom big as a closet, only one tiny window, and bring my own cot and pillow, not even furnished. Twenty percent out my pay, cost too much! Hall bathroom and a walk-to-it kitchen ain't even a real kitchen, just a sink and microwave. No stove." Sonny points a grin at K.O. "Got a nice big fridge though, lots of drinks in it."

Unable to conceal it, a spark lights up his eyes, he coveted that space for the past month, ever since the first day he traded, but figures it requires a bitch and a moan, and bargain before a deal. The way of the world, his world anyway, always has been, even before the mom event that tore a huge hole in his life.

"Nice big gym-size showers too, got to give it that." K.O. counters, cuts just enough slack that Sonny saves face. "Window that small keeps you safe from burglars. Besides, furnished room costs more."

K.O. embellishes the good side, keeps his off-the-ropes humor in all he says whenever he can, knows nothing in life was quite as bad as some places he lived, a jail cell for one, state juvenile homes for another. Nothing too fine or uppity about any of those bedrooms, and even a closet feels better than a tent when a freeze hits with no warning.

"Okay, then give a raise … been working a month already without one, work hard too. Two dollars raise a week, or work extra hour a week – wait – extra hour a month."

Sonny never sells himself short. Wants the best part of the deal even though he already owns the best half of this bargain, and has been on top since that first day when he traded four hours cleaning for each week of gym time, and he gets the ten bucks. He plays it out regardless. Otherwise, he might appear soft and mushy.

"Split the difference. Two hours a month, utilities included." K.O. plays his final chip, and knows Sonny will accept no matter what he offers. Played this game for years, K.O. has, and mostly wins. K.O. knows kids, knows how to bargain too.

Sonny rubs his head, apparently deciding something much tougher than it appears.

The demon voice bangs at him again. *Don't do it. Don't do it. He's screwing you! Get more. Get more! Give less! Punch Willow. Kick K.O.* Its screech echoes in his brain, its paranoid punch pops out and gives orders every chance it gets.

Sonny flexes a fist, looks down at it, shakes his head, and cups an ear in each hand, circles the clearing, stops behind the tent." No! Get out!" He steps back out, plops down on the stump.

Perplexed, Willow and K.O. watch him struggle, then glance at one another, eyebrows up, both wonder why this decision appears so difficult. A win-win for everyone, no one loses.

"Okay, but only if I get the raise." The demon screams again but Sonny shuts it off this time and smiles at his win. He bumps a fist at K.O. then Willow, cementing the deal. Willow offers a hug. Sonny accepts, embarrassed at her first touch ever, his ears redden and his heart thumps, a pale blush fills both cheeks. In the darkness, no one hears or sees it.

The demon demands violence. *Punch her! Slap Willow! Grab that branch, hit K.O.*

The stress builds. Sonny shakes it off.

7

The meal bell rings twice. Twenty-four doors in the residential units unlock at once and Thirty-nine inmates follow the green boundary lane and file into the dining hall.

Walter Ferguson enters last, same as always, number forty. He edges into the lane, and pokes the last man in the line. The man looks behind himself and steps aside. Ferguson takes his spot, pokes the next man in line, and takes his spot too. He fills his tray as he walks along the line, poking and moving up, his obsession, his compulsion, his daily routine. Everyone knows it.

A tall and very heavy convict with long stringy hair and a full beard stands alone, leans against the wall beside the gate that leads into Unit Two. Chase Nickels waits until the line forms, then pushes his bulk off the wall, walks over and grabs the first man in line, shoves him aside, and steals his tray.

Nickels angles backwards along the chow line, forces the each man sideways, and fills the tray, an instant replay. He repeats this behavior every meal and every day. No one objects, his obsession, his compulsion, his daily routine, and his size and manner leave no room for a challenge.

The first man simply walks away, gets another tray, and steps back in line. No one in the facility tests Nickels, ever. At six foot four and three hundred twenty pounds, and mean as a mad-dog with rabies, he collects his own meal first every time and always walks backwards from the front.

Halfway down the line, one inmate refuses to move aside, a new man, his first meal. Hardcore and defending his spot, the new man knows nothing about this daily routine yet.

Nickels stands completely still for ten seconds while both men engage a staring contest. Nickels suddenly set his tray on the counter, snatches the man by his belt and collar, spins in a circle, and lets him loose. The man slides fifteen feet across the slick tile and bounces off the wall.

Nickels hollers. "Ha! You're off the line! You stepped out of bounds! You crossed the green boundary! Ha! Ha! Ha!" He sniggers. "You eat in your room today and git no dessert." Then he laughs louder, a bizarre cackle fills the room then shuts off, then silence. Nickels adds food to his tray then finds a seat alone, ignoring the new man.

The new inmate rolls to his feet, shakes his head, and whines at Nickels, "Christ! You're fuckin' crazy!"

The new man gets another tray and walks to the end, packs his food on it, and glances at Nickels over his shoulder. The remaining inmates merge back into a line. Ferguson dumps his food into a garbage can, grabs a new tray and starts over. He walks back to the end, and once again begins poking and moving up the line. The men and the staff ignore the violent event as if it never happened, or maybe happens often. A routine.

*

Teaching a little responsibility, K.O. wrote a brief rental agreement, and both signed it. Two days later, Sonny spent three hours patching and painting the bed-closet as he affectionately named his new room.

He sits on his cot and organizes his clothes, fills three drawers that run down one side of a small reading desk that serves as his dresser. He pushes a chair under the desk section and watches the door swing in.

Willow enters dressed in her uniform and carrying pair of dark blue curtains for the window. "Here, hang these, they'll keep the boogie-man out."

Sonny glances at her, wonders how she knows about his demon, guesses she calls hers a 'boogie-man'. Makes sense, although she should call it a 'boogie-girl'. He says nothing about it. She can call her spook whatever she wants. She owns it.

"Could hang these towels I got here instead. Or you just

busy being a girl?" He says the wrong thing at the wrong time to a female ranger in full dress uniform, a nine millimeter Glock 17 hanging on her hip.

"Yup, just busy being a girl. Actually I'm being a friend, and brought this side-arm so I could shoot you if you made any kind of sexist comment about my sewing."

A very odd look jumps into his eyes. He pulls up a sincere face and says, "Sorry."

His demon pops up and screams. *Never say sorry. Punch her. Slap her. Don't let her talk to you like that. She deserves a kick.*

Sonny stands up and flexes his fist, looks down at his shoe, feels the rage, works hard to control it. "No!" He says it, softly, under his breath and sits down again.

Willow aims an odd look at Sonny, wonders why he said 'No', but exactly as it happens, K.O. pushes his head in through the door and hears the 'shoot you' comment. K.O. and Willow crack up laughing, find a bit of humor in the odd exchange of words.

Uncertain why they're laughing, Sonny laughs with them anyway, his own weird giggle as the rage dissipates, and his fist relaxes. He wonders why Willow would shoot him for calling her a girl. She is a girl, definitely, no doubt, no lie, and no guessing, a definite fact.

Sonny thinks literally, as he matures and his distorted male hormones kick in, a less concrete thought process develops, and when someone says a thing like that, he believes it exactly as said. His mind works that way now, a little different and more directly than most young male minds his age. He knows that already, wonders about it, but pays it no attention. Sonny believes all brains work like his, including its demonic voice. Sonny believes everyone has a spook, just like his, but no one talks about it, so he keeps his a secret as well.

*

K.O. says, "Come on, let's get a workout." He holds up boxing gloves and hand wraps. "Let me show you." Sonny holds out his hands and K.O. wraps the knuckles then pushes the gloves in place and ties the laces.

Inside the ring, K.O. bats aside the punches as fast as Sonny swings and his first attempt at what looks easy ends in frustration. Sonny swings harder and harder, faster and faster, but each time K.O. easily bounces away and stress begins eating at Sonny, a little anger pushes at his mind. K.O. watches it arrive, has seen it before in other kids, and stays loose and balanced, totally in control.

Sonny never gets close, and K.O. never swings at all, just dances around and weaves in and out, wearing Sonny out in twenty minutes, bringing out a heavy sweat in both athletes.

Finally, Sonny drops his arms. Two wet spaghetti strands hang loose off his shoulders, and he says, "Well, a little tougher than it looks." The demon idles back in the corner of his mind, but says nothing. A good workout always shuts it up, the heavy sweat washing away its demands.

K.O. grins. Sonny pushes his anger aside and grins back, heads down the hall into the showers. K.O turns his eyes toward a couple gym rats. "What the hell are you gawking at?"

Lucas laughs and says, "Looks pretty good K.O. Might have a bit a talent here, almost tagged you a couple times."

"Bullshit!"

Lucas laughs harder. "Watch it in that wall mirror next time. You missed it this time. Getting a bit long in the tooth, are we? Eyes getting a bit weak?"

K.O. grins and shakes his head, knows he not only saw something good today, but something very different, a unique style Sonny engaged even his first time in the ring, but something in it bothers him a little too. He keeps it to himself for now. "Not yet Lucas, not yet, long way to go. Good kid though, needs a break."

8

Even in heels she seldom wears, Catherine Morgantholavich stands much shorter than her name and hums a pop-tune while she scans a stack of documents related to her research. Straight black hair cut short and shaggy and bright green eyes stand out as the most noticeable hand-me-downs from her Irish and Russian genetic mixture. No Irish lilt evident in her speech from that line of decent four times removed, but the Russian accent sticks with her no matter how hard she works at it.

These ancestral features, a petite build, and a pixie face grab a man and open his eyes wide immediately. Each man she meets, professionally or otherwise, thinks of her first as a woman second as a doctor, a big mistake in her mind.

Her great, great Irish grandfather believed in remaining true to his heritage and that of his wife. The unique and strange, but short-lived concept of hyphenated names had not developed yet, so the grand old gentleman simply merged both names into one regardless of its letter count or pronunciation issues. He personally saw no problem with it.

In subsequent generations, the paternal offspring consider it sentimental and carry his tradition right on down the family lines despite the tongue-twisting surname and fifteen characters. The single women as well, some even marry and keep it anyway, pride in the heritage.

Doctor Morgantholavich shortens it for her patients, especially the young ones. The black tag on her clinic gown confirms her title and a three-letter shortcut, Doctor Cat. A smiley face kitten her five-year-old niece once drew with a green crayon sits beside it, etched into her nametag.

Cat plops into a chair and flips open her laptop, starts tapping keys.

Biological memory, the record of a lifetime, a weird and wonderful wizard projecting full-color videos into the mind of its actors. Instant replay on-demand, no fees, no hidden charges, one complete history. Surround-sound included. Individual copyrights apply, bootlegs and forgeries forbidden.

Cat taps the letters and grins briefly at her humor. The odd wording she includes in her field notations occasionally sparks her thoughts and invites metaphor and artistic harmony into her hard science world. She acquired that rhetorical expression through her relationship with Professor Maxwell Whitetail, an undeniable respect for her mentor and his profound influence on her work, and it grabs the fleeting attention span that her students exhibit as well.

She continues typing lecture notes on thought processes, preparing for an advanced medical seminar at Harvard when the next term opens. Cat runs her fingers across the keyboard, her words track up on the screen nearly as fast as she conceives her thoughts.

Cat opens the Ferguson file and records her opinions and conclusions, adds a question.

The instinct for individual survival unconsciously rules all behavioral choices, producing protective actions first, and foremost, then a search for sustenance, nutrition, shelter, and rest. Secondary behavior choices include courtship and procreation, followed last by diversified social and cultural activities.

Instinct defines a natural and unconscious reaction to a specific event or action, particularly in the threat event. Conscious choice via learning often over-rules instinct, but instinct rules as first priority actions in any behavior, such as response to danger.

Why does Fergie punch his friends? Why is Parker a threat?

Cat shuts the laptop, heads into the basement and completes a short workout, then connects with her supervisor during a strategy meeting after lunch, time to review his package. Doctor Aaron Clark spent several weeks developing a new attack on some legal issues that stifle objective research and slow her progress.

*

Upon a written request and staff approval, men confined at the Stark facility may share a cell. Chase Nickels lies on his bunk, fully dressed with a knit hat pulled down over his ears, staring at several photos of his family, a mom and two brothers, no dad.

He frowns, climbs up off his bed, and tells his cellmate, "Git yourself down here Josh, I need a little therapy."

"Not up for it now, I'm reading," Joshua Barnes responds.

Chase reaches over and slaps Josh very softly on the cheek. "Can't wait, missin' my family. Lights coming up fast, popcorn too," he says and grabs Barnes, hauls him off the top bunk then slaps him softly again, almost a caress.

Barnes weighs a hundred thirty-five pounds, Nickels over three hundred, not a close match at all, no opportunity for resistance from the much smaller man.

"Okay, a short one." Barnes suddenly punches Nickels then punches him again, and again, hard as he can hit. Nickels quickly unbuttons his shirt, pulls it off, throws it on his bed, his knit cap follows. Barnes works his way around the larger man, punching and bringing up a light redness each time a fist lands. Barnes circles Nickels three or four times, landing rights and lefts on the hairy arms, the chest, stomach, and shoulders in a staccato rhythm. Nickels grins and giggles as each fist lands.

After four or five minutes, Barnes works up a light sweat then suddenly quits. "Enough." He climbs back up on his bunk and opens his book, leaving Nickels with bright red blotches all over his body.

"O-h-h-h-h-h man, that feels so good," Nickels groans, basking in the pain. "Thanks Josh, but too short. You owe me later."

"Yeah, right," Josh grumps.

Josh clicks on his overhead light, begins reading. Nickels pulls on his shirt and hat, rolls back onto his bed, hugs himself, and smiles, shuts his eyes.

*

Cat quits humming and fits a grim frown on her face, waves a set of papers at the project director. "There's just not enough information here Aaron, privacy laws curtail our ability to collect base data for solid research. Everyone hides behind the HIPAA as if the privacy law is somehow tangible, like a huge granite blockade. We can't talk to anyone directly, and can't even know the patients names so we can ask and get permissions signed. What a mess."

"Warden Brooks out at Stark squawks privacy too, although he'll lose that battle. He's stretching his power band and puffing his chest up again but it's still our project. The State and Feds will step all over him, like last time. Public dollars and they want the answers they paid for. Besides, he cheated on the budget and the medications. He'll probably lose his job over that misstep even though he took nothing out for himself. It just takes weeks screwing around, wasted time that we could spend on patients and treatment instead of fighting legal battles with him and his goons."

"Ha." Aaron chuckles, "He's just a little schemer then, not a real crook?"

"Ignorant clowns." Cat waves her hand, brushes Warden Brooks and his cronies off the table. "We need to share treatment information so doctors and nurses can practice medicine instead of producing paperwork in secret no one else can read, well can't legally read. HIPAA definitely interferes, especially with late teens and young adults."

She tosses her documents on the desk and walks out, shaking her head. "I'll be in the basement." Two at a time, she hops down fifteen concrete steps, jumps on the treadmill and runs for twenty minutes.

*

Back in her office later, Cat pops the lid on her laptop and begins documenting the stories Walter Ferguson shared this time. The demons in his mind, demons he sees in other men, his violent contact with Harry Parker. He shared how his mind reacts with different medications over the past year since her last contact with the Stark monitoring group and her sponsor clinic. Some chemistry works a little, some not so well, some reduce stress, and some push more stress into a system. It's a very slow and emotionally painful process.

Cat spent three very productive hours alone with Ferguson after the strangling incident. First time a killer choked her, a new experience, one that really shook her up. She ran that scare off in a half hour at a local park near the facility then returned and spoke with Ferguson and two more of the five inmates that remain in the Harvard program, two refused her invitation, including Chase Nickels who responds well when he takes his meds, but then simply quits with no explanation. Like many patients, he waffles back and forth, in and out of his psychosis, in and out of his rage episodes, on and off his meds.

Joshua Barnes and Chase Nickels share a cell, but Barnes has never officially participated in the Harvard program. Barnes randomly starts and stops medications prescribed through the state medical officer, with Harvard team support. Cat has a few minimal records of the man, and documents Barnes in her study whenever she can. He piques her interest due to a rare and very odd behavior. Small, light, and relatively weak, he likes punching men, and that violent action releases a deep destructive desire in his brain that Cat hopes she will eventually understand.

Chase Nickels exhibits a manifestation in hallucinations Cat has never seen documented anywhere. He experiences vibrant flashing colors and loud noises in his conscious mind, a multicolored lightning collage as he describes it, and crackling noises, like popcorn exploding in his brain. He claims it drives him crazy, a strange interpretation on his part. In an interesting but unique relationship, Barnes beats on Nickels enough to bruise the skin but never really does any damage. He's too small. The punches stop the mental exhibitions in Nickels' brain temporarily.

"Why does that violence stop his hallucinations?" Cat asks

herself the question, has no answer, wonders.

Both men experience a weird physical release. Josh Barnes likes beating men and Chase Nickels mentally relaxes when he receives beatings. Not a treatment Cat would prescribe generally, but interesting from an observation and medical standpoint.

"How would a doctor write that prescription?" She ponders the notion aloud. "Punch a friend as needed, once every four hours. Drink lots of water." Her lips tip up at the thought.

Both men stop and start meds erratically and frequently self-medicate with street drugs anyone can buy on the facility yard. Visitors routinely smuggle it in for patients, and one or two staff jump on an opportunity to pad the payroll as well. The mental routine in his brain varies enough that Nickels blames Barnes for the colors and noise but accepts his fists as a temporary cure. Bizarre relationships emerge in a prison environment, not easy to predict or understand.

Receiving the punches makes Nickels happy. It makes no sense in the medical labs, but chemistry and neural circuit distortion and cross-connections in brain biology often create strange responses. Cat believes the punches mimic a heavy workout and may trigger the endorphin complex in his brain, and allow Nickels a relaxation period, like a morphine injection, similar to the 'runner's high' athletes often experience during training and competition.

After the interviews, Cat had approached the main offices and Warden Brooks as well. She inquired about the illegal medication switch Ferguson revealed, and the budget. His staff declined contact and comment, and told her Brooks was unavailable. Extremely upset about the medication change, Cat knows it harms Ferguson and it hurts Harry Parker too, indirectly.

*

She types a directive demanding a complete medical review for Walter Ferguson on the state level, and an order that he receive the proper medications her Harvard medical team developed with his help six years ago, the same medications that minimize his battle with the demons. Ferguson generated a significant amount of insight into the psychotic mind for more than two years during her psychiatric internship, and two years after it with the follow up medical panels, and still gives input whenever Cat asks. He deserves at least the courtesy of its rewards, whatever minimal peace it brings his soul.

Cat jumps up and heads out the door and down into the mail office, hands the package to a courier. "Get this package to Senator Winston today, no delay, in his hands no matter what time. He's at the Sheraton this evening, Dalton Street."

The courier hops on a sleek racing bike, pedals it through an automatic door that springs open as he rolls across a metal trigger on the floor, and disappears into the night.

Two monitoring teams watchdog the Stark grant program. Back in her office, she clicks the online buttons, opens the ports, and confirms the falsified medical orders. Ferguson supplied accurate information about his prescription changes, she notes.

The warden modified the medications without an approval from her Harvard team, reducing his multi-million dollar budget. A couple hundred dollars a year per inmate for sixteen mental patients hardly seems worth it. Harvard accountants simply missed it because the prison clerk claims he accidentally mislabeled the pharmacy restocking requests. The auditing official found evidence of file tampering while cross checking the prescription documents after Cat requested an audit.

Approaching the seven-year mark now, four quit and transferred, two died, and three she stopped treating as non-responsive after one year, six inmates remain in her program, but she only counts five in the monitoring process.

Josh Barnes starts and stops meds, and often takes standard psyche meds instead, mixed with street drugs he buys inside the facility, but he shares no verbal information. She tracks him when she gets a chance, but his data offers little value, too incomplete. She stores it anyway.

Cat and Aaron Clark tagged Warden Brooks with the fraud results two days later, the same day she received the official report.

*

Her phone dings, Warden Brooks returning her call, just to push her buttons. He knew his goose was cooked as soon as the monitor caught his medication change. "Cat here."

"These guys need aspirin, or some sugar pill they imagine

works, just don't tell them what it is. They eat it and smile or eat it and frown, doesn't matter. We waste our money. They're crazy anyway, we don't need you or ..."

Cat disconnects his call in mid-sentence, immune to his continuous denigration toward her patients after six years. Her lips bunch into a knot, Cat barely contains her fury.

All that additional mental pain these men experience now for a couple of thousand dollars per year savings on medications Harvard actually supplies to the institution at cost for its psyche programs. Cat opens her phone, punches the speed dial button that connects her to a personal cell phone.

Senator Winston answers on the second ring. "Hello Catherine, it's been awhile."

"Too long, Miller. Nice to hear your voice. How are Jennifer and the boys?"

"Jen's fine, and raising two hellcats, it seems. Just got your notes, how can I help?"

*

Sonny adds a few customers each month, eventually the bike can't keep up with the work. A year and a half after Sonny moved into the gym, K.O helped Sonny find a truck and outfit it with more equipment. The silver GMC born the same year as Sonny sits in the back lot, ding free, shining, and meticulously maintained.

Bart Bailey steps through the door and finds Sonny hitting the leather speed bag uncountable shots a minute, the bag a blur bouncing off the top-plate. Bailey hooked up with K.O. three years ago just for the workouts, no boxing. If Bailey actually boxed in a weight class he might make featherweight if he wears boots, a heavy winter jacket, eats two double Whoppers with fries, and cheats, sticking two rolls of quarters in each pocket before he steps on the scales.

"Little Jumbo took the money but skipped with the tin. Couldn't help it Sonny, he's too big, and he knows it. Ain't afraid of me, I couldn't do nothing." Bailey admits his failure. A slight shake in his fingers and a tear creases his cheek, acknowledging his loss.

"It's okay Bailey. Shoulda known that crook would bust your balls. Shoulda gone myself." Sonny slaps the bag, pulls off the pads, and heads for his truck. "Come on, we'll find him." Both climb in and Sonny spins out the driveway.

"He's over at the Bomb, with the three B's."

The silver truck swings in to a slot at the Bomb Burger, a teen hangout. Sonny climbs out and walks directly at a group gathered in the rear parking lot, six boys all eighteen or nineteen years of age, big kids and looking tough. Teamwork keeps the town kids scared. These wannabe mob-boys hope it's enough. It usually works but not always, like this time when it fails completely. Sonny feels no fear, shrugs off the mean and tough each gang boy projects, knows it as mostly bluff and bluster.

The gang calls itself Big Bad Boys and wraps its boy-shield around Little Jumbo, protecting the top dog. Its members all run tall and too heavy, but each owns a nickname that mimics a pint-size item, reflections on a wish, maybe.

A single wooden toothpick sticks out the corner of a sly grin Little Jumbo aims at Sonny as he approaches. Six-foot two and two hundred sixty pounds, the gang leader stands four inches taller and outweighs Sonny by nearly seventy pounds. Little Jumbo ain't afraid a much, mostly because his thugs surround him except when he sleeps. Slit-eyes watch Sonny close the gap, and Little Jumbo recites the gang slogan. "What the fuck!"

Sonny pushes through the boy-wall. He knows Little Jumbo's just a big, fat bully. Sonny puts his whole shoulder and nearly two years of training behind it and drives a left hook directly into the grin. No words required.

So quick and so hard, Jumbo never sees it coming, topples over backwards, and hits the ground hard. Jumbo spits out a tooth, and blood bubbles out the side of his mouth. Punch drove the toothpick clean through his tongue. Stunned, Little Jumbo rolls around a bit, groans, starts to get up. Sonny knees him back down, a minimal effort, holds out a paw, wiggles his fingers, and growls, "Gimme."

Little Jumbo rolls up on an elbow, slips his hand into a back pocket. Sonny steps closer into him, knees Jumbo again. "Bring out that cutter and I'll stick it in you so far you won't shit for a week."

The gang mentality shuffles toward retaliation, but in that same instant a collective thought ponders what kind of penalty the gang will pay once K.O. learns it. By the time that thought solidifies, the time for engaging it passed. Unconsciously, the collective mind decides no one wants that answer. The slowest thinker of the group, Mini-Mark takes a step forward. Alone.

Sonny catches movement in his right eye, keeps his chin aimed at Jumbo, and raises his right fist straight out the side, points a finger at Mark. "Don't think it."

Mark thinks it anyway. The idea bobbles around in his brain. Still working on a gang mentality, his eyes seek an ally and probe the group one at time. One more step and he gives it up. A little bit of coward exists in each gang member and Mark's the only one moving except Little Jumbo, and Jumbo just rolls around on the ground bleeding. He glares at his tooth lying in the dirt, and projects a less than scary image.

Little Jumbo slumps back, looks at Tiny Tingle, smallest of the six but still a size or two bigger than Sonny. Not a single gram of courage exists between them even when adding it all together. Jumbo spits blood again, nods his head. Tiny Tingle withdraws a small tin container, opens it, and counts out a few wraps.

"Uh-uh. All of it." Sonny wiggles his fingers at Tingle. "You guys picked on Bailey, made Sonny Bones drive all the way out here and hurt Little Jumbo. Sonny don't like hurting animals, so you gonna pay for it. You chose it, not me."

Tiny Tingle glances at Little Jumbo. Jumbo nods again. Tingle snaps the lid shut and tosses the silver tin. Sonny catches it and opens it, inspects it. Satisfied, he points his eyes at each member of the gang one at a time, all look away but the heaviest.

Small Sammy, largest boy in the group, meets his stare. "You want some Sammy? Step up now, otherwise we're done here."

Sammy thinks over his answer then finally drops his head, points his eyes toward his feet. Unable to see past his belt, he examines weeds three feet in front of him instead, not a new experience for Sammy, the too fat belt.

Sonny spins around, heads toward his truck. Back over his shoulder he barks, "Taste better be right or it won't be a tiny tingle you feel next time we cross paths." Sonny grins at his own warped humor. No one else gets it.

The spook claps and giggles. *Nice punch. Good one, drew blood. See? Feels great, doesn't it? Let's do it again. Find K.O., he's next!*

"Shut up spook. Didn't do it for you."

"What?" Bailey asks, and climbs into the truck.

"Nothing. No big deal." Sonny turns the key and backs out, accelerates toward home.

*

An imaginary save, the drugs help briefly, but never long enough and the dollars simply trickle away. Steadily, day after day, Sonny wins a losing battle, gaining spike holes in his arms and nosebleeds that burn.

Fight chemistry with chemistry, makes sense, right? Sonny believes it, fakes it, denies it, and knows it won't help, but can't restrain himself. A pill drops, the scream shrinks into a whimper, the hallucination grows fuzzy, and pain dribbles away. The spook fades at last. The vision dissolves. Chemistry buys time, and quiet - what Sonny needs most when the demons rage. A few seconds emerge, a few minutes, one entire hour free of haunting when he gets lucky - priceless - and good enough for now.

Peace masters his life and Sonny rejoices, basking in the briefest comfort street drugs allow. He heads out toward Baxter Recreation Center, looking for action as long as it engages him physically. Never slows down though, the demons might catch him.

*

Her phone dings and Cat glances at the tag line, Stark Medical. She ignores it, thinking Brooks may be trying to squash her investigation. Not a chance. She logs in the Ferguson choking event and begins evaluating new information the convict shared with her, his experience over three years with multi-medications, as well as additional information two other inmates enrolled in her project offered last month.

Each man receives a different chemical mixture, and each

responds in uniquely different ways. Some negative results and some positive, but always controlled and under the guidance of the Harvard team during quarterly monitoring and its follow-up, but an extremely enlightening weekend in her eyes regardless. It got away due to falsified ordering protocols.

Cat opens her phone and pokes a number, starts giving orders. "Set up a complete review and audit from on the entire Stark project. Go back four years, at least. Let me look at it, we may go back farther. Interject its data into our new TC909-44 theoretical model, including Ferguson and the four remaining patients in this study. I need it yesterday."

She hits end, punches another number, but gets no answer, leaves a message. "Erin, let's play hardball with the prison staff, and get the Stark medical program back on track. Call Jerry Curtiss and engage his new security protocol too, on the medical records and the pharmacy so this kind of budget burglary short-circuits itself before it begins. Call me when it's done."

Cat punches speed dial once more. "Hey Aaron, guess what?" She waits for his guess. "No way, the Jets will never beat the Patriots Sunday, but that's not the correct answer so you pay for lunch. I've got an interesting story so wear your serious ears and bring a recorder."

Cat has no idea a young athlete named Sonny Bones trains hard every day and night in a gym eight hundred miles southwest of Boston, and confronts similar mental demons as those her patients in her Stark medical panel experience. His brain chemistry pushes him closer and closer to intense and uncontrollable violence as each day passes.

*

Sonny climbs up into the ring, a slight haunting presence remains after his run in the park earlier today. He spars seriously now only with K.O. after more than eighteen months with Lucas and other pro boxers in the training program.

Sonny develops too quickly, learns technique too fast, and adds his own patterns and style. No one can keep up with his hands and reaction time. No one else can stay in the ring with him and teach him anything new, so K.O. and Sonny spar twice a day, six days a week. Sonny continues martial arts training two nights a week as well. Brian Santoro teaches self-defense classes for kids and higher levels for a few special adults. Sonny joins Brian for both, enjoys it as much as boxing, and he loves working with the kids.

K.O watched Sonny and his unique style emerge over almost two years, and sees a truth in that natural talent and skill Lucas spotted that first day.

Sonny never hits K.O. A dead spot in technique fails every time. K.O. carries solid physical abilities and skills into the ring, an indefinable punch blocking magic that exists in K.O.'s boxing style. A special knowledge born in a fighter makes him untouchable, and K.O. has had it from birth. It made him unhittable early in his career, and remains with him now. Some athletes have it, some lack it, and no one can teach it or learn it, it just exists at birth, or not, an innate skill few fighters can claim. K.O. recognized it early on in Sonny too, a natural grace and insight great fighters possess, and the speed in his eyes and hands. That quality, combined with heart, makes most anyone that has it a winner.

Sonny swings and K.O. dodges, bats it aside and smiles, bats a right cross, a left hook and another cross, one punch after another misses or K.O. brushes it aside, easy as swatting a fly. K.O puffs out his cheeks and smiles around a bright blue mouth-guard after each whiff.

Frustration emerges and Sonny swings harder and faster, slides in closer then slips away. His eyes suddenly spark, the anger rising at his own failure. Still swinging, still failing, as his rage emerges.

K.O. keeps that bright grin in its normal place. Every miss brings it out. He shows his blue plastic grin after each punch and finally pushes the wrong button.

Sonny attacks, putting everything he has in it every time he and K.O. spar, and wears himself out. K.O seems at idle, a resting technique K.O. learned early in his career and never forgets. Rest and relax every second you can, even in the ring. You always need it.

Then suddenly a combination punch-set Sonny worked in secret fools K.O. Sonny misses two hard left jabs and a left hook intentionally then nails a straight right that stands K.O. up on his toes, drags a little blood out of his grin.

An unusual and mean glint flits across his face and hardens his eyes briefly, but Sonny pulls his mouth-guard and follows the punch with his trademark tongue-flip and grin, and both men laugh aloud at his success.

K.O. bows. Sonny backs away, and salutes, tips the glove off his forehead. Sweat and effort keeps his demon invisible at workouts, the strain shuts it off. It sits quietly in the background, like smoke in a mirror, a slight rasp in his mind, just a bare whisper, but its anger overcomes Sonny quickly whenever he lets his guard down.

You got him. You got him. Let's hit him again. Hurry! Draw blood next time!

"Shut up!" Sonny says it under his breath. He turns around and points the gloves at Lucas.

"What?" Lucas asks.

"Nothin'." Sonny sticks out his hands. The old fighter tugs off each glove and unravels the wraps. Sonny lies down on the bench and runs a lightweight bar up and down for twenty minutes. The voice fades, slowly, but the intensity grows and grates in his mind.

Sonny pushes harder every day now, disregarding the demonic orders, ignoring its unquenchable thirst for violence. Sonny hates it and works until he tires it out and the spook departs on its own. He adds thirty pounds and counts the lifts aloud, "Nineteen, twenty"...a breath..."twenty-one, twenty-two"...a breath..."twenty-three", breathing hard, sweating harder.

*

K.O. drops onto the bench next to Willow. A smile slips onto her face, "Tagged you good. First time, right?"

"Getting a bit tougher gauging his punches now. Was able to see it coming early on, but he gets quicker every day." His early on means a tenth of a second faster. "But now, can just barely tell, he's always had quick hands, but now he brings tricky too, even harder to see that. He keeps it up and he'll tag me hard, which will *not* feel good."

Willow laughs, "What's this, an ego spat?"

K.O. laughs with her. "Maybe time I retire these old fists.

Let the kids take over."

Uncertain he means it though, at barely beyond his prime, K.O. reflects a moment at a glint that crossed Sonny's eyes when he tagged K.O. for the first time ever. Unsure if he likes that look, K.O. wipes wet drops off his face, then wipes again at a little bit of worry. The sweat disappears. The worry remains.

*

Upset today, Chase Nickels lies on his bed, tossing and turning every few minutes, his mind filled with noise and light. He has no clue what causes it, a regular and routine day in the clinic and nothing occurred that would change it. His brain biology pushes aggressive behavior some days, other days it acts relatively passive, and he skipped his meds the past couple days, a choice he makes each time - take it, not take it, take it, not take it - depends on his mood, like others in his situation with similar mental conditions.

Like nearly all mental patients, Chase picks and chooses the days he takes medication. A typical attitude, when he takes it, he feels better, and that elevates this confidence, makes him believe he can live without it, then he stops and the stress picks up again. The past week he took one a day, but skipped two of three on his medication orders. The stress levels in his brain gain traction when he skips some or all medications.

The choice to take or not take medications affects every activity men like Chase Nickels and Ferguson and Barnes engage in each day, and how each feels emotionally and physically, and in random and unpredictable patterns.

The cell lock clicks, Josh Barnes pushes in through the barred steel door, crawls up on his bunk, grabs his paperback. The bunk bounces and wiggles as Nickels rolls over beneath him a few times, and Barnes says, "You feeling a little uptight today Chase? You take your meds?"

Nickels contemplates an answer, takes a minute, and mutters, "Some of 'em."

"Yeah, right. You talk to Medina?"

"Yup. Same thing, she tells me, 'Take your meds', like a fuckin' recorder. You know, the meds, it ain't the same Josh. Just not like the real thing."

Barnes says, "Yeah, I know, not the same, we all feel it. What do these doctors know? Nothing, right? They read it, don't live it." A burst of laughter bleats out the side of his mouth. "Treat us like cattle, run the process, collect the fees."

"Never hear us, we know, not them. Should hear us, should listen better, use both ears, like Fergie tells it," Nickels says. "Well, been waiting here, it's time."

Barnes shakes his head. "Not feeling much like it lately."

"No fuckin' way. Been too long, you gettin' lazy, stress keeps lightin' me up, and pops comin' too ... big ones, too loud. Can feel it ragin', Josh, come on!" His voice cuts an edge in it, and rises with his complaints. Chase starts agitating, pulls up out of bed.

Barnes watches, sees the anger begin, understands it. "Okay, so let's get it over with. Try for eight this time?"

Nickels barks out a laugh. "Never happen, you skipped lunch. No way, you ain't lastin' eight minutes. Bet two Xanax and a cookie you can't even make six."

Barnes began a new medication several weeks ago and it works well. It calms him and softens his brain issues more than many other compounds his doctors tried in the past. Cat gave input to his doctor on the last chemistry batch. Josh started the new combination three weeks ago.

Josh lasts two minutes and quits then jumps up on his bed, suddenly loses interest in punching Nickels, as if he no longer finds joy in, as if he no longer needs it.

Disappointed and still upset, Nickels barks, "Not enough, not enough, you'll be sorry Josh. We have a deal. Four days in a row now, you quit on me. You owe me Josh, this ain't no game. You'll be sorry, Josh. Sorry. Sorry, you will be really fuckin' sorry."

*

Later that same evening, just past midnight, a uniformed guard wanders the Stark residential corridors alone, and punches his station meter at each checkpoint. The vent system expands and contracts, and ticks softly as the heat kicks off. The night settles in, as quiet as it gets. Most felons lie on the bunks, asleep. The entire wing smells like an old athletic sock.

Inside his cell, Joshua Barnes rolls onto his back and a snort breaks the silence, then another. Whenever he sleeps face up, Barnes snores loudly. It happens often, and when it happens, Nickels barks at the noise, shakes the bed, and punches the bottom of the mattress. Barnes usually turns over and breathes quietly.

Upset tonight for some unknown reason, Nickels opens his eyes and listens for at least a minute. The pops and colors in his brain rage, much higher activity than normal tonight - if one can ever actually label his odd psychosis as normal. He decides his cellmate snores on purpose and keeps him awake intentionally. The thought upsets Nickels even more, lays a pinch of stress on that final nerve.

Nickels grabs the crossbar, hoists himself up off his mattress, reaches over the end rail above it and grabs Barnes by the throat. The skinny weakling struggles, kicks his feet wildly beneath the sheets, and bats his fists at the powerful shoulders above his head.

Chase Nickels - two hundred pounds heavier and much stronger - works his way around the bunk. Holding Josh in place easily with his left hand, he gently and steadily increases pressure with his right thumb, crushing the esophagus.

The snore shuts off immediately but the struggle continues for two or three minutes, Barnes coughs up blood, coughs again, and then relaxes completely, lies still and quiet on his sheets. His legs and feet twitch and wiggle a few times as Josh Barnes settles into eternity.

Nickels reaches over and smoothes a few hairs, and caresses both cheeks a couple of times each while Barnes lies motionless. Chase frowns at the blood on his hands, pulls the sheet up and covers his victim, wipes his fingers on it, then drops back into his bunk and fluffs up his pillow. The colors and pops vanish. Nickels eases back on his bunk, pulls his knit cap down over his ears, and smiles at the silence. "Told ya' Josh, you'd be sorry. Told ya'."

A clock sitting on his dresser ticks off sixty seconds. Nickels falls into a guiltless, dreamless sleep, his hands still splotched with fresh blood.

9

Eight voices yell, "Surprise!" Fright flashes briefly across his face and his heart thumps a few hard beats then quickly fades into a smile and a steady rhythm as Sonny steps into the snack room and recognizes his friends waiting.

Sonny sucks in a breath and blows. Seventeen candles blink out on a large birthday cake Willow places on the table. A space ship and three weird creatures decorate its top. Six teen-age gym rats and K.O. join Willow singing Happy Birthday, mostly off key. Willow cuts the cake.

"You believe in aliens K.O.?" Sonny points at the cake design.

"Don't know, may be somebody else out there. It's just a decoration the baker drew. You chatting about space and ships and space aliens sometimes, and odd demons, kids thought you'd like it."

Sonny grins wide and buries his fright, waiting for this surprise day to end so he can sneak away and hide in his room. How would these kids know this date, and how would they get here? Must be reading his mind? Sonny gave out no invitations. He knows that for sure, he would remember if he told them.

Must have been those aliens told or haunts, those demons, whatever they are, brothers of those three nasty jokers setting on his cake or sisters maybe? Sonny can't tell the difference. Damn alien demons beginning to piss him off though, won't stay out of his life lately, sitting in his brain, getting stronger, harder to kick out. Keeps telling him to punch walls and hurt people with alien brains stuck inside their heads. The demon told all these kids about his birthday, he told no one so he knows the spook read his mind.

*

His imagination runs wild as his brain biology matures and hormones short-circuit across his thought patterns, the dysfunctional mind creates monsters in his memory cells now, and adds faces occasionally. Sweat keeps the demons at bay and he works out harder and harder and pushes the stress. Exhaustion finally tires his body as well as his mind.

*

Big hand on six, little hand on five, his clock lies on the floor, its face smashed, a little dent in the wall where the clock struck it and broke at five-thirty this morning when the alarm kicked on.

Seventy-one minutes pass and no more wakeup dings, then the phone drags him out of a dead sleep. "What?" Sonny blurts, rubs his eyes. "Whoops, sorry Mrs. Greene, alarm didn't ring. Sure, an hour, maybe a little bit more, got one other chore first."

Tell her to go screw herself. She pays too little. Make her pay more, she's cheap. She reads your mind – that's how she knows. You're worth more, make her pay it! Punch her if she won't. Punch her anyway. Kick her brat, he deserves it.

"Get away!" Sonny barks at it, annoyed. He stretches and yawns, hauls himself into his morning, kicks off the blankets.

Voices in his brain bark more often now, sometimes one, sometimes two, the first one brings a friend with it lately, teams up on Sonny if he ignores its chatter. Sometimes it wears a face sometimes not. Voices have been coming around for years, the faces only about six or eight months, and not every time. Voices get louder, give orders, and try to boss him around. Sonny pays it little attention today, knows the run will dissolve it, this one this time, at least temporarily.

Sonny slips out of bed, pulls on his sweats, stops in the hallway, stands absolutely still for a full minute staring at the paint, then punches a hole in the drywall. "Get out!" He moves a foot to the right, punches another hole. "You too, both of you, get out."

He looks at his knuckles, rubs his fist, sticks his hands in the hoodie pouch, heads out the door, and jogs five miles in the cold. A light dusting of snow and the scent of November chill the air.

Breathing hard, frost-breath still pushing between his lips, he grabs his Stihl and heads out again, his second chore today. First chore every morning - a run - clouds, sun, rain or snow, he runs, chases away the demon that greets his wake-up every day.

Heavy wind split an oak down its center, and it blocks the client's garage. Sonny yanks the cord twice. Chain teeth bite deep into tough meat and chips fly everywhere. He works up a heavy sweat stacking the wood. Cut, split, stack, sweat, cut, split, stack, sweat, and the demon shuts up once more, at least for a while.

Sonny bites into a sandwich and chugs a drink, puts a little more burn in his belly for later. He'll need it. The demon will be back. He knows it, no doubt, but his work will push it out again. He knows that too, run, lift, spar, cutting, split, stack, and pedal, no matter which as long as it brings out sweat and kick-starts adrenaline. He tosses the last wedge on the pile, packs up his saw, collects his fee, and heads toward the gym.

*

Sonny sneaks around back, slips inside, and creeps into his room. Silent, lying on his bed, he watches the door swing open. He pulls the blanket up around his shoulders, scant protection if an alien enters. K.O. steps in and Sonny relaxes.

"How'd this get here?" K.O. asks and points at the fist-sized hole in the wall.

"Yup, me," Sonny admits. "Tripped and fell against it. Hit it with my elbow."

"Pretty rough trip you ask me. Looks more like a punch hole to me."

"Tripped over my socks." Sonny sticks out his tongue and tries his lop-side grin again. It fails.

K.O. aims real scare-eyes at him, a very tough glare, but conceals his confusion, unsure what triggers the anger and mean attitude lately. The last few months or so, two clocks broken, fist-size holes in the wall, three bent lamps, cups and glasses smashed and cleaned up, but broken chips hide in corners and missing crockery gives the secret away.

Sonny folds up his grin, tucks it away. "Stuff happens, K.O. No big deal, just a hole. Besides, it's my wall."

"Nope, my wall, you just rent it."

"So, add it to the rent." Sonny turns his head and pushes his face into the pillow.

"A pair out in the hallway look just like it, twins." K.O. remarks, "You trip over that other sock out there?"

No answer.

"And, what happened to your cell, pieces of it lying all over the gym floor? How you gonna get work, no one can call? You miss a payment, lose your truck."

No answer.

"Broke two clocks, you don't want it ringing you awake, don't set the button." K.O. has concerns about Sonny, but a little irritation too, about the damage.

"Been bouncing anger off everyone around here lately Sonny, better get a hold of that. You want a talk, you come see me, or Willow. You know that."

Still no answer.

K.O. shuts the door, pauses a minute outside, then opens it again and sticks his head in.

"You training tonight? Jacki expects you sparring her at eight. Coming a long ways to learn. She worships you Sonny. Don't disappoint her. She's a nice kid."

"Ain't earned worship here, still just a kid too, Remember? You tell me that anyway, still just a kid too."

"That's so, huh? Maybe old enough can take a fact or two now without your head swelling too much." K.O raises his voice, pushes out the truth. "Okay kid, how's this? Toughest work ethic here, quickest hands, stiffest jab and hardest right punch in all my years training, all of 'em. Got it?"

He softens his words. "And, biggest thing Sonny, you got heart and you teach heart. That earns worship, even if Jacki's only twelve. She watches how hard you work, how well you share what you know, and dreams that for her own future."

K.O. points a finger. "So, act like an adult. She deserves that much, at least."

Sonny rolls up on a shoulder. "Got it, K.O., I won't let her down. She's cool, I'm cool."

"You been working harder than ever lately, but acting feisty toward everyone, all your friends this last month or two. Your first sanctioned bout comes in a week and under the lights. It's just a boxing match. Don't let it bother you like that. You slack off now though, get your butt handed back to you on a plate. All that training and sparring and running and lifting the past two years, just be wasted."

Sonny cuts a little mean into his face, even though deep in his heart he finds no good place for it, but he lost control. "So, maybe one day we'll find out about this 'best punch' in the gym," Sonny says. "A little pre-best punch this afternoon maybe, you missed it K.O., look in that wall mirror next time. Reflection catches everything happens in this ring."

Sonny pushes his first challenge ever toward K.O. and he regrets it immediately but says nothing more, pulls the pillow up over his face, hides his worry and his anger. His worry feels real, but Sonny has no idea why anger pops in his life so often lately, demon usually accompanies it though, so he pushes some of the rage toward the nasty spook that sticks itself in his brain each time he rests.

*

K.O. believes stress causes Sonny to break things, and his anxiety lately. Sonny has his first sanctioned fight next week, but K.O. guessed dead wrong about the reason. He waits and stares, but his scare-eyes fail this time and he shuts the door again. Drooping eyes and a sagging jaw fits a troubled look on his face. K.O. walks down the hall shaking his head, puzzled. "Kids!"

Sonny kicks his chair across the room. He stares at the wall a full minute then punches once, controls his fist and leaves a very small dent in the drywall. He falls back on his bed, grabs his head in both hands and hides beneath his pillow, tears running down both cheeks.

10

Eight hundred miles northeast of the KNOCKOUT, Cat struggles with information her assistant provided, evaluating the data for her psychiatric research. She keys page down, page down, page down, shakes her head, pushes a pager button, "Are you busy, can you come in here a minute?"

A blond-haired, blue-eyed, Minnesota girl tucks her roundness into a multi-colored granny-dress every day, and brings phenomenal technical knowledge into the office. She steps in through the door and pushes her rimless glasses back on her nose. Married to a stay-at-home dad who care-takes both children while she works in a field she loves almost as much as her kids, Erin McCord says, "What's up?"

"I need you to run these clinic notes." She hands McCord a list. "Set up a capture that grabs only cases with these four key words in the workup."

The tech wizard says, "Okay. What're we looking for?"

"Brain chemistry, distorted memory circuits or hormone interactions that produce a violent response under conditions where it shouldn't or wouldn't. Generally, we want case notes that describe unprovoked and uncontrollable violence that occurs in an otherwise safe social setting."

"We're looking at young adults with an imbalance in brain biology that triggers hormone-induced violent reactions. The imbalance in communication channels creates distorted visual and auditory function in the mental eye and ear inside the brain. These visions and voices produce high stress levels, and drive these kids into elevated levels of violence to offset the chemical reactions inside the neural pathways."

"The endomorph interaction in flight or fight choices in a threat situation dampens it. We're trying to duplicate it medically as a part of the treatment chemistry."

Erin responds. "What if it backfires, and produces more intense violence? We ran two field trials a few years ago in Africa and India. Male baboons and macaques exhibit some nasty behaviors when the females hit an estrous cycle. And, that's totally hormone driven."

"Oh, that's right. You went with Max on that one, didn't you?" Cat remembers it well and read the raw field data after the trials concluded. "We're controlling for that, trying to anyway, watching it close."

"We're importing data from the Stark cases too. According to the records, two cellmates developed a very odd relationship."

Cat explains it. "Barnes liked to hit men and Nickels likes getting hit. We have a little skinny weakling beating on this huge bear of a man. And each man finds some strange kind of mental release in it."

"We're making sure we don't miss any behaviors similar to Walter Ferguson, or Nickels, or Barnes. These men often hide it, although it remains transparent to the observers, but only when we get to watch it. Nickels actually beat up Barnes every day for almost a week because Barnes refused to punch him and stop the colors and flashing. Chase Nickels exhibits a lightning effect and a popping noise in his brain and it initiates huge stress factors. Punching and bruising shuts it off, like closing a toggle switch. How's that for unusual?"

"Definite failure in Nickels, you'll see it in the notes. He eventually killed Barnes right in his cell. Not sure if it was med related, or if he stopped taking it, or if Brooks messed up with the medications orders. Nickels generally cooperates. Sometimes he talks, sometimes he babbles, but when he finds focus and opens up to me, what he shares is extremely useful."

Cat never verbalizes it, but it hurts her emotionally every time she fails with a patient. Her mentor always tells her, '... never get emotionally involved with patients.' Practically impossible, and she wonders how any doctor acknowledges that advice, or lives it. Maxwell Whitetail ignores his own advice as well, a dedicated softy that treats all his patients like family.

"Nickels killed his brothers and his mother five years ago. He thinks they still live in Springfield, and ignore him. Then Nickels accused Barnes of plotting with the warden to add years on Nickels sentence, but he's already serving three at life without parole."

"Nickels admits Barnes was snoring that night, says it 'sounds like a freight train' in his cell. Claims a voice in the dark asked him to stop it, ordered him to just '... put a little pressure on the windpipe'. Nickels later told us he choked the devil out of Barnes so he would lose the paranoia and beat on him again. Keeps changing his story. I believe he wanted the relationship back on track, the beatings, but Nickels strangled Barnes instead then crawled back on his bunk and fell asleep. No guilt at all, claims Barnes broke the bargain."

"Similar issues exist with Walter Ferguson, but he tempered his violence a little over the years. The medication he helped us develop works well with him once he got back on it again. He finally finds some relaxing time, and he quit punching the walls."

Erin asks, "You and Ferguson became friends, right?"

"Not exactly best buddies, but we developed a relationship, not a true friendship but I respect his honesty and he gives us a lot. He's open with me and with Aaron too. Nothing we find tells us he's making up any of it. It doesn't excuse his violence, but it does explain it in one sense."

"So again, what if it backfires and brings more violence into the equation?"

"That's what the grant committee wonders too. They push us hard on that possibility. We're careful with it. Aaron says I can choose anyone to assist in this one. You game, or you still tied up?"

"Absolutely, count me in, sounds like a challenge. Will finalize the Turner and Worthington reports this week, then I'm all yours. Where's this new data coming from?"

"All up and down the east coast. We sent out requests to all emergency psyche clinics, requesting behavior records on young adults that exhibit unprovoked violence. We know the clinics but get redacted names, just merge the data so we can quantify for now."

"Eventually, we'll request names and a release from each clinic when we identify patients we may involve in this study. The clinic needs a signed HIPAA release before we can even know who it is, and then we contact each one that agrees and insert into our field study. It's very tedious at this point, but if you can key-word this search, might speed it up."

"One more thing, pull up all raw data from the old study at Stark and see how it correlates with this new stuff but keep it separate. Particularly Ferguson and Nickels at our Harvard program three, four years ago. Include this file too." Cat jots a file number from memory on a scrap of paper. "I've seen Fergie a few times since then, that info's in this new file." She jots down another file number.

Cat pops a thumb-drive out of her laptop and hands McCord a stack of forms and the disk. "Some sent a printed form, some sent a web reply. Scan the forms in and collate with the electronic responses, then run a sort program and give us a total count and the ER location for each patient that fits our criteria. Select from those and send HIPAA releases blind, hope we get the right responses. Give me a separate file on the Stark study Aaron and I ran five or six years ago, up to current. Exact dates are on this disk as well."

"A lot of this data's worth a bit less for us here and now, but we'll see what pops up in this search first, before we store it." Cat gets frustrated with her search technique, but runs into legal difficulties if she collects data the way she wants it because HIPAA interferes and stops medical facilities from exchanging health care information, even between clinics.

"We often get diagnostic information, but no names without signed permissions. Here we go, data that only tells us we have a sick kid, which we already know, but no name unless we ask permission first, and we don't know the name so we can't ask and can't do follow-up. Typical Catch-22 bureaucratic nonsense." She shakes her head, the frustration evident.

Most social workers find little time between meetings and mileage to answer her queries and those that do it send information that illustrates how untrained many are in this field today. The health care workers document individual behavior illustrating simple everyday activities, eating, sleeping, walking around, reading, and none of that helps Cat understand what goes on in the brain when these kids act out and respond with violence during normal and non-threatening events.

Observing a sedated patient in a set environment illustrates only what happens with sedated patients under controlled conditions. The field workers see clients only on best behavior outside the clinics too, because most patients choose to live at home, or in a car, even in a field or a box, anywhere but locked up in the clinics.

"Makes sense," McCord says, "Even homeless vagrants want the freedom to live outside a cell or without the confinement of a clinic setting. They pick a cardboard cabin over a medic white-coat telling them how to live every time." McCord laughs, "Better hang up that gown Cat, you'll lose all your clients to a refrigerator carton."

Cat must observe the kids that exhibit unprovoked violence in person, so she can identify the biological triggers before the violence gets out of control. Cat believes she can develop a formula that chemically offsets that violence instead of the brain forcing it to act out physically in a violent manner.

"So take your time with this search, double blind it in the program if you need it. We have a good budget as long as we stay inside the guidelines. Although I don't know how this committee expects us to harvest the veggies without planting a few seeds first."

Cat and Aaron Clark had a very difficult time convincing the grant committee that she 'won't create a monster' like the movie Frankenstein or Jekyll and Hyde with her chemistry manipulations. The committee worries, expressing a reasonable fear that her chemistry interjections might trigger intense and uncontrollable violence instead of comfort and relaxation, and a patient may end up with a deranged mind capable of hurting or even executing innocent individuals at any moment, and unpredictably.

A very tough sell, so her research team walks a tightrope. "Feels like we're dancing on a molecule," Cat admits, "a very slick one."

Even now, as the state begins an investigation, trying to decide if Nickels choked Barnes because his medication triggered it, or if Barnes pissed him off when he stopped punching him. Cat knows Nickels stopped his medications for at least a week prior, but also knows Barnes quit punching Nickels when he began his new medication a few weeks prior as well. Still, she has no proof of cause and effect. No one can prove it one way or the other in cases like this. The same old chicken or the egg question.

11

Lefts and rights snap in and out, headshots and uppercuts, both fists strike with the speed of a snake. Blue ink decorates his left bicep, swirling spikes and pointed wire link an artistic 'BONES' tattooed beneath the sleek left shoulder that drives his jab.

A body shot, left jab, a right cross, an uppercut, more body shots, relentless combinations. Sonny stalks his prey, his right fist connects, a power punch that stops his first bout almost before it begins. Ronny Hutchison hits the mat at one minute and twenty-nine seconds. Sonny stands above him, making sure. The referee pushes Sonny into the farthest corner, twice, and then starts his count.

In the middle of a very brief Round One, his opponent rolls around on the deck and the referee shouts ten, waves his hands. Not even a hard workout. Sonny barely broke a sweat, but smiles at it anyway. He counts his first win. His record begins, one and zero, a great start. Sonny circles the ring, celebrates his victory, the bright red gloves bouncing above his head.

No contest this one, Sonny believes it anyway, his brain tells him that, and his heart concurs – just a thing he knows – a thing resigned as if nothing can interfere, ever, and his confidence shines, always on the attack, never backing away. Heart, belief in himself, a thing K.O. drilled into him the past two years, though he brought a lot of heart with him, confidence he learned in a tough life, surviving alone - a child in the forest.

Character, he earns that too, works hard, sweats hard, lifts hard, and bangs the bags harder. He runs long and fast, defeating the demons. K.O. trains him well though the voices remain his own, Sonny's secret from the external world as he hides the spooks that live in his brain.

A flashbulb pops! The crowd roars, cheering its hometown boy. Friends and fans scream his name repeatedly. "Sonny! Sonny! Sonny!" The contagious chant echoes off the arena walls.

*

Two months pass. Miles from home in a strange town the final bell ends Round Three - his second match. Two young athletes shuffle at center-ring awaiting the tally, both men stoic and still. Both teens clone a mental intensity while masking identical thoughts, a shared intimacy warming the night. Two maturing fighters connected in body and spirit wait, hiding impatience as only an athlete can. A thirty-second eternity seems longer than the match itself. Two teens stand mute, each hoping for the result only one can receive.

Finally, the referee scores the card and barks, "Blue corner, the winner!" The official raises the winning fist high above his head, still dressed in its bright red glove.   A huge cheer erupts. Sonny raises his other red glove. Both fists bounce in the air, both feet dance on the mat, the stout, vibrating kid that never stands still. A winner! Unanimous! Age seventeen, his second match, his second win, this bout lasting the full three rounds, nine whole minutes, unlike his first, which never rang Round Two. Elation sparks his grin.

Sonny peeks at K.O. holding a stool in one hand and a thumb up on the other, both hands high above the ropes. Sonny grins and turns back to center ring.

"Good fight," both boys harmonize.   The athletes hug sweat, pop gloves, bump shoulders and grin, exhibiting true sportsmanship, like the idols both worship and the champions both admire.

A name tickles a corner of his mind, briefly turning up both ends of his lips. Confident, sure of himself, almost cocky, 'The Dominator' stands in simple colors, black and white, with dark red trim, nothing fancy, nothing flashy. Sonny Bones has arrived, a young challenger in an old fight game. Sonny grins at K.O. and barks, "Bring it on!"

A great amateur beginning … Sonny rolls his shoulders, tightly muscled, smooth and powerful from years of work. Sweat drips off his brow. He dances in the ring, still up on his toes, no effort, adrenaline pushing his nerves, his energy boundless for the moment, and his smile bigger than life – elated, he claims his reward.

Two fights, two wins, and his fingers curl tightly into his palms, looking for more, daring the next opponent to split the ropes and climb up on the mat he now owns. Both fists bounce in the air once more while Sonny jogs the ring a final time. All that sacrifice finally pays off. His new record reads two and zero.

A very young boxer stares over the ropes and grins at his sister, his duplicate mother, his trust friend, whatever Willow represents. He jumps off the platform, clicks knuckles with K.O., and hugs Willow. "Least this guy can fight." Sonny recalls his first opponent, who never got beyond round one.

"Golden Gloves! The Olympics!" K.O predicts, as the cheers continue behind him. K.O. dances a figure eight twice, a huge smile on his face.

An incredible dream, a young athlete nearly released from the task of his birth – an unwed mother once pushed to choose. Bathed in unawareness and her secret wetness, the calm of her womb, he wiggled his fingers for the first time ever. Her decision but his reward, he won that fight with no words and no fists, though Sonny never knew it.

Adopted instead of aborted, and Sonny Bones welcomes the cheers.

The demons hide in the shadows, completely silent tonight.

12

Back at Stark Medical Facility, Cat sits in the same meeting room with a different patient, Chase Nickels. No change in furnishings or decor since last time she met with Ferguson and Nickels more than a year ago, and more than two years since the Ferguson choking event.

"Hey Cat," Nickels says. Nickels squeaks, a brief giggle escapes. He chuckles again, enjoying his joke in a place that seldom jokes. "Walls need new paint, looks the color of pee."

Cat sticks a smile on her face. "Hey Chase." She looks at the paint, shrugs.

Nickels cooperates less well with doctors than some more agreeable patients, including Ferguson, and his personality exhibits more nastiness than candor. Sometimes Nickels hides it, sometimes not, but nasty always lies in the background, a term he earned almost from the cradle. He aggravated his mother, forcing his brother to punch him even as a young adult, as equally strange a relationship as the one he later developed with Barnes.

The convict eyes Cat across the table, smoke filters out between his lips and curls up around his eyes, a demand he made before he agreed to meet her again. He sits in a no-smoking room in a no-smoking facility, smoking a cigarette and grinning. His one condition for meeting Cat and talking about his violence again means he gets a smoke in this room. One more violation of facility rules, and one more power trip he claims for himself and aims at the prison administration, thumbing his nose once more.

Looking like a big old fat hairy bear sitting on a toy chair, his dark brown curls hang long and filthy, streaked with blonde highlights. Nickels squints through the smoke, his hands cuffed behind him and a cigarette between his lips, obviously uncomfortable, with no way to control the gray cloud drifting into his eyes and up his nose. Nickels coughs and giggles.

He coughs again, harder, and spits the barely burned unfiltered Lucky Strike butt onto the floor. In a nimble flash of agility with both feet chained together, he twists the chair, elevates his legs straight out like two thick logs hanging off the edge of his seat, and drops his boots, crushing the red coal with one heel.

No one objected when Cat approached the new warden with this odd request. Staff here knows her influence reaches as high as the governor's office, and Aaron Clark reaches even higher if he needs it. Doctor Clark declined a federal political office on several occasions because he loves his work and wants to make a difference on a meaningful level. So staff pretty much leaves her alone and give her what she needs and wants. Cat has no wish to flaunt her authority, but believes her results offset any minor bend in institution regulations.

Nickels wanted a cigarette as payment for his chat. Cat brought one with her and lit it as part of her weird agreement, but stood clear of any possible contact after her narrow escape with Ferguson and his chain choker. As usual, information carries a price, especially in prison facilities. Cheap enough this time, although Cat had to buy a whole pack for the one she owed Nickels. Once it cost her a hundred twenty bucks for a twelve-inch television, her most expensive bribe so far. She feels lucky this time, one pack of smokes, under four bucks, and nineteen remain she can freeze in case she can bribe with it again. She laughs inside herself at that thought. What are the chances?

"Nice one Chase, feels great in the eyes, right? Good for your lungs too."

"Fuck it Cat, quit smokin' years ago. Hate them suckers, but just want to screw with the officials, had no time to think of anything better. Got little enough to laugh at here, might as well choke smoke, and break a rule." Nickels shifts this three-hundred-twenty pound bulk and kicks his legs out front, his restraints rattle against the chair.

"Bastards got me back though, light me up and chain my

hands behind my back." Nickels grins then coughs again, shifts his weight, in obvious discomfort. Too large for the small metal folding chair the warden sent in for this specific occasion. A little get-back aimed at Nickels and Cat for pushing his button about the cigarette.

"So, I hear you got another life tag a couple months ago? Want to talk about it?"

"You already know, don't you? Talked to Fergie first, right?"

"Yeah, he told me what happened, but not how it happened or why or how you felt. Only you can tell that part."

"Felt same as always without the bruising. Joshua started his new medication and quit hitting me. Couldn't stand it anymore, colors and noise, noise and colors, colors and noise, louder, flashing, flashing brighter, just wouldn't quit. Nearly drove me crazy."

Nickels cackles, loud and boisterous, then sings, "Drivin' me crazy. Drivin' me crazy, drivin' me crazy," his voice rings out, sweet and true, a total surprise, a tenor exactly on key. Then he laughs and wiggles his large bushy eyebrows up and down a few times. Cat laughs aloud at his antics.

"So, I just choked him and got me a single cell, then started my meds again. Serves him right, he quit fixing me, paid the penalty." His words kicked the interview back into a serious mode.

"No reason to kill him," Cat says.

"Didn't, just stopped his snoring. He choked. I didn't mean it, exactly. He couldn't breathe, his fault not mine. Spit blood on me too. Warned him. Told him he'd be sorry."

She buffers her emotions. She understands the pain these men cause others or themselves, but carefully hides it. She laughs with one, cries with another. She lets each man believe she condones it or agrees with it so the men talk and tell her the truth. Some will, some will not. She still feels it inside though, no matter that she remains helpless as well, but on a different emotional level.

Nickels ignores her critique and stands up but the cuffs loop through the rails behind him and the chair lifts with him and hits his thighs below his buttocks and high up on his back, keeping him neatly bent at the waist. He sits again, kicks out his feet, squirms in his seat.

"Bet the warden got a laugh out of putting this chair in here. Guess I owe him one." He shrugs, indifferent, accustomed to minor abuse, already plotting some way to repay Paul Acheson. Acheson took over as warden when the committee fired Brooks. A change in personnel brought no change in attitude. The typical institutional mentality remains.

"New pills work better, just make me itch a lot, and gotta pee more too. Switched my meds to bedtime, puts me to sleep. If I take 'em in the mornings, it knocks me out in an hour. Was never gettin' out anyways, so who cares, two lifers or three lifers, still sleep in the same cell and eat the same grub, look at the same green walls."

"Joshua deserved it, teasing me, made me feel good then just stopped hitting me. His own fault I had to choke him, and he snored besides. Can't be having that loud breathing, not in a double crib anyways, keeps a guy awake. Besides, we had a deal, he broke it."

Cat feels his discomfort. She knocks on the exit door. The escort enters.

"Unlock those cuffs, lock them in front. He can't even sit down."

Escort looks at the chair, looks at Nickels, looks at Cat, says nothing, walks back outside the door, shuts it, locks it, dials a wall phone, speaks and listens, unlocks the door again, walks back inside, unlocks the cuffs, relocks the cuffs in front, exits and locks the door behind him. Never says a word.

"Thanks Cat, now I owe you." He grins. "What can I tell you?"

"Explain how the colors work, and the pops. Tell me what happens when the punches land. What happens when he stops hitting? Where do the colors go? And the noise?"

So Nickels grins and tells it, describes the hurt, the sting, the bright flashing colors slowly fading, the popping noise slowly dims as the bruising comes up. His arms and back and stomach and his chest redden and swell slightly as the punches urge blood toward the skin surface.

"Never hit on the face though, never there, that's too personal." Nickels grunts at the thought, shakes his head, his curls float around his face and tangle in his beard.

Nickels smiles, enjoys the memory. "Harder Josh swings, the faster the flashes fade and noise disappear, the harder Josh works, the quicker I get relief. Took at least fifteen minutes on his best days, but he's so light and weak he never hit me hard enough to hurt me no matter how hard he swings. It just stings and relaxes the flashes and pops. Clean wore him out finally, so he quit hitting me after he went on a new med."

He tells it exactly as he remembers it, his eyes glaze over, as if he feels it happening again right now in this room, not months ago and in the past with a man he killed. He easily recalls the experience up into his mind, projects it on his mental screen, as if he performs this action often, and nearly as real as the days when it occurred, but it appears dreamlike now. The pills lessen his emotion and the colors and noise hide along the edges of his consciousness, hovering in the background, dim and quiet, as if awaiting the day he stops medication and needs the beatings again.

"So, you see lightning flashes, different colors, and hear a pop each time it flashes, right? And the colors and pops recede when someone like Josh hits you, that release, can you explain that feeling?"

"Weird, like a flood of warm, or comfort just runs all over my body, kinda like a drug in my blood, you know what I mean, like a heroin high when we shoot up. Then the colors fade and the noise quits."

"No, I don't know. I never shoot heroin, Chase."

He grins, "Don't know what you're missing Cat." He looks at his feet, then around the room, then directly into her eyes, then wipes his mouth, the cuffs rattle. "Want to punch on me a while Cat? Wish I'd thought of that, been better than that waste of smoke. You're smaller than Josh, probably hit just right." Nickels squints, grins, chuckles, and shifts his weight.

"No thanks, I'd just hurt you." Both laugh out loud at that one.

Cat decides the beatings trigger the endurance hormones, so he feels less pain, and the relief. Researchers call that experience the 'runner's high', the endorphin complex that releases in the brain under heavy physical exertion and acts like morphine, and gives long-distance runners or hunters a lift in energy and a suppression of pain when engaged in intense battles or a predator escape or an endurance marathon.

"Gotta find a new punch partner if this new med don't work, 'cause Joshua ain't coming back." He chuckles at his ridiculous comment, but Cat detects sadness in his gaze and his lips turn down at the ends. As odd as it may seem, both men engaged in behavior that brought each one comfort while enduring a biological condition few people understand.

*

Cat sits at her desk, reviews her narrative, and interjects her newest notes from interviews with Ferguson and Nickels. She begins applying her theory to the violent events in the lives of the two men she knows best of all the men in her studies.

She met Ferguson and Nickels first, and both men have been forthcoming over the years. Nickels expressed extreme violence recently, but jumps in and out of his agreement with her. He shares his actions and motivations, but only at his whim, sometimes he does and sometimes not, completely unpredictable, and unreliable.

Ferguson remains the most violent and the most sharing, the most truthful as well, an unusual contradiction in one sense, and the most trusted. He never refuses meeting with Cat. She knows Ferguson loves her, but like a sister, not a wife. He tells her often although he often comments on her sexuality as well. That negates the factor of an emotionless mind when dealing with the violence attributed to the mental condition, as some researchers claim. She believes the emotions remain, but the brain contains those emotions beneath an overlay that allows protective mechanisms - like survival instincts - to exhibit and control behavior when fright or a threat appears, even a false threat.

Although Nickels exhibits extreme violence too. He choked Barnes to death because the man stopped hitting him. Nickels strangled his brother for the same reason. His younger brother stopped hitting him. Then, he shot his older brother and mother because they both witnessed it and started dialing the cops. He shut them up, hid the bodies in the closet, and ran away. Sheriff caught him an hour later, down at the bar, playing pool.

So small and weak, Barnes could hit Nickels all day, and Nickels received nothing but light bruises and some kind of mental release. Barnes did as well, and felt a stress release when he punched a man, a weird but equal exchange between them. In a mental oddity Cat does not yet understand, it worked well for both men until Barnes accepted new medications and it relieved his urges. At that point, Nickels no longer needed Barnes nor does he feel remorse for killing his friend. Nickels never considered Barnes a friend, only a method, a tool to stop his mental hallucinations, like a unique medication, true physical therapy.

In an odder tweak of ethics and morals versus science, Cat wonders briefly if she should feel any guilt. She medicated Barnes, stopped his psychotic desires - the punching - and he died because of it. Very complex philosophical inquiry for certain, but Cat shakes it off. Not her fault Barnes committed the crimes that got him sentenced. Still, she ponders … did she miss something important? Could she have stopped that violent act?

No one knew it until the evening count the next day when Barnes refused to stand for the tally. The count guard unlocked the cell and hauled Barnes off his bunk, got a real surprise when Barnes just flopped down onto the floor, motionless.

Is any part of his death her fault? No, she decides, and drops that subject forever. Tears fill her eyes regardless.

13

Sonny stands at the library checkout desk with several magazines in his hand, the covers facing down. He needs a card to operate the copy machine. "So, you're Brian's sister, right?"

The clerk continues writing in her ledger, long dark hair tied up in a bun, spare pencil stuck behind her ear. A badge pinned on her shirt spells Lisa.

Discretely, Sonny examines Lisa Santoro while he waits. Her Italian heritage accents dark feminine features and a soft peach tone brightens her lips. A small scar on her chin adds character. Almost as tall as Sonny, a bit slim in the hips and bust, she passes his visual exam with points to spare.

She continues writing. "Nope, I'm Lisa. Brian just happens to be my brother, an accident of cohabitating parents."

Six years the younger sibling, this female counter clerk defends her identity, weary of the 'Brian's little sister' label that tagged her growing up years in this small rural hometown.

Sonny grew into middle school same year Lisa moved up to high school. The two never met officially during those years - even in a small rural town it happens - and Sonny dropped out during tenth grade.

Sonny decides he better stay away from the brother subject even though Sonny knows Brian well and trains in the Mixed Martial Arts class Brian instructs every Thursday at the gym. Keeps his feet loose and conditions his reflex time to any kind of punch from any angle. Sonny tries again, just wants his copies, but feels stuck, knowing her brother and seeing her around town occasionally over the years. Not wanting to push any rudeness at her, he just needs an access card for the copy machine.

"Um, you're Ricky's girlfriend right?" Sonny tries a different tactic, creates a chat, seeks comfort, but feels an edge. His brain begins stressing out.

"No, I'm Lisa, remember? Ricky's gone." She stops scribbling, looks at Sonny. "Oh, you're K.O's friend, from the gym, right?"

"Yeah, right K.O.'s friend, also known as Sonny Bones," he says, defending his individual identity too, paying her back, "but not related." Both smile, tit-for-tat, quick minds think alike. "So, what's up with you and Ricky?"

"Nothing. Just decided he's too redneck for a Berkeley girl."

"Whoa, you're kidding. You going to Berkeley? Cool enough!"

"Not yet, but if he's too redneck for a Berkeley girl, he's too redneck for me out at Blue Ridge too. Besides, he's from across the border."

Across the border, you mean an illegal alien? Here?" Sonny pops his eyes wide open. Alien demons never admit it. They all hide. "What border? How'd you know about it?"

"Not that border, the North Carolina border, it's a real border, not just a state line in his case." Lisa hands Sonny the copy card. "Ain't one tiny smidgen of sweet ole' south Virginia boy in him, that's for sure."

Puzzled, Sonny stacks four magazines on the counter upside-down, hands Lisa a dollar, signs the index, gets the key card and makes his copies. He restocks the magazines, drops the card in the return slot, and waves his fingers at Lisa on the way out. In a hurry now, he feels the anger suddenly emerge for no apparent reason.

Punch her, she laughed at you. She thinks you're weird. A distorted vision, a face stretched out of shape pops up in his mind and screams at him. He struggles with rage, it grabs him without warning, but Sonny pushes the words and thoughts away, relaxes his fist.

Lisa turns away, smiling. She knows high school boys copy Playboy Bunnies, not news journals, and hide them under face down news magazines. Not her business, she just works here and part time at that, student a more important word in her life than clerk.

"Strange conversation though," she comments. No one else hears it.

*

Sonny opens his eyes and greets a weird green space alien floating in a corner near the window. A black knot of tension eats at his gut. Similar alien presence visits his mind each morning, his demonic delusions. Same black knot sours his stomach too. Nerves and frustration chew on him and degrade his comfort, step on his hope. It makes him angry.

Willow's not your friend, she fakes it. She wants what you have. She reads your mind, and tells everyone else your secrets. An alien lives in her brain ... she arrived on that space ship, the one on your cake. Remember it? K.O. and Willow, both aliens now and destined to control the earth. Only you can stop them. So, train, run, fight! Kill them both!

"Go fuck yourself! Willow's nothing like that." Sonny bats at a form hanging in his face, his hand passing through it like smoke. The spook fades away.

He both resents and admires the alien power, and believes if he destroys a demon, he gains its power, transforms it into himself, learn its ability to read minds, and fight the others. The contradiction confuses him. Unsure whether he should join the aliens or fight the aliens, Sonny waffles and makes no choice.

Recently, the voices add wavy multi-colored faces almost every time now instead of occasionally. Distorted monsters encourage his training but cajole, demand, lie, force, and abuse him, ignoring his wishes as well. Hallucinations and holograms fill his soul, but Sonny knows he can beat them. He outran the voices for years, now he needs a way to beat the faces too. Confidence, he embraces it and sweats it out, using it against them, and will win again this time. Positive, he feels the win coming. It just takes time and energy but the effort often wears him down.

Sonny hops out of bed and hits the ten-mile loop before breakfast, accelerates past the five-mile mark in under forty minutes. Both demons chase his tail but lose wind and spiral out of sight behind him as sweat trickles down his body. Sonny smiles at a mind with no monsters, at least for the moment, an effort he embraces nearly every morning. The phantoms hide behind mist and mirrors, or his fractured imagination, no one knows for sure.

A simple run wins. The demons always fall back when he sweats. He simply blows each into the breeze, one by one. It takes effort and will power, and staring each in the eye. If the run fails, kick a chair, punch a wall, or smash a lamp, any object he breaks cuts the demon loose, pushes the adrenaline home. Heavy action and the chemical rush bites into his brain, deep and clean, and the demons disappear, at least for the day, or a morning, or an hour.

Emotional pain, it begins at random and ends with sweat, but the monsters scream often and order him to perform violent acts, and now the run occasionally fails. *Kill her. She's not an ally. Stab him, K.O's not your friend. He's an alien, save everyone else. Train, work hard! You are the protector, the only one. Save the earth, save everyone, kill your false friends! Kill the aliens!*

"Get out! I don't believe you! I ain't doing it!" Sonny barks right back at them, turning the rage against his enemies. The stronger it gets the more he believes, but the harder he fights. Kill the demons. Join the demons. Conquer the earth. Which is it, whom does he fight, whom does he protect? The voices tell him both. How does he know? Which should he choose? Confusion and turmoil fill his mind, no way to know, no one to help, no one to answer. The demons kick him into a hole and leave him to rot.

The run fails today, so Sonny hits the gym, pushes iron fast and hard, and washes that nasty image out one more time.

He accepts his reality. He grows into the sounds and images as his brain and body mature and hormones begin affecting his behavior. He believes all humans experience alien entities, even his friends, even his enemies. Each person sees its own screaming face inside its mind. He believes a spook lives in all minds, a natural human experience. Right? He knows without asking, why would he ask? He's human. He sees it, doesn't everyone?

14

Oblivious to Sonny, his boxing efforts, and his mental condition, Cat rolls up a chair and logs onto her laptop, begins cultivating her lab notes and the biological and behavioral data her team collected from clinics and interviews. She documents her preliminary conclusion.

An hour later, she takes a break, stretches, and rubs her temples, organizing the information mentally before she continues. Her phone dings and she peeks at the caller label and punches the speaker. "Hey Max."

A voice in the speaker responds, "Got your notes. Fergie's a real character, got him in the right place, Nickels too." Papers rattle over the speaker. "Let me read this, you can ask me anything now, and I'll pop this in an email later in the week. We're in the woods with some friends, collecting tea and fruit, and watching for bears." Max laughs, "Hope we don't see any, getting too old for running away. Maybe just toss some berries at it."

Her favorite college professor and mentor says, "Butt in if you have a question, it's complicated and long, but worth it. First, you asked about dysfunctional memory and distorted sensory input, here goes."

Max begins explaining how the brain works, and how it sometime fails. "Pretend Harry, a friend, hands Fergie a lemon. He takes a bite and puckers his lips. His brain uses its senses and collects information about that lemon, an elongated round shape, its yellow color, soft and juicy, tart citrus flavor, rough skin, tangy citrus scent, and transfers that knowledge biologically to individual neurons in his brain. Billions of neurons sit in a brain at birth, unused, empty, each one waiting for the brain to find a use for it over its lifetime."

"First, his brain locates empty cells, then it builds proteins, it hooks the cells together – like a sense tag – using as many empty neurons as it requires. It creates one memory circuit - a lemon and its perceivable properties - and fills these cells in a way that connects all the properties of this individual experience, in this case, a lemon."

"His brain stores that specific memory, one lemon. In theory, those brain cells, the neurons, remain connected, linked or tagged forever, and it develops as one memory circuit with the input from that particular experience. He can recall any memory whenever he needs it. His brain triggers those bonded proteins. Same thing occurs continuously in his brain, in all brains. New perceptions and memories record everything he experiences every second he's alive, like everyone else. Like a hard drive with a list of files, each one equals a memory with a file tag to call it up."

"Then, later in the same day, Fergie watches a science film and the narrator discusses hemlock, a poison plant, and a couple hours later, he plays a space alien video game."

Cat interrupts. "Fergie has no space video games, he's in prison."

"We're pretending Cat, it doesn't matter. Just imagine it, like your patients do." Max laughs at his own joke, a great sense of humor. A bumper sticker on his Austin Healy reads: 'Our other self is Bi-polar, we charge twice for consults.'

"So, Fergie now has a lemon, a hemlock plant, and a space demon experience stored in his brain, collectively as individual bonded memories. Whenever a lemon appears, even in a photo or as a written word, or a friend speaks that word, it triggers one or more tags and his mind recalls that lemon experience, the tart taste, the rough feel, the juiciness, and he experiences a lemon again. Obviously not quite as dramatic in recall, more of a recognition process in a mental video projected inside his mind."

"When a normal brain stores each memory it stacks the experience in the order which it happens in life, all of its life, not just today, with most recent on top or maybe the most intense on top, like stacking records where each one contains an amount of information and intensity. You will 'notice' it first while the mind browses back over its life, as it does while resting or during minimally intense activity."

Cat says, "Like layered memories with the newest on top, a stacked thinking model?"

"Correct. Although when a brain creates a memory the intensity of emotion makes it faster on recall, and more complete, very angry or very passionate events will store as more intense memories, and may pull those first. Then when a normal brain thinks, it fills the conscious mind in that instant with direct sensory input from everything around it and in its environment, and recalls any memories related to it. It combines memories from yesterday, today, last year, and years ago, then correlates it with input immediately as it happens in real time as well."

"Thought processes then engage, combining these qualities into a full spectrum lemon inside the conscious mind, and includes everything associated with that memory. It recalls the lemon and everything that surrounds that thought right at that moment of recall. The brain collects new sensory input and recalls memories at the same instant, then combines that data and projects this collective information into the consciousness, like a mental video, and that interaction emerges as conscious thinking."

"But an abnormal brain, like Fergie, recalls his memory with 'holes' in it, like a disconnection in one or more segments. And, because a mind requires itself to fill all the blanks and project a complete mental video during the thinking process, it fills the 'holes' with what may be faulty information, faulty recollections. Unrelated incidents may fill the holes just as easily as related incidents because the original memory link broke, and the connections distort."

Cat breaks in again. "So, the mental video, lies flat and the 'holes' just pop in it?"

"Not exactly, just think a second when I say 'lemon,' what do you see? A lemon, as you know it, right? And, you visualize lots of peripheral noise around it, leaves, a branch, maybe a plate, other vague images of al lemons in your life flitter around it while a lemon idles in the middle."

"Then, as soon as I say elephant, the lemon disappears and a large fat gray brute with a tooting trunk fills the mind screen, right? The consciousness exists as a constant jumble of memory and experience that a normal brain sorts and uses when we think or act, or when we need it."

"In Fergie's recall, let's imagine his lemon memory recall misses 'fruity' this time, so his mind opens a 'hole' in that mental video where 'fruity' should exist. It fills that hole with 'hemlock poison', a random choice from a different experience in his memory stacks, the science film. His mind recalls a lemon, inserts 'hemlock' instead of 'fruity' and creates a separate but inaccurate memory that his conscious mind recalls later and uses during specific thinking events, but he believes it's a real and true memory."

"Fergie engages in these experiences and his brain collects all that information. Except, in his case, his brain either misdirects or distorts that information and those images, producing and storing a memory that combines those features into another new memory that mistakenly contains some properties from each separate experience. His brain now has a new memory, two new memories in fact, that contain what he thinks of as a lemon, both different, but each one just as true to his mind."

"Now, when he picks up a lemon, an erroneous memory may pop into his conscious mind, 'this oblong yellow fruit contains hemlock poison', and he equates the fruity taste with hemlock poison. He incidentally recalls the distorted memory and its properties of lemon and hemlock mix, combining real memory with faulty memory, and recalls a new but unreal or inaccurate memory of a lemon."

Cat breaks in again. "And, this one scares him. Poison, right?"

"Right, and in addition, Fergie recalls a memory of the space alien in his game as a demon, and the demon as a threat then embeds itself into another 'hole,' this one in a different memory, that of his friend Harry."

Cat nods her head, working it through. "So, in the memory of his friend, Harry Parker, his mind falsely installs poison and a demon into holes in his mental video, and recognizes Harry as a threat, a false threat. Harry offers a lemon, Fergie thinks it's poison."

Max continues. "Exactly right, as this new recall emerges

his brain collects but distorts the properties of a lemon, his friend, a space alien, and a poison hemlock plant and creates another new but partly inaccurate video in his conscious mind containing real and unreal perceptions. A week later, if Harry hands Fergie a lemon in the mess hall, Fergie may recall that new distorted memory sequence, a lemon, his friend, a poison hemlock plant, and a space demon all on that same afternoon. Thus, the conscious video image that his mind creates differs from the original experience, but projects just as clear and intense, and just as real to him."

Cat butts in, "So, why Fergie and not everyone, if all brains fill the holes."

"Every brain works the same way, but some brains create more holes than others, and some short-circuit in the electronic transfer. Some brains interpret more emotion in the activities it remembers. Brains operate fundamentally the same, but genetically different. If an abnormal brain reaches a certain level of dysfunction, it chemically destroys neurons and memory circuits during certain phases of development, or when the chemistry invades some circuits and damages the bonds, or in other ways breaks the memory link."

"And, remember Catherine, this lemon might appear as a behavior trigger with holes in it, so the behavior emerges with new triggers in it. Then, we have a behavior that responds to odd clues, and so it triggers either an inaccurate response – fright when no threat exists – or punches a wall, like Fergie does, and for no valid reason. In fact, the punch releases frustration because the individual can't control the images in his brain, and some odd way knows its faulty but can't do anything about it."

"But, the frustration level remains high in these abnormal memories as they confuse the mind, and are not what the mind expects. In survival or social situations, a brain then acts erratically. Eventually brain chemistry may destroy enough cells that it can't function at the survival level, no heart function, no lungs, and no internal systems."

Max says, "Hope that helps Catherine," and the phone clicks off, his normal method, an eccentric dismissal as usual. It rings immediately, Cat pokes the button. "Come for lunch I'll buy."

"Something else too, reconstruction of any experience in our memories never records an exact copy, nor does it always replicate that experience without error even in otherwise totally normal brains – if we ever actually find one totally normal brain exists." Max laughs at his qualifier, always a qualifier with science until evidence certifies it as fact, and no scientist ever makes that claim, not without numerous duplications."

"Back to it. Abnormal brains will make more and greater errors and add more intensity to those errors through emotions. A malfunctioning brain often adds fright, the most intense emotion of all, as the default emotion. Fright emerges from the survival instinct, but Fergie's mind misinterprets his memory and perceives it as a new memory when it appears in his consciousness – his distorted mental video projects an alien handing him a poison fruit. Fergie exhibits acute paranoia, punches his friend to protect himself and, in fact, to protect his friend as well. Pretty simple Catherine."

"No, it's not Max, what about the demons he sees in Harry, on his shoulder? That's not a Fergie memory."

"That's a mistake in the recall and the mental video. Memory bonds superimpose different and distorted visuals in his mind. It's a different function, biologically, but very similar. It's the sequence in delusions, hallucinations and illusions, and for another time. Got to go pick a berry, or chase a bear, will be in the office next week." The phone disconnects abruptly as usual. Max simply hangs up when he finishes talking, a personal quirk.

Cat shuts the phone, picks up a pencil, taps it against her forehead as if knocking tidbits of sense into her brain, and suddenly it clicks. "Yes! Got it! So this is it?" She pops her fist in the air and shouts, "BINGO!" She arches her back, stretches, sips her coffee, and verbalizes her thoughts. "What a nightmare Fergie lives. No wonder he punches walls."

It seems so obvious now that she 'gets it'. She leans back in her seat and shuts her eyes, nods her head, worn out. Her phone dings and she punches the speaker button, "Cat here."

Erin asks, "Break for lunch?"

"Yeah, see you in fifteen." Cat logs off and shuts the laptop, hops down the basement steps. She organizes her thoughts well when she jogs, and often works out problems or dilemmas, or develops connections between mental and biological relationships while she runs on a treadmill or on a natural trail whenever she finds one available. Anyone walking Boston Commons sees her footprints all over it. Fifteen minutes later, she heads up to the cafeteria, sweating and hungry.

15

K.O. stands behind the weight bench, spotting the bar as Sonny pushes a hundred fifty pounds, grunts, repeats up and down, up and down, as fast as he can, a grunt between each lift. "Brian's sister asked about you, if you got a girlfriend."

Sonny eases the bar down into its clip, takes a breather, panting. "What you mean, asked? She's old, twenty at least, nothing about me that's twenty. Brian's sister too, pretty tough dude, wouldn't want to mess with her. Don't call her that, call her Lisa or nothing. Works at the library, sensitive about the little sister thing, seems like."

K.O. holds up his palms. "Don't shoot the messenger."

Right, good idea. Shoot him. Why didn't we think of that?

The demon starts in again, just advising this time, weak voice, rarely screams when Sonny works weights, no compensating power against the heavy sweat. The workout sends the spooks packing nearly every time. Getting a bit tougher lately though, each time that sucker adds energy between workouts, and it takes longer to kick it out.

"Shut up spook." Sonny pushes the weights harder, faster. The voice shuts up and fades. Sonny drops the bar into its holder, rolls off the weight bench and walks down the hall, hits the shower.

Half way through his seventeenth year, every evening the devil brings its dance, a nightmare mimic, a personal Halloween. The voices bark, demand, and order him around. Each time one appears it gains intensity as hormones invade his brain in higher concentrations as Sonny matures. The neurotransmitters push home a distorted message. Sonny works out as long and hard as it takes and finally rejects the conflicts. He wears himself out just so he can sleep.

His neurons arc over, his blood boils and his mind reels, his edge begins slipping away. Frustration and the desire for violence fill his days, like a wide-awake nightmare. Identical tears spill down each cheek, driven by sadness and madness, and frustration at the rage that sparks his anger and denies his control. He punches a hole in the wall, knocks a lamp across the room, bounces a cell phone off the floor, dial buttons and plastic fragments fly everywhere. The tension finally eases off.

Joe Cocker chimes in and croons his advice – '*Sometimes a little help from my friends*' – And Sonny grabs the release, a quick puff or a pill one day, a snort, or drain a spike into a vein the next. No problem, just use up the burn each day and drive the demon away, like dust in the wind the drugs simply blow it away, and it disappears. He knows it, has done it before, uncountable times over the past couple years.

Keeping his mind straight and focused gets tougher every day. Sonny stands before a mirror outside the showers. He stares at himself, locks eyes with a demon inside. "Get the fuck out of my head!"

A straight right nails the glass and it explodes, scattering chips all over the sink and floor. Sonny looks down at his knuckles, cut and bleeding. He holds his head in both hands, and blood drips along his arm.

He opens a Red Cross kit, disinfects the cuts, and wraps his hand. He sweeps up the glass fragments, vacuums the particles, then hops in his truck, fires it up, drives eleven miles, and pulls into his campsite. He never gives it up, saves it for time he needs alone and unobserved. He picks up the first limb off a pile of dead wood. Swings hard, grunts, and breaks it across the tree trunk, grabs another, grunts, breaks it, another, grunts, breaks it, tosses the chunks onto a pile destined for his fire pit. Each swing stings all the way up his arm and his knuckles bleed through the bandage.

Lisa pauses on the pathway, watches Sonny busting wood, the evening still and quiet, the silence broken only when a limb pops.

The demons fade. Sonny grunts each time a branch hits the trunk. He swings again, a grunt, vibration stings his wrists and elbows, the branch cracks, one more swing and it splits into two pieces.

She knocks her knuckles lightly on a pine tree and slips around the last bush, stands at the edge of the clearing, watching.

Surprised, Sonny jerks erect, recognizes Lisa, his face brightens, and he sits on his stump. "Hey, Lisa."

"Why you busting up wood like that?"

He tosses both limbs onto the burn pile and grabs a towel, dries sweat off his head and neck. "Need some firewood, forgot my saw."

"Chain saw sitting in back of that truck cuts wood a lot easier."

Busted, nothing slow in her brain, Sonny thinks fast. "No fuel, forgot to stop."

"K.O. thinks you came here, and he gave directions. Hope it's okay? I just came to visit, didn't mean to blow you off at the library."

"You didn't. Got my copies, all I needed."

"Yeah, I know, you just read the articles." She smiles at that ancient Playboy joke.

Sonny says, "How'd you know?"

Lisa ignores his question. "Mind if I sit awhile?" She plops herself down on a thick log Sonny had rolled up beside the fire pit months ago just for that purpose, a seat for his guests, his very few guests, two in fact. Now Lisa makes it three.

Lisa points at the bandage. "What happened to your hand?"

Sonny looks at his hand a few seconds, remembers the bandage and the mirror. He shrugs it off. "Cut it chopping wood."

"You come here a lot?" She glances at the tent. Her eyes wander around the clearing. "It's very peaceful."

"Come here and sit, eases my mind." He allows some truth but not the whole truth of it. Easing his mind ain't all that peaceful, takes a lot of energy keeping these aliens quiet. He stacks a few branches and weaves in a couple sticks, ignites the kindling. Flames soon shoot up and reflect off the trees, the bushes, and the tent wall. A few sparks fly up into the dusk.

"Be right back."

Sonny heads toward a narrow dirt path that makes a half-mile circle out around a small pond and back to the parking area. He jogs it quickly, stops at the pickup, grabs his cooler and carries it back, sets it down. Sonny digs into the ice, pulls out a beer and a soda, points both at Lisa. She accepts the beer and twists its top like a pro. He replaces the soda and uncaps another beer, both too young to buy it but old enough to enjoy it.

A bum in town everyone calls Shanty buys it for underage kids if they pay him something extra, food usually. Shanty drinks no alcohol, although he uses a drug occasionally, when he can steal it. 'Just a nut', the kids say. He hangs out around town, stands in front of a deserted store, and chatters at his reflection, draws strange maps on the window with chalk then washes it off. An old bike with metal baskets hanging on it holds everything he owns.

Sonny finishes half the first beer, drops down beside the tent, counts off twenty-five push-ups, squats under the bush and rolls his rock, wraps up a smoke.

Lisa makes no comment about the joint, just accepts it, and fires the end. "Why the push-ups? Weird place for a workout."

"Not weird, part of my routine, do it all the time here, relax after." Sonny makes certain the demon stays absent tonight, counting on that little extra workout and the run, along with smoking the buds.

After two hours chatting, laughing, joking, sharing the third and final beer, half a turkey sub each, some pretzels and chips, two chocolate chip cookies, and a little smoke, Sonny no longer cares why Brian's little sister showed up tonight, but finds joy in it as the night edges on.

The big and tough brother factor and her twenty years on earth fade from his thinking. Sharing her company brings a good feeling to his male side. Few female companions enter his life. Willow, but more like a sister or a duplicate mom, and the girls he meets at the gym, mostly younger, a few older and married, even a couple grandmas keeping fit, carting in toddlers while the mothers earn a paycheck. The moms arrive later and finish the day. Working out, and winding down sets them free for the evening and the kids, dinner, then a husband romp after the ball game.

Sonny finds no interest in all that, not at his age. All act friendly but have no girlfriend potential anyway, not that he sees.

All older and taken, and most of the women have kids.

He quit school at age fourteen, not a lot of socializing in his life, and no siblings he knows about. Sonny never dates, uncomfortable and inexperienced, shy in a boy-girl relationship, but confident and friendly with both genders under his trainer guise.

Sonny teaches physical fitness, trains kids and a few adults, runs, cuts trees, rakes leaves, lifts weights, hits the bags, and suffers his absent social life in silence, enjoying life. Not without a wish though, but he's still very shy around girls.

Usually alone at his campsite, he comes here often when he feels its pull. He sets up his tent every time, a minor obsessive behavior his brain forces upon him, and he often sleeps over. It only takes five minutes, but resisting that compulsion pushes the stress up a notch, so he pitches the tent, a harmless obsession. Willow still pops up here occasionally, knows he hangs out here or at the gym, or at the Town Center basketball court. Both meet here often, enjoy the memories, 'the good old times' as Willow terms it.

Peering down a short road toward his eighteenth birthday, the few months Sonny lived here includes very little of his reminiscing and covers a brief time span in his life. He tries to forget some of his history, but this clearing and its fire pit and Willow always holds a special spot in his heart regardless of the past, present, or the future, whatever it may bring.

Lisa scoots closer, sits down cross-legged beside his stump, slides one wrist and a forearm down this knee, offers her hand, and grins. "Feel like a little tent sparring tonight?"

Unsure exactly how to respond, he peers into two large brown eyes glistening in the firelight, recognizes her sincerity and her fire. A dark brown ponytail bobs behind her ears and drapes over one shoulder or the other whenever she turns her head, the peach tint on her lips begs for a taste. One turquoise stone set in a silver feather dangles from each ear, a matching necklace sparkles each time she moves. The scent of violets surrounds her, subtle, barely perceivable, even more enticing for its near absence. Spellbound for a few seconds, Sonny locks eyes with his guest and feels the heat.

"Don't mean you have to marry me Sonny. Don't need that 'committed forever' stuff. Let's just enjoy ourselves for the night.

Okay?"

Lisa grabs his fingers and pulls him toward her, sharing the sweetness of peach briefly then backs away, then eases toward Sonny again. This time Lisa proves the soft pink muscle hidden behind her smile offers an activity other than word making and honey sampling, although Sonny imagines that sweet nectar the bee gods produce tastes exactly like Lisa at this particular instant, and both savor the moment.

Three years older and two years more experienced, Brian's little sister steals Sonny Bones' virginity in the rural Virginia countryside. Sonny never tells her that secret though, so she never knows it. Not a girl that maintains her silence when she engages in sexual frolics, a few encouraging murmurs float out the tent flaps and rise above the coals, drifting off into a moonless evening sky.

"Oh, like that. No, here … like this. Yes, m-m-m-m-m ... exactly."

The demon leaves it alone, not even one tiny peep the entire evening.

Sonny and Lisa lay side-by-side on the sleeping bag. Sonny speaks, still a young boy timbre, but one giant step older than yesterday. "Not that I wouldn't marry you, Lisa. I mean later, after we grow up some. I mean you're really nice, and all, and pretty."

A nugget of knowledge and a spark of humor settle her voice. "Shut up, Sonny."

Sonny stops talking, snaps his eyes open wide, wondering why she said that. Sounds mean at first. Lisa snuggles into his shoulder and slides her arm across his chest, so he ignores it. Soon enough both nod off, and awaken with the sunrise, arms and legs comfortably entwined.

Sonny comes to understand a new social term over the next few months – friends with benefits – and takes it to heart, definitely a nice term. Sonny likes it just fine, cradles it right down in his word basket beside hope and comfort as one of his favorites.

Most folks never use the words savage and tender in the same sentence when describing the coupling of two young adults enjoying the physical side of a relationship. Sonny attaches those two words to the memory of his first night with Lisa, and every night she spends at his camp after it until she packs her bags, follows her dream, and heads off to Berkeley on a full academic scholarship. The night Lisa Santoro departs, Sonny Bones realizes this tiny state park campsite just hogged a much bigger spot in his heart.

Sonny stands beside a maple tree, watches Lisa swish down the trail. She glances back over her shoulder once then twice then disappears around a curl in the bushes.

Sonny looks above the path, spots a spook sitting in a tree. *"Should've ripped her clothes off, hurt her, cut her, she's using you, She'll come back and steal your tent.*

Sonny barks out a note of anger, bounces a punch off the pine tree, and dislocates a knuckle. He grunts, grabs it, pulls it in against his shirt. "Get the fuck out of here." Sonny cuts loose, a long drawn out wail as he grabs the knuckle and jerks it straight, pops it into place. He doubles over in pain then plunges his hand into the cooler filled with ice.

"Damn, that hurts! Damn! Damn! Damn!"

16

Sonny lies on his bed, denying those distorted masks hiding in his mind. He never shares the visions that haunt his soul. Hallucinations, holograms, monsters, screaming voices live inside his mental video. An indefinable bruising thrives in his brain. The turmoil began the date of conception. Unknown biological forces twisted his genes the moment fertilization occurred. Complex biology, DNA, chemistry in action, raging hormones, disjointed signals, crooked genetic structure, and tweaked neural pathways now enrage his mind, his mental video sticks on rewind.

Kill her, stab him. Don't trust anyone. Even your friends ring false, they all fake it. Violence will release you! Punch, kick anything, hurt someone, anyone - it's the only answer. Destroy the aliens, all of them. The aliens came from outer space to conquer the world. Only you can stop it. Train, lift, run, punch a wall! Kick a chair! Kill all the aliens, and fake friends the demons control!

The voices scream instructions, driving his emotions toward an uncontrollable urge that initiates violence toward inanimate objects, but lately toward people too, his friends. He begins experiencing a greater fear too, that he might hurt someone he loves.

Months pass. His friends shift shapes, and begin looking like enemies one day and friends the next. His brain chemistry mingles thoughts and memories, and actively juggles his perceptions. Odd bug-eyes, big ears, green skin and long thin arms and legs, tentacle fingers reach out and pick at his thoughts. Panic invades his mind. He runs and the demon runs with him, he circles back and slams branch after branch into the tree trunk, and finally finds relief, for short periods. Odd combinations of vision and sound fill the holes in his mind, and he develops strange pairings in his consciousness.

Confused, mystified, uncertain, unsure what choices he should make, he simply accepts it and runs and runs and runs until his mind clears. Gets tougher though, he runs faster, runs longer, pushes more weight, and still the demon lingers.

A nasty distorted face screams. *Kill something! We need blood! We need blood!*

The stress grows daily, the demons act particularly nasty today. Sonny begins ingesting and injecting street drugs more often, and embraces the temporary relief it brings. The voices push him harder, and for the first time, it attacks Willow.

A demon screams her name. *Choke her. Choke Willow. She plots with K.O. to steal your saw. Choke her. She'll be gone. She'll fail, and you keep your tools.*

A ball of fright consumes Sonny and for the first time he scares himself. He truly believes he will never hurt Willow, but the voice insists and uncertainty emerges. The thought of it frightens him.

Choke her, rip off her clothes. Do it. Do it. You...Want...It! We want it! We need it! Fuck her. She craves it! You can't get free if you don't do it. Never free. Never free. How does that suit you? Cackling laughter follows the demonic demands.

Sonny kicks the door open, races outside, and runs directly into K.O. who wraps his arms around Sonny. Both men struggle a moment. Escape on his mind, Sonny swings and misses as K.O instinctively dodges the punch, and grabs Sonny again. "Whoa, whoa buddy, what's this?"

Sonny bounces free, stares at K.O. for a split second, and swings again, driving two gut punches into a very surprised trainer, catching K.O. twice before he can react and K.O. bends over, grabs a breath. Sonny aims a knockout punch at K.O.'s jaw. Wide-eyed and quick as a snake, K.O. raises his forearm. Sonny's eyes pop open and he pulls his punch halfway. K.O. bats it sideways anyway, a reflex action.

"Get away, get away. Leave me alone!" Sonny yells at a

demon he imagines on K.O.'s left shoulder. Sonny breaks away, runs across the lot, jumps in his truck, and spits gravel on his way out. Tears run down his cheeks as he realizes he just slugged K.O. several times, his mind out of control, an intense frenzy engaging. "It's like punching my dad," he cries, and aims his pickup toward the forest camp eleven miles away.

Twenty minutes later, Sonny slams a branch over a log, another one, and another. "Don't make me hit K.O." Another limb cracks, "I can't hit K.O." Another crack, "Don't make me hit K.O. It's not right, I can't hit trust friends." Another limb splits in two. "You can't make me! Aaarrrgggghhh!" He screams at the demon, refuses its orders, and takes off running down the trail, a long circle through the forest and back into his camp.

"I'm going craaaazzzzzzy!" Sonny falls to the ground, rolls around in torment. He wraps his arms around his head. "Crazy, crazy, going craaazzzzy!" he yells. He jumps up bends over and grabs another branch, changes his mind, sits on his stump and pulls out his hit kit, burns up his last bubble. Tears stream down his cheeks. A minute later, he hits a vein and the tears dry up, his eyes lower half-mast and he grins, leans back against the stump.

*

Sonny jumps in his truck and drives around town, looking for relief. He hates it when the kit sits empty, no release when he needs it the most. He tries the Bomb and Jumbo's boys, nothing. Tries Melanie, finds her parents locked her up in the clinic for a week. He even tries Shanty, a last resort, no luck. He asks around and stumbles onto an undercover cop setting up Small Sammy in a drug sting outside the gas station, and floats right into the middle of it flying high. The narcotics cop busts Sonny too, a wild coincidence, but the officer calls it in, a lucky break for the cop, unlucky break for Sonny.

Sheriff Mike gets the squeal and picks up Sonny but takes him to a clinic instead of the jailhouse. A bit of luck hangs with Sonny this time, if that idea makes sense with demons banging on his brain and heroin in his arm, and rage in his mind. Sonny has been to the clinic a couple times for check-ups, evaluations. Willow forced it a month or so ago when Sonny began destabilizing and his violent outbursts became less controllable. Sheriff Mike knows Sonny from middle school lectures and workouts at the gym, and understands a little about the mental issues that bug his brain. Mike and K.O. are long-time friends.

It takes an hour and forty minutes. Mike fills out papers and checks in, exchanging custody for admission for the third time in two months. Then Sonny flops on a bed, coming down, a little discomfort settles in. He knows this will take at least three days - maybe more - before he gets released. And, the doctors again begin a medications treatment Sonny will ignore as soon as the clinic releases him again. Routine.

Sonny always watches his dose and frequency, never allows himself to fall into heavy addiction and withdrawals. He successfully mingles heavy workouts and street drugs, always has, beginning with the smoke. He figured it out early on, a bright kid, maybe too bright for his own good.

Willow made Sonny take a few tests at the social service office in town, and those tests indicate an extremely intelligent and very street-smart kid.

His brain tweaks, confusion and conflict jump in when he finds no street drugs to support his workouts. Then, he floats all over the place, violent and ranting when the brain disconnects kick out, but subdued and social otherwise, with no control of his actions at odd times with no specific or definable behavior triggers, and no defined length to the manic episodes. The patterns arrive and depart at random. Most manic episodes last minutes but often extend into hours. While days may pass between each one, the timing remains completely unpredictable.

Sonny was assigned one of the single rooms. He and other mental patients or addicts like him spend the medical evaluation days locked up in a building that contains eight single rooms, and four doubles, sixteen patients when full. The wing houses male and female patients, but forbids opposite sex room partners. Three full bathrooms at one end allow private showers but no locks.

Locks violate security protocol and patient safety laws, but no one sneaks into an in-use shower except when a patient plays a harmless trick on another, and when that happens everyone knows it, enjoys the joke and applauds, so no one gets in trouble for peeking.

Sonny rolls off his bed, grabs his towel and steps into the hallway, heads for the shower. A door opens as Sonny passes and Shanty creeps into the corridor, turns and bumps into Sonny.

"Was looking for you outside, hell of a way to find you Shanty, had to get busted," Sonny says. Both giggle, an odd humor bond exists between locked up and whacked out mental clinic companions. "Was looking for a pop."

Shanty shakes his head. "Got nothing." He quickly sticks a towel behind his back and grins. "You seen Allen?" His voice sounds like sand scratching on a floor tile. His eyes open wide, his forehead wrinkles, his lips curl into a false grin, the untruth written all over his face, his knees shake, his eye twitches.

Sonny says, "Nope, just got here."

His real name, Theodore Purdue, like the chicken packer. Most patients find humor in his name, especially when a new patient meets Shanty, but Melanie tagged him Shanty almost three years ago because his image presents like a hobo. The nickname stuck.

A few years older than most kids at the clinic, his appearance reminds folks of a bum wearing ratty clothes and living in a hobo village, and even when he acquires a new shirt, Shanty carefully rips it along the bottom edge and one sleeve, same rips each time, like a personal fashion statement, an obsession, irresistible. His clothes all look alike except the drab faded colors that match only if he gets lucky at the trash bins behind the Salvation Army thrift store.

He never complains about the nickname, even answers to it in the clinic. No one knows where he lives or with whom, or what name he uses outside the walls. Many believe he lives in an old shack down in the woods, a true story according to Sheriff Mike. Shanty built it himself out of metal sheets, scavenged plywood, sticks, and salvaged rope. Most kids in here dislike him and no one trusts him. Most know he's a thief inside and out, but they all tolerate him, got his hang-ups like everyone else. No one throws that first stone in a mental ward.

Shanty shows up at the clinic every few months and dries out, gets his addictions treated, eats a few healthy meals, puts on a little weight, then heads back into the streets where he immediately stops his medications and triggers the cycle again. Rides an old rusty Schwinn around town with two wire baskets bolted on the back and one up front, and his gear sits inside those baskets and a small nylon backpack he straps over one shoulder. Shanty installed vintage multi-colored streamers on his hand grips, very proud of that lucky find at the dump years ago. No other bike in town has them, his most valuable possession.

Deputy Mike always takes the bike home with him so it stays safe, and brings it back when Shanty gets a release. Equal treatment for all and even though Mike dislikes Shanty and his theft habits, the bike gets protection, like everything else in his town that needs it. A good cop, Mike is, and the baskets contain everything Shanty owns.

Shanty just wanders the streets, and rides around, an odd town character that causes little trouble except when he steals or decides he needs health care for a few days. Then he starts banging on cars and trucks until he gets himself locked up. Shanty never provokes violence, so generally hangs out on his own, provided he keeps his hands off other folks' property, a nearly impossible task for Shanty even though he promises every time he gets released. Like everyone in here, tell counselors what they want to hear and go home, even if home resembles a cardboard box or a mix and match shanty shack.

He hangs out in the clinic until the doctors kick him out, or his Medicaid agent squawks after three or four days of evaluations, then doctors label him harmless and non-violent. When he needs a few days in the clinic again, Shanty runs out in front of a moving car or truck and starts acting crazy, like he's suicidal, slams his fist on the hood or slaps at the windows, kicks the tires, freaks out until someone dials the sheriff.

Same story every time, but generally harmless, seems the sheriff would remember it and know it's fake, but he keeps hauling Shanty here and he gets a psyche release after a couple days. Seems almost like he hires on here, almost a part-time job for Shanty, like reporting for work once every couple months when he gets real hungry, or tired of living in a shack down by the river, if that's where he actually lives.

Checks himself in more often when cold hits, stays outside when the weather warms up, and always finds the clinic when a major storm heads up the Atlantic coast too. Shanty overlaps enough trips in here where any repeat patients know him, and all share his story. It never changes much. Might be a harmless character and a little odd, but nobody trusts him. He steals.

His socks seldom match, long greasy hair and stringy brown whiskers decorate his face, the shirts and pants he wears always look old and shabby, even new ones he retrieves from thrift store dumpster every Sunday. Shanty takes a shower only when the staff threatens him – no TV or no treats – then he soaps up and washes off and actually stays in the shower until staff orders him out. Kind of weird, refuses to get in it then refuses to get out. Must be nuts.

Patients make fun of him, until a patient receives a gift pack. Then he sneaks right in and helps himself, even though most patients share with others, like comrades, like pals, like patients all fighting separate skirmishes on the same battlefield. Unfortunately, Shanty cultivates an irresistible steal fixation, but most patients know it and hide the chocolate bars and cookies.

Sonny reads the lie on his face and grabs Shanty, pushes his shoulders against the wall. Holding Shanty in place with his left hand, Sonny slides up his right, his fingers circle the thin emaciated throat and slowly squeeze. "Can't steal from Allen," Sonny growls.

"Didn't." Shanty manages a squeak. He pulls at the right hand clutching his throat but his weak muscles change nothing. His face turns red, he loses his breath, he shakes and sweats, and his airway constricts, the gritty voice now mute.

"If that word 'Didn't' was my last word in this life Shanty, I'd pick a different one and say it nicer. Like 'Sorry,' and aim it at Allen."

Sonny reaches his left hand behind Shanty and removes the towel, shakes it out. Two packs of chocolate chip cookies and four Hershey bars hit the floor.

Shanty tries to shake his head, but Sonny holds it tight against the wall. Shanty attempts the word sorry, but it comes out a hiss and urine runs down his legs.

"We'll except that piss poor attempt," Sonny says. "Got a demon in you Shanty, makes you steal from our friends? Look at it, that little green sucker with big yellow eyes and a pointy head hides right behind those flap ears you got, hides inside that stringy hair you wear. Gotta cut it off, then that demon can't hide in it. Squeezing that spook outta you this time Shanty, get you healthy again. Then you can cut your hair and keep that spook out. What you think, you like that idea, me helping you this time?"

Shanty tries shaking his head 'no,' but it remains frozen against the wall, tries a mini-shrug, but it fails too, another hiss, more urine.

"Those demons make you steal from Allen or you doing it all by yourself? Come on, Shanty, tell it, 'fess it up. Which is it, you, or that nasty old spook? Allen don't deserve it. Told us some of his package disappeared yesterday too. That you too, or did the spook get it that time?"

His eyes open wide and roll back and Shanty shakes harder, shudders top to bottom, his feet twitch, his arms flop sideways, useless against Sonny in his manic state. Slowly losing oxygen, no blood reaching his brain, Shanty quickly becomes a casualty of his crimes, right here on the clinic wall, a bit of street justice.

Sonny opens his eyes wider, grits his teeth, his jaw bulges, the brow knots, and he suddenly grins, but the face surrounding his grin shows mean and rage all over it.

"Got it Shanty, watch its eyes pop." Sonny stares into the eyes as both glaze over and Shanty loses consciousness. Sonny continues squeezing slowly, as if hypnotized by the power. His personal demon takes control and Sonny transforms into a killing tool. He grins at Shanty, watches his life drain away, watches the demon expire.

"Let loose Sonny or you'll kill him." Melanie stands at his right shoulder and whispers in his ear. Sonny eases off the choke, but keeps his fingers in place.

Melanie checks in and out of here more than any other patient. She began about age sixteen, her first time here, and celebrated birthday number twenty-two this week, in here as well. Her parents, both career professionals, carry great insurance. The clinic likes her, she pays well and immediately, so she stays longer than most others each time, gets a nice rest, never gets kicked out like some, has seen a lot, knows a lot, knows how things happen and don't happen. Many new patients believe she's a nurse until a few days pass and truth emerges. Patients that know her help her fake it then everyone shares the chuckle bug after a new client discovers the joke, but all enjoy the laugh.

Serious now, Melanie moves closer, gently drapes her fingers across his forearm, wraps her arm around his waist, puts her lips right next to his ear. "Let him go Sonny, please."

"This demon makes him steal Melanie, see it, hiding behind his ears? Get a little tired of these spooks hanging around, bossing people, giving orders. Got one finally, right here in my fist." Stress squeaks in his voice, Sonny wants it over, done. His first chance. Kill a demon, watch it up close, feel it die between his fingers. "Gotta kill it, Mel."

Melanie leans in, observes Shanty. "Nope, don't see anything here but stringy, dirty hair could use a little soap." Melanie lightly massages the forearm, reaches up her other hand, and pries at his fingers. No chance. Sonny anchors in place like a stone, a steel fist still squeezing. Melanie, a little whacked out socially, with addictions keeping her coming back here, but the violence sickens her. Her voice pitches higher, terrified she that might witness an act she despises, and she fears Sonny may get into trouble for it.

"I get its powers if I kill it," Sonny says.

"See no demons here Sonny, but he got blood leaking out his nose and mouth, bit his tongue, maybe? Better let him go now." Her voice pitches toward shrill, she pulls a little harder, but Sonny locks his fingers tight, much too strong for her.

"Nasty fucking thief deserves a little pain for stealing, but you'll never get out of here if you hurt him. Besides he's nuts and doesn't know any better." Her voice squeaks, hits its highest note then she backs off, smoothes out her words, talking Sonny down. Melanie continuously glances back and forth down the hall toward the locked entry door.

She tries again. "Security patrolling through this wing in about two minutes Sonny – will catch you anyways, even if Shanty earns this pain by stealing." She squeals the final phrase, stress pushing hard at her words. "You get the bigger penalty, not him, the main penalty, you want that? Shanty ain't worth it Sonny."

Sonny squints sideways, glares at Shanty, peeks at Melanie. "You see nothing, no demons hanging on his ears, don't hear spooks yelling?"

"No Sonny, nothing. Nothing. Please let him loose."

His anger dissolves and Sonny releases his grip. "Good, guess I killed it."

Shanty slides along the wall and flops down on the floor unconscious. He stops breathing. Sonny picks up the towel and the stolen candy, carries it into the room, and hides the snacks in a drawer. He returns and march-steps into the shower stall, his lips curl back tight in his cheeks. Unfocused, his eyes aim at an object a thousand miles away only Sonny can see.

Breathless, Melanie sprints down the hall and punches a red button by the access door. Clinic staff pops open the door and Melanie explains quickly. The nurse runs out, returns with a breather bag, and hovers over Shanty, starts pumping his chest, slides a tube down his throat. Count and blow, count and blow, pump his chest. Ninety seconds later Shanty opens his eyes, and coughs blood all over his shirt.

*

Shanty survives. Three days pass but he refuses to discuss the incident or the bruises on his throat. Tells everyone he tripped and fell. Melanie admits nothing. Sonny spends eleven days in clinic evaluations while doctors and security argue, but finally release him. No hall cameras and no evidence, bunch of nuts acting out. K.O. picks Sonny up and he immediately jumps in his truck and hits the running trails, same as every other time he leaves the clinic. The workout releases the stress build-up he experiences in the lock-down rooms.

*

Eight hundred miles north, Cat punches the buttons on her cell as Erin sits at the table with her. After a couple rings, Professor Max Whitetail speaks. "What?" One word barks through the cell speaker.

"Hi Max, it's me and Erin. You get my email?"

"Yup, only got about ten minutes, meeting with budget, gotta get my paydays, so I'll get right to it."

"Fine." She nudges a button. "Go! Speaker open."

"Okay Cat, a normal human mind realizes that hurting

friends is as natural as hurting enemies to achieve a goal. Unlike other animals, humans develop organized culture that allows certain behavior patterns, and enforces laws and rules and policies against other behaviors. That's learned behavior, unlike instinct, which protects self and family at all costs and passes on in the individual brain genetics. Early on in brain development, about five years old up to and during adolescence, the brain interlocks moral and ethical patterns that a person begins learning early in life, our cultural and parenting values, and transposes those to counteract against some protective actions in dangerous situations."

"Thomas Hobbes, a sixteenth century British thinker, maintained that humans will always resort to brutality and violence against every other human or animal or situation unless some kind of social order controls our behaviors. He means we need a threat of policing or collective protection against an individual for the basic social good - some sort of reflex harm to an individual or, even ourselves if one of us gets out of line. If not, we could all revert to violent self-preservation and self-gratification no matter what behavior it requires. And most often, it provokes violence because it engages brutality on the first order if it's necessary to obtain what a human wants, or more rightly, needs for survival. Think carnivores here, big cats especially, or raptors."

"Neither Fergie or Nickels feels anything remotely like remorse nor guilt. That chemical reaction never engages in abnormal brains like these two. It's either absent, or too low a level to make a difference. Both men believe the demon exists, and each man hurt his friend thinking he was protecting that friend. Like Fergie when he nearly killed Harry, and Nickels when he choked his cellmate. Neither man feels guilt, but both tweak a friend into the hallucinations as a danger - it fills the video holes with negative data."

"The easy answer, they're both nuts Cat." Max laughs, knowing the theory contains truth, but with such severe consequences that he either laughs or may go crazy himself. Humans exhibit intense and uncompromising brutality once we remove the social constraints we learn on the laps of our parents."

"That's it, gotta go. Let me know if you need more. I can give you time later … I'm on the road speaking starting tomorrow, maybe in a couple weeks we can take an hour or so." The phone clicks once and a dial tone returns.

"Could listen to that man forever," Erin admits.

"That's why he gets so many speaking engagements, and why I can't get him on the phone for more than five minutes."

*

Sonny opens his eyes and pokes the message button. A client called him last night while he raged in the park, but he ignored it. Wind blew a tree down in her yard. He likes windy days, at least the first few days after a storm blows through, keeps him busy. He hops out of bed. He knows a spook masquerades as the mother, and lives with her alien son. She tells everyone he's six.

Sonny believes aliens created her son two centuries ago on another planet and slipped him into her family. The son speaks no words, just flashes his hands and fingers, but Sonny knows the boy signs just to keep his space birth a secret and he actually speaks several languages, including alien and demon. Sonny hears him mutter in the sandbox, playing, but understands none of the words or syllables - sounds like a foreigner talking too fast. The voice rings hollow and makes no sense.

The woman always pays him immediately and feeds him lunch. Sonny decides working for the fake alien mother will get him some pay. He needs a little uplift today, a pill or some spike powder works just fine, whatever he finds on the streets later. The smoke just softens the voices lately, and he needs something stronger. Heroin or a few Percocet pills to crush and snort might work.

Best go get those Hamiltons. Repair yourself, no one else will. The demon rags at him again, a redundant activity occurring nearly every day and more frequently now.

Sonny runs outside, pops the shed door behind the gym, grabs his saw and his tool kit, jumps in his truck, and peels out, the tires spitting gravel behind it in his haste. He slows as he approaches a dirt driveway, turns in through the open gate, calm and rational outside, raging inside.

He fires up the Stihl, knowing work shuts it up, even

cutting and splitting this small broken tree, well maybe. Sonny pays it less attention, learning to ignore it as best he can. If the tree work fails, spike juice may do it. If he finds no one selling, he has plenty of time. He can run over to the campsite and bust more firewood. He needs that extra action more and more lately, knocking those demons out.

17

Sonny checks each bill as he sits by his tent and counts his pay. He began noting money by name instead of amount a few years ago right after he lost his mother and set up his tent camp. It keeps his mind occupied, passes time in dim fire-lit evenings or full moon nights when he visits the camp. He often stays overnight, even thought he lives in his room at the gym. He like it here, he knows sometimes the spooks kick him into a uncontrollable rage, and he can run, break branches, and generally keep it secret when he loses that control, and, no one here to hurt.

He tosses a few sticks in the fire, drops and runs a set of a hundred pushups, breaks eight branches over a tree trunk, then sits on his stump, sweating. The spooks vanish.

Sonny recognizes the historical figures on each configuration. A low voice in the background assists when the demons depart. His spiritual brother speaks each word quietly in his ear, the name instead of a denomination as he examines each Treasury note – George a one, Abraham a five, Alexander a ten, Andrew a twenty as he totals a hundred six dollars, four Andy, two Alex, an Abe, and one George he earned today. Sonny likes Ben Franklin best but receives him so infrequently he stores each one in a separate pouch, his private savings. It now contains three. He never spends a Ben Franklin.

The date this soft and friendly spirit voice first appeared escapes him, but he recalls no memory of a time when it was completely absent. His spirit brother helps him count, but the demons always engulf it, boisterous and commanding, the demons send his spirit brother into hiding nearly every time it appears lately. Sonny worked the tree hard today, collected his pay, ate a sub, and scored some spike dust. He counts out what money remains, sixty-four dollars.

An internal advisor, he remembers its voice years ago, his acoustical conscience, a personal voice he hears, and the memories it contains. A spirit brother, he recalls it in his life before the demons began screaming and yelling, absorbing his mind and pushing everything else away. Now the hushed spirit brother hovers in a vaporous shadow while dark demanding haunts scream louder and shout orders, overwhelming it. The spirit brother whispers only when Sonny rests after sweating the demons out for the day, and it speaks so quietly he barely hears it now, but when he listens carefully his spirit brother advises and guides him toward the good things Sonny enjoys in life.

Ignore the demons. Take the medications. Ignore the aliens. Engage no violence.

The nearly absent voice counsels, the internal advisor all humans acquire at birth tells him the demons only bring hurt. But the alien entity gains strength and it requires more and more sweat to control it. Conflict continuously floods his mind. Drugs assist the sweat, and his mind turns toward that release more often lately, chemical support for his heavy physical workouts.

Sonny carries his counting practice over into his odd way of stating his billing to each client, one Andrew and one Abraham, 'an Andy and an Abe,' he says to each one, slaps on his sideways grin and hopes for a tip, maybe two Andy Jacksons instead. A tweak in his mind believes a client may sooner cut loose a green paper he calls Andrew than a twenty-dollar bill. Makes little sense in the employment world, but sometimes it works as he believes, and he recalls a few times when the statement produced a nice result, a tip. Sonny makes logical sense of it in his own mind, no loss to him if it fails.

Playing a brain game at night sitting alone by his fire, Sonny adds Alex, Abe, and Andy in his head, stacking different combinations in his mind, checking it with a calculator afterward – always dead accurate. Even tries to fool his brain and get the total wrong, but he always hits the number, exactly. It's a thing his brain does all by itself oddly enough, with help from one friendly, undistorted, misty spirit that minimally resembles what his brother might look like if one exists. Perhaps a truth, a sibling might exist in his birth family. The passive spirit always appears in his mind as a vague shadow with a soft voice and no real substance, and only those nights he chases the demanding demons out for a while.

Is it strange? Is it weird? Sonny wonders if other people count money as an historical portrait instead of a number or an amount. Might account for his inability to balance his bank statements when checks remain outstanding, or when a deposit delays for a day while the bank finishes its internal accounting. In his brain, he automatically converts his total, with no digital manipulations that delay a date and a time with the inert monetary balancing equations that all bank computers apply to online accounts.

*

Sonny pops into the basketball court and his friends each bump a fist and set up a game. "Pick up tonight, or what?" Vibrating in place as usual, Sonny craves activity, even more lately, no rest ever ... what a bitch!

"Let's do it." Just in it for exercise and fun, lifelong friends automatically section off into even teams. Each teen knows the players, so no one stacks a side. All kids, all skilled athletes, great competition without the stress. Points never count, only the effort – make the hoop, a cheer, miss the hoop, nice try – either way the action continues until lights out and lock up. Every player wins.

Two young athletes race down the court, Sonny trails Bucky Henderson, a simple competitive chase – sink the basket or bat the ball away – the only challenge. Same chase occurs ten or fifteen times in a game, each time a kid steals a breakaway. Nothing fancy, quick one-on-one, fleet feet down the court. These kids almost never miss a hoop.

Sonny plants his foot and swipes at the fat brown sphere, swats this one away. A minor twist at the line, a sharp pop beneath the hoop, a single acoustical note sings out and his knee crumbles. Sonny stagger-steps, hits the wall and bounces, grabs his right knee in both hands and drops down beneath the basket, moaning. An anterior cruciate ligament ripped loose, and lays Sonny out, changing his life forever.

18

Sonny lies on a bed, knee up and iced over, guard down, wasted and whipped. His knee repaired after an hour in surgery, a pharmacy tech dopes him up and intravenous fluids seep into his arm, Sonny feels groggy and lightheaded. An exercise mechanism strapped across his thigh and around his calf pushes range-of-motion mechanically, once an hour the nurse instructed. Nothing else moves, in all practicality it anchors him to the bed. Hours pass at idle, lying flat in a hospital bed, hurt, no running, no lifting, no sparring, no burn, he waits for healing.

Sonny drives that machine every waking minute, relentless, pump the knee and pump the knee, and pump it again. The only exercise available, identical motion, repeat and repeat, it extends his range-of-motion. Pump the knee, pump the knee, the pain continues, he counts the cycles and rotates his leg trying to work up a sweat but the machine spins freely adding flexion not muscle, and his powerful thigh cycles through it with little effort and no sweat. Six weeks on crutches lies ahead, six times an eternity.

"Physical therapy, that's all you need now." The nurse smiles, believes it. "Keep at it and you're up before you know it."

That belief dries up and floats away. Sonny knows better, takes more than a little physical therapy to slow down these spooks. He lies limp and corralled, hog-tied in a hospital bed. No running, no biking, no sparring, and no way he can chase these demons tonight. Sonny stares at two crutches leaning against the wall, shuts his eyes, then snaps them open and watches for spooks, afraid they might capture him now.

After years popping in, popping out, jamming him up, jamming him down, and often simply hiding, awaiting a chance, the darklings emerge in full force and no warning. Side-by-side, full strength, four distorted masks sneak up on his mind and peer down at his youth, screeching louder than ever. Four nasty faces harmoniously warp into his mind.

Got you! Got You!! GOT You!!! WE GOT YOU!!!! You can't run away now!

Sonny believes it, hides beneath his pillow. Peeking above it, he shakes and throbs, tears run freely down his cheeks while terror envelops his mind. Four dysfunctional bandits rob him of soul. One chemical batch mixed in his genes on the night of conception and random confusion scrambles his thoughts. His mind slowly disintegrates, no sweat available, and the demons win.

Suddenly and completely, the fright emerges. Terrified, Sonny stares at a paranoid world most humans never experience. Afraid to come, afraid to go, afraid to stay, afraid, afraid, afraid. "The demons can read my mind!" Sonny moans the words and shuts his eyes, but the skin shield fails. The spooks live in his skull. Gray-streaked beards and pointed heads and powers beyond belief fold him into delusion.

*

The door swings open. K.O. and Willow peek around it. "You awake, can we come in?" Willow almost begs, but not quite. Sonny exhibits a little hostility toward both since his surgery four days ago. Nothing intentional, nothing mean, he simply has no choice. Chemistry in action.

"How you feeling, Champ?" K.O. asks and grins. "We're taking you home."

"Sucks. Can't run, can't work out, can't push iron. Just this machine, that's no workout at all. Besides, can't do much here to protect anyone. Everyone's after me. Everyone reads my mind, demons know my weakness. Want me to kill people I don't want to hurt."

Confused, Willow takes his hand. "Who's after you?"

Sonny jerks away. "Don't touch me Willow. It will break your fingers."

"Who reads your mind? No one can do that. That's crazy," she says, immediately regretting her word choice. "No one wants you hurt, or you to hurt anyone."

"Who will break my fingers, no one here but you?"

"The spook will make ME do it Willow - it orders me to hit you, and cut you up. It's in my brain, yelling at me. K.O too, tells me to hurt him, cut him up."

"Town leaders now too, demons took over, the Gray Leaders own beggars and doctors and farmers, the cops, and all read my mind and want me to work for them, defending them. They plant thoughts in my mind. They all work on me, working on me, testing me all day and all night. Always sell me short. Always lure me along. Always tell me only I can save the people. One demon tells me to kill the same people his spook pals tell me to save. How do I know what's right?"

Completely confused, K.O. asks, "What you mean? Who's working on you?"

Sonny studies K.O. first then shifts his eyes toward Willow, his mental video running wild, the holes filling with random memories. Physical activity that normally shuts off the imaginary demon fails him here, and a biological dysfunction in his brain overwhelms his control, triggering intense distorted images in his mind.

"You know it. You both read my mind. You stick thoughts in there. Make me want to hurt some people, save others. Then suddenly want me to protect everyone. Weird K.O., nothing helps, except the pain shots sometimes, but it's never enough. Just a small dose, just a teaser, doctors playing me, that's all. The demons still order me around, telling me to hurt Jacki, and Randy too."

"Why do you think I hit it with spike juice? Well, so I don't hurt you, it's getting too strong. I need the help. Meds you give don't work. Don't need a doctor, I need a street corner. "

"You're making no sense. No one wants to hurt you. No one wants you to hurt anyone." Willow says. Neither she nor K.O. understands yet the experience Sonny describes.

"Right, Willow, Jacki too. She's really a demon faking me out, faking us all out. She's one of the top Masters, she's a Gray Leader. She's supreme, not young like you all think. She's nine hundred and three years old. She's testing me, checking me out. See if I'm good enough to rise up. The next level or two maybe, can read minds then too, like you all."

"Think about what you just said. Jacki's only twelve. She's just a little girl." A tear shines in the corner of each eye. She loves Sonny like a brother, like a son, like a combination of both. Tears stream down her cheeks.

"Aliens from another galaxy flew in here ten years ago, left demons and spooks here, plan on taking over the earth in a few years, maybe sooner," Sonny claims, accepting every word as truth. Convincing others, failing, wanting everyone to believe him. Conflicted between love for his friends and the biological disconnects that cause such rage and hostility in his mind, he describes a giant paranoid conspiracy engaged in conquering the earth.

Fright fills his mind completely.

"Unless I can stop them." His thoughts switch to confident. "So I got to train, got to train harder and faster. Only one way I can get strong enough to beat them and save all my friends, got to box, and fight, learn the ways of war against these aliens, and defeat these demons. I'll become a Warrior and join with other Warriors, like me, a secret society that kills the aliens and protects the earth. We all keep it secret too, no one knows us. Brian too, he trains me, we train together, Warriors, but no one else knows."

"Brian denies it, and laughs at me in public, keeping it secret, but I know better. Every Warrior denies it. Keep the secret, get it? Why do you think we train so hard and so long? We will beat the aliens when they bring in the take-over teams. Right now, only the scouts are here. We see them in our brains, and on your shoulders, and sometimes in your head. They hide everywhere, in walls, in windows, under beds, in the trees out at my tent site too. That's where they sleep, when they sleep, but they don't really need sleep."

His eyes spin around the room. "Don't tell anyone." His momentary confidence departs and his fright resumes, his head swivels back and forth, his eyes dart about.

"You know what they look like. You just read my mind and you can see them. You probably put them in there. These demons are your friends, not mine." Sonny shakes his head, confusion wears him out. His brain exhausts itself seeking the truth but finds conflicted delusions instead. "You know them, one lives in your brain too, some of the time K.O., so watch it, don't let it get control of you. You too Willow. I can see it sometimes, not always."

The phantoms sneak in again. Sonny missed it, concentrating on his story. Suddenly all four emerge, giggle and point. *"We win! We Win! We Win! We Win!* Aliens chant repeatedly. *Strike Three! Strike Three! Strike Three! Strike Three!* All four scream at once, dancing, and cackle insanely while Sonny stares at the wall then hides his eyes.

"Can't run, can't bike, can't lift, and can't face it." Sonny bats at the air. "See it, right there's one." Sonny swings a fist, waves at it again, points at empty space above his head.

Sonny rolls over, rips the needle and lines off his arm, blood leaks down his wrist and across his hand. The knee machine clatters to the floor, still strapped to his leg in places. "Get this off me, get it off! Get It The Fuck Off Me-e-e-e-e!"

Sonny pushes up off the bed, trips over his harness, hits the floor and slides across the slick tiles, his head bounces off the wall. He grabs his knee and cries out in pain.

K.O. bear hugs Sonny, easily lifting him off the floor, and strong-arms him back into bed, holding Sonny stable with no small effort. Extremely fit and very muscular, but no match for K.O., Sonny struggles while Willow bolts for the nurse.

A haunting ghost rears its ugly head and the demons jump for joy. *We got one! We got one! We captured you Sonny! You'll never escape us!*

Sonny wraps his pillow around his head, moaning into its fluff. "I can't beat them K.O. Can't beat them, can't win. Not strong enough."

Sonny recognizes it as truth. A nurse enters and injects fluid into his arm. A few seconds pass. Sonny embraces its relief and his eyes close halfway.

"What's happening to me, K.O? What's happening in my brain?" Sonny slurs his words. K.O. says nothing. "I'm doomed! These aliens read my mind. They know all my thoughts, know everything. If I leave my room they'll grab me and haul me away and hide me in the stars." Tears run freely down his cheeks. "I'll never get back Willow, never."

Willow wraps her arms around Sonny, holds him tight, and matches him tear for tear. "I'm going Craaazzzyyyyyy!" Sonny cries out and wraps his head in a towel.

*

Bewildered and frightened after Sonny explains his wild nightmares, alien visions and delusions, Willow punches the call button. She and K.O. arrange psyche consults and recount his story. The doctors offer no immediate answers, but keep him several days and run a battery of biological tests that reveal little. The staff psychiatrist at the clinic prescribes stress medications, hands Willow a script. "Go home tomorrow Sonny, relax, get some rest, he says.

"Relax! Rest!" Sonny blurts the words. "Relax! How can we relax, the aliens are taking over." Sonny cackles harder than ever at that order. "Relax." He laughs again, "We can't rest, we need to train, or they'll win. Don't you guys get it? Relax? Fuck that!" Sonny pulls the pillow up over his head and screams into the mattress.

Later that evening, the doctor reads his chart, prescribes sedatives, a psychotic relief medication, and rest. Orders him released in the morning, if he has a ride and a home.

*

Sonny awakens the next morning when the nurse arrives with his soap and water, cream for his back. "

"My name's Alice, she says. Her badge proves it. She begins rubbing ointment into his skin, protecting it from bed-rash.

Alice asks, "How are those meds doing, helping at all? Probably too soon."

Sonny says, "How would I know that? I seem normal to me. It's you all who tell it, 'Sonny ain't normal', not me."

"You feel normal when you punch a wall?"

Sonny says, "Well, yeah of course, otherwise, why would I do it? Feels right to me, see a wall, punch it, when it feels right, or when the demon tells me, or when I see a demon hanging on something, I hit it." He looks her in the eye. "Don't you, if you see one? They hide in walls sometimes, even in trees."

"Nope, I don't see demons."

"Why not, you don't have one?"

"No, I don't." She pushes at his legs, "Here, turn a little, let me get your legs."

"Well, you have a voice in your head, tells you what to do, right? Go eat. Mow the lawn. Get up. Brush your teeth. Go to work? What about when you read? Do you hear words, or what? And what do you hear when you look at a clock?"

"Well, guess I hear myself sometimes, yeah, of course, a little voice. That's my conscious self. It says 'four o'clock', or whatever."

"H-u-u-u-h, weird, mine tells the time too, but never says, 'or whatever' after." Sonny contemplates that for minute, looks at the nurse, and chuckles, grins.

"Must be like the one I had earlier in life, the nice one, the spirit brother, but you don't have a demon one now? You didn't get a demon one when you got older?"

"Nope, don't see a spook in my brain, or a demon."

"See? That's your problem, if you don't have your own demon, you're not allowed to see the other demons. You don't have your own spook, you ain't normal. You only live half a life then."

Nurse Alice Waggoner looks at Sonny as if he's the strangest person she's ever seen. And, she's seen some real weird ones in her time in the psyche wards and clinics. Never heard this one though.

Sonny says, "I hate it, want to kill it. The mean one yells at me and tells me to do things I disagree with, like hitting K.O. and Willow. It yells and gets mad at me, but I ignore it usually. Hard to stop it sometimes, when the spooks hang around, barking loud orders. If I have trouble, I run away or hit something else, or push weight until it leaves me alone." He keeps the secret about his street drugs. No trust here.

19

Six days after his hospital discharge, Sonny crutches down the hall and into his room and lies on his bed, unable to exercise hard, unable to work the sweat that over-rides the demon visions and voices. Sonny peeks over his pillow, watching his door, staring, afraid it might open. No talking, no driving, no shopping, afraid to leave his room, and fright fills his life. Silent, he lies on his bed wishing his mind would collapse.

Midnight finally, and Sonny crutches down the hall, empties himself, cleans himself, grabs a sandwich and a drink then hobbles back, slams the door and hooks its lock quickly, hoping he beat the spooks into the room. He lost the race. One nasty face hangs from the ceiling and points a giggle at Sonny. *Kill someone or we never let you go!*

Paranoia attacks him body and soul. Sensory perceptions cross-connects its signals and triggers fright chemistry in his brain. Fear up-charges his body and prepares him to defend his life from a false threat that appears real. Terror streaks across his mind and digs in, ripping his brain apart bit by bit. The darkness consumes his essence. All day and all night, week after week, Sonny huddles beneath his blanket, safe and protected only inside his room.

Fear fills his eyes whenever his door opens, and he barricades himself in every night before he can sleep. Colored cloth covers the only window in his very small bedroom, keeping prying eyes at bay and protects him from investigating spies that giggle soundlessly and point while enjoying his tremble.

Sonny sneaks into the gym at night, working the lightest

weights and only in darkness, pushing iron, punching the bag, hiding in shadows. It does no good. Aliens can see in the dark, he races the fright back to his room and slams the door behind him. Too late. Slow on his crutches, the aliens sprint in before him and hang on his curtains, watch him twist the lock. Sonny turns and listens.

One alien bleats laughter, and floats above his window. Sonny realizes he lost the race, dives into his pillow, pulls it over his head and screams, "Leave me alone. Leave Me Alone!" His crutches hit the floor. He pushes himself up and swings at a demon. His fist penetrates the glass and opens a jagged cut from wrist to elbow.

*

A light knock, the door swings open. Sonny relaxes slightly as Willow sticks her head in, smiling but unsure how Sonny feels. Sometimes Sonny welcomes, sometimes Sonny rejects, confusing himself as well as his friends.

"Hey Willow."

Two words, a safe entry Willow believes, at least for a few minutes. "How's the arm? You lost a lot of blood. Hundred and eight stitches, a nasty cut."

"Yeah, bled all over the floor, got a spook though. Nailed it, felt like smoke. I'll get him next time. Then you'll see one. I'll save it for you."

Sonny sits up, grim and solemn. Salty wetness streaks his face. "It's not safe Willow, not you, not here, not now, not with me, K.O. too. Tell him to stay away too. No one is safe, especially K.O. The demons chose my target, K.O. Then I get his powers, and the mind reading. I refused, at least so far, but the demon has a lot more power. It can force me. Tell K.O. to stay away."

"You can't do it. You cannot hurt K.O. after all he's done for you. And he has no powers to get." Willow glances around the room. "And why is it not safe here? You look healthy, you're crutch-walking now, almost ready to start running again. You lift, work out, and take your meds. That's important."

Sonny looks at the floor, ashamed. "Sometimes I do, sometimes I don't. Meds don't help. Just poison me. The demons want me to die because I won't follow orders. Doctors just working on me, finding stuff inside me they can use, experimenting on me, working on me all the time, but stay invisible so I can't see them, can't protect myself."

"You hear them at the meeting Tuesday? Told you all and me they worked on me Monday and last Friday. Well, guess what? I saw no doctor, or nurse, or counselor Friday or Monday. So, either they're invisible or reading my mind, or lying. They were not in the room with me, and I was not at the clinic. They were not working on me, but they said it, claimed they worked on me Friday and Monday. That's lying."

"The doctors work with others in the medical offices, working on you, defining treatment. They talk about how to treat this brain illness Sonny. The doctors believe you have a chemical problem in your brain. Makes you imagine things, the demons, mind reading, taking over earth. It's in your mind, imaginary, it's not real."

"Nope, aliens, working on me, sit in the offices sending waves into my brain. That's what they do. Read my mind. Been doing it for a while, but running always chased them out, they can run but can't keep up. I can't run fast enough now." Sonny buries his head in the pillow then peeks at Willow when she speaks.

"There are no aliens, Sonny. Aliens don't exist. It's in your brain, it's an illness. It's biology and chemistry, a mixed hormone imbalance. We can help. The doctors can help, but only if you take these medications."

"No Meds! No Meds! It's poison. The legal woman at the clinic told us we don't have to take meds. Law says we don't, so the doctor can't make me."

Sonny wraps his hands around his chest, and rocks in place. "I'm going crazy Willow! What's wrong with me?" He grabs his head, his arms cover his ears, his mouth a tortured frown. Once again, he buries his head in his pillow, lifts it, and mumbles as if speaking it softer denies its truth.

"Go ask Melanie, she knows, she'll tell you. Pills, the demon poison. Ask her, she knows everything."

"Who's Melanie, a doctor?"

"No," Sonny replies, "she's a patient, one of the good ones, been in that clinic the longest, she's a little freaky and flips out once in a while, gotta be locked up alone for a bit, but she knows this stuff, just ask her. Melanie knows all the answers."

Willow throws her hands in the air and shakes her head, "You tell me a mental patient knows everything and you believe her!" Willow spins in a circle releasing her frustration. "You believe her and not the doctors."

"The alien wants me to hurt you, Willow, and K.O, too. If I do it, it'll free me, it'll leave me alone, quit haunting me. It promised. It reads my mind. The doctors read my mind. You and K.O read my mind. I can't read anyone's mind. I'm weak. I'm not worthy. Unless I execute you or K.O. and receive your powers, then I gain the next level. If I kill both, even more power and gain two levels. Then I can read minds too."

A savage grin flicks across his face. Wildly manic, his mind mimics a video game, fighting, winning, gaining power and higher levels with each battle scene, each voyage, each episode, finally cashing it in as a Leader, a Top Dog, a Gray Supreme, its final goal. Sonny kicks his legs over the edge of his mattress, sits up, then changes his mind and falls back on this bed, wraps his arms around his knees. His body curls upon itself, a fetal implosion. His voice a tragic moan, "What's happening to Me-e-e-e-e-e-e?"

Complex panic contorts a fine-tuned athlete, his muscles and fitness no match for the rage and anger as hormones spill into his brain and bio-systems. His dysfunctional biology creates holes in his memories and fills his mind with images that trigger intense visual, auditory, and emotional distortions only violence will cure.

The alien screeches an order. *Got your chance, easy. Kill her now, a quick twist. Break her neck.*

Sonny balls a fist, struggles with the rage, conflicted, stares at Willow, the anger nearly impossible to control when he finds her close. He wants to end it, but his conscience refuses, he will not harm Willow. Instead, he punches himself in the jaw, twice, splits his lip. Blood runs down his chin.

"Go Willow! Now! I love you, you're like my sister, and K.O., I don't want to hurt him. Please go and come back later, when it's safe, help me kill these aliens. They brought a space ship. They want me to take a trip. It scares me. How Will I Breathe?"

He hugs hard, both arms wrapped tightly around Willow.

She returns his embrace and copies his tears. In the truth of it all, he has no idea how to protect his friends.

Break her neck. It's easy, a quick twist. She's an enemy

"No! Get out!" Sonny pushes Willow away, swings at smoke above the window.

The spook barks. *You have to kill her first.* Wild chatter echoes in his mind.

"Run Willow, run away!" Sonny yells, turns and punches his fist completely through the wall.

20

Aaron Clark waves a letter. "Good news, your grant funded again, another two years." He hands Cat the proof. "Congrats."

Cat bounces up and down on her toes, ecstatic. A Russian citizen continuously renewed on a research visa, she finds it difficult to gain grant approvals in the United States despite the fact she nearly aced Harvard Medical School and works a research fellowship at McLean at the satellite mental health clinic outside Boston she and Aaron Clark developed six years ago. Her mentor, Professor Maxwell Whitetail pulled a few strings too, knowing in his heart every dollar will be well spent, and gain sound and beneficial results for science, and her patients.

Currently helping develop a new wing at McLean that offers treatment and care for children and young adults with biological brain disorders, Catherine Morgantholavich and Aaron Clark operate a pilot research program under the McLean Trauma Unit. She earns every penny of her grant, her dedication evident in every project she attempts. She gives it her all, virtually obsessed with finding a mental health treatment that works.

Aaron and Cat and other investors developed and support a biotech research firm as well, a non-profit research organization currently developing an electronic microprocessor.

A surgeon will implant the micro-device inside a skull temporarily, then read blood chemistry internally, inside the brain, and send signals to a chemical evaluation program it also developed contiguous with the wireless device.

Aaron and Cat will use that information to create a drug

complex that attempts to mimic the individual brain chemistry and simulate electro-pulse sensations when anger and rage exhibits in clients. The drug compound will allow a patient to release anger and enter a relaxation state, like filtering the input and creating less frenzy in the information a brain senses at any given time. The project tries to stop the violence, not cure an incurable disease.

That idea pushes research to the edge, and remains extremely experimental, and unlicensed for human use anywhere in the world. The implant device works on rats, and monkeys, with no discernible damage to the brain and no observable change in behavior.

Aaron flattens a haunch upon the corner of her desk and lays an elbow on his knee, his hand filled with grant papers. "So, what's next?"

"I'm not sure yet how we'll complete the next step. Bits and pieces emerge when we gather data, but we need the entire picture. We need full reports on each patient from a competent detailer, one that knows how to document responses from sick kids who trust no one in this system. We have no issues with 'mom told me not to talk', that's not relevant. The rejection comes chemically engrained in the biology – brain chemistry triggers fright, so we're unable to talk them out of it. It takes accurate chemical and hormone conditioning, but if they have that, the fear disappears. Then they're healthy not sick, and don't need us. How frustrating is that?"

"And HIPAA again, interferes with data gathering. Damn privacy laws may hide proof some idiot wants to keep an infidelity secret or an employer in the dark, but that poorly developed law completely undermines the potential for treatment in a child that can't think rationally."

"These kids can't make sound medical decisions because their minds don't reason properly and they fear everything. Legal students looking for credit on a college paper hover in state health clinics explaining laws that claim sick young adults own the rights to refuse medication. It completely undermines the best treatment, the only treatment."

"Worse yet, civil rights advocates encourage the same sick young adults to refuse treatment just because they can, just because it's legal. Problem is, the paranoid brain wins, and the sick mind believes we try to poison it or trick it, not heal it. We gain no trust."

"But they're still children, regardless of that 'reached age eighteen' drivel. It's just a number. One day, a parent signs, a kid receives treatment, the next day none, simply because a child blows out an extra birthday candle. One minute later he becomes an adult, and the only one who can sign off. There are thousands out there Aaron, just like Ferguson and Nickels, and Barnes, but much younger. They've not begun killing people yet."

"Most of them may not, but a few will. We've got to stop that, and give these kids a chance at life, which says nothing of the victims." Cat tosses the HIPAA folder in the trash can. "It makes me sick myself, almost makes me want to kill someone." She shakes her head in denial.

Cat continues her rant. "Everyone claims it's too expensive to house and treat all the mental patients. Well, that may be true enough, but if we can focus on and treat our youth and young adults *before* we lose them to criminal lifestyles, and at least stabilize these kids, they might become productive adults at some level beyond what happens if we don't treat it. The cost to insurance claims and damaged property, and damaged families compared to the cost of medication and socialization clearly outweighs that fact in favor of treatment."

Frustrated, Cat blows out a breath and grabs a financial record, waves it at Aaron.

"Read this. Government agencies spent eighty-eight billion dollars housing prison inmates last year. That's a 'B', Billion! One Year! No figures here for country jails, or court trials, or enforcement even. No telling what that would add. Imagine this, even if mental illness causes only ten percent of that crime – and the percentage probably runs much higher. If we could treat that disease before these kids turn into criminals, we'd have eight billion dollars to support mental health issues instead of building prison cells. Just ten percent, that's eight billion for research and treatment!"

A calming influence as usual, Aaron responds. "Not letting a bit of attorney-speak get in the way of proceeding, are we?"

"Nope, we'll find a way around those laws, and the costs." Cat bounces up on her toes, her energy level rises, almost limitless when she touches a goal. She heads toward the stairwell and the workout room. "We got our funding, we'll find a way." She repeats the words back over her shoulder, at once confident and positive, and dedicated.

*

Willow crosses and re-crosses her legs, swinging one foot back and forth, her frustration evident, "So, what can you tell us?"

Eyebrows arched, forehead wrinkled, lips pursed, Doctor Andrew Anderson successfully conceals his own confusion, puts a frown on his face. Mental health and brain issues confuse most people, including many professionals that treat it, and he finds it nearly impossible to explain it to parents and friends, and annoyed that he needs to explain it at all.

"Heavy exercise produces endorphins and probably balances the active hormones, but his brain chemistry remains disorganized. His brain engages fright and confusion as soon as he quits pushing himself physically. Some kids are like that and some adults too. Whatever happens is just human nature, some chemistry is missing, or maybe his neurotransmitters overload the system, neural connectors misfire, we think, or maybe too much of one or another, or some combination."

Willow frowns, dissatisfied with his answer. Frustration edges her reply, "Probably? What do you mean, 'probably' and 'whatever happens'? You're a brain doctor, the psychiatrist. You're supposed to know this stuff."

"Well, we don't know for sure. Every person's different, every brain different. We don't know yet what's missing."

"Yet? So, what do we do? How do we find out? Seven months and you're still guessing?"

Anderson spouts his memorized monologue, as if Willow's comments mean nothing, and in his mind, it's true. Families have no understanding, no knowledge. He believes it's a waste of his golf time to meet with a parent, let alone a friend, but one of his office chores requires explaining his patients to families, and that fills his checkbook and pays his country-club dues.

"That's why this condition exhibits itself most often during adolescence, the maturing process, and new hormones it introduces. Unfortunately, the bad news, it's incurable, but the good news, it's easily treatable. Medications temper the violence and control the outbursts. We'll teach him to interact in his world, watch him, test him, wait and see."

"Test him? That's what Sonny says. The doctors test him, experiment on him. It supports what he thinks in some strange way, doesn't it? The doctors work on him, he says. So how long? He could become dangerous. He's already dangerous, with what he talks about, all this violence, punching walls and kicking doors, breaking things. We're lucky it's all inanimate. As strong as Sonny is, he could really hurt someone, even accidentally let alone if a person really pisses him off."

"What else can we do?" The perpetual mental health rhetorical question emerges once more. "We don't know, six months, a year? It's not like surgery, cut it out or mend the bone. Brain chemistry just doesn't work that way," Anderson says.

"He waffles on the meds, sometimes he'll take them, sometimes he won't. Nothing right now, he's refusing. He says it's poison. He thinks aliens live here on earth and plan on taking over the planet." Willow shakes her head, aggravation sitting right on the surface.

"That's not unusual. Voices, delusions, hallucination, chemistry pushes his instinct, works inside his memory, his brain cells and circuits, take bits and pieces of his own life experience and combines them, triggers a mental picture of his reality, often times a very distorted picture." Anderson looks at his watch, twice, a hint her time's up.

Partially right and partially wrong, Willow has limited knowledge, so she expects the doctor's right, but his answers dissatisfy her. She wants to know a medication will cure his brain soon. Just as many parents inaccurately believe, Willow expects Sonny will eventually take the correct chemical combination and end his illness, bring him back to a normal kid.

No cure exists. The hormones damage or destroy brain cells, and neurons never regenerate. An internal component of biology degrades, brain function degrades, and the cells disappear, dead, unrecoverable. Biochemistry treats it, and can control future damage even eliminate future damage, but it cannot repair damage already done. Sometimes, a patient can relearn behavior though, if the correct learning sequences remain undamaged.

Anderson exhibits a haughty demeanor, falsely calm and reassuring. Like some, and unlike others, this doctor leaves work issues at his office each evening, passing into an orderly, organized household, while most of his patients endure anger, rage, frustration, and strike out blindly, finding small comfort in the 'probably' or 'maybe' he offers during office visits. He looks at his watch again, frowns.

Willow ignores the time-over hint. "What happens if he refuses the medications?"

"Cell deterioration probably continues. Hormones may damage more brain cells, may disconnect the communication channels. Eventually, he may be unable to care for himself, or may hurt someone, or himself. How long, or even if that will or could happen, no way to predict, possibly something in the middle. As unlikely as it seems, Sonny could recover tomorrow, or next month, move on with his life. It's a crap shoot."

Anderson shrugs, his indifference apparent. "But Sonny will probably survive, with some care. His prime motivation rules his behavior, same in all animals – survival first, then procreation."

"Animals? He's an animal now! May, possibly, maybe, could? A crap-shoot?" Willow snarls the vague qualifiers back at him. "So, as long as we feed and water him and find a woman to fuck him once in a while, he won't hurt anyone? Is that it? Is that your answer?" Willow vents her frustration, bangs the door open, and leaves the doctor sitting at his desk.

"We only see the failures," Anderson says to her back, without comprehending that his failures may be mostly his own fault.

21

The knee heals. Sonny works hard, and he begins training as soon as he gets back on his feet. He recovers much quicker than anyone expected. Driven both physically and mentally, he thrives on physical therapy. His great fitness and conditioning prior to the injury allows his body to heal much faster than non-athletes, and his courage and confidence push him nearly to exhaustion. Then rest, and back at it.

K.O. schedules three more boxing matches in the next five months, normally a short time-frame for that many bouts. So quick and powerful, and Sonny trains so hard, K.O. finds no issue with the frequency of his fight dates, and Sonny always answers the same way, "I'm ready K.O. I'm ready. Sign the match, sign it." Anytime, every month if he could find a bout, he would challenge his opponent, and beat the demons.

Off and on, he takes the medication, but his ability to train again, the hard workouts and sweat, supports the body chemistry and assists the fight with his imaginary demons as well as his competition skills. As an odd side effect of this brain chemistry issue, fighting the brain disorder pushes him even harder to train and heavy physical activity drives the demons out. His extraordinary physical efforts offer a unique reward - it calms his mind - and one reason why he works so hard, and it coincidentally improves his conditioning and his abilities as an athlete as well. In eight weeks, he hits his peak, runs ten miles every day and completes intense physical workouts and sparring at the gym.

An interesting derivative, when he trains for a fight he

stops all street drugs and alcohol with no withdrawals. He just runs and trains, eats and sleeps. For some unknown reason, a chemical escape becomes unnecessary, perhaps a by-product of the continuous adrenalin rush.

*

He dominates a match in Atlanta and knocks out his opponent at two minutes, twenty seconds into the third round. His fourth match follows quickly two months later, and earns Sonny a unanimous decision in Tampa, dominating that bout as well. A knockdown in the first and third rounds, and his opponent barely toed the mark a few seconds before the final bell. The referee almost stops it twice early on.

Sonny sees the end coming and slows his attack, knows he has the point win. The referee recognizes him backing off, and lets the final seconds tick out right at the end. Sonny recalls K.O.'s advice, 'beat your opponent clean but never cheat and never hurt another athlete.'

His record now stands at four and zero. His nickname 'Dominator' moves toward reality in the fight ring, and becomes a buzz-word in the amateur boxing circles. Sonny has begun a great career, well on its way up the chain as he counts the days until his next birthday.

K.O. scheduled his next bout three months from today in Richmond, where Sonny will carry a four and zero record into the ring, his fifth sanctioned bout just one month past his eighteenth birthday.

*

K.O. sits at a table in the nearly empty Baxter Café chatting with Johnny Sparks, an amateur fight sponsor. Sparks drops his arms down across his extended belly, a lot rounder and out of shape than he once was as a young Golden Gloves boxer. The trainer stares at K.O through dark warp-eyed shades set beneath a brown fedora with a blue band on it that matches the tie hanging loose at this neck.

"Nope, can't do it Kenny," Sparks says. "Carson's got ten

fights, nine wins and a draw he shoulda won. You got a natural athlete. No way my fighter's gittin' in the ring with Sonny now … we'd just come out nine, one and one, unless Carson got lucky, and ain't betting my fighter on luck. He's young, got a good start on a great career, no sense in shooting himself in the foot just to make you and Sonny look good again."

"Sonny ain't *that* good." K.O. lies with the straightest face he owns, knowing he wants Sonny in the ring with Carson Brown, the next big step and a shot at qualifying for the Olympics. K.O. knows it, Johnny Sparks knows it, and both know they both know it. Both men grin at the dilemma, good friends passing the time, each man wanting the best for his own boxer.

K.O. wants Sonny to fight Brown, and Sparks wants to save his fighter an almost certain loss. Too early in his career, Sparks knows it. He'll let Brown mature a bit and earn some wins. No fighter at this level can touch Sonny now, and he wants to keep it that way as far as Carson Brown goes.

Sparks took a slight detour on his trip home to Atlanta, and stopped to visit K.O. while passing through Baxter on his way south. The men carry a friendship back almost an entire lifetime, since third grade. Alley-fighting, candy-stealing, sneaking smokes, joyriding as youngsters, selling nickel pot and dime pops on the streets as teens, growing up closer than brothers. "Had your back," Sparks says.

"Had yours," K.O. repeats. Both men chuckle at the shared history each time they meet, both men recalling the truths of life in the mean ghetto streets of downtown Buffalo, New York.

Johnny Sparks drove out to Attica at least once a month to visit K.O., made damn sure he was serving his time right and short, and that his best friend needed nothing during his eighteen-month vacation with the state authorities.

"Just ain't gonna happen." Sparks laughs. "Wish I'd found Sonny first. You probably got to go outside this area to git him a match now. Find some trainer ain't seen him fight yet, not one around this southeast district anyways."

Willow pushes in through the door, spots K.O. He waves her over. Willow grabs a cup and sits, shakes hands with Sparks. "You the trainer? Sonny's next match?"

"Me, a trainer? Yes. Sonny's next victim? Nope." Sparks

chuckles past that item. "Maybe someday when both these kids sit a little higher up the food-chain, but right now we'll take a pass. In two weeks Carson fights Joey Morris in Atlanta. He'll win that one and earn a shot at regional. You guys come on down, watch the fight, enjoy the weekend."

Sparks finishes his coffee and pushes his bulk up out of the chair, throws a ten on the table. "I'll git this."

"You're welcome too, Willow. Got a spare room at the house, y'all come and spend the weekend. Tap a cold one and listen at Kenny and me swap some almost true stories. You're even allowed to laugh at our dumb kid days."

K.O. picks up the ten, tucks it into Johnny's shirt pocket, and grabs the check. "No way, not in my town." Both men share a hug, brief but intense, and Johnny Sparks heads for his Jeep.

Willow looks at K.O., raises her eyebrows. "A spare room?" she says. He looks back and grins.

Both laugh at the odd conclusion. A surprising tick hits K.O. between the ears, and he takes another look at what Johnny Sparks thought might be his party partner. K.O. ponders it for a minute. In the past, he always stuck Willow in a daughter category just because she and Sonny act like sister and brother, and Sonny feels like his son.

K.O. suddenly realizes only twelve years lies between Willow and himself. His ex-wife lives outside of Las Vegas, chasing money. Willow suddenly emerges as one fine young woman in his eyes, and he surprises himself with his thoughts.

"Hungry, want dinner?" K.O adds little spark in his eyes and shows his teeth this time, unlike the casual relationship between them that surrounds Sonny at its center. A change in the way he defines Willow emerges in his brain. These two friends frequently catch a bite together whenever convenience leaves it out there, often including Sonny or a couple gym rats, almost never just the two alone, depends upon who's hanging around.

Willow pops to her feet, "Sure, where? Meet you at Antonio's?" The top local Italian eatery, one of the best spots in town, but limited competition in Baxter means few choices and nothing fancy at all in town. Low cost, good taste and portion size rules for most country folks. Antonio's fits that category and serves great taste on a country budget.

K.O. names an upscale French restaurant two towns over near the golf course, the locals save it for special occasions. "What about the Rose Tower?" His eyes definitely give away his goal this time. "You can change, I'll pick you up."

"Oh." A light blush appears in her cheeks. A slightly embarrassed Willow says, "I thought you meant eat, like food."

K.O. comes right back, "Did mean eat, that's what we do at Rose Tower, we eat. It's a restaurant."

"I know. We've been there, Danny..." Willow stops...finds no words, this unique invite from K.O. completely unexpected, catches her off-guard. "You mean like a date?"

K.O. takes her hand, holds her fingers for a few seconds. "Yup, pick you up and everything. Just in my truck, course, only wheels I got." He holds her gaze briefly then Willow turns her eyes away.

A bit puzzled, K.O. removes his fingers, both hands land in his lap. He wonders at her odd reaction. His lips flatten out, "What?"

She raise her eye, aims them at K.O. again. "K.O., I don't know what to say here. I'm very flattered and really care a lot for you, and we're really great friends, best friends. You're like a second brother, but I'm married K.O., I thought you knew."

K.O. sits speechless for the first time in his life, then embarrassed, then confused, and no sound fills the air, a little tension slips in. "Oh," breaks loose, and he catches himself as best he can. "Well, knew that, just want some company and change of menu. Food gets boring here, these same few places in town all the time." He covers his error and attempts to save both from strangling on more words.

Willow lightly rubs the area around her left finger right below the knuckle where a wedding ring normally fits, "No, K.O. you didn't, and I'm touched, really touched. Danny wears his on a chain around his neck. He's an Army Ranger serving in Afghanistan, with four months left on a two-year tour, his second. It's very personal, K.O. Not a thing I share easily, and no part of Sonny and his issues either. It just never comes up."

She pulls a gold chain from beneath her blouse, shows him an engraved wedding band hanging on it. "Near our hearts, he wears mine and I wear his, until he comes home for good."

Willow stands and pulls K.O to his feet, wraps her arms around him, hugs him tight. He returns her affection and in that instant the relationship moves away from a common friendship and takes that uncommon intimate step a man and woman almost never take, bonding like adopted siblings, like kindred spirits connected through convictions and truth. A brother and sister in essence and choice, the hug lasting several minutes while each recover the attachment and comfort between them that exists through Sonny, acknowledging the trust in two mature adults with feelings, a complete bonding that requires no vows or blood tie.

"Of course, why didn't that register? Danny Parks. Ain't seen him in years. We'll wait for him together. Hope he stays safe."

Willow says, "I fall asleep every night wondering if I'll ever see him again." Her tears give a clue to her emotion. She shakes it off, wipes her eyes, grins, and says, "Come on, let's go eat."

"Okay, Antonio's?"

Willow aims a grin at K.O. "So, not a date and you get cheap on me?" Both share a laugh and head out to his truck. K.O. shuts the door, twists his key and turns left out the parking lot toward Rose Tower, not a right toward Antonio's Eatery. "Fuck it," K.O. says, "It's a nice night and a nice drive anyways." K.O. looks at Willow. "And nice company too."

Willow rolls down the window and a breeze floats in. She leans across the seat and briefly presses her lips against his cheek.

22

Sonny lies on a couch in the snack room, curled up and napping. He opens one eye, turns an ear, and listens. A slight disturbance edges in through the open windows, kids playing in the street, yelling and laughing. The howl of a skateboard rolls and thumps, its wheels clattering on pavement. He rises quickly, ignoring Willow, jerks the door open, leaves it open, runs outside and jumps off the porch, returns fifteen minutes later breathing hard, enters, shuts the door, locks it, pulls the curtain across.

Sonny checks the room, peeks out a window, creeps into the kitchen, circles the refrigerator, periodically looks over his left shoulder down the hall. Finally, he grabs two sandwiches and a can of juice, sets both on the coffee table then curls up on the couch. He shuts his eyes.

Otherwise motionless, he opens one eye every few seconds, rolls his eye around the room without moving his head, aims the eye at his meal and, after a few minutes, uncoils his body and sits upright, glances over each shoulder and down the hall. As if guarding his food, he curls both arms around the plate, looks over his shoulder again, protective, invoking the poise of a carnivore.

He eats one sandwich quickly as if another predator might sneak in and steal his lunch. Hunger sated, Sonny places the second sandwich back in the fridge. He grabs a washcloth and covers the sandwich, stashing it for later. Sonny coils up in his lair again, shuts both eyes. He opens one eye at every sound, listens intently. No threat apparent. He shuts the eye. No wasted motion, Sonny finally relaxes, curls up, and sleeps undisturbed for two hours. Basic instinct hard at work, survival first, hunt and eat a meal, socialize second, if at all. At least Anderson got that survival instinct part correct.

*

"Sat and watched this entire episode, K.O. Was like I didn't even exist yesterday afternoon. Sonny never spoke, never acknowledged my presence. I was invisible. No threat, so he ignored me. Reminds me of that cougar study we did in the Sierras a few years ago, extremely primitive predatory behavior, like a hunt, a stalk, a kill, and cache some for later. We set up in blinds above her lair and along her hunting routes, followed her whenever we could, a very elusive cat. Only reason we saw her at all was her kittens. We knew she had to feed them, so we tracked her out whenever she left."

"Took us months and months to interpret how she hunts, eats, feeds, trains her kittens. Sonny acted out a replica of that film, so real it was almost scary. He reverted into a primitive man in his mind. Acted just like a hunter on the prowl, total instinct, but somehow based in our home culture. It was real strange K.O., almost like watching an Attenborough nature film in real life starring a stone-age human."

"So fit and so powerful, he stalked that sandwich like animal on the prowl, like his hunter-gatherer heritage slipped in and stole his humanity." Willow explains the predator activity that she observes in Sonny lately, like a recurrent instinctual awareness and response to his environment, lacking the culture. "Extremely primitive behavior and he's been acting it out for weeks. Almost like he's reverting instead of developing social skills."

Tires crunch across gravel. Sonny parks, slams his truck door, takes two steps, turns back, opens the door and shuts it gently, "Sorry," he says to himself, kicks the trash can, circles around the rear, enters. He stops halfway down the short hallway, stands motionless, and stares at the wall briefly. "No, get out," he grunts once with each punch, and knocks two dents in the drywall, rubs his knuckles, and bangs into his room, slams the door.

Sonny hides under his pillow, ignoring K.O. when he follows Sonny into the room. Shame fills Sonny, but he loses control of his actions when phantoms rage in his brain and he rages in return, striking out, pushing the adrenalin as often as he can. "Get away, get away! Leave me alone!"

"Uh-uh, Sonny, not gonna happen today. Owned this place longer than you been alive, so don't you go busting it up. Ain't no place for anger like that in my gym. You got something to say, say it, no more violence. That's enough, it ends now."

"No K.O., not you, these guys, these aliens. See them hanging on that wall in the corner, laughing, pointing, barking at me? Won't leave me alone today, chased me thirty miles on the bike path. Stayed with me all the way up Stony Ridge, couldn't pedal fast enough, still in here, yelling at me!"

Sonny points to a vacant spot near the window. "Look at them, hanging on that window rod, barking at me!" Sonny jumps up, approaches the wall, and cocks a fist.

K.O. grabs Sonny from behind, and twists him around face-to-face, envelopes Sonny in a bear hug and pushes him back on the bed then stands between the bed and the walls, protecting both his property and Sonny from more damage.

Sonny jumps up off the bed, points a finger, "Watch it K.O., it's grabbing you, it's hanging on your ear!"

Sonny swings, a right hook aimed at the alien he perceives, but K.O. blocks it and grabs the fist, twisting it sideways.

"Wait, wait K.O. let me kill it!" Sonny swings a left, K.O. blocks it again, and both men scuffle, banging off the walls and the table, until K.O. finally wrestles Sonny down on the bed again.

"Settle down, settle down, Sonny," K.O. growls, holding Sonny on the bed beneath his full weight. "There's nothing in me, nothing on my ear! Relax!"

Sonny suddenly shakes his head, calms down and, as quickly as the scuffle began, it ends. The brief struggle released the stress and his arms flop down beside his hips.

"Sorry K.O., sorry, sorry, sorry. Saw an alien grabbing you! Now it's gone, they just disappear, turn invisible." Sonny ducks under his pillow then peeks above it. Finally, the hallucinations produce a threat too real, violence too strong, and the tweaks in Sonny's brain scare even K.O.

"It's back! Get away! Get away! Leave me alone!" Sonny groans, squirms off the bed and slides onto the floor, holds his head, rocking back and forth. Tears dribble down his cheeks again.

A spark of anger flits across his face again and Sonny jumps up, slips past K.O. and races down the hall, hops on the treadmill, spins the dial to its fastest speed, and runs, and runs, and runs.

23

K.O. spins out the gym driveway and heads north out of town, cell phone stuck on his ear. He drives a hundred eighteen miles non-stop into the Blue Ridge foothills that edge southwest Virginia. He slips into a space outside a municipal building the size of a small market. Sign above the doors reads Blue Ridge County Offices and Municipal Courthouse.

K.O. hustles inside, passes greeters, points a wave at each but no words, and turns down a hallway. Conflicted, he pushes through a door. A plaque on the door announces the occupant: Superior Court Justice Eleanor Archer.

"Kenneth Olsen." The judge holds out a hand. She pushes up on her tiptoes then adds a foot to her eyes just to match his, and K.O.'s not all that tall. Gives a hint to her size but reveals nothing about her extraordinary spirit and dedication.

K.O touches her fingertips. "Judge Archer."

Judge Archer accepts his touch then grabs his hand and squeezes harder, pulling K.O toward her. Formal greetings over quickly in those first four words, K.O. sweeps the diminutive judge into his arms and she returns his embrace, both enthusiastic and affectionate.

"Hello Ellie, still pretty as a teenager I see," ignoring the gray-cut granny-looking legal scholar and more than thirty years court experience appearance. Judge Eleanor Archer stretches her embrace out more than a minute. "Been way, way too long."

"Your fault, K.O., not mine, door's always open here. It's the law. I can't shut you out even if I want to," she jokes. "Still drink scotch?" Reading his mind, already pouring one each, over ice.

Glasses click, ice tinkles, a sip swirls on each tongue. "How's Jake doing? Still working those greasy monster trucks?"

"Yes, doing great. He stopped all that physical stuff right after the medal. Got caught up in old-style mechanics just watching you drive that GMC around town. I saw you park it outside, still looks brand new and it's old as you."

"So, this old trainer don't look brand new anymore, Ellie?" K.O. laughs and the judge joins him, dear friends enjoying time together after too long apart.

"But Jake fell in love with big engines, not the gloves. He wanted to steal that sweet blue truck every time he rode in it." Ellie wiggles one finger at K.O. "Lucky he didn't, been tough sentencing my own son."

Ellie laughs again, a sense of humor running high with her friend, like always when they meet. "You never knew that, did you? Too young for a license when he first saw it. Was always plotting some way to steal that truck for himself. Runs his own shop now, builds custom race engines for anyone can afford him. Does pretty well too, hasn't begged money in years. Guess what he drives?" Two smiles light up. K.O. knows it's blue and built the same year as his own.

"But that's not why you're here K.O." Judge gets down to business, wasting no more minutes with chat when a long-time friend carries his troubles all those miles. "So, what's up? Sounds like you got a problem."

K.O. drops more ice, pours two refills, sits, sips, and tells it all. Sonny, his mom, the state park, Willow, the gym, training, world-class boxing potential, the out of control rage, madness, the biology, the brain damage, the frustration, the drug abuse, and what the doctors say he needs. Takes him an hour, leaves nothing out. She asks a question occasionally, fixing clarity in her mind, but never interrupts the flow, her legal mind working as fast as K.O speaks until he finishes his story. The scotch and words finally run out.

Hoping she has answers, K.O. stops talking and looks her in the eye.

"Sounds like a very bright kid with some tough breaks,"

she says. "Experienced all that turmoil and found a way to survive with no help and no family. Found a safe enough home, ate healthy, and bought a tool that kept him alive and working. Then he found you, made a deal, got a room, got food, works hard, and extremely street smart as well. No hair growing on his soles."

"Then that demon illness bit him, now he needs our help," K.O. says.

"One good thing, Sonny's a minor, no parents, no relatives we know about, be a lot harder if he's an adult, but he'll need his own representation too. I'll arrange a quick hearing, tomorrow even, right here, you stay over. We can make you and Willow his guardians. She can drive him up. George will feed you a fish and tell you a whopper while you eat it. Can't stay off that lake since he retired. Get an attorney in your area, if you can't, Jerry Briggs will do it. Do you know Jerry?"

"Heard the name around town, never met him though."

"Well, you should. He does juvenile casework anywhere in the state. Got a small cabin over at Peanut Lake, be glad for any reason to come up here. Does great work for kids, paid or not, child abuse, family law, very dedicated man, doesn't need the money."

"Hunts and fishes all the time here, weekends mostly, out of season even once in a while. Bubba with a law license and a cocky-ass grin," she confesses, "an original home-boy. But he's a lawyer not a judge, so he gets away with it." A three-note chuckle cheats any serious out of her comments. "Besides, local game warden, Sissy Briggs, she's his youngest sister."

"You and Willow, joint custody in two days, get yourselves helping this kid K.O. Sounds like he needs it. We'll generate a court order enforceable by both his guardians, a judgment that he takes medication and enters a psychiatric program."

"He needs someone with medical training to point you two in the right direction, and stop all that violence. Social programs help a fuzzy brain that needs training, like patching up social interactions and poor lifestyle training, which won't help him much at this point."

"Biology, chemistry, physiology, that's a completely different matter. That's medicine. You make sure he takes all those meds, and gets his brain balanced. Get him a good doctor, and I mean a good one. And keep him off street drugs. That horrific junk breeds nothing but hurt."

*

After Judge Eleanor Archer's custody hearing the day before, Sonny and Willow sit at a table inside the gym. Both heads turn as one and look out the window. K.O. pulls his truck into the parking lot, climbs out, heads inside.

"Where you been K.O.?" A bit stiff with his greeting, emotions push hard all the time now though Sonny contains it when he can. Releasing it in secret, he beats dead tree limbs in his tent retreat when he's not running or punching bags in the gym, or lifting weights several times a day.

"Went up to see a new doctor at the Morrison Clinic over in Gatesville, gonna get you the right meds. Will keep you calm until we get a handle on this anger you carrying around all the time now. Breaking things, punching my walls, calling people names, mad at everyone, makes no sense."

"Not me, no meds. Don't need 'em. Just run and train, lift, that's all."

Afraid of help, afraid to admit his brain is unbalanced, unable to admit he's different, Sonny believes he's normal, like everyone else. Unwilling to accept an alternative, he fears the possibility. He has no true frame of reference for normal or abnormal. To Sonny, it is what it is, same as every other human mind knows about itself.

"Wrong answer Sonny, walls here can't take you anymore. New holes, old holes, busted lamps, broke your cell phone again. You go along a few days, a week, training, and working out, acting normal. Then, suddenly you jump all over things, like a different person hiding inside you, a mean nasty one."

"Just dropped the phone K.O. Got out of my truck and it slipped out in the rain. Can't find it." His weak attempt at hiding the phone he smashed on the floor after the court hearing and the anger he carried home yesterday falls flat. "Need a new one or I can't get work."

"Yeah, what're those plastic chips on your dresser, black ones with tiny letters and numbers on 'em? You just pop a few souvenir buttons off the phone before you lost it?"

Sonny snaps, flapping his hands around, pain in his voice. "What's happening to me? What's in my brain, Willow?" Sonny jumps up, rages around the room, kicks the trash can again.

"Alien face yells at me, all the time, orders me to stab you, K.O., wants me to kill those aliens hiding in your head too, always screaming it in my brain." His words make little sense, and he frequently repeats himself, believing that if he states his personal truths often enough, people will believe him and understand what he knows.

"That's my reward, K.O., if I kill your alien, or anyone else, Jacki, Randy, Brian, even Lisa, these aliens will leave me alone and I get its power, rise up with the Gray Masters. It's almost worth it, gets rid of the aliens, and saves my friends."

Sonny holds his breath, looks at the ceiling, working something out in his mind, "Gotta pick one, gotta pick one," he mutters, "… better not try Brian unless sneaking up behind him works. He's way too tough, besides, he's a Warrior too, and Lisa's brother, can't hurt Lisa's brother."

His mind wanders a bit, Lisa's brother he is now, instead of Brian's sister she was then. Lisa took off out of state, gone, safe. He knows where she lives but not how to find her. Could call Berkeley and find her that way, maybe she hangs out around the big golden bear in that photo she sent? Confuses Sonny for a minute, then he pops out of it, knows he'll never intentionally harm anyone, especially Lisa after all that sweetness and passion she shared.

Starting to scare him though, the space aliens never let up, and the workouts help less and less lately. The smoke helps little if at all, the spike drugs work best, and narcotics – Percocet or Vicodin - drain his wallet and sap his energy.

Willow sobs through her tears, "How could you say that about K.O. He's like a father to you. Jacki and Randy, they're just kids, your friends. How could you even think it?"

Sonny sits down and bounces his forehead off the table, once, twice, three times, then wraps his arms around his head.

"Don't mean that K.O. Never hurt you guys, never ever hurt you." He bangs his head on the table again, and again and once more harder.

Distorted faces demand action, barking into his brain, claiming violence and anger cures his rage. Sonny tries it again, holds his breath, hoping the calm arrives in time. Hope fails again. Sonny jumps up, slams his forehead and knocks a dent in the drywall. He yells at smoke and throws his fists at shadows, then punches himself in the jaw, twice, three times.

The fourth punch splits his lip and Sonny draws his own blood. He cries out again, "Don't come near me K.O. Aliens picked you. I don't want to hurt you. Stay out Willow, only hurt for you here too. Go, leave me alone!" Sonny runs into his room, slams the door, blood on his lip and his cheek swelling, truly afraid he might hurt Willow or K.O.

Willow grabs her cell phone. K.O. holds the court order Ellie signed, waits for the emergency response unit.

Hands cuffed behind his back after resisting three medics, Sonny puts hate-eyes on K.O., turns around, slips his pants low down, exposing his underwear, a fashion style K.O. hates. Sonny bows out his knees, swagger-walks as he approaches the ERT van then gives it up as his pants keep slipping. He hooks one finger through the belt loop behind him and keeps his low pants from sliding down his thighs.

Deputy Mike Mitchell, the local sheriff teaches kids at the middle school about drugs and the associated dangers, helps Sonny settle into the ERT van.

"Thanks Mike. Got it." The rage gone now, often disappearing as fast as it arrives.

Deputy Mike unlocks one cuff, relocks it in front, and Sonny lies down on his back. Mike pats his shoulder, holds up a fist, Sonny bumps his knuckles. "Take it easy Sonny. Be right behind you, no worries."

The squad car idles behind the van. Deputy Mike climbs in, flicks on his flashers, and escorts the ERT van. Both vehicles turn left toward the mental health clinic, lights blinking, siren silent. Ambulance backs into the ramp, patrol car rolls in beside it. All the lights shut down at once.

K.O. follows both in and parks his truck. Deputy Mike escorts Sonny into a secure room, unlocks the cuffs, and exits the door. His anger absent for the moment, Sonny follows the deputy back along the corridor, like a playful puppy.

Clinic security patrol arrives, a rent-a-cop type in a gray uniform, no military or police experience apparent, his walk a spindly strut on new cowboy boots, stiff jeans, and a gray security shirt. The plastic nametag stuck on his pocket spells out Stanton. Deputy Mike and Stanton block the hall then lead Sonny, the puppy, back into the security lock-up.

Stanton shoves Sonny from behind, unnecessarily rough, but expressing a little unearned machismo just because he can. The push annoys Sonny but he ignores it. The action lets Stanton believe he's in charge, that he's tough, that he's boss of the security wing. Untrue, and everyone else knows it but most ignore him, which always upsets Stanton. No one else recognizes his importance, and that bums him out. Folks do recognize jerk fits him well though, and that bums him out even more.

Deputy Mike watches Stanton push Sonny and says, "Not a good idea, Hank."

Hank Stanton glares at Deputy Mike, grunts and shoves Sonny once more, a little harder. "Git in there," Stanton demands. Pushing the puppy once more.

A gray and black streaked comb-over partly covers his head and his arms dangle, twin twigs with no muscle tone. Tall and string bean thin, several inches of paunch sag over a large silver belt buckle. His body language an easy read, Stanton decides he'll act out the tough guy role and impress this youngster while everyone watches. He plants himself between Sonny and the door. A raunchy stench rolls off Stanton and into the six feet by eight feet holding cell, yesterday's beer and stale cigarette smoke. The stink of too much cologne and a wad of Double-Mint attempt the cover up. Both fail.

Sonny takes a couple steps toward the door again, heading out into the hallway. He wants to go home now. *Slap him, he's an asshole. He ain't worth a whole punch. Do It ! Do It!* The spook cackles. *Do it, teach him a lesson.*

Sonny bunches a fist, his rage building. "Shut up Spook, I'll handle this."

"What? Stay right where you are," Stanton orders, pushes out his chest, stretches taller. Immature and childish, his inexperience and attitude gives him away. Stanton pushes Sonny once more, harder, the puppy disappears.

Stanton mistakenly awakens the dog and launches the rage.

His face contorts, his brow wrinkles, his eyes glare, his face turns red, Sonny clenches a fist.

Stanton crouches, right foot behind the left and left hand above the right, he extends both arms. He stretches his fingers forward, bent hooks, a scary martial arts stance he believes, but a ridiculous giveaway for anyone that knows the sport. Stanton mimics a snarl. "Git your ass in there!" He completely fails at 'scary'.

Sonny looks at Stanton and suddenly laughs above his anger. He can't help it. "You're kidding, right?" One quick motion, Sonny relaxes the fist and slaps the upper arm sideways and Stanton staggers and stumbles, his shoulder and nose bounce off the wall. Stanton grabs the wall for balance and swears, "Son-of-a-bitch!"

Sonny slaps Stanton again, harder, and the security man staggers sideways, catches the wall for balance once more.

His lack of fitness apparent even in the tight quarters, and more upset with Sonny now, Stanton pushes off and spins in a half circle too quickly, pissed and coming for Sonny. He trips over his own boot and Sonny slaps him again, a bit of muscle behind this one, and Stanton's nose and forehead hit the wall hard.

Stanton grabs his face with one hand and pushes himself upright with the other, but Sonny swats him again and Stanton staggers sideways and his head clips the edge of the door, so far out of the tough-guy league he might just as well wear cloth diapers and knit booties. Definitely, the center of attention though, a clown at the circus, not exactly the attention he craves and it all happens in less than fifteen seconds.

Gaining his balance again, Stanton grabs the doorknob holds himself upright, then pulls a red rag out of his pocket, and wipes a trickle of blood off a pencil thin brush he cultivates above his lip. Upset and hurting, a red swelling above his right eye, his nose bleeding slightly, and extremely embarrassed at his lack of coordination, Stanton hitches up his pants and starts after Sonny one more time. A lot of anger fills his strut this time, he aims at getting even with the wise punk who has said or done nothing truly out of line. Stanton has not learned his lesson yet.

K.O. slides in behind Stanton, shows his teeth, moves

quickly, and holds out an arm, slows Stanton down, spins him around with very little effort. "Better not. You'll just look foolish again."

Mike and K.O. turn the guard away, before Stanton really gets hurt, and more importantly, before Sonny gets in legal trouble.

The fright disappears as Sonny sits on the floor and giggles for two full minutes. The cell door clicks and locks. Satisfied for the moment, Sonny leans back against the wall, willing to wait it out one more time. He accepts his confinements, redundant rest periods, pretty much a normal occurrence lately, new custom in his life, another habit he'll kick someday he hopes. Sonny bangs his head lightly, rhythmically, against the padded wall behind him, keeping a beat in his head no one else hears.

*

Sonny pushes his empty breakfast tray away. His door opens. Willow steps in, but no K.O. this time. Sonny refused K.O. visits because K.O. helped the cops cage him.

"What you want Willow? Got me in here, didn't you? Like the aliens want, working on me again, trying to make me fight for them. Your new space buddies, right?"

Paranoia works against his social network, occasionally forcing Sonny to reject his friends with no true evidence of betrayal.

"No one's working on you, Sonny." Willow repeats what she said numerous times in the past months, arguing against his delusional thinking. "No one wants you to fight for them. No one wants to hurt you either. It's your imagination."

"They put me in jail first, locked me in a cell, fighting with a security guy at the clinic they said. All I did was push him back. He pushed me first, twice, the security guy, one that came after we got there with ERT. Mike took off the cuffs. Security guy, probably another alien wannabe, shoved me into the room."

Sonny grins. "Weak-ass sucker though, tripped and fell, gave himself a bloody nose and tried to blame it on me. His lack of coordination ain't my fault. Should practice more, he wants to push people around. Not a very smart alien, should send him home, and order a new one, little more fit. Jacki can train him, and Bart

Bailey can probably whup him."

Sonny giggles at that thought, a twelve-year-old girl training a forty-something failure. "If that Gray Leader alien pays Stanton, it's wasting its money. He couldn't take over a closet." Sonny thinks about that for a second, "And he better leave my closet alone."

Willow grins, wipes it off quickly. "The Sheriff just kept you a few hours, until the clinic transferred you here. The nurse was afraid you'd hurt yourself. You're not arrested, no record. K.O. saw the whole thing and told the supervisor to keep that guard away from you. Willow hides her smile. "As soon as his nose quits bleeding."

Sonny starts rambling. "Illegal aliens, here every day. Hear it on TV all the time. Border Patrol fighting aliens, kicking them out the country so they can't take over. Me and Randy, we play video games, watching the news too. You think we're not listening. We hear it, Willow. Hear all about those illegal aliens."

"Border Patrol? Those are Mexicans, Sonny. Mexicans sneak across the river into California and Texas, trying to get jobs and free medical care here in the States. They're not from outer space."

"Yeah, why don't the news call them that then, Mexicans, if that's what they are? They don't, news guys call 'em illegal aliens. Get it? Aliens from another planet, sneaking in, trying to take us over." Sonny sits up straighter, appealing, almost begging Willow to agree so he can believe he's normal, so he can know he's just like everyone else.

"And gorillas taking over Panama, what about that? Shoot people, looting stores, taking over the government, the highways, and airports." Sonny stands up, extremely convincing, and describes his distorted thought patterns and interpretations in amazing detail.

"You think I don't know? You still fooling me? You and K.O., and the doctors, reading my mind, planting stuff in my brain."

"Not gorillas. Guerillas. Men, Sonny, rebels, not gorillas invading Panama. It's spelled different, and has a different meaning. Gorillas are not like that, they're animals. They're not smart enough for that. They're not part of some alien space culture taking over the earth."

"You told me before, they're smart. Gorillas. Remember that night at the camp? The night K.O showed up. Smart you said, like chimps, now not so smart. Tell me one thing then tell me different now. See? Just trying to confuse me."

"You're already confused Sonny." Willow throws her hands in the air, no idea how to confront the disorganized logic Sonny fires at her quicker than she can respond. Almost sounds like an odd truth in a weird sort of way.

"So, gorillas taking over Panama, and illegal aliens sneaking across the border, taking us over. Can't deny it Willow, all you got to do is listen, watch TV. Look at the news sites, all kinds of evidence. Look at Roswell, those guys found space ships. You'll see I'm right. Tell K.O. too, he'll see. You tell him for me. I'm not talking to him today. He pissed me off, turning me in. Ain't fair, his alien did it ... made him do it."

24

Four days later, Sonny parks his truck and walks into the office, meeting again with Derek Morton his social services counselor, a generally unpleasant man. Twice a week event, supposed to meet twice a week anyway, most often ends up more like once in two or three weeks.

Morton arranges a clipboard, asks the same questions. "How you feeling? You eating right? Keeping your anger in check? How's everything with your family? Oh right, you don't have a family." Morton puts a checkmark inside each box – yes, no, slips in a few N/A – not much real or useful information gathering.

A frumpy looking man wearing a frumpy sports coat and a wrinkled shirt open at the neck, and needs a haircut, needs a shave. Morton checks off the list, no emotion, less caring, bored with the dead-end he makes of his job. Actually writes a note or two in the space labeled opinion at the bottom this time. Most often, he writes something derogatory about his clients whenever he does it, no positives in this counselor. He hates his job, has no respect for his clients, but embraces the paycheck, takes advantage of loose supervision.

Sonny peers across the desk and tries to read the note, Morton shields the words. Sonny spots a lunch smear on Morton's shirt, ketchup or some sauce, ignores it but looks down at his own shirt, checks it, finds it clean as usual, shrugs. Sonny showers every day and wears fresh clothes, keeps himself very tidy.

"Need some help, got a check confused at the market, some

mistake the bank made. Can you come explain it, the bank over-charged me. Tried to explain it myself, but just can't make sense of it. Willow's working today, K.O.'s out of town and she said you'd help me."

Sonny tried numerous times, but simply cannot make the bank balance function correctly, one of the odd memory blocks in his brain. He's usually great with numbers and money, especially his own, but the daily bank balance correlation between an actual balance and outstanding payouts or online deposits not yet cleared somehow eludes his reasoning.

"Can't do it, have another meeting in a half hour across town, out by the mall. You'll have to do it yourself." Morton told him the same thing earlier on the phone, makes an excuse each time a client asks for assistance, each time a client tries to learn something old that becomes something new due to the mental workings of a brain with medication side effects or a chemical imbalance.

Sonny hoped he might change his mind, that Morton would assist with a little begging, which Sonny hates but needs his accounts fixed. Sometimes works with folks, but not this time, and never with Morton. "I tried, but can't figure it out. Won't take long, it's right on your way, down from the mini-mall."

"No time now, Sonny. Got other clients too, you know."

Morton hustles Sonny out the door, exits his office, signs the Out-Log, checks 'Client Meeting,' heads for his car. Morton punches the speed dial, sticks his cell on his ear. "Cindy, we have a meeting in a half hour." He lights a cigarette. "Well, yes we do, unless *you* want to cancel?"

He takes a drag, inhales, blows smoke out the window. "Okay, see you next time then." Morton disconnects, smiles, "Works every time," he mutters, congratulating his own cleverness.

Morton takes out his notebook, writes 'Client Cancelled' next to Cindy Wells, shifts his car into gear and drives to the Town Cinema, cashes in a free ticket the theater donates to the clinic for two mental health patients every week. Morton scuttles inside and views a movie, eats two candy bars he smuggled in his pocket.

Two hours later, Morton exits the theater, stops for coffee and the grocery store, drives back to the office, collects his paycheck, and signs out for home. No one remembers the coming and going of each counselor on any specific date, so no one will remember that Morton never came back after the cancel, and never comes back on other days after the same set-up with his clients either. His regular work routine, a weak loser dedicated to the hustle.

25

After a half-hour at medium speed, Cat hops off the treadmill, grabs a towel, and runs up stairs, drops into her chair and wipes a towel across her face. She begins reviewing her phone notes and clinic responses, and emails again. Cat organizes her research, seeking a connection between brain biology and violent interaction within the social environment at the instant that violence occurs.

She hopes she can find that biological trigger, whatever it is in a specific brain that forces it into unprovoked violence under certain social conditions that normal brains perceive as harmless. Quickly, her fingers tap across the keyboard, transforming evaluations and notations into a cohesive theoretical application.

A human brain arrives at birth with a combination of instinctual behaviors intact and separate from conscious actions. During the sexual maturity state, if an abnormal brain chemically breaks down, the newest memories go first and action responses eventually revert toward instinctual behavior, and that result creates dysfunction in social areas and prioritizes survival activities. Filtering mechanisms break down and every social contact seems threatening.

Cross-connected signals might force instinct to the surface as a protective behavior when a less aggressive behavior will accomplish the goal, but the brain thinks it needs the high protective level and defaults to

it -- the mind then has no time to make a different, less aggressive response based on immediate sensory input and memory.

The brain makes its decision almost immediately, and the defense releases. The high-energy level remains for a period. We're unsure yet how long. We believe the intensity of the threat relates to the length of time it lasts and strength of the chemistry.

Aggressive and protective triggers stall, but bio-systems remain up-charged and unaware until sensory input completes its evaluation - possibly in less than a tenth of a second if the defense level interpretation determines a low danger element.

Under abnormal brain conditions, the release fails, the fright remains, and the up-charge chemistry remains active much longer, creating a defensive posture or actions even after the brain should have evaluated the threat as a false danger.

An extended duration in an up-charged state initiates a violent behavior - punching walls, punching cell bars - dissipates the energy and releases that stress and allows a calming effect to emerge.

Note to self: Evaluate 'runner high' effect here.

Cat stops typing, squeezes her fingers together, rotates her palms, and stretches, all five feet five inches if she tips up on toes, and cheats. Flat footed, she stands five feet two and a quarter, and always marks the quarter inch, taking credit for every molecule of her being. Once, at age fourteen, she pulled on three sets of heavy wool sox, one over the other, and gained another quarter inch for a sports event.

Her colleagues all laugh at her quirky behaviors, but she laughs with them, so it's never degrading, and her sense of humor over-rides any implied loss of character. Cat's simply a winner.

Working with a research team based at Harvard, Cat and Aaron developed a chemical complex for five remaining mental patients at Stark, all volunteers. She had twelve when she launched the program. One died of natural causes, two transferred out-of state, one hung himself, an inmate executed one in a fight, and two simply quit assisting her for unknown reasons.

The ethical, moral, legal and medication dilemmas the team engaged in with the state corrections system and the legal system delayed her progress. The last legal debate centered on whether mental patients are rational enough to understand the voluntary agreement and its medical ramifications.

Cat and her legal team turned the same arguments back on the state legal scholars that the legal scholars used against her medical team - the constitutional right to refuse treatment. She carefully installed that shoe on the other foot, and argued that if these patients are rational enough to refuse treatment, they are also rational enough to accept it. Her team won, it took eleven months, nearly a year wasted.

Walter Ferguson, a felon with a major brain dysfunction explained it in an extremely articulate narrative on the witness stand in a temporary courtroom set in the Stark Medical Facility. He claimed his demons are absolutely real and alive, that he fights them alone and with little success. Ferguson insisted that he could and should receive any treatment he chooses to assist in his fight and, in a rare burst of bonding, Chase Nickels testified the same way and claimed the same thing, that he needs her help stopping his personal sideshow.

State officials and the general public might stigmatize Ferguson with the label, 'nuts,' but he's one extremely bright nut, despite the erratic, irrational, anti-social, and violent behavior he often exhibits.

The legal scholars won the first skirmish, the right for state agencies to reject a choice that often interferes with the best treatment for specific patients, and based it on security issues as well as medical. Cat won the war and her research team took one giant step forward, gaining another foothold toward her goal - an individualized chemical complex that will treat every violent behavioral disorder that initiates itself in brain biology.

Now, it remains for her to convince patients and doctors it's the best treatment when it applies. Some violence emerges through gang-training and other social activities including family, and alcohol and drug abuse, as well as other issues. Cat knows and understands why she cannot treat those behaviors medically. She only wants the biological cases, the patients with chemically and biologically dysfunctional brains.

One interesting idea emerged from that battle. Cat and Aaron both realized the fight against treatment for the mentally ill relies on the underlying concept that treating patients becomes too expensive. Both know most of the waste comes from paperwork duplicate, triplicate, and quadruplicate for the same patient during the same admission. Four minimally trained employees on the payroll with one skill, asking the patient a name, address, birth date, and how will you pay. Although staff asks the payment question first, and checks that box - no payment, no treatment. If insured, a patient sees a nurse, and sometimes but not always, a doctor.

Cat and Aaron now believe treating patients costs less than the legal fees to fight that battle in the courts, especially when you add into that cost the economic destruction when these mentally ill individuals pursue crime to get money for the self-medication they desire or even require for stability. Add to that state and local budgets providing crime control just for drug crimes and criminal acts related directly to drug use these mentally unstable addicts commit, then the true costs of denying a socially funded treatment base rise much higher in comparison.

She knows it's too late for Walter Ferguson and Nickels, and other volunteers whose minds deteriorated too many years ago. She cannot repair, or reproduce the brain cells previously damaged by hormone invasion during the maturation years and later in life.

She can ease that pain now, and allow these men some peace in the remaining years, regardless that they will spend those years in confinement for violent crimes. More importantly, she can use the information each man contributes to define a program that assists teens and young adults who develop this disease, and get treatment to them early in their lives and stop the brain damage and thus the violence, and the toll it takes on those kids and their families.

Cat remains under no illusion that all crime, gang behavior, social injustice, and violence stems from brain dysfunction, nor will all crime disappear in our cities and towns with medication and treatment. Much street crime and violence in gangland areas begins in and is encouraged within that culture itself as a social mechanism, similar to tribal warfare in Native American cultures where violence and physical abilities brings honor and respect despite the harm it delivers to another tribe or person.

Today, she directs her team to treat only the mental pain that develops when brain dysfunction creates a mind that triggers violent behavior, and allow those individuals to rest, and curtail the destruction it creates in family units.

Three for five in the facility Cat claims, not what she hoped but at least two steps in the right direction. The program succeeded on some level in two cases, in one case, no change, but passive behavior, and it aggravated the brain further and initiated more violence in two individuals. With the two violent patients, she stopped treatment and both returned to the original demented state within three months, and both continue serving life sentences. The one who exhibited no significant change still has hope for his future. Two active men remain in her program, not a great outcome, but success in medical research advances in miniscule steps, and the ultimate reward far outweighs the financial cost if it's defined appropriately in terms of human pain and suffering.

Walter Ferguson and Chase Nickels find hallucinations and demons, and the orders and demands controllable, though it remains inside each mind. The demons become less harsh, demanding, and allow some semblance of life that mimics a real life, a stable life absent the fear and violence each directed toward any person that entered either man's world. That journey continues, although Nickels jumps on and off his meds often, and operates violently and with little control at times, even while incarcerated.

Cat logs out and heads home for the evening. She combines her medical training, her personal experience, the field research data, and discussion with her own patients into her theoretical constructs that may eventually offer a successful treatment plan to many mentally disturbed clients in every clinic across America, and back in her own homeland.

The prison inmates intrigue her, and assist her in understanding the long-term effects of mental illness, but those few exist as a research platform. Her real motivation and focus for her work fixates on the teens she treats, and how she can help each of them before the faulty chemistry breaks down the brain cells. It breaks her heart every time she meets one and no treatment or cure exists, and she simply watches and cries while brain damage destroys a child.

Cat holds no illusions that her prison patients will ever achieve release from the life sentence even if treatment succeeds, nor do the inmates in it. But the research proves invaluable for younger victims, and in some strange way, no matter how distorted the brain chemistry becomes in these older men, some recognize that her work benefits children and young adults, and assist Cat with that altruistic result as its only reward. It touches her heart, and adds another reason for helping these men who will never see freedom again.

She suspects it allows some to escape the boredom that a lock-down environment creates as well. New people from her research teams meet the participants, professionals that bring conversation and respect into the prison yard instead of authority and derision. The men get a break from the monotony and tedium as well.

Well, sometimes the Snickers bars help too, or some other benefit within the walls. One inmate wanted a small television as his reward so he could watch soaps. Hard to figure what drives one individual mind and not another. Cat tweaks her budget. Tinker Perry watches his soaps and Fergie gets a Snickers six-pack in the mail a few times a year.

Cat has been collecting data and researching mental illness non-stop for more than two years as an intern and four years as the lead psychiatrist, but the biological component that triggers these recurring and unprovoked episodes under certain conditions in a specific violent individual still eludes her.

She recently began unraveling the complex electrical circuitry and hormonal interaction of behavior triggers. She realizes the answer may be unique in every victim, a prediction she never imagined as a truth when she began this project. The word 'individual' stretched the boundaries of its prior definition. Occasionally, a path one chooses arrives at an unexpected destination.

26

Sonny, Willow and K.O. sit in the clinic office, discussing new medications with the lead prescribing nurse. Sonny acts a bit surly, withdrawn, moody, the alien presence bothering him more today for some reason. Another clinic visit contributes added stress as he listens to one more identical lecture about his imaginary aliens. That he's making it up, and the perpetual 'take your meds' and 'check this box' many social workers spout as each meeting proceeds.

Sonny tires of the charade. "You're all aliens, from outer space. You experiment on me. Gray Leaders look inside me and study an earth person so you can capture all of us and take over our world."

His face reddens and lines crease his forehead, a mask of anger and frustration, confusion and fright emerges, his belief a repeat of its personal history, obsessive and redundant. Brain chemistry warps his memories, but Sonny knows no other truth. His reality remains his reality regardless, and if his beliefs prove as accurate as he explains, "Just read my mind. You'll see it and know it too." He believes that odd contradiction as well.

"And you're one of them," he yells at the nurse, "and I'm not taking these pills." He throws the paper cup at her, the pills scatter across her desk, and Sonny runs out the door. The nurse grabs her phone. The cops pick him up two hours later jogging down the road toward the gym and his truck, and find four Percocet pills in his pocket. Court order again, and once more he fills a jail bed overnight, then the clinic.

He sat in jail overnight and the clinic for three days lockdown after another release just a week ago. "Nine times in eight months, Sonny. When will it sink in? You have to take your meds and balance your brain chemistry. That's how you keep your temper under control."

Willow pleads with Sonny again, a repeat of the last eight times.

A drug possession charge now hangs over his head. His ability to control the rage deteriorates as he ages and matures, the hormone balance increases in a lop-sided mix. The unbalanced circuitry in his brain strengthens the chemical dosage inside his body, converts fright into anger when fright finds no release.

Willow has a conversation with the director of social services, and checks out fees for services in the insurance payout literature. Director Terri Birch explains the variations in clinic services, and that over-crowded clinics discharge patients as quickly as possible when that patient has a home and supervision. A strategy driven completely by budget and not by treatment needs.

"These short-term patients need more than a simple assessment," she says, "and some are sicker than others. We have no easy way to know which is which with the medical technology that's available today. Mental illness is extremely difficult to diagnose and treat, unlike virus or bacterial infections, or broken bones, or organic disease."

Admission fees and initial mental health consults bring more revenue in than clinic beds, so does a discharge consult. Admitting and discharging a patient raises the bottom line on revenue and finances. The treatment fees charged to the resident patient falls below those lines when expenses and overhead costs float into the budget picture, but the clinics need revenue to succeed as clinics, regardless of treatment results on short-term patients.

"And," Terri continues, "in addition, insurance companies limit the days of assessment annually, so after a set period, the income shuts down, often in as few as twenty-one accumulated days over an entire year."

"How's that float your boat? You got a sick kid and the state tells you it only treats a mental admission for twenty-one days and claims that as a normal and customary stay. He's not sick after that, goes home and packs his mind in a box, refrigerates it until the next season renews his eligible days?" Birch frowns.

"Bring him back in three-hundred and forty-four days, and the magic wallet opens again, if he's still alive." She shakes her head, frustrated.

The director fights the system, and tracks her clients, intervening when she believes it will benefit a specific patient. First priority, she's a doctor, second an administrator.

"Refuse to accept Sonny when the clinic sets his discharge date, just don't sign it. Clinics can't discharge a mental patient into unsupervised quarters, especially a minor. That's the law. So, if you refuse, the clinic holds him and continues treatment, at least until it finds supervised housing for him. And, locally, that's in short supply so Sonny will remain in the clinic for awhile and you can play that out as it develops, but at least he gets a little more evaluation time here."

Birch shifts in her seat, looks directly at Willow. "You didn't hear that, Willow. I'd deny it, and it would get me in trouble regardless. I'm certain Sonny will benefit from at least another week or more of intense observation, even minimally. Three or four days in a clinic bunk over a weekend gives the doctors too little information, if they even see him. We need a little more time, and maybe a lot more time in his case."

*

The discharge nurse pushes release paperwork across the desk and points at a blank signature line. Willow and K.O. both say, "Nope, not this time." Both refuse custody after another warehouse weekend and minimal treatment, and a simple revolving door.

"Keep him and treat him this time," Willow demands. "The medication calms him down, but does nothing for his hallucinations and delusions. Fix it," she demands, as if all it takes is her order. Willow and K.O. push up out of the chairs and walk out the door.

Sonny fits a look of astonishment on his face, tears squeezing out beneath his eyelids. Willow explained it earlier, that she will leave him here and force his treatment, but his action proves he did not believe her or understand her strategy.

"You're leaving me here Willow, with the aliens?" His disbelief and despair hovers naked in the room. "They'll test me and look in my brain, find out stuff, and use it to win Earth. They'll work on me."

Sitting at the desk with an alien nurse in an alien environment, Sonny watches K.O. and Willow depart, his only friends deserting him. His brain fills with fright and he pulls his sweatshirt up over his head, peeks out through the neck hole. Slowly spinning his body in a circle, he finds no escape possible. Tears run freely down his cheeks.

"You're not friends. You want my saw, my tools. You hate me now because I figured out you're aliens." Sonny yells his paranoid thoughts out the door as it swings shut behind K.O. and Willow, and locks him inside.

27

Derek Morton dusts the donut powder off his shirt and slithers into the meeting room, the last counselor to arrive as usual, and ten minutes late. The odor of cigarette smoke follows him in. He sets his coffee cup, his clipboard, and several folders on the table. Out of breath, he flops into a chair. Apparently, the four-minute marathon stroll from the parking lot to this first floor meeting room stole all his wind.

District manager Maggie Murray looks at the clock, "Nice of you to join us Derek."

"Traffic," Morton spouts, his standard remark when he's late. A traffic jam in this rural and spread out community of nine thousand citizens means a retired grandmother or a couple produce trucks heading toward a market pause an extra minute at one of two stop signs in town and chat, or a horse or a cow crosses a highway too slowly. Maybe Old Man Perkins pauses a minute and eyeballs the resident buzzards polishing off some fresh road kill at the water ditch cafe, unhappy because the vultures got there first. Any one of those incidentals could have made Morton late. The truth is, lazy and slow fits his style, and it takes no reason at all. He figures the later he arrives, the less work hours he must complete.

Maggie turns her eyes toward the six health care workers present and begins. "Janice, you want first shot today?"

A phone chirps behind the desk. Everyone ignores it, a message machine picks up. A mother asks, "Please ask Mister Morton to call me back as soon as you get in. The pharmacy has not renewed the medication for my son. It's urgent, my third call.

He ran out today." The phone clicks off, rings again a minute later, another message taped. No one pays it attention.

A slim, dark-haired, forty-something woman originally from San Francisco opens a folder. Wrapped in a rainbow-colored granny dress hugging a figure that obviously spends time in a fitness program, she pulls silver wire-frames off the top of her head and perches them on the end of her nose. Janice Merchant flips through the pages, one of four folders lying on the table.

"Gary Parsons, age nineteen, in our client base for eleven months, had a major relapse last week and kicked back heavily into depression, freaked out in the park. Had to call ERT and send him in."

"Stopped taking his meds a couple weeks ago, so we checked him into the Gatesville rehab station for a few days, happens every couple months with him. Not dangerous, but very moody and wears military clothing he bargain shops at the thrift store but never has been in the service. Maybe wants it, but didn't get in. He exhibits a low-scale learning disability in reading. His social interactive ability scales minimal. He works odd jobs around town, moves furniture, cleans attics and barns, and bargain-sells stuff he finds instead of taking it to the dump. He scares people with his actions and manner, but he has no violence in his record. Depressed though, presents as a conflicted personality when off his meds, but for some unexplainable reason, displays no violent tendencies to date, harmless, never hurts anyone. Had a job delivering pizza for Antonio's, but each one arrived with a slice gone, so he lost that one. He pushed the remaining seven pieces around so it looked like a whole pizza, sorta."

She laughs aloud at her own comment, which kicks starts the brains and the rest lose it for a few seconds too. "We're trying the gas station. Hope he doesn't drink the fuel." Janice runs her grin around the table.

Janice continues her monologue, discussing the symptoms and treatment, and client history, names his medications, and tells about two meetings with her client the past three weeks. Takes thirty-five minutes and the group hears nothing new this week, same discussion as last week except she added the relapse information, generally another repeat activity in his case.

"Derek, you're up."

In the background, the phone chirps, again ignored, again records a voice requesting help for a patient.

Morton begins. "Cindy Wells, age twenty-two, our client for nineteen months. I only met with her once this month. She often cancels our meetings at the last minute, or doesn't show up. She exhibits several learning disabilities and needs reading and comprehension training, lacks concentration and gets distracted easily. We found her two jobs – Baxter Market and the Quik Stop – but she forgets her hours and misses too much. Both let her go after less than a month. She just stays home and gets stoned all the time, reads romance books."

Morton runs on about her background, medications, history, meetings, her depression, and fantasy dreams. He wastes forty minutes with his repetitive monologue, almost a recording of last week and the week before that. He seldom meets his clients, so adds little new information at these team discussion sessions.

Janice pops up, "She was mine for seven months, a nice young girl, but obsessive, needs light supervision and once she got into the pattern of work, she'd remember it easily. You should see her rooms, spotless, and she obsesses about the dirt, you never find a grain of sand on her floors. Never smoked pot when she was on my caseload Derek, where did you get that info?"

Morton looks down, responds with a lie, "Caught her with it. I try with her, but all she wants is stay home and smoke pot." He fails to mention she fits his 'always easy to cancel' list, and he has no idea if Cindy really smokes pot. He attributes a street drug habit to all mental patients. He does a phone cancel routine often with Cindy, gives himself lots of free time at the expense of her counseling sessions. She's very passive and easy to manipulate.

Morton changes the subject, afraid Janice will bust him for ignoring a client that she knows well. He looks at his checkbox chart, says, "Sonny Bones, a real character, still making up fake stories about aliens taking over the earth. Trying to get more drugs, my guess, like all the rest, won't take his meds but loves street drugs."

"Drug abuse, violent behavior, skips meetings, wastes all his time at the gym. Thinks he'll win a boxing title someday, very scary physically, but lacks character and very slow mentally. Ask him a question and it takes a minute or two, he processes information slowly. Probably a low IQ and we have little hope he'll recover. I think he's in the rehab clinic now, ought to keep him there or send him up state. He never listens. Some crook ex-con and a state ranger help him out, and interfere with my counseling all the time."

Janice butts in, knows Morton well enough, knows he's self-absorbed, and most often shorts his clients in areas they need help the most. Morton believes he hides his lazy incompetence, but Janice picks it up easily, as do others. "You think he's in the clinic? Don't you know?"

Morton ignores her this time. "Fights medications, says we're poisoning him, makes up stories that aliens and demons possess everyone, and read his mind, and plan to take over the world. A real nut case, we have to watch him close. We need forced medication here, and I recommend a long-term hospital sentence next time he flies off the handle. Only reason he's not in secure housing, he never hurts anyone, only things. So far, he's lucky. Cancels meetings a lot, just a druggie trying to use the system, slips into the clinic, and picks up his come-down drugs when he can't score on the streets."

Janice jumps in again, unwilling to let Morton slide, "He's yours Derek. Do you know if he's in the clinic or out?" Pushing Morton a little, letting him know she knows he lacks dedication. She also knows Sonny a little bit, not well though. Her husband works out at the gym several times a week, tells a different story about Sonny, and about Willow and K.O. too. Janice knows Cindy even better and she acts very unlike the young woman Morton presents.

Murray breaks in, "Okay, okay, ease up."

The meeting runs another couple of hours and Murray says, "It's almost eleven-thirty, let's stop for lunch. Meet back here at one and head out for afternoon client meetings. Everyone log in working on Cindy Wells for one hour and Sonny Bones for an hour, and Channing, O'Connor, and Montclair a half hour each."

Murray looks at the phone as it chirps again, the eleventh time since the meeting began. All messages record a parent or a client asking for a call back, all messages usually sit ignored until late in the afternoon, if returned at all. Even those calls that a clinic worker returns usually find a message machine as well, and leave the same message, 'call me back'. The staff member checks it off the call list. A machine calls a machine in the electronics world, and no one in the clinic shares cell numbers with clients. It makes no sense to ask a client to call back if only a machine answers. If the machine always answers, the requests simply run in a circle unless a caller gets lucky.

Murray picks up a list and runs her eyes down the names. "Tomorrow we discuss Parker, Estrada, Eastman, Herriata, and Marks, so we have a full morning as usual. Try to get here on time Derek."

Jones Johnson perks up, raises a finger, and starts speaking. "Just a second, before we head out. I've only been here at this unit about two months. Seems like we spend lots of time sitting here talking about our clients, same info each time unless we get a new one, but I wonder if anyone else thinks we should shorten these discussion times, and spend more time with our clients. We could easily take ten minutes not forty minutes to review anything new about each client, and get into the field by ten, not by one, not after lunch." He shrugs, looks around the table. "Discussing symptoms with one another here in these meetings like we do, that won't help them much."

"And, hour and a half for lunch? Never had more than a half hour at the Tanner clinic, and we don't add it into our work day either."

Janice Merchant jumps in, a tag-team effort both counselors agreed upon earlier. "All of us sitting here talking about clients won't help us learn about our clients, or help our clients learn lifestyle skills."

"Our clients need hands-on behavior and social training. We're not treating a cold here, or an infection. We're assisting our clients in the socialization and survival processes. They need field help, lifestyle training. Sitting at home attending half hour meetings with one of us every two weeks teaches a client nothing useful."

"Last week six of us, plus the unit manager, spent four or more hours every day, that's at least twenty hours each week, times six – or seven counting Maggie – more than one hundred forty man-hours per week discussing mostly things we already know. Then we go out and meet two clients for a half hour each day, and log in travel time each afternoon four days a week. That's six trained field workers at two-hundred forty work hours, and we give twenty-four total hours per work week counseling all our clients combined!"

"Service time seems a little out of whack to me." Janice Merchant speaks again. "We learned different fieldwork techniques in San Francisco. We took our clients out for coffee, a beach walk, bike ride, at least those that could. It loosens up the chat. Not so formal, we got to know each one, developed trust, treated them as friends, or at least not as odd characters."

"Our base here totals only sixty clients, all under age thirty, and in three counties. That's not many, ten each, that's nothing like the cities. If we have one hundred sixty work hours a month each, and ten clients, even if we spend twenty-five percent in meetings and paperwork, that's twelve hours a month each, not one or two hours every two weeks like now."

Jonesy and Janice both feel the same way, and discussed it last week, deciding this two-pronged advisory would make the point better than one.

"And, we haven't even counted Maggie and her time in management, and Terri Birch too," Janice implicates two more forty-hour weeks in the calculations. "Once we start counting supervisors, and managers, we get into fifteen hundred paid hours a month, to get a hundred forty hours of counseling, and only three hours, often less, with a client in a month. How's that helping them?"

Johnson speaks again, the tag team tango works well. "Walking in with a notebook each time and filling out forms doesn't build much trust – that's what we need, trust, so we open a true dialogue and allow us to understand what problems exist, and what our clients need and want right from their own lips." He looks around the table. "Make sense?"

Janice closes her folders. "Cindy gets well into her meds, and she will stay there if we hang out with her a little, spend time walking her to the store on time. She obsesses, so make it an obsession to arrive on time and do her job."

"Look at her room, clean space, an obsession with her as well. She needs confidence and comfort, not meeting a clipboard and checking off how she feels, and asking about her meds. You do that, she'll just tell you what you want to hear, not how she really feels if all you do is check boxes. Nothing's normal in questions and notations, it's too much like confinement or probation. These kids aren't criminals, they're sick and confused, and they need our help."

"Once medication stabilizes the brain, we need to re-train these kids, re-socialize in areas they need. Not tell them, show them. That's how it works." Janice looks at Morton. "I don't know why she got transferred to you Derek, but I like her and she seldom missed meetings with me, and she never smoked pot either. Not one drug fail that I know about, and her record shows it. I'll take her back in a heartbeat."

A little frustration and embarrassment at her calling his game in public brings a little redness to his face, and Morton replies, "They all do it, manipulate the system, manipulate you, that's why she met with you. You let her get away with things. She can't be a friend, she's a client, a nut-kid. She never gets that with me. I make these kids toe the line or they always take advantage if you let them."

"Telling us these kids aren't smart but still manipulate us and the system. Little contradiction there don't you think Derek? Maybe you're in the wrong business," Johnson offers. "Transfer yourself into the jailhouse instead. Those criminals don't need friends, just watchdogs." Johnson disliked Morton and his counseling methods the first time he met him, and two months interaction changed nothing about his opinion.

"Okay, knock it off. Snapping at one another won't help." Maggie adjourns the meeting.

By the way, we have a rep coming in Thursday afternoon at one o'clock for a one hour panel on balancing our hourly budgets with our mileage, so cancel your client sessions that day. It's important we get this right for our annual accounting - no excuses, be here. Clients can wait a week."

Once again, she illustrates that budget concern sits higher on the food chain than client care and training. Individual health care workers like Merchant and Johnson feel differently, but changing the system alone never works, even two people, and the person signing the paychecks gets the final word, and that person has no contact with patients.

Janice Merchant and Jones Johnson pick up the folders, look at one another, and shake two heads in tandem on the way out the door, watching another twelve hours of counseling time fly out the window for a one hour training seminar on a subject they should already understand – log your mileage. Merchant mutters, "How difficult is logging mileage anyway?

28

Eight days have passed since his last outburst and Sonny remains locked down in the rehab clinic. Willow forced the clinic into a full evaluation and release hearing after Sonny punched his own face and cut his lip, drew his own blood. Legally, the clinic cannot release a mental patient unless a responsible party signs him out, a less known law, and one the clinics fail to explain or encourage. It's even more difficult releasing minors.

K.O. called Judge Archer after his chat with Willow. The judge explained the legal position that exists as a countermeasure to continuous three-day observation periods. Often patients admitted over a weekend endure two days of dead time that produces little results, particularly when a patient has no supervision or assistance at home. Home care becomes an important part of mental health care too, or in a few cases, if a person has no home at all, it becomes even more important to make good use of any time available, even weekends. That fails when the skeleton staff performs only basic care and limited evaluations.

She told K.O. "If no one accepts custody, Sonny will stay in the clinic and continue evaluation, or at least the clinic must find him a place with supervised housing until his doctor clears his condition. Few doctors willingly assume that responsibility when a patient exhibits violent or self-destructive episodes."

It's a legal position Willow and K.O. never knew about, so each time the clinic called for a release, one or the other signed him out, and Sonny returned home without a true diagnosis or an effective treatment plan. Clinic just supplies sedatives and medications that no one verifies as effective for a specific case, in general, a one-size-fits-all pill group that may or may not work. Give the patient a pill and discharge, standard practice today in mental health clinics. No other choice and, generally, minimal follow up if any.

Mental illness exhibits unique characteristics in each patient, needs a unique medication blend to work properly, and requires innovative research presently unknown to many practitioners in the field. The treatment teams that know it and accept it have the best success in the field. Cat and Aaron dance directly on that cutting edge, and define it in the psychiatric field today.

*

"This place does nothing for us. We sit all day, drugged up, talk to a different counselor asking the same questions. Takes fifteen minutes every time, same answers, same green clipboard with the same crack in it, each writes them down, all check the boxes. 'Observing us', they tell us. Ha, while we observe them, then we're stuck inside all day, two hours a day outside in the patio, one morning, and one afternoon."

"They don't believe me, about the aliens. Tell me I'm making it up, so I quit telling it. Same thing every time K.O., nothing happens there. Take your med, take your med, that's all we hear. Might as well record it and save the energy, or just make a sign, wave it around. The med helps nothing, some make me dizzy, some make me shake, and most make me tired, one made me puke."

Sonny slurs his words, a response to sedation. His eyes droop, his body reacts in the chemically induced stupor that most patients in the clinic exhibit. "So, we tell doctors what doctors want to hear, and we leave. Pretty simple, K.O. We don't like it here, and nothing's wrong with us. Ask Melanie, she knows, she's here a lot, got plenty of experience. No reason for us to stay here, just lock up the space aliens and let us go home. Everyone be happy then, and no aliens be taking over the earth."

A pill nurse monitors the ward and security personnel assist, assuring every client remains calm inside the walls. No one bothers the gatekeepers and the pill pushers watch carefully, wise to patient tricks. Everyone eats a drug. Any patient that hides a pill or capsule in a cheek or under a tongue gets liquid. No hiding that. Dribbles right down the old throat, no spitting allowed.

Staff stays happy. Patients stay numb. No one causes trouble. A brief doctor visit and generic medication drives new-age health plans with pint-size budgets – HMO – the magical cure-all management companies work as quick as a blink, even when it fails medically, it still fills its till. A macro-economic policy works fine in a collection of micro-clinic environments, a processing plant for continuous billings, treatment almost an accident.

*

Alone in a single room, Sonny shucks his clothes and settles back on his bed, watches a shadow pass by the glow line beneath his door. Security makes a pass each night after lights-out, inspects the dorm, clicks off the television, stacks books and magazines, checks the showers, and verifies everyone tucked in properly for the night.

Sonny shuts his eyes. Two minutes pass. A light squeak intrudes on the silence. He opens his eyes as his door swings open. Sonny blinks, hard to focus. Only the dim corridor nightlight shines behind a shadow slipping in. He rolls off his bunk and cocks a fist, then blinks again.

A giggle, then a soft feminine voice with a slight southern accent he recognizes tells him, "Hey Sonny, it's only me. Please don't punch me."

"Okay, I won't. What are you doing Melanie? It's past lights out." Almost indiscernible, a definitive womanly shape poses inside the door, backlit in the dimness.

The door swings shut behind her and she takes three steps, holds her hands out, feeling her way in the darkness. "I know, I know. I waited, security just passed. We have at least an hour, let's don't waste it." She grabs his hands, wraps his arms around her waist, a thin cotton gown covers her body, nothing else. "Been wanting this a while Sonny, watching you, liking you. Hoping you'd be here this week when I checked in."

"Why didn't you just call me at the gym?" Sonny wraps his arms around her, almost an instinct. An extremely well-proportioned woman, Melanie leans in tight and presses full length against his body.

"Don't know. Guess I'm just weird, one of Derek's nut-kids, like you. Like us." She giggles again.

Sonny discovers the difference between an athletic, muscular female in a park camp and a fully mature and voluptuous woman in a hospital bed. Two hours later, he watches her definite womanly shadow slip out his door, leaving Sonny lying on his bed wearing nothing but a smile and a little sweat. A hard decision now, which one he likes best, Lisa or Melanie. Figures if Melanie hangs around a few more times, he can figure it out someday. Ask his trust cards. Not in a hurry though. Besides, Lisa lives in Berkeley, Melanie lives right here, ten feet down the hall. Sonny smiles and shuts his eyes, not a difficult choice.

*

On the ninth day, K.O. and Willow join Sonny and five people sitting around a conference table, notebooks, or notepads set before each one, ready to discuss treatment options and a release date. Individual chats fill the room.

Head psychologist Louis Ingram leaves and returns, passes around coffee, juice, and water, sets a plate of cookies and buns on the table. Some dig in. Some leave it.

Sonny grabs an orange juice and grins at everyone as he quickly eats two cookies and a bun, and chugs the entire bottle. He rolls a second unopened plastic container in his hands, sets two more cookies and a bun on a napkin between his arms as if protecting his snack. His eyes dart around the room, checking everyone out. His personal field examination put names on faces and watches for haunts.

Social worker Jose Morales, Derek Morton, Med-Assist staff supervisor Larry Boone watch clinic director and lead psychiatrist Anne Winslow enter and begin speaking. The session quiets. "We're here today to decide if we can send Sonny home."

Sonny perks up, interrupts. "Why don't you just ask me? I got a perfect answer for that one." He looks around the circle, grinning at everyone.

Winslow glances at Sonny, "You'll get a chance."

She turns back to the group. "This back and forth, in and out of this clinic isn't helping him. He's having a problem with medications, and skips doses when he's not monitored. His blood readings go up and down, inconsistent. The court order says he must take his meds or he lands in the clinic and lockdown again. But he says he's ready to go home and will take his meds."

Morton speaks up, exhibits his characteristic negativity. "He said that before. He always says it when he's here in clinic, but he won't take meds when he's home. And, he skips meetings, cancels, don't show up, just like all the rest. We waste time working on these kids. They never listen. Don't hear anything we say. I really try to get Sonny to fix his life, and take his meds. But he won't pay attention."

Morton lies with a straight face, not a hint of embarrassment at the untruth. Almost fifty percent of his logged out time with his clients he spends on other personal activities, and to top that off, he cheats on his mileage logs, adding mileage for clients even when he skips a meeting.

Boone chimes in. "We work on Sonny a lot. Trying to help them out, help them learn new skills, recover lost skills, help them find employment and housing. Med-Assist counselors spend lots of time working on them."

Sonny breaks in, his voice rising, "What do you mean working on me! You work on me? How come I never see you working on me? You reading my mind, put stuff in it when I can't see you, poking your ideas into my head, ordering me to hurt my friends! I see all you guys, what? ..." Sonny aims his eyes at the ceiling, as if counting tiles or contemplating his next statement, glances at his wrist as if he wears a watch, "... maybe fifteen minutes sometimes a half hour every two weeks, that's it. You come into the gym and put a checkmark in each little box on a page, and leave. Two hours a month?"

Sonny loses the grin, his facial muscles tighten, his eyes narrow. He releases the juice carton and drops his hands in his lap, makes a fist, his knee jumps nervously beneath the table, stress setting in.

"That's not what we mean." Boone covers his tracks. "We spend time with other issues."

Willow leans in toward K.O. whispers in his ear. "Notice Boone said 'we' and 'them' not 'him'. The team approach, right? Spread the blame for any fuck-ups."

Silently, Willow rails at the counselors, but truthfully wants to understand the purpose of these non-profit groups that supply in-field counseling services paid by the state but spend very few hours out of each month in personal client contact. She wonders where that time goes. Who pays for it? If it's not spent with clients, then it contains little value.

Frustration and lack of progress takes a peripheral toll on the friends and relatives in mental health cases, and the ability to treat these cases reaches technical limits quickly in the medical field, research and treatment expenses remain high, and results vary widely with limited success as well. The impact destroys families, friendships, and working relationships to some degree, as well as the patients.

Willow sticks a little challenge in, brings some attitude, "Like what, Larry? Sonny's been in lockdown nine days this time? Finally, more than a three-day observation and evaluation, and how many times have you been in here Larry or you Derek?"

No one speaks.

"How many times? Maybe we should go look at the log book."

Sonny blurts out, "Hey, I can answer that one. Mister Morton, one time so I could sign a paper, Mister Boone zero." Sonny nods, aims a knowledgeable smile around the table, stopping briefly at each face. "See, you never ask me." He shrugs his shoulders, pops his hands out, palms up. "I'm the only one that knows." He returns his hands to his lap, bunches his fists again, the anger begins asserting itself.

Willow also knows the case workers spend very limited outside time with the clients, at least with Sonny. Morton logged in only once in nine days according to Sonny, and Boone not at all, and K.O. told her that Sonny sees Morton at the gym very seldom, meets him there once a month – if that – and maybe once at Med-

Assist offices in town.

Sonny breaks in again. "You're never around much, Mister Morton, you either Mister Boone." An edge cuts into his voice, illustrates a lack of respect emerging, a bit more stress pushing his attitude suddenly, the manic spells come on unannounced and unpredictable. The meeting begins pushing at his stress level.

"So how can you know what I want or what I do? Do you both read my mind, maybe that's how? You work on me invisibly and plant negative thinking in my brain so I'll hurt some people and protect others? Make me break things?" His frenzy ratchets up a notch. "That proves you're an alien. Can't see you, but you're working on me. Sit in your office and work my brain waves, sending nasty signals into it over the air."

Sonny picks up his unopened orange juice container, flexes his forearm and squeezes his fingers together, tightening his grip until the cap explodes and shoots straight into the air, bounces off the ceiling, juice splashing all over the table and notepads. The plastic cap spins into a corner.

Sonny stands, circles the table. "Let's take five," he spits the words out and grabs a handful of napkins, passes them around. Everyone helps clean up the juice as if Sonny rules the group, as if he's suddenly in charge. He circles the table, holds out the trash can. Everyone drops in the napkins. Sonny grabs a cookie, takes a bite, "Extra energy." He smirks, drops down on the floor near the wall and starts a push-up count, grunts the numbers aloud.

"One, two, three, four, ..." retreating into his physical routine while these people he places in his no-trust card index discuss his life without asking his input or opinion.

He speaks as he pushes up and down. "You talk about me as if I'm absent," he takes a breath, "or can't hear you," another breath, "as if I'm a puppet or a pet dog." A breath, "Well, I'm here, this is my case and I know the answers, you don't."

He pauses at the up peak, arms stiff, "Anyone else? Get down here and do some real work, instead of sitting in your office sending mental waves out to us in the clinics, or at home. This is work, sending waves ain't helping us any. Maybe we should take ten instead, work you all into it a little easier, slower. Think you can do even ten pushups? Looks like you all need it."

He inhales again, resumes counting"...twenty-six, twenty-seven," a breath, "twenty-eight..." He pops up and down, a slight sweat but no strain with his physical ability, not even breathing hard yet, effortless. "Go on Derek, eat another donut instead, you too Larry."

The tone of this meeting upset him so he works out the stress, counting toward fifty aloud. Every eye watches him, spellbound, up, down, up, down, barking out the count as he builds the numbers, his voice the only sound. No one says a word during his session, all curious and worried at the same time. Each one all but frozen in a chair, but somehow fascinated by this intense psychotic exhibition right before their eyes, one with intensity like this one most have only read about in books until today. They just sit and stare, a little bit shaky about his intent. The tension mounts.

"Forty-nine...fifty, not so hard, you should try it sometime. Works better than those pills you feed me." Sonny rolls over, sits cross-legged on the floor.

"Boss demon orders me to kill all the spooks inside my friends, the ones that fake it. The Gray Leader screams those orders into my brain. Left me alone in this clinic for a while so I can rest up, just checked in a few times this week, but now it's back and bossy again, yesterday and today. Could it be one of you all sent it in, or brought it in with you? Which one did it? Come on, claim credit for your input!"

Effortlessly, Sonny rolls upright, bounces on the balls of his feet, grits his teeth and says nothing for a few seconds, puts a glare in his eyes, grunts, a muscle knots across his brow, the rage emerging. Like a tiger in a cage, he circles the table slowly, cracks his knuckles, and stretches his fists toward the ceiling. Sonny stops briefly behind each person. Once behind K.O. he turns his back to the table and punches the wall twice, a quick one two, but his knuckles barely touch the paint, perfect fist control. He stops behind Willow another quick one two.

Tension increases each second, almost thick enough to breathe. A little nervousness fills the air, staff unsure about Sonny, his anger and his intent. The group shifts uneasily in its seats, very aware of his history, his strength, and his physical ability, all suddenly wary.

Sonny continues his circle, touch-taps the wall behind Willow and K.O. Each time, his fists barely brush the paint. All these counselors read reports that describe his delusions and know he currently believes he's training to kill aliens, and he receives mental orders from demons and spooks that invade his friends as well. Every person sitting at this table knows without a doubt that Sonny absolutely believes within each counselor in this room an alien life form exists, and it hurts his friends. The conflict in his thoughts means nothing in his manic state. His beliefs transition from moment to moment.

He flexes his fists, the muscle on both forearms tightens and releases, tightens and releases, rhythmic, as if preparing him for action. He stares at each one individually, selecting his first victim. Every person in the room knows two locked doors lead to one exit in the hallway and the only unlocked door opens directly on the internal corridors leading into the dorm rooms. No way out, no one willing to lift a phone and call security, no one willing to step up and unlock the door, no one knows how Sonny will respond, so no one makes the first move.

Checkmate.

Sonny exudes power and confidence, its potency electrifies the air. The group shifts in its seats again. Complete silence envelops the room.

K.O. prepares himself, will intervene if necessary, but he lets Sonny play it his way. Decides it might benefit Sonny if these medical professionals finally observe in real time the exact symptoms each one denies Sonny exhibits when K.O. and Willow explain it second hand.

"So, you read my mind, plant alien thoughts in my brain. Your demons order me to kill my friends, and some nasty aliens – the ones you don't like, the ones that disobey the Gray Leader – then you lock me up unless I eat your poison."

He locks his eyelids wide open, his eyes dart around the room, sweat beads his forehead. Pausing briefly at the door, he quickly squats and glances under the table.

"Just checking, see if you hid one of your buddies under there." He aims a grin around the table. "Nope, lucky for it." Sonny giggles, flexes his fists again then hardens his stare. "Probably time to kill one. Steal its powers."

He stops. This eyes circle the room. "I got about one nerve left here today, and you're on it." Sonny brays laughter, "Ha, just heard that one on radio-talk. Think it's funny? Well, I did." He chuckles this time, and giggles then cuts it off, as if a hatchet chopped it in half, and his face tightens into a glare.

Amazingly, Anne Winslow documents every action, scribbling notes continuously on a yellow pad lying on the desk in front of her. Sonny walks behind her, peeks over her shoulder and says, "See you're taking notes, checking boxes. Good, check that alien box, Doctor Winslow, so everyone will know they attended too, especially Larry and Derek."

Sonny hardens his face, glares at each one individually, his mood jumps in and out of his manic component, stronger now, an idea that the clinic may decide to keep him longer pushes his stress higher. Once the manic stage hits, it sometimes lasts minutes, sometimes hours and he rages at everyone and everything. His strength and power scares even his friends. The people running this meeting know he feels no friendship, no kinship, no passion, and no trust toward any of them. No clinic staff here has earned his respect.

Sonny keeps stalking, pauses behind each person for a few seconds, skips past Willow and K.O. this time but stops behind Morton. "How about it Derek? Five, think you can do just five? I'll even count it out for you, save you some breath. That's real work, nothing like you do for us, sending out waves, checking boxes on a page." Sonny points at the floor. "Go ahead, pop down on the floor, and show us your work Derek."

Panic beads his forehead, sweat runs along his cheeks and his chin, Morton remains motionless. He stinks of fear and his personal fright radiates into the room, his face reddens and Morton says, "Didn't mean anything Sonny, nothing bad for you, just trying to help you."

"That why you call us 'nut-kids,' cause you're trying to help us Derek?"

Sonny uses the call name today for the first time in the relationship, always offered the respect title in the past, Mister Morton. Under these stress conditions, a sign of his growing disrespect emerges.

"Pretty odd nickname for kids you're supposed to be helping. Think we all don't know that? Well, we do. We're smarter than you think, or, maybe you're dumber than you think. Or, are those equal postulations?" Sonny giggles briefly, a private joke. He read that word once in a psyche article, looked it up. Couldn't wait to use it on one of these guys.

Again, he installs his serious face and looks at everyone once more. "Don't you know that word Derek? You ought to read more."

"How about a hypotheses? You know that one? I hypothesis if you read more Derek, you learn what that word means, both words." He glares at Derek Morton. "And, you'll learn more about psyche patients too, and how to treat us like clients, instead of 'nut-kids', and show some respect too."

"You must be one of the weak aliens Derek, still in training, don't know much yet, sweating here now because you have no powers. You never help us, you disrespect us, steal our movie tickets. Well, no worries, we're even, no one respects you either, always degrading us nut-kids."

Morton turns his head, but cannot look Sonny in the eye.

"Think we don't know that? Think we can't count who gets a movie each week. Can't count two tickets, pretty simple, even for us 'nut-kids,' right? Don't even need all our fingers, don't even need any fingers. And, we all got two thumbs, all we need. Only need one thumb actually, you steal the other ticket so we can't even count it. We can save the other thumb for hitch-hiking a ride out a here."

His voice rises and falls now, bouncing between a high squeak and a deep rumble with each sentence. Sonny has Morton right where he wants him – playing him – as Morton plays his clients. Sonny places one hand on each shoulder and Morton opens his eyes impossibly wider – fright consumes him and sweat pours off his forehead, large wet circles appear beneath his armpits, his hands shake, his cheek twitches.

"Well, keep it up Mister Morton. We 'nut-kids' need all the help we can get, even that tiny puffer you offer us, me and my mental buddies in here. Besides, not to worry, you ain't on the alien kill list, you have no powers, nothing to gain if we execute you. You're safe."

Sonny suddenly blinks, his face relaxes, he pats Derek Morton once lightly on each shoulder and turns away, laughs out loud, almost a cackle, and walks around the table, opens the door, slips through it into the hallway that leads to his room.

"You all don't need me here. You all talk to yourselves not me. You don't ask me nothing. Don't ask me how I feel, what I need. Just tell each other how I feel and what I need without knowing the truth. Half the time, you ain't even right. You got a question for me just spin a mind-ray through that wall. My room sets right on the other side of it."

"Wait," he pauses, "all you aliens might not have mind-rays yet, you weak ones. Here, I'll make it easy for you." Sonny hops back through the doorway, and stands beside the wall.

"I'll bust a hole in it so you weaker aliens with no mind power yet can just yell through it." Sonny hauls back and aims his right fist at the drywall, drives it forward and pulls back just as it touches the paint, again perfect fist control. "Just kidding," he says, snorts a laugh, a cackle and rolls it down to a giggle.

"Make a note of that Doctor Winslow, check a box. Sonny restrained himself today." He giggles then shuts it off, circles his glare around the table once more.

Sonny steps into the hallway, turns and punches the door as its auto-closer compresses it toward him, left right and left right and left right combinations. Barely touching his bare knuckles on the metal face as it swings toward him, he taps a perfect rhythm and distance as he backs away into the corridor. He giggles again and grins at the group, his face disappearing as the crack in the doorway shrinks into a narrow slot then closes tightly and isolates him in the hall behind it.

K.O. and Willow look at one another, both shrug. Both have seen it before but when either one describes it, the doctors or health care workers never believe it, never accept it as truth. Here it is in living color and surround sound. Let these professionals deny it now.

"Any one find that interesting?" K.O. asks, almost certain that he'll get no answer. He's right. Silence fills the room.

The discussion begins and continues without Sonny. "Well, we've been involved with other things. Housing, employment counseling." Boone pops out a catch-all phrase, justifying his services in his haste to protect himself, forgetting Sonny already has a job and a home.

Willow and K.O. learned a lot tracking and logging Sonny

during his attempts at and his rejections of medical care over the months, watching the 'who pays' mentality, obscure the treatment benefits. A lack of dedication in some misfits offsets the true professionals, the best of whom aim first at healing the minds and second at a bankroll, the way it should work, but more often fails.

K.O. reminds everyone. "He has a home, and he works at the gym, and he cuts trees and cleans yards." K.O. rotates his eyes between Boone and Morton, back and forth, waiting for either one to claim additional time logged in on services Sonny has covered.

"And, Sonny's right. You don't help these kids much if you sit and talk about this stuff in your offices. That's no help to your clients. Sonny needs someone to show him how to cope with these demons, the voices, and counsel certain social areas of his life, not tell him to go do it himself. His memory fails often, he can't concentrate, forgets things. If he could do it himself, he wouldn't need you folks, would he? Save the state a lot of money if we accept that as a truth."

Willow follows his thought pattern, "Like that bank problem you ignored Derek. You people need to go in the field and get to know these kids, how they think, what they feel about life, how they interact in their world. It's different from yours - neither one of you think like Sonny - none of us does."

"True or false, his world contains aliens, these space demons speak to him and order him around, and he needs to understand why that happens and live with it, and not hurt himself or anyone else because of it."

"Sonny and others like him live a wide awake nightmare every day, and if you think your dreams seem real when you're sleeping, try living one with demons screaming violent orders at you every minute you're awake, and that's all day folks, every day. And, it's as real in his world as any world you all experience every day. No wonder he gets angry."

K.O. tosses a set of papers on the table. "He needs help Derek, like these state insurance papers, the ones you gave him four months ago, and again three weeks ago then never follow up. Found these in gym, Sonny left them. Very complicated and confusing even for Willow or me, and it needs professional evaluations, things you have and he doesn't, and can't get. Especially confusing to a kid with issues like Sonny who has a tough time making transitions from one thought pattern to another and keeping his mind focused."

"He forgets where he's headed on the way to the store, forgets what he needs too, once he arrives. Sometimes he leaves for the store and never gets there, forgets where he's going. Goes down for milk and comes back with Kleenex and soap."

"Physically, he could tip a dime off your nose and you'd feel nothing but breeze. But once he did it, he may lose the dime and forget he had it, and sometimes forget why he had his fist up." K.O. pauses, looks around the room, "I know, I know, he can complete any physical routine, but that's an obsession, something he finds safe and comfortable, eases his mind, gives him a release. Training becomes a reflex, no thought involved, a routine in which he finds comfort and it relieves that stress."

Willow breaks in. "Sonny can't control that process with all the duplication and factors that interact with his illness and more paperwork, and rules. You're supposed to help him with this stuff. Isn't that what why you both draw a pay check?"

Morton and Boone choose silence. Hoping the team leader will quickly push this discussion back on track and get both men off the hot seat. Each man squirms in his chair and looks away, neither one able to meet K.O. eye to eye. Sonny brought some innocence in and dropped it right on them at their own meeting, kicked it right out of the control they normally maintain.

Doctor Anne Winslow says, "We need to decide if Sonny can leave tomorrow. That's why we're here. Let's keep on that track for now." She looks around the table, waiting for comments.

The door opens. Sonny pops back in, his obsessive personality wanders the loop again. "Working on me, you working on me, you said. Well, that just proves it. You can read my mind and stick thoughts back in it. You work on me but I never see you, so that proves it." His words hang in the room.

He stands behind K.O. and Willow looking for support, and drops one hand on a shoulder of each, drawing friendship in close. Sonny points his eyes at Morton. "You all tell me I'm making it up, ain't no aliens, right? Okay then, if not, then I'm one of your 'nut-kids' Derek. Aliens exist, or I'm a 'nut-kid', right Derek? Counsel me for aliens or counsel me for being nuts, one or the other. And, it ain't happening. Either way, you phone cancel our meetings and watch our movies. It ain't getting your job done, is it?"

"Invisible mind-rays right? Well, if you all just admit it, we can get down to business today. Get these aliens the fuck off our world. But I need a little help, can't do it alone."

Sonny drops down into his chair, slides a huge smile across his face, flicks his eyes at each person.

"So, am I going home today or what?"

29

After ten additional days, and a detailed and thorough evaluation according to staff, he's ready. Sonny promises he will take his meds. K.O. signs release papers that allow Sonny back into the gym and his room. Makes Sonny promise he'll curb the violence too, leave the walls and the lamps in one piece, and the cups and dishes too. Sonny agrees, even though he has little control over the behavior he exhibits during his times of stress, seems the right thing to do when he does it, at least to him at the time it happens.

His release consult time arrives, after another staff meeting, a little less stressful, the team finally agrees and sets his discharge date for the next morning.

Sonny sits alone with a nurse at the desk inside the release office and answers the 'check-out' list. Nurse Burkhart reviews the questions and Sonny marks the boxes. Sonny feels only dislike for Nurse Burkhart, but at least she treats all patients the same, no favorites. Everyone gets a full dose, just her regular nasty and bossy self.

Burkhart begins each day crabbing about clean rooms and clothing, even if a patient just swept the floor and pulled clean clothes out of a drawer. Sonny won't miss her at all. She smells like a no-shower day, wears over-powering perfume on her neck, and flirts with security a lot but fails with all three men even though all are older and not much of a catch – no real winners among them. Hard to pull off a sexy flirt when she resembles a tank and stringy brown hair floats out around her ears. Sonny usually backs away when she talks too. Sonny decides against offering her a toothbrush and a comb. He might end up like Allen.

Allen was just trying to be nice. A truck hit him when he was riding his bike and cracked his head on the pavement a couple years ago. His brother tells everyone it scrambled his marbles, and Allen pops in several times a year. He's young, almost sixteen, and knows nothing yet about women and attitude, so he offered Nurse Burkhart his used toothbrush when he got his new one last Friday, like everyone gets every Friday, and every new patient gets at the check-in desk upon arrival. Allen even put half a squirt of his favorite striped toothpaste on it first.

She really lost it at that one, made Allen scrub the sink in his room with it. Allen seemed very sincere at the time, but Nurse Burkhart has no clue about the sincere parts of Allen, nor apparently, no clue about her breath.

"Do you have a home, Steven?"

"Sonny," he says, squeezing his fists and directing his disgust elsewhere. "Yes, at the gym, and my own room."

"Oh, that's right, Sonny ... sorry." Sorry she says, but not sorry she means pops into his brain. He ignores it. She stays here. He leaves after nineteen days this time. He likes that idea just fine, plants the smile on his lips she wants but with no real sincerity in it. She earns sincerity from no one.

She points at a line. "Write the address and phone here. Write who else lives with you on the next line." She watches him write it in the box.

"What about work, do you work? Check that box yes or no." She points again.

"Yes, at the gym. Train kids, teach workouts and healthy habits, and clean up, and, cut trees and brush in season, or storm-blown all year. " Sonny checks the box and writes in his jobs. His eyes track down the list. He checks the yes box at 'Do you have a ride home', and checks the next two in a row beneath it.

"No, don't check that one, or that."

"Why not? That's how I feel."

"Doctor Winslow won't sign you out if you feel that way. Erase that and check this one instead, so you can leave. We can't keep you, other patients come in today. We need the bed. You need to go home. And check this one, and this one, and this one."

"That's not how I feel, those aren't the right answers."

"Trust me, Steven, that's how you feel if you want to go home today."

"Sonny, that's me, Sonny Bones." He points the pencil at his name. Nope, no trust for this nurse, a bit annoyed she forgets his name. Sonny snaps the pencil in half, a bit of anger pops out at her ignorance. He hides it quickly, and grabs another one, pushes too hard and breaks the lead point. He takes a breath, slows his heartbeat, grabs another pencil.

He dealt her a no-trust card into his brain pack the first day she entered his room and started bossing him around. A mean one, she called him Steven then too. Smiles sometimes, not often and never a real smile, just a frown stuck upside down on her face, a little super glue hard at work.

Now she makes him lie, well, sort of lie, only a box checked, like all other counselors check whenever he meets one, new ones or old ones, all the same paperwork. Sometimes counselors lie too, he knows it, he sees it, checking the wrong boxes so a thing looks done, even if it's not really done.

Lies must be all right in the counseling business, happens a lot, and he's in that business at the moment so Sonny feels no guilt about bending the truth. Must be the reason they use pencils and erasers instead of pens. Sonny figures these offices could save a lot of work if they just copied the same lies from last time he was here and let him sign the bottom each time. He checks the boxes she tells him anyway. He wants out of this clinic today and back on the running trails, no argument here. A couple lies, no bother for him, seems a regular habit in the clinic.

"Give me the box, I'll check it." He chuckles at his joke then installs his serious face and points it at Burkhart, marks the last box, then turns away and chuckles again, that weird cackle, like when he left the meeting last week. Burkhart pays it no attention, just reviews the checked boxes to assure Sonny gets his release today.

"Check, check, check." He grins and decides if she calls him Steven again, he'll ignore it. She seems unable to fix that mistake in her mind. Her boss alien probably programmed her brain with the wrong translations. He imagines for a moment her name translates into Checkbox in alien jargon, thinks he'll call her

Nurse Checkbox if he ever comes back here. She'll get upset, he figures, but she can't make him scrub a floor or a sink with a name. Besides, if she thinks he's Steven, he can do anything he wants and get away with it. Steven gets the blame. Sonny likes that idea, pays back Nurse Burkhart for Allen too. Allen didn't deserve scrubbing his sink with a toothbrush, the penalty she gave for Allen being nice.

At least the demons stopped screaming these past five or six days, but the nurse alien still hangs around in here, sending him back out there where her spook buddies live, and so he can start his training again, build himself up to fight the demons, and to meet his next opponent in the ring.

An escort knocks once, enters, and grins at Sonny. "Ready, Sonny?"

Sonny bumps a fist with Carl. "Boy, am I ever ready Carl? Ever-ready, Ever-ready, Ever-Ready!" Sonny repeats both words aloud a few times, and chuckles, imagining a pink battery bunny bouncing around the halls here. Bring in some entertainment and liven up the depression clinic staff feels all the time. Turn all those frowns upside down.

Only the patients laugh here, though not all the time, only when something neat or weird happens to staff, or even to the patients. Then all patients get it, the old chuckle-bug. Staff never gets it and the patients never clue them in either. If staff cannot figure out the fun, let the staff suffer a no-laugh life.

Carl leads Sonny out the gate and K.O. fires up his pickup, pushes the door open. Sonny climbs in slams the door, opens it quickly and shuts it gently, "Sorry," looks at K.O., frowns at the door but then grins at K.O., bumps knuckles.

The day Sonny promised no violence or breaking things he meant it, the same with other promises and statements he made in the social worker offices. Sonny remembers the false entries in those documents and the fact that telling the absolute truth means only occasionally in this world, depending upon the results that any individual desires at that specific moment. Ask Nurse Burkhart, she knows, just look at her paper, lies all over it but she signs it anyway, or ask Morton, or Boone. Same thing, lie and sign, no penalty.

30

Four days later, Derek Morton sets the phone down and stuffs a pizza crust into his mouth as Willow blasts into his office, her anger boiling over. "What kind of counselor tweaks the client into cancelling a meeting so his books show 'client refused meeting' and then blows off the conference?"

Morton chews, sips his coffee, two sugars, two creams. Office smells of stale cigarettes, Morton ignores the no smoking regulation in Med-Assist Health Care offices most days. He says nothing.

"You know these kids will skip for any small reason. You give them one, don't you? Led Sonny right into it, twice so far that I heard directly. Didn't know he usually listens on speaker when he gets counselor calls, did you?" Willow speaks soft and low, but her voice leaks grit and mean into the room, something she learned from K.O. It gets results.

"...unless *you* want to cancel, Sonny?" She repeats the comment she heard when Morton called Sonny about a meeting after his release. "Now I know what Sonny was saying in that meeting. You steal movie tickets too?" Willow barely restrains her anger. "Set that cancel right on these kids, don't you?"

Morton says nothing, swallows the crust, wipes his mouth on his sleeve, and sips his coffee again. Willow stares at him long enough. He finally squirms in his seat.

"You don't know about these kids. They never tell the truth, why waste my time. Been doing this for twelve years, I know the score. Kids just look for attention, and every kid thinks violence gets it. We can't fix them. They don't want to be fixed."

"Twelve years. Just because you put in the years and claim experience doesn't mean you do the job right. Do you even know Sonny, what he's like, what he needs? We know you skip most meetings and now I see how you do it, blaming the kids. Mark it as a 'Client Cancel'. Do you even read his file?"

"How can I read his file? He's been in three institutions in two counties, with five counselors, eleven trips to the ER clinic, and how many files from all that? And our files, too much, don't have time. And some don't even share with us, no HIPAA release so we can't even get it half the time."

"How do you expect to know your clients? How you assist them or understand what to do, what not to do?"

"I just do my job, I know about these kids. All the same, don't have to read files to see what they want. A free ride, that's all. Druggies looking for a come-down fix or a weekend away from a family that either beats them or ignores them and drinks, uses drugs, don't work."

Morton takes a slug of cold bitter coffee, spits it back into the cup, curls his lips. "They're not sick they're just junk-punks."

"You think that fits K.O. and me? We don't care about Sonny, we drink and do drugs!" Willow loses her temper completely, her voice rising as the anger bites deeper. "If that is what you think Derek, maybe you should spend some time in your own clinic, and get your head stuck on a little straighter! And, you say that around K.O., you won't walk straight for a week, he won't be as soft on you as I am!" Willow turns around, aims herself at the door, takes two steps, and spins back around.

"That's why you're stuck at the same level all these years, Derek. These twelve years you claim glued you right in that chair, no vertical movement. Must be no 'down lower' from that seat you're sitting on!"

"Were you born an asshole Derek, or did you grow into it?"

*

Willow whips out the office, slams the door behind her and heads upstairs, sticks her phone on her ear and dials K.O., fills him in. Willow hangs up and K.O. calls Ellie Archer.

Later that afternoon, Judge Archer recommends a different

social worker after chatting with a colleague local to Baxter and finishes a brief phone chat with the new counselor as well, personally checking him out, and hearing it with her own ear.

That same afternoon, the local director assigns Sonny a new counselor, one Willow and K.O. approve after an okay from the district supervisor. The next morning, Jones Johnson finds a new folder in his workbox, the name Sonny Bones lettered across its top.

*

His friends call him 'Jonesy,' a humanistic oddity in a workforce of grazers, mild manners outside, but tough at the core, a hole-in-one stifled by a volley of bogies. One dedicated man trying to gain traction in a system smothered by itself and very cumbersome, highly motivated toward the status quo. No rocking the boat please. Just keep the books current and the boxes checked. Money fountain leaks just fine now, all players own a cup so leave the holes unplugged. Jonesy works around that quagmire for the benefit of all the kids assigned to his caseload.

Willow and K.O. walk into the main offices and find a meeting room, wait for the new counselor. Jones Johnson, carries two thick blue files in one hand, coffee cup in the other, and finds a seat. "I read a bit of this at breakfast, and will review a little more today. My daughters have soccer practice after school. It's a pretty thick file, but I can finish it tonight after kids hit the sack. I can meet Sonny in the morning and see how we feel about us."

*

Sonny waits for Jones Johnson at the bank, exactly at its opening hour. Once again, he believes his account over-drafted, third time in two months, so he wants to understand how it happens so he knows why and can stop it in the future. Sonny evaluates his new counselor as he approaches.

Tight dark curls cut short, a clean shave, though a neat soul-patch accents his chin, dresses casual, no tie, but neat khaki pants and soft-cut pullovers, white running shoes nearly everyone wears nowadays. Little heavy in the middle but he works an office job, walks when he can in the personal time three active daughters spare him.

Johnson accompanies Sonny into the bank, helps him fix his account, no error, just computer timing on his electronic deposits. Jonesy shows him how it happens, runs through it a couple times with the teller and shows that it overdrafts each time for the amount difference between one deposit and one credit of exactly the same size. When he spends on his debit card, it charges instantly, but it takes computer time to cycle with deposits. Occasionally, it appears an overdraft occurs, but it really balances, and Sonny misinterprets it.

The sense of it eludes his brain. They compromise with a connection between his checking and savings, and the savings kicks in and covers when he misses the money count. It satisfies Sonny because he always gets the figures right, never makes the timing work on crossover deposits and time the computer needs, but he knows it will read exactly right after a day or two and agree with his figures, so he buys into it and perks up.

After the bank effort, Jonesy buys Sonny a coffee. Sonny chalks Jonesy a plus point in his friend box for helping him out at the bank, another because he looks cool. See if this new social worker makes the trust friend level in his mental card pack, but probably not, at least not quickly. That takes a lot more than most folks are willing to give, and based on Sonny and his personal history, most counselors and health care workers begin in the hole.

He asks Johnson, "Bet they call you Jonesy, don't they?" One more person in his life Sonny gets a laugh with about names, and Johnson laughs too.

Sonny always likes social, some folks like it back, some not. One of the good ones, Jones Johnson likes social just fine. Social helps Jonesy help kids that need it, believes the definition of social worker includes socialize as an operative verb. This counselor carries no notebook, no clipboard, no checklist, no pen, just dictates his notes into a recorder later – the important parts, the notes that help him help his clients – discards the rest.

Jonesy strives for comfort between himself and his clients. Getting to know a client rides very high on the Jones Johnson job description. Jonesy sits and sips the dark brew, listens to Sonny the person not Sonny the patient, and hears his words, a nice departure from the lack of communication with Morton or Boone. First priority for Jonesy, develop a friendship and a person-to-person trust. Treat the patient as an individual first, and a client second.

31

Six months pass, and after five more three-day sessions at the clinic when he briefly refused his medications on occasion and exhibited disruptive behavior, Sonny bangs the fat bag. Dancing sideways, punching hard, he teaches two new kids the fundamental boxing skills, the right way and the wrong way so each knows the difference first hand as both youngsters follow his moves, watching carefully, missing nothing.

Judge Archer intervened earlier, and the court cleared the drug possession case, got him supervised probation. Lucky for Sonny and he knows it, hates the lock-up psyche ward, though he makes a new friend there each time, another nut-kid.

All these kids repeat in it, like old home week each time one arrives, a way of life for kids and young adults whose brains disconnect with reality. Most take medication sporadically, but some take meds according to the doctor orders. Seems it makes little difference as some psyche medications work on some patients, some work on others, some work on no one, and usually it's a mixed bag. And nearly all drugs engage one or more side-effects, some minimal, some very intense.

It often takes months for a psyche team to determine if one drug works on a specific patient. Unlike a painkiller or an antibiotic, it takes time for the medication to adjust the brain chemistry, and the side effects often make the kids uncomfortable. All patients struggle with inconsistency. Sometimes it takes several years to find the one medication mixture that works on a specific patient, and with tolerable side effects.

Tremendous conflict lives in his mind, a moral and ethical dilemma Sonny faces every day, and the hurt his space alien aims at his friends offsets his happiness whenever he sees it. Sonny smiles beyond it, teaches, loves his work, his friends, likes his life, the healing, building a dream, or so it appears on the surface. Sonny illustrates it today, and yesterday, and most often during the past six months.

Hold your patience. Bide your time. Your turn is coming! A haunting voice advises each time he forgets and listens, a weak whisper this morning, in one ear only.

Sonny shrugs it off. "Not today." He growls deep in his throat, then laughs aloud. The kids chime in, enjoying the lessons, the budding competition, the hard work, the fun.

K.O. delays signing Sonny another boxing match as long as he's in treatment, or at least until he gets that legal point clarified, so keeps a vigilant eye on what Sonny does, where he goes, how he acts, how he lives. Court order gives K.O. those rights, Willow too. Meds and home or meds and confinement, Sonny gets a choice.

Sonny chose home and promised, so he eats his meds, sometimes, but only when his tricks fail, he still figures counselors lie a little and accepts it, reliving the check boxes and his answers, he bends his accuracy a bit when counting his medications, just a small lie and no one cares, just like Nurse Burkhart and her fake-out checkmarks.

He knows medications work differently on some patients. Kids at the clinics share that info, and the side effects often bring discomfort, dizziness, itching, twitching, and the diet suffers, no appetite or over-eating. Doctors take months deciding if a specific medication works on a specific patient, and it takes weeks just to observe even minor changes. If it proves unsuccessful, try another, and take another six months. No one wins every time, and the side effects bring discomfort while the 'testing' continues.

Sonny yearns for the next match, disappointment hides deep inside him for now but his dream continues. His aliens tell him, play a game, skip the meds, and he takes his medication promise less serious than when he gives his word on other events or situations.

Either Willow or K.O. watch Sonny each time, at least one tracks his pillbox right on schedule, opens it, and hands him the meds. One problem, no one trained the watchdogs. Willow turns on the tap, her eyes flick left, watching the glass fill. Sonny watches her watch the glass and cheeks his pills. He chugs the water, smiles at Willow and walks into the rest room, spits the poison into the toilet, flushes.

One alien claps. *Nice one, you did it. Fooled her again.*

"Shut up, leave her alone." Sonny bats at the mirror, an imaginary spook hangs in the reflection. The alien sits on his shoulder pointing long sharp fangs at his ear, threatening. Sonny ignores it.

Sonny gets away with it almost half the time, whenever either watchdog fake alien looks away for a second. In his mental video, Willow and K.O. often appear as aliens with strange faces hovering above, like halos or vaporous masks, but as often appear as friends with no alien presence. Sonny never knows positively which one is which and which time, but he always acts as if he accepts both as friends, hiding his knowledge of an alien disguise.

He figures both K.O. and Willow fight the alien presence, same as he does, so sometimes the aliens sit in, sometimes not. Never certain which, he remains on guard all the time. Both friends always stay in his trust box, because he knows somewhere inside each body his friends still exist, even when an alien takes over for a brief period.

K.O. and Willow medicate him unsuccessfully, untrained, unwise in the way of clinic veterans who teach Sonny each time he hits the hospital lockup for a few days. The partial doses work, at least minimally. A few days with liquid medication in the clinic when he acts out again works a little, softens the alien presence. Some medication hits his system despite his rejection and it balances his chemistry, and sometimes the brain chemistry itself creates a temporary balance, less stress and more activity allow him some control of his motivations and thoughts. Finally.

Why that control comes and goes without his conscious direction eludes both Sonny and his doctors. True healing never occurs spontaneously, nor does suppressing the alien visions completely. Dosage remains insufficient, haphazard, low strength, and no strength, while destructive chemical reactions slowly but continuously digest his brain. Sonny meets doctors, counselors, real friends, false friends, and bides his time. The aliens simply advise him at this point, an up cycle at present, no orders now, orders come later.

Wait, patience, your time coming. Wait, wait, wait, you get your chance. Teach the kids, teach the kids, stay out of jail, stay out of the hospital. Too confining, you hate it. Can't run, can't walk, can't stand it indoors, always locked up. Nurse Burkhart bossing you around, and can't reject the poison when you're inside those walls. Hate it, hate it, stay out, wait your turn. You can still win. Punch someone, kill someone and you'll be free! Kill a child, it can't fight back!

Sonny denies it all, an intense struggle - his personal ethics and morals win the battle, for now.

The voices soften, speaking quietly and tempting now, the faces less bizarre, the partial dose medication weakens its impact. Aliens disguise themselves as friendly, smiling, selling the goods once more, but never give up completely. Sonny obeys, mostly because it fits his needs at present, but he believes this strategy will only last a while, so he rests when he can, and shuts the voices and faces out of his mind.

Night hides his truck. Sonny slips into his old camp space, sits on the stump, watches spooks glow, one each in three trees. He pushes to his feet. A loud pop pierces the stillness, then another. Sonny swings hard, breaks a thick branch against a tree, then another, then another, working the rage again, sweating it out, easing his pain, hiding the damage, tossing the wreckage aside, saving it on his burn pile.

Advice again, no commands, as if the alien plays carefully. *No more trips inside, no more confinement, no doctor drugs, no pharmacy chemicals, no more poison, make that promise every day. Bide your time.*

Sonny hates confinement, will do anything to remain free. Aliens gain strength but he works harder, keeping it nose to nose down the stretch. He rolls his rock, sparks a match, fires up a bud, inhales, grins, inhales again, knows he can beat it, just knows, he wills it, just two months left and freedom, a word he loves equally as much as hope. Fifty-nine days left, he counts it down every morning, fifty-eight tomorrow, his deadline approaches.

It's poison, don't take the pills. Freedom's on its way, getting closer, counting the days.

Sonny breaks out his kit again, fires up the spoon, and boils off his own personal treatment. He still hears its whisper, one alien advising but no new demands yet, still just tactfully convincing. His prescribed meds work a little, no way he can spit them all, smoke helps a little too, just enough, and keeps Sonny rational, sane at least most of the time. He sticks his vein. The liquid instantly spreads warmth and relaxation throughout his body. The nasty vision disappears then its voice chokes off. A blood dot forms on his forearm and Sonny grins and nods out, a brief but peaceful respite from his rage.

*

Hormones push his brain, aliens attack his soul, friends become his enemies, enemies stay enemies, or enemies become his friends. Confusing and conflicting, his frustration boils over. Anger and violence offsets his fright, so he strikes out at his world but keeps it a secret, smashing things he can hide, embracing its power, protecting his self, admiring his work. The rage still grabs him for minutes or hours or even days.

Sonny walks into the break room, slaps a lamp off the table. He grabs his head with both hands, "No!" Then quickly sweeps up the debris and hides it in the trash. Two young men hitting the bags and two teenagers jumping rope stop and stare but say nothing.

Demons quietly applaud. *Great job, you killed a lamp. Take a bow.*

No bow, he refuses the idea that breakage brings a good thing into his world. He loses control some of the time but the physical attacks release the stress. Unable to stop the damage, he hates when he breaks things but that action helps controls the urge, releases that stress and silences the voice commanding him to hurt a person. Hurting a person would cost Sonny too dearly, and fry his emotions. At the core of human spirit, his heart and soul provide the guilt, and he refuses that kill order every time he hears it.

32

Aaron Clark and Cat sit in her office, discussing how she can best approach the next stage of her research. Stifled by a less than organized and less than effective national medical community, often under-trained and under-funded, and secretive due to liability issues and federal privacy laws, she lacks the ability to change its character alone.

Cat struggles with her research but maintains slow and steady progress toward her goals. Her inability to receive the data she needs to understand each of her patients affects her capacity to assist in the healing. Her personal insight often runs contrary to current treatment theory and that bogs down her ability to gather the information she needs as well.

Health care workers often lack true understanding and document patient data improperly, and thus, an essential element in her data collection often fails. Mute and frowning somewhere in the fog, Captain John Yossarian applauds her dilemma and shares her frustration. Catch-22 anomalies live and breathe in the mental health clinics across the nation.

*

"These patients live in a chemically unbalanced world, and with a brain unable to make rational decisions on medical care, and then harm themselves, refuse the best treatment, and the brain deteriorates further. The illness itself interferes with the proper thinking, and thereby creates failure in the treatment plan. These kids and young adults simply make the wrong choices out of fear for the consequences." Cat vents her frustration. Aaron Clark listens. Equally familiar with the problems, he simply watches and frowns his understanding while Cat releases her own stress.

Aaron feels it as well, as do many that work in the field and experience the same problems, at least the dedicated professionals that care enough about it. "So, what exactly do you need at this point?"

"Written releases from the subjects, or parent or guardian. It's impossible to decide which of these kids will bring value to the project and benefit from treatment, or at least prove the theory works - and the treatments - without harming one of them, or more. But we've got less than half the information we need, and the least valuable half at that, and the patients that will help our research the most live all over the east coast."

Cat palm-slaps her forehead, her irritation evident. Her grant funding and research depends on her understanding the conscious brain patterns and chemical imbalance of mentally ill patients, so she can interpret the effects of minor biochemical adjustments directly from the patient, not just from field notes taken out of context.

No observer can explain it better than an individual directly experiencing the transition from paranoid and angry to confident and comfortable, and how the electro-magnetic and hormonal balance affects mood, personal choice, the physical body and most importantly, the mind and its perceptions.

"What practical good is it to know she wore a green shirt yesterday or spilled a drink at lunch? What's with observers in this age, no training? Observing and gathering worthless information brings no value, makes it more like baby-sitting. Looks like a tattle-tale telling mom, not the observation notations documenting internally motivated behavior patterns."

"We need to know how it feels inside a mind when a sick teenager breaks a chair over the porch railing or throws a cup across the room. What kind of chemical stability does that create in a brain and a body when violent behavior releases that anger and calms the brain?"

"Only the patient can tell us that, not an observer, the data collector must ask directly in this research, and the patients must be willing to answer, not frightened by a social worker. We need to be there, right with them Aaron, get to know them personally."

"Checking a box tells us nothing. Why ask? Why do it? It has no value."

Aaron Clark adds, "The patients know that too Cat, better than we do. A client may be schizophrenic or bi-polar but also very bright, matter of fact, many patients test extremely bright. Experiencing an odd sequence of disconnects in the neural pathways creates conflict, but the patients often find unique methods to cope. That takes a very bright mind."

"Patients generally tell us what they think we want to hear, but not what we need to know to treat them. Remember, these kids all fear us, they fear most counselors and doctors too. Fear is one constant component of mental illness in these violent cases. Many even fear family members. That's a symptom of the disease. Simple chemical reactions inside the brain direct powerful emotions and major behavioral responses in an individual."

"Learning disabilities, speech impediments, perception transitions illustrate a different type of disorder. Screaming demons bring danger to the table and make diagnosis and treatment more critical. These kids will hurt other kids or adults, or themselves. That sometimes elicits a grim finality we can never revisit."

He adds a little caution. "Careful how you screen your patients Cat, some of those fears you identify are real for other reasons. An alcoholic parent beats a child, that's not the same fear trigger, but it's real fear. Inexperienced observers frequently label those fears inaccurately. It's a whole different complex of behaviors."

"I know. We see those too." Cat says. "Plus, the legal system and the medical system disagree, often fighting with one another in court. Strange thing, Fergie and Chase give us the most useful information and the most honesty. Hardcore criminals no less, but give us our best source of live data. Who'd have figured that?"

Lawsuits, malpractice, new laws that restrict solid research fill the news media, never enough money to fight legal battles and fund current medical inquiry or treatment as well. Cat just wants to make a difference without all the fuss. Partial statements, clinic refusals, and lies or simple mistakes, even contradictions on the same page in some records impacts any chance for solid data collection. Untrained or uncaring health care workers that either don't know or don't care if it's correct limits her ability to see how mental illness affects the patients and social interactions in areas where they live.

"Health care workers just submit paperwork, make it neat, and meet the funding requirements for grants or medical insurance payouts. Patients look great on paper, perfect angels. But they would be at home, not assigned to a clinic and bounce in and out of it if these records contain accurate notes, so these cannot be accurate. Impossible, it makes no sense when we read it."

"So, go out in the field and get it." Aaron Clark shrugs. "If that's what you need."

She jumps off her seat, dances in a circle, fists in the air, and hugs her boss. Really, really, how many?" Delight bubbles over. Cat loves her job and thrives on fieldwork. It challenges her abilities and her dedication, brings a huge personal reward when successful, and helps validate her theoretical models. "How soon can I go? Who can assist?"

"Tomorrow too late?" He grins and waves a hand, no worry on his part. He's confident Cat will make it work.

"Take what time you need, just meet the grant deadlines. Pick as many as you want - we charted twenty-six. Pick the most responsive five or six and go with that for now. See how it proceeds, see how quick they respond, and even if they respond. You might overwork it otherwise, especially if you run too quickly and concentrate on too many. Use one assistant in-house, whomever you work with best. We can modify that later if you need more."

Cat hugs her boss again. "I'll keep Erin McCord on it, no doubt about it, she's works well on her own, and has the psyche background, and no one here can touch her data coordination and tech skills. She worked it already, a little. She ran a few searches and coordinating drills on Ferguson, Nickels and our Harvard cases. Pulled some back studies, and integrated the data with this new stuff. A great mind too, she sees a big picture even when she reviews small data batches."

"Good enough, I'll tell her tomorrow, and cut her loose from everything else. Go get 'em Catherine. Good luck, just keep me in the loop."

33

"Better, at least. That's the word I'd use, not cured, not perfect, not like when we met him." Willow condenses the changes she saw in Sonny over the past few months. "Confused sometimes, frustrated often, but happy too, especially when he hangs out with the younger kids. He loves the workouts, watching each kid improve. He expresses less anger."

K.O takes his turn. "Like magic in him, anger tempered some, a lot less rage, some kind of spirit transcending all that pain. Not the old Sonny, not the wise-mouth humor, that one vanished, but certainly a new version, a dedicated companion sort of, not a confused maniac like he was six months ago. Most trainers never see a touch that soft with those kids, as much as he hurts inside. Sonny maintains a great rapport with those younger kids again, Jacki and Randy, and the others."

Willow says, "Scared Jacki to death. He called her a Master, some kind of Gray Leader alien, asking her, almost begging her to raise him up a level, said he's worth it. Told her he'd prove it. No wonder she scared off all those weeks ... would scare me too. Did scare me, but in a different way of course, more afraid for Sonny than for myself."

K.O includes his observations. "After all those accusations, all that turmoil, right back almost normal, like nothing happened. Sonny has that way about him, earns that trust, even with his wildness, like some spirit inside never fails him, even in all this darkness."

Doctor Anderson sits upright, arrogant, suddenly a 'know it

all,' his smooth talk claims all the credit. "Well, there's no cure, but I knew I could fix him, at least."

After all the 'not sure' chatter in past meetings, Anderson suddenly takes credit for his earlier failures, what he claimed he never knew, what no one in the mental health field knows for certain. Now he takes his bow, an unearned bow in reality.

"By the way, his insurance cancels in a couple weeks, so if you'd make other arrangements for payment before you leave, that will help."

"Knew you could fix him?" She lets that comment stew a minute, upset that Anderson suddenly takes credit for success. He maintained from the beginning he was hit and miss prescribing, guessing, testing medications, and unsure about actual treatments and related success in this field, excusing his failure before the fact just in case, and because most cases are nearly impossible to treat, let alone cure.

She switches to a more important topic for the moment. "What do you mean, his insurance cancels?"

Anderson explains his office rules. "Well, no payment, no treatment. His mother received an employer insurer plan at her job, pays very little as it is, you know, like Medicaid. It's good until age eighteen. That's why we can't do much with these kids. We medicate, keep our eyes on them, keep violence under control, and read the counselor reports. Do the best we can on a limited budget."

"His insurance cancels in a week. He's an adult then, and no more family visits, and we can't share medical information with you anymore unless he signs a new release. That's everyone, all adult patients, HIPAA privacy laws, it's federal." Anderson places his reading glasses on the tip of his nose and tilts his head back, looks through the glass and past the end of his nose at them.

K.O. and Willow pick up the attitude, the blind lack of knowledge, a 'we wait and see' posture. Both want to believe, both embrace the possibility, the potential that Sonny will recover soon, as if he caught a cold, not developed a major biological dysfunction in his brain. Both running out of patience and annoyed at this doctor and his arrogance, and Willow remains very upset about the last meeting when Anderson called Sonny an animal.

Convinced Anderson cares less about treating his patients

than collecting his paycheck, Willow decides to change doctors again. Failure feeds frustration, frustration feeds failure. Both K.O and Willow hope to change that and find something, someone, anyone that works and treats kids, and cares about the kids more than a paycheck, a nearly impossible task. Regardless, mental illness remains fundamentally incurable, and often but not always at least treatable.

Both leave the office side by side and glance at one another. "Change doctors again?" K.O. nods his agreement, ready to voice the identical thought but Willow beat him to it.

One week before Sonny turns eighteen Willow sits in the gym office and reads the insurance termination aloud. "The health insurance benefit through his mother covers him until he reaches adulthood, age eighteen according to the policy rules."

Willow found the policy in his room when Sonny injured his knee. He did not know it existed. The gym takes care of his annual physical and any injuries during training periods, same with all its boxing students, so Sonny had no reason to seek insurance coverage. It never crossed his mind.

Willow and K.O. examine his treatment plan and agree, "We'll pay medication costs," both say the words at once. Sixteen hundred dollars a month if Sonny has no insurance, three hundred and sixty a month if an insurance company pays it with a co-pay of only twenty-six dollars from the patient.

"What bullshit!" Willow shouts, "How ridiculous! Medication and health care systems charges the highest rates for patients that need it the most and can afford it the least."

Unable to afford doctors and psychologists and medication and clinics, K.O and Willow agree medications seem the most important tool in his treatment, and rightly so. Biological malfunctions gain little from psychologists talking about problems. He needs chemistry, not words. Words and training may come later.

"Seems odd, why not the same rate for everyone? Almost borders on reverse elitism in a sense. The least paid and lowest income citizens work the hardest and get charged the most." Willow tosses the pages on the table.

Sonny accidently overhears parts of the discussion, though it always stops when he appears. Obviously, an alien conference, he decides. He hears conversation as he walks down the hall, silence when he enters the room. Makes it a mission to listen whenever he can but he receives a copy of all notices too, mail comes to him personally as well as the guardians. The law requires it. He decides to act on his own and begins a plan, his brain unbalanced enough now that he believes he can accomplish it alone. He slides onto a stool.

"You read that Willow, about my health insurance? You don't have to pay it. You're guardians, not parents. You just guard me, you don't pay my bills. Insurance over, that's it, the end, eighteen, makes me an adult next week."

'Don't need the meds anyway, don't need doctors, don't need counselors or clinics. I'll just workout harder, use heavier weight, more reps, run longer, bike farther, kick those spooks out. Works fine. Besides, aliens live inside most doctor brains now anyway, taking everyone over, can't trust them, all trying to poison me."

A look passes between K.O. and Willow, the message clear between them. Sonny now knows the medical costs will become a financial drain on his friends. "Bummer." The word jumps out of both mouths simultaneously, close friends thinking alike.

Sometimes Sonny believes he needs the pills, sometimes not. Deep down in his heart, in that hidden place where he protects his soul from the demons and aliens, he knows he needs medication. He hides that knowledge, afraid to admit aloud that his brain malfunctions, refusing that social stigma. The consequences of an admission like that presents a huge social cost in his culture, a culture that allows little space in it for less than perfect individuals, a culture that comes down especially hard on weak or damaged minds.

Depends on the dose Sonny gets and how often he spits it, but he realizes the truth enough times that he wants that option, but more than a choice, he wants to please Willow and K.O. even if he decides the medication helps nothing, that he needs no pills, just the heavy workouts. He believes Willow and K.O. too, at least some of the time, but confusion reigns. No reason for lies, he thinks, unless both his friends really converted into aliens, and that too remains unclear.

Continuously conflicted in his mind, he now frets over the medication costs K.O. and Willow pay, and it dumps more stress into the mix. If he loses his medication option, he has no choice. Sonny likes choices. Unable to understand his world the way others do, he plans a change in his future. Qualify for federal insurance or state assistance, whatever it takes. Not sure how yet, but he begins a plan based on everything he reads and everything he hears, including the 'in-house training' he acquires from his buddies in the hospital and clinics. Whenever the court sends him on a visit, his mentally ill but surprisingly bright comrades, many exactly like him, share experience and knowledge.

Many doctors and nurses make a huge mistake. They listen but never hear the words. Sonny listens carefully and hears what his clinic pals say, a big difference. He believes doctors should pay more attention to the patients. Doctors could learn a lot. Who better knows what goes on inside a person? It takes trust, trust between doctor and patient, and most often, the health care workers never give it enough time, and believe clients have little to offer.

Course, not all are equally bright - his mental clinic friends - some a little thin in that department, but everyone gains experience each time the doors click behind him, and all share it willingly. Patients against staff, always patients against staff in the institutional world of locked down weekends. With little to gain personally, the health care guardians generally lose. With nowhere to go and little to do, the patients spend all day planning a score, even the smallest victory – a single pill hidden in one cheek or beneath a tongue brings joy and laughter during an otherwise boring day in the mental health wing.

For some indefinable reason, many mental health patients refuse medication, an almost universal behavior. Some doctors believe an admission from a person taking psychotic meds becomes an acknowledgement he or she has an abnormal brain. Because society thinks less of a person with an abnormal brain, most patients refuse to take meds and by default, refuse that admission as well, refuse that stigma.

Although most people quickly accept an antibiotic or a cancer drug, for some social reason, an individual accepting a faulty body feels less shameful than accepting a faulty brain. Many psychotic drugs cause uncomfortable side effects as well, and an upset mind acts quite unlike an upset stomach.

Sonny smiles when he recalls one incident he cooked up in the clinic. A casting director seeking a movie-star body and cover-girl face would hire Melanie in a Hollywood minute, despite rainbow hair spiked on top, beads in her ears and nose, and an addictive personality she cannot control. Melanie spends more time in this clinic and knows more about it than anyone, including half the staff. Her brain and mind work just fine, but she loves highs, the altered mind, the alcohol, pot and pills, and occasionally gets hooked on addictive drugs. Melanie needs no psychosis treatment. Overly shy in social areas, she embraces the lightness and spark street medications inject into her personality. When she finds it and addiction strikes, her parents tuck her away in a clinic, display the insurance card, hug Mel and depart. She signs in and dries out.

Her parents carry a very good insurance policy and it pays the tab. Melanie lives at home, but her parents travel a lot working as technical consultants out of state. She launches herself into her drug world as soon as the front door shuts behind her folks. Whenever her parents return, they check her in for a few weeks, a little ritual 'clean up the kid' action.

She arrives at the offices and joins the group hovering around the med desk, all expecting a daily dose. They giggle and point, and Melanie joins right in, 'hide the pill, and spit it'.

Eventually, she signs herself out and starts it all over again. Her folks tried live-in house help, but Melanie just ignores it, and trots out her addictive behavior any chance she gets as soon as her parents depart. She knows so much about treatment she could become a nurse here if she was not an addict - but she'd eat all the sedatives herself, even admits it.

She opened two buttons on her low cut blouse, and rehearsed an act a couple times with Allen – much to his delight. Then later, she popped an extra button, and pushed up into one very big-eyed view while Antonio Vargas vigorously checked her mouth for pills and delightfully checked her cleavage for his own pleasure.

Melanie teases Antonio often, knows he's married to a

heavy Italian wife he loves dearly, and has three teenage kids, and two toddlers. "Nice huh Antonio, damn things, always popping my blouse, can't help it, won't stay shut. Gimme a hand, buttoning this up, will ya'?" She offered, and he almost had a heart attack, but locked his eyes on the buttons, or maybe between the buttons.

Red-faced and embarrassed, Antonio lifted his hands, then drops each one slowly, then lifted again, failed, and dropped them again, this time forcing both hands into his back pockets, keeping himself out of trouble. Melanie laughed, and winked, popped her blouse open wide briefly, then buttoned it up. Antonio nearly wet his pants.

Allen hid two capsules in his ear and got away with it while Antonio enjoyed his view. A pill nurse always checks each mouth after a patient swallows, makes him lift up his tongue and wiggle it around, inspecting for meds the patient hides in a cheek or under the tongue. Antonio definitely failed his monitor job this night.

Everyone laughed about that one for hours. Allen hiding pills in his ear was even better than when Gregory stuck two meds under his armpit. No one figured a way around the liquid yet, but they all work on that dilemma during free time, lots of that in every day.

Patients discuss the pill-hiding Olympics, voting awards each weekend, an extra pudding or cake at lunch. Melanie and Allen split the prize, half a piece of cake each for great teamwork. Sonny has a new idea. Commission a badge of honor for 'best pill hider' and pass it around weekly. Create a beaded emblem shaped like a medicine capsule hanging off a tongue in Art Learning sessions. Patients laugh for ten minutes, drawing stick figures in the air, depicting the new tongue badge with a pill stuck on it. Anything to erase the boredom 'locked-up' creates.

*

Sonny has another violent episode, punches a couple holes in the wall again, and K.O. checks him into the clinic once more for a three-day evaluation. He pops back into his room.

Nothing slow about the brains in this clinic despite the general attitude regarding mental patients, course the aliens know better but never share that information publicly. Many mental patients own demons, and spooks, and aliens that order them around, some even own spirit brothers that share guidance as well. Games like dominos and cards take the boredom out of clinic life, along with pill hiding, and video games for those that can afford it, and a wide-screen in the lounge area runs morning wake-up to lights-out at night.

An odd mixture of brain chemistry creates a unique selection of visions, delusions and hallucinations in a mental clinic, and hoards a fountain of knowledge no one taps into, a stream of information no one records. Listen to your patients, listen to your patients, but hear the words. Patients will teach health care workers more than books or meetings if the staff just pay attention.

*

Released again earlier this morning, Sonny kicks the door open and steps into his room. Three spooks hang on his closet door, in conference, muttering at one another. Sonny swings. The visual blows apart like smoke then forms up again, still hanging, still muttering.

Suddenly, one aims a finger and screams. *Hit him, punch him. We choose K.O. first, we need his heart. You need his power. You get his mind-reading power and we leave you alone, but you have to kill K.O. Our choice, K.O.! Kill him and be free!*

Aliens continue hollering at Sonny, bossing him around, informing him the medications contain poison – confusion fills his brain, the conflict continues. Emotions run him ragged and he can no longer outdistance the rage when it hits. Sonny begins fearing himself, afraid someday his resistance may weaken and follow the orders, hurt someone he loves.

The aliens chose K.O. Tears fill his eyes when that command hits Sonny.

Aliens increase the pressure, gaining strength every day, every week, every month, yelping louder and louder, adding shrillness until the alien shrieks completely overwhelm Sonny, demanding violence. He crawls into his bed and pulls up the blankets, but the thin green cloth offers scant protection from harsh spooks that live in his brain.

Sitting at the table with his back toward Sonny, K.O. scans a boxing magazine, his phone stuck on an ear. K.O. speaks then listens. Sonny stands at the counter behind K.O, slicing a tomato, glancing at K.O.

A warped face appears, a nasty voice demands. *Cut him, bleed him out. Skin tight there, at the throat right below the chin, easy, one slice and it's over. Wait until he hangs up. Just one more minute! Someday he'll hurt you if you don't kill him first!*

The voice rises slowly, convincing, tempting. *No one will know. You'll be free. We'll take you home with us and sooth your brain.*

Seductive now, the voice whispers. *Kill K.O. Slit his throat. You'll gain his alien powers and the ability to read minds. You'll gain his strength, and become a Warrior!*

Sonny finds it nearly impossible to resist the urge, voices and rage soak into his brain. He draws the blade, another fruit slice falls away, his hands tremble, a single bead of sweat trickles down his cheek. He glances back at K.O, another slice, another glance, another slice.

K.O. winds down, ending the call. Sonny turns, takes two steps, eases up behind K.O., the knife angled to slit K.O.s throat as soon as he hangs up. *Cut the alien out and kill it, cut the alien out. Kill it! Help K.O. now! Kill his demon.*

"Okay, let me know." K.O. shuts the phone.

Sonny drops his arm, stands behind K.O. Five ticks, an eternity. His eyes blink back and forth, the knife, the throat, the knife, the throat, his forehead beads up, his hands shake, his fingers twitch, sweat drips off his chin.

The voices screech. *Cut him, Kill K.O, He's an alien, he wants what you have. Bleed him out, it's so easy. You get his powers! Execute his demon, he'll be safe. Help your friend, cut his throat!*

K.O. flips a page, without looking up. "Cut me off a couple slices while you're at it, will you?"

Sweat runs down his back, soaks his shirt. Sonny shakes his head, "No ... No!" He spins on his heel, drops the knife into the sink, kicks his way out the door.

K.O. glances up, watches Sonny stomp out, shrugs. "Wasn't that hungry anyways."

*

In his camp twenty minutes later, Sonny begins a heavy workout. He breathes deep and cracks a branch, cracks another, wipes his brow and cracks another. Fright-eyes turn toward the trail between swings.

He reaches in his pocket, launches his medications into the brush. Sonny sits on the stump and opens his kit, removes a clear baggie and needle, heats up a spoon. A minute later, warmth and relaxation flood his body, consuming his fright. Stress rushes up his arm and floats away on the cool night breeze. No faces, no voices. Sonny relaxes, his head nods forward. He grins and his eyes slide shut.

34

Tiny boxing gloves that fit on a finger decorate his cake. Sonny blows hard, the flames blink out. Thin gray curls spiral up above eighteen wax candles. He fits one small boxing glove on a fingertip, dips it in cake icing, taps K.O. on the nose, and laughs.

Sonny spent six of the last ten days in the clinic, two trips, two days apart, three days each and then a release yesterday. The clinic admitted him on two no insurance consult visits that ended as soon as he saw a doctor in the free care wing, and promised he'd take his meds.

This small and private party celebrates his eighteenth birthday nine days late.

K.O. grabs a finger-glove and taps frosting on Sonny's nose, back and forth, K.O and Sonny, quick mini-jabs with mini-gloves, a midget matchup. Willow joins in, tapping both Sonny and K.O. Dots of icing stick on the foreheads and cheeks of all three. Laughter and happiness fills the room.

Sonny began a different medication ten days ago. The accumulated affects of this new chemistry help slightly after a few days, but creates an upset stomach, dizziness, and periods of anguish difficult to control, even with heavy workouts. Sonny told no one. He decides these side effects hurt his brain more than the medication helps. Once again, he hides the med and spits it whenever he can.

He tried explaining these side effects, the discomfort it brings, the mental pain, but Doctor Turner, one of the temporary fill-ins at the mental health clinic ignored his input and continued the same prescription. One more doctor listens to his patient, but never hears the words. The clinics often rotate a different doctor into the urgent section each weekend. Clinic personnel vary nearly as often as do patients. In a fairly lucid period, Sonny wonders how a doctor can treat a patient when the doctor only sees him once or twice.

Two large hologram faces suddenly appear in his mind, and two distorted voices shriek louder than ever. Sonny grabs his head with both hands.

K.O. fakes it, he wants you dead. Willow poisoned the cake and put rat juice in the frosting. The aliens stole the real Willow and flew away. Watch K.O. curl his lips and fake a smile. His cheeks hide long yellow fangs, proof an alien hides in his head. Look!

Suddenly the play intensifies. Sonny grabs a fistful of cake and throws it at K.O., grabs another chunk, throws it again, another slice hits the wall, another hits the window. He grabs cake with both hands, throws it again, a left and a right, one splatters Willow and the other K.O.

The spooks applaud. *Great pitch. Throw it again! Good idea, piss off the aliens.*

K.O. wipes frosting off his forehead and shirt, more cake and frosting sticks on the wall behind him. Sonny runs down the hall, yells back over his shoulder, "Eighteen, an adult now. No more meds!! You can't tell me what to do anymore!"

He kicks at the door on the way in, no hole this time. An experienced property owner bought this one. A metal-faced door hangs where hollow wood doors once hung, the ones Sonny kicked holes in three times. K.O. learned about kicking holes and punching walls, expensive lessons, and he now practices solid maintenance with Sonny busting things up the past year or more.

Sonny pulls out his chair, sits, rhythmically bangs his head against his table, gets up, walks to the wall, nails it a very light one two punch, no dent, another one two punch, no dent, each fist mimics a gut punch but lightly taps the wall instead of a heavy punch banging a hole in it. He pulls it back just as his knuckles touch the wall, perfect fist control, then he walks in a tight circle, sits down again, bangs his head on the table three times then stares out the window. His eyes glaze over. A thousand-yard stare emerges.

K.O. appears in the doorway, briefly, and backs away and watches for a few minutes then punches a button on his phone.

Sonny repeats the series again, his body lock steps like a robot. He appears unaware of the sit and stand, the circle steps, the punches, the head bang, the stare, but repeats it over, and over. He sits, bangs his forehead on the table three times, stares, stands, circles, punches a one two combination at the wall twice, and sits again, his head bangs the table three times during each routine. Sonny continues this repetitious behavior until the ERT arrives. He rejects Officer Mike, struggles, pulls away, repeats the wall and circle behavior. Mike and K.O. team up, forcing him outside, across the parking lot.

*

"He refused his meds." That's all the court needs. Willow signs the admit order, the saddest thing she's ever done. She feels like she betrayed Sonny, though she knows it's best for his health.

Deputy Mike leads Sonny back to the ERT van once more and stops, pulls the door open. Sonny stands in one spot, walking in place, up step, up step, up step, up step, alternating his feet. An extremely confused Sonny points his eyes at the dirt, predicting an overnight jail cell and three fruitless days in the clinic. Mike eases Sonny up into the van. Sonny lies down on the stretcher, stares out the window at daylight. He settles down a little once the cuffs bite into his wrists and the straps cross his chest. He contains his emotions, but his glare packs more power than any punch. K.O. and Willow both look away, steeped in sadness. His eyes lock again and glaze over, his mind empty, no spirit, no soul. Brain dysfunction steals his heart. Aliens suck him dry.

Maybe Stanton will unlock the cell. You can break his nose again. The demon whispers, filling itself with glee.

Sonny lies on the stretcher, thumping his head on the pillow, lift it, drop it, lift it, drop it, his eyes stare straight up, locked on vacant. His feet attempt a walk motion, but the leg and chest bands anchor him horizontal so his feet just wiggle instead, and his forehead alternately pushes and releases the strap, as if still banging the table, and his arms flex and relax, flex and relax, as if punching the walls in a boxing rhythm. Sonny remains mute during the entire trip.

*

The processing clerk checks her screen and looks up. "Here, these forms, you have to fill these out," she says. "Whoops, wait a minute, Sonny has no insurance now. The policy expired."

"Same as last week both times, so what do we do this time?" Willow asks. "Admissions shredded those and sent us here, *AFTER* we already filled out the same paperwork earlier you're giving us now."

"Right, processing did it, if you have insurance. You don't, he doesn't," she says.

"Go sit in there and talk to the self-pay and financial coordinator desk."

"We did that last time too. Can't you use the same forms he signed?"

"Ask them," she points, "it's not my job. I'm processing, they're financials, inside that room." She points again, turns back to her screen. She wiggles her fingers, motioning the next couple forward.

Willow sits in a room, awaiting her turn to speak with the financials clerk.

K.O. walks out and finds the security room again, looks in through the glass port. Sonny spins in circles, randomly walks back and forth, then suddenly punches the wall twice, softly, a one-two each time, then sits on the floor and thumps his head against the wall behind him, thump, thump, thump. He smiles at the locked door, his eyes glazed and vacant.

He stops and starts, wraps his arms around his head a minute, then thumps, thumps, thumps his head again, and again. He smiles at the locked door. Stands up, circles the room again, two steps and turns left, two steps and turns left, two steps and turns left, punches the wall twice in a four step sequence, left right and left right, and sits on the floor again, thumps his head three times against the wall, a repetitive action syndrome, compulsive and impulsive. Sonny behaves like a robot with a crossed circuit, his brain randomly mixing hormones and signals, an organic soup sparking odd behaviors that feel normal inside his mind. He smiles at the locked door, pushes up off the floor again, and repeats the sequence.

*

K.O. returns and tells Willow about Sonny and, after three applicants complete the papers and leave, both settle into chairs across the desk from a nervous and jumpy financial evaluations clerk.

The clerk drums his fingers on his desk. He picks up a pen, puts it down, picks it up again, tugs at his tie, removes his glasses, slides his glasses back into place, waves K.O. and Willow into a chair even though both sat before his signal.

He licks his lips twice, and says, "Well, no insurance, we need to fill out these papers, and these too, stating lack of employment, and his work history, and show bank statements that Sonny has very limited funds. And we need this declaration that he has no insurance with any employer or private coverage, or if he has parents, certify they have no dependent rider." Adam D. Adams III takes a breath and grins.

"And we write all that in five minutes, and carry all those documents around with us just in case of an emergency, while Sonny bangs his head against the wall! Get real!" K.O. unloads his frustration on a clerk that simply abides the rules.

Anyone describing an office wimp could use this clerk as a model, an attempt at helpful but a bureaucratic brainstem wearing a health care worker suit and unable to change his patterns. His nerves get the best of him and he squirms around on his seat, crossing and uncrossing his legs as if afraid he might slip off the chair if he sits quietly, a very odd character, but not yet a complete jerk like some.

Willow jumps in again, reading the nametag. "But he's sick, Mister Adams, he's thrashing around in that room banging his head against the wall – he's hurt. Why can't someone help him while we do this?"

"We have to figure out who pays first."

"But we know some organization will pay, it's the law in an ER. It just depends which grant department picks it up this time, right?" Willow again nearly in tears, her frustrations leak out. "We've done this before, last time, twice in fact."

"Got to do it every time, things change." A nervous grin passes over his face then disappears. The clerk frowns, taps the pen on the desktop, and points it at a form, seven pages. "If you come again, copy it all this time and we'll only need the admit form if nothing changes." He looks over his shoulder, lowers his voice. "Don't tell anyone I said that."

"Then why can't you just copy what we brought last time?" Frustration grabs K.O. again but he holds it back as best he can. Expressing his annoyance won't help Sonny.

"Because you have to give it to us, we can't assume it's the same. He might have insurance now, or changed carriers, or got a job." Pen taps, taps, taps, Adams adjusts his tie, pats his hair.

Willow looks at the first set. "We just filled this out in the other room, same forms. She said 'no good', and shredded those. Why couldn't we bring them here?"

Adams taps his pen. "Well she had to watch you sign. No good if you bring it from somewhere else. We can't see you sign it there." He states that fact as if it sounds normal, and not absurd, as if it makes sense.

K.O. leans in closer, as if confiding, "Or, he could've strangled his rich old aunt and got her house and all the drug deal money since we left that other office three minutes ago."

K.O. pushes out his scare-eyes, in case it works, "And, he gets her cat, too, Jezebel." He flexes and relaxes, clenching his jaw. Torn between getting these forms finished and a desire to lift this wimp off his feet and illustrate how it might benefit him physically if he finishes this immediately, or skips it until later. K.O. struggles within himself because he knows in this situation a physical altercation will slow things down and only hurt Sonny. This clerk would probably just drop his pen and pass out, no benefit gained here from that tactic.

"I know he needs a doctor, but we need to know who pays first. We have to do the paperwork. Only takes a few minutes."

K.O. leans in, a low growl in his words, "Already been forty-two minutes in this ER and you don't even have his name wrote down on that page yet. Good thing he's only flipping out instead of bleeding out, ain't it?"

Adams stops shuffling the papers, looks at K.O., then looks at Willow, looks at K.O. again, looks back at Willow. "Well, we can skip the bank statements for now. You probably don't have those with you."

The clerk smiles then frowns, and tap, tap, taps the pen again. He glances at Willow. His eyes track a fat tear down her cheek. "Okay, here, we know him, he's been here a few times, fill his name and the contact stuff, promise me you'll copy and bring this information back to me today, before midnight, and I'll check him in with a state aid payout." He hands her a list and a stack of papers. "Promise?"

Willow nods her agreement, wipes her eyes, and grabs the list. K.O. quickly fills out the contact information, hands it back.

"And here, a HIPAA release for Mister Bones to sign, or I can't even take his papers from you." The clerk crosses his legs again and removes his glasses, then tap, tap, taps his pen on the desktop. "And the doctor won't talk to you either." Adams grins, a rapid twist of his lips twice, then stares at K.O., the lips become a flat line.

Adams holds up his hand as both rise to leave. "You know, it's really a problem for our clinics too, the payment. Federal law says the ER clinics must treat everyone, paid or not, insurance or not. Many people come in every day with no insurance, and no payment. They come in because they have no insurance and we must treat them, even kids with a minor illness, a cold, sniffles, a cut finger, and they know it, but the kids are sick and parents have nowhere else to go. Never pay a thing."

"Our doctors and nurses truly want to help people, but we have families too, and mortgages, and kids. MBA's with no medical training decide treatment, and count pennies instead of medical need. We exist in a Catch-22 world today – damned if we don't, broke and damned if we do."

"Hard to fix it, nearly impossible, and we're lucky if we collect thirty percent on our billings over a year."

"My assistant is out for a week, and I'm the director here. I know about these problems, but can't do much. We're short staff, and I take over when anyone's out for any reason. Sick, vacation, or training, it's always me."

"The kids are sick. We're doctors. We want to heal people."

He frowns, his frustration evident.

Surprising and caring words come out of Adam D. Adams III and tweak both sides of a very tough issue in health care. "Go take care of Sonny. I'll take care of this paperwork. Just make sure you bring back copies okay, or I'll be the one in trouble with the Medical Director." He glances down at his badge then back up at Willow and grins. The badge reads: Medical Director - Dr. Adam D. Adams. He shuffles his too few papers into a stack. "You promise, right?"

Willow nods her head and means it.

35

After communicating by phone and email numerous times, Willow and Cat meet face to face for the first time in an office at the park headquarters where Willow works. The clinic had returned an evaluation form that listed Willow as his contact. Two coffee cups sit between them.

Cat explains why she wants Sonny in her program. She spreads some information flyers out on the table, but it's only a chore that keeps her hands busy as she gathers her thoughts. She needs no notes or reminders to prime these discussions. Her theory and her work descriptions lie on the table, but Cat understands it completely. She needs nothing but the knowledge already inside her brain for these discussions.

Cat says, "So, you read that info I sent about the lemon, poison, demons and Ferguson, and how his mind fills the holes in his memory recall and his conscious mind with variations of other memories. Sounds very similar to what Sonny experiences according to clinic files and your notes, his mental images seem distorted and he communicates with aliens and demons."

Willow nods her agreement.

Always excited when she discusses her methods and goals, Cat explains, "We all communicate internally, inside our minds, we use a mental voice and vision, sort of a spirit inside our consciousness. We all do it, and we all have it."

"That voice and vision generates an inner awareness, we compile all memories and experiences from the time we can remember events. Although we cannot consciously recollect every memory all the time, we can recall any single event or related events we need when we need it. We all do that. Our personal mental video. We don't always pay it attention," both women smile, "but we all hear it and see it."

Cat stands up and walks around the table and chairs, stretches, spins on her toes, caught up in her narrative, she paces from one end of the room to the other, back and forth, back and forth. She refills the cups to keep her hands occupied, as if activity calms her thoughts, allowing her a continuous monologue.

"You read it. As we travel through life, neuron circuits in the brain collect every physical or mental experience and, through its interpretation of our senses – see, hear, touch, smell, taste – it creates our individual memories and combines those memories with immediate sensory input. That's our daily experience as we wander through life."

"We use these memories to make decisions about every activity we choose during our lives, but one brain component rules all others, the primal instinct – survival. The strongest of all brain activities pushes every other behavior out of its way and protects itself first and foremost. Survival, the most powerful behavior stimulator of all, and it's passed down biologically to every human offspring. Survival over-rules any social activity, especially ones that appear as a danger or a threat to the body or brain, even if it's not truly a danger. The brain defaults to the defensive strategies and the body protects itself and its brain until it decides. And the brain maintains primary control in all actions that we physically engage in our lives."

"But, a normal brain can learn to overcome those instincts with conscious choice, which combines information from our senses and our memories, and the learning process, and then decides what actions we need. So, even when instinct automatically triggers a defensive behavior, we can consciously choose a different response or we can decide it's a false threat."

Willow wrinkles her brow, puzzled. "I never studied brain thought process and motivation theory in quite this way,' she says. "I follow the biology so far but, I'm ready for a break." She opens the fridge, pulls out two salads and some juice.

Cat grabs a fork, spikes lettuce between words. "Okay, I have to leave soon anyway. We'll keep filling it in as we go. I'd like to meet Sonny, follow up on all these notes and put a person with his name. We only know him as field reports so far and would love to change that."

"We're picking Sonny up from the clinic again tomorrow. It's probably better we do that alone, without you. Give him a chance to settle in at home first."

Cat nods her agreement.

*

Willow signs his release and escorts Sonny back to the gym for the tenth time in the past year or so. She talks about a new researcher she met. "Doctor Morgantholavich wants to speak with you about medications and the aliens and spooks you see and hear."

"Pretty weird name, is she an alien too? Sounds like it."

"She goes by Doctor Cat." Willow explains Cat's interest, and that she's not a practicing psychiatrist, like Anderson, but a specialist that works at her own research clinic out of state, near Boston. "She hopes you'll explain some things about your brain so she can help you and others like you to control the anger you feel and settle those aliens and demons."

"Just a couple meetings," Willow almost begs him to agree. "She's very nice, not adversarial like some others, nothing like Anderson, nothing like Morton and some clinic workers."

Sonny cups both ears, walks back and forth, his face scrunched with worry. *Don't meet her, she's an alien, she'll feed you poison like the rest. Willow lies!*

"Shut up. Leave me alone," he speaks quietly, as if only to himself and his spook. The medications help a little, not enough, but at least he can still deny its orders if not the anger it sparks.

Sonny stops, looks at Willow. "Okay, will meet her once and decide, that good enough?"

When his brain functions correctly, he knows Willow does everything with his best interest at heart. He wants to please her and K.O. whenever he can and right now, the meds work minimally as he's been in the clinic several days. His body continues filtering out the sedatives too, but it takes a little time.

Willow pulls out her phone, and Sonny sets an appointment

with this new doctor in an office Cat borrowed at the town center.

If she talks boring, or if she acts like all the others, making lists and checking boxes, he'll bail out and run downstairs, shoot some hoops, work up a sweat. Sonny decides it's a good idea, and he needs a little practice under the basket anyway, so he can't lose.

The clinic confinement allows little time for exercise. Push-ups and sit-ups work a few muscles but leave him with unreleased energy and stress. Sonny closes the phone, and hits the running trail, the first thing on his schedule every time he leaves the clinic.

K.O. and Sonny climb into the ring. "Okay, let's take it easy, you been in the clinic a while." Lucas and few gym rats stop working out, sit and watch.

Sonny spots a demon sitting on the ring post, turns away, takes a few warm up jabs at air then walks over to the corner, pokes a fist at the spook. It floats out of reach. Sonny gears up, ignores the demon presence. Pushing all the accumulated stress out, he comes up to speed quickly, both men sweating heavily in ten minutes.

Sonny jabs six in a row then throws rights and lefts, an uppercut follows. K.O. keeps batting the punches sideways, watching carefully, knows Sonny might want to prove something today. All his fighters eventually show a 'beat the trainer' confidence. K.O. never had a problem before, not even with Jake Archer, his first and only Olympic medal winner.

K.O. always blocks everything, speed and experience winning over youth and enthusiasm, and K.O. has the most heart and confidence, years of it.

Sonny developed a unique style, and he has very, very fast hands, the fastest hands K.O. has ever trained.

The demon hovers back on the post and shrieks from across the ring. *Punch him!*

A mean look kicks up into his eyes, his forehead wrinkles and a muscle knots, the rage and torment reveals itself bit by bit as Sonny speeds up the action. A left jab K.O. bats away, a right cross K.O bats away. Another jab series, very quick, K.O. dances sideways this time and bats each punch away, slides the ropes.

Sonny pushes hard now, determined he will hit K.O. and teach him a lesson this time, and swings harder and faster, tries a few new tricks he worked out alone that K.O. knows nothing about yet.

The mat dance continues, both men circle the ring, slide the ropes, bob, weave, strike, and bat punches away. Two feather-light touches brush past, a close tip at the peak of his chin, but nothing solid and first time between them. Sonny comes on very strong, grunts each time he swings, left, right, left right, left, right, almost losing it and swinging wildly but still in control, slowly losing his temper. Both men drip sweat.

K.O. survived on the streets, in this gym, and in a tough boxing world all these years, and hides a few tricks of his own in his personal fight box. He calls upon all his experience during the last six minutes of this workout and, as Sonny loses focus and clearly drops down into the brutality of street fighting and hurt, the killing game, punching harder, and grunting.

K.O. finally drops his hands and says, "Enough Sonny, take ten."

The trainer never observed that kind of rage in Sonny before, and again, it sparks a bit of worry, as Sonny seems lost in a different world, stalking the ring as if nothing will interfere with a final confrontation here. Sonny takes another step toward K.O., and K.O. wraps him up, pushes Sonny against the ropes, then into a corner. Sonny struggles, tries to push out of the powerful embrace but K.O. holds Sonny tight in the corner until the anger and frustration release.

"Take it easy Sonny, relax. We're not here to hurt anyone."

Sonny stands there in the embrace, rigid, breathing hard, watching two nasty spooks fly away, hide up in the heat vents and ductwork as his imagination plays complicated tricks on his consciousness.

K.O. releases his grip, pulls away.

Sonny turns around and punches the posts three times with each glove, then drops his fists and walks away with his head down, splits the ropes, climbs out and heads for the showers.

Lucas asks, "Whoa, what's that all about K.O?"

"Nothing, no worries." K.O. worries anyway.

36

Meeting Sonny for the first time, Doctor Cat shakes his hand, offers him a seat and a bottle of orange juice, his favorite drink. She read a partial file before leaving her main office in Boston, a file the court and his clinics supplied, and supplemental information, and releases Willow and K.O. signed off. An incomplete file unfortunately, as complete files are difficult to obtain, especially on short notice. HIPAA protects much of it. She read everything the clinics sent. Her staff processed a signature card and mailed it to every clinic, nurse, and doctor that treated Sonny, as it did with four other patients she wants for this independent clinical study, five subjects.

Many clinics take too long with a response if it sends one at all. She's particularly interested in the notes from Anderson, who treated Sonny the longest. He failed to respond so far, and Willow believes he probably will not send his records, and she cannot force it.

Although she never met Anderson or his colleagues, she's read some of his 'required for a license' publishing and judged it 'unprofessional' and full of 'blow hard fluff'. Her best information comes from personal observations K.O. and Willow recorded, and a few notes from Sonny while the guardian release was in force.

Cat has a good idea about the Sonny Bones he shows everyone, but wants to know the secret Sonny, the one that hides in darkness and fears his world. She hopes she can help him fix that part, but needs face-to-face interaction and trust first. The rest of him is good as it gets, a great young adult, but truly locked in a tragic life.

Sonny and Doctor Cat bat a few introductory phrases around, breaking the ice, testing the water. Then Cat moves on to the reasons she's here, probing the tricks of brain chemistry and memory, the upsets in biological balance that create such heartbreak in young adults and families. She describes the concepts that drive her passion.

"It's not often I meet a client with great physical skills and knows a heavy workout knocks out those aliens. Good thing you figured that out, huh? Sure helps you beat those nasty dudes, right, keeps them off your back."

Sonny stares at her, his eyes widen in disbelief, the first doctor that admits she understands his mind, the first that believes he sees and hears demons and aliens, and makes no fun of it. Then his paranoia kicks in. "So, how'd you know that, you read my mind too? What, you another alien?"

"Nope, no alien here, I'm a brain doctor. I know how a mind works."

"Read my mind, knew about orange juice. How'd you know it?"

"I asked Willow, it's not complicated or tricky. We don't sneak around hiding stuff." She grins, a great smile. "We're not creepy old doctors like in the movies."

Sonny says nothing, watching her, comparing her to Willow. Definitely not creepy, or old, like he thought she might be. A voice barks in his ear. He drops and runs fifty push-ups on his knuckles, counts it out, jumps up, sits back in the chair, wanting no alien interrupting the moment. Wants to explore this new doctor, see what makes her tick, see if she may be different, if she respects 'nut kids'. He grins, waits for her comment.

"Something bothering you? Aliens ganging up on you? That why you ran those push-ups just now? Sends it away, right? Kicks it out the door, gone?"

"Maybe I just like to work out in a doctor's office, feels pretty good. Not like a gym floor, carpet got nice padding, easy on the knuckles."

Cat keeps her eyes locked on his. "Maybe, maybe not, but it helps, doesn't it. Kills the stress, those workouts, sweat lowers the voices, fades the faces. Helps you ignore the orders, right?"

Sonny squirms in his seat, her frankness a bit challenging, different. No one else believes him. "Everyone tells me I'm making it up."

She looks about twenty-two, maybe a year or two older, could easily stick her in a spot he once reserved for Willow now that Willow fits in his life as a sister or extra mom. Always did actually, but lately he accepts it as a fact, despite two years older, and now more experienced when he includes Lisa and Melanie in his world of women.

Lisa filled that spot few months ago, briefly but very nicely. She took off, gone now, attending college at Berkeley. Cat the doctor, must be a little older, finished college and all, probably same age as Willow, at least. Too bad for him but maybe not, Sonny never gives up.

Those hormones that burn his brain and tweak his mental videos originate in his reproductive biology. Doctor Carter explained it last time, at the clinic. Every woman he meets interests him at this point, especially Melanie. That wonder word 'hope' still lives in his word basket, sticks itself back into his life whenever he calls it.

Might be trouble if Willow made a mistake though, and Doctor Cat turns out just another alien trying to fool him. No aliens hang in her ears, or hide in her hair, a good sign. He trusts Willow, but not quite ready to give up his life story yet, not to a stranger. Tread easy, see if she gives up her life first. "So, how old are you?"

Cat keeps her eyes on his. Each man she meets, even a young adult like Sonny, thinks first of her as a woman second as a doctor. Never fails, never changes, but she tunes it out. She goes with what she has, one attractive researcher confronting a challenge. Dead serious about her work though, always. She bore no biological children, but she mothers every patient as if she gave each one birth through some indefinable non-physical method. She cries real tears for the pain each feels as well, even Ferguson and Nickels as violent as both men behave.

No busting out of her t-shirt either, though her trim, fit body pushes the clothes she wears in all the right directions. Nothing she can do about that either, wear a bag maybe?

"I turned thirty-four last month." No evasion, direct

answers work best, she learned that fact from personal experience.

Sonny frowns at his error, ten years off. "You're kidding."

"Nope, not cheating a day and much too old for you." Cat interprets his body language easily. Cat the expert, Sonny the novice. "I know how teenage minds work too, especially young men your age."

She flashes even white teeth, a small chip in one incisor, mars this otherwise perfect female, a small scar on her left cheek adds character.

Aliens limit perfection, Sonny believes, at least the one that haunts him the hardest, perfection would give it away, so it makes itself all weird and spacey, they all do.

Almost perfect fits fine in his world, good enough anyway. Not cute exactly, not beautiful, not pretty, but not plain either, just an aura about her that sets her apart from all other women. It sets her apart as an individual, almost as if her upbeat character creates an aliveness that illustrates a humanistic bond between Doctor Cat and everyone she meets, male or female, normal and abnormal.

Males address it differently than females, and Cat has fought that battle all her adult life, a few times as a teen. But everyone recognizes that special character within her that makes her a great doctor, one that believes in healing above all else though most never define it in exactly those words.

Sonny believes her, senses her honesty, her passion, mostly because she hits right on target about his thoughts at this particular moment, but wonders if she really can read his mind. She sure knows what he was thinking. Sonny stares, frees his concentration, caught up in fantasy for the moment. His grin and eyes give it away.

A young maturing male compares Doctor Cat and Willow Parks, drops Lisa in there briefly too, and Melanie. Glad at least some hormones don't eat his brain as he experiences a surge of pleasure when the womanly parts pause for inspection and Sonny enjoys the examination. After a minute, he stares at the wall, lost briefly in his own masculine world.

Cat calls him back. "It's in our genes, my family tree. That's exactly what we should talk about today, my genes and your genes. We both have genes. Every human gets half from each parent. Genes makes us tick, and grow, and colors our eyes and hair, and most important, lets us think and behave in specific ways. Some of our genes, yours and mine, might even be the same family a long time ago."

"Irish and German and Swedish blood in you maybe, looks like it, lot of Swede in you maybe. Half my family came from Ireland too, a few generations ago, and mixed with Russian, the other half. So, what do you say? We talk about us today, our family bloodlines – our genes, what we have in common. What makes you a great boxer, and what makes you angry, and what makes you laugh or cry, what brings on the rage."

Sonny spaces out for a moment, lost in his thoughts. Tie score so far, but Willow maybe wins it by default, extra points for sticking by him in tough times, and never ratted him out in the park campsite. Course the sister-mom issue might take some points away too, only one or two. Sonny suddenly wishes his life contained a few more years, little extra experience with women. Tagging on a little age and wisdom would help.

Doctor Cat wins a few points for speaking directly. Willow and Cat tie again, despite her 'too old for you' comment that turns him off a little until he discovered she really is too old for him. Lisa scores more points than any female, ever, but she moved on and chased her dream. No winning it from a distance, least when Sonny makes up his own rules, after all, in his contest he picks the winner. Melanie pops into his head, pops out again, the Lisa memories flit through.

Cat asks him again. "Want to talk about it? Our genes, how we're built, how our biology functions I mean, not my age."

Not ready yet, Sonny won't give himself up that easily, been traveling down this road alone too long. Counselors, doctors, nurses never believe him. Always recite the same repetitive story, no spitting meds, no punching walls, no hurting patients, sleep now in the dark, wake now in the light, watch the clock tick and eat now, completely boring activities for an adolescent coming of age and full of sexual energy.

No life, no excitement, no connection exists between his life and the care clinics offer. More important though, no drugs for his alien delusions – just medications that cure nothing but always meet a schedule. Even K.O. and Willow, his favorite and most trusted friends believe he imagines demons that do not really exist.

One suddenly appears. A misty shadow barely whispers. *Don't trust her. She's not a friend.*

Sonny shuts his eyes, holds his breath, shuts it off and says, "Okay, you first."

"Let's get out of here, it's too stuffy." Cat steps around the desk, peels off her doctor jacket and reveals light green above-the-knee running shorts, a matching tight knit work-out blouse, and dark green Nike running shoes on the smallest feet Sonny's ever seen on a grown woman. Cat ties a sweatband around her hair, its color matching her shoes.

Combination looks cool enough, Sonny admires her choice a minute, decides it looks neat and stylish rather than the color conscious rural teenage environment of caps that slew sideways, over-sized shirts that hang near the knees, and pants that bag and slide off.

Sonny grins at her outfit, wishes now he wore his new sweats, the gray set with wide blue stripes stitched down the thighs and end in a sharp flair. Instead, he wore his old black basketball shorts and an orange tee shirt with its sleeves ripped off. He guessed wrong, guessed that he would skip chatting with this doctor and wind up shooting hoops.

Figures now he made the wrong choice in clothing today, but it's no bother to Cat it seems, so Sonny ignores it. Decides he'll choose different clothes next time, and dress himself a little less raggedy. She's worth it so far, even if a little older than she looks. Sonny hides a grin.

Cat points her flat round key guard at a dark green Volkswagen Beetle she bought four years ago from a fellow med student at Harvard. He upgraded the bug then dropped out of school and had to sell it. His loss, her gain, and she loves it. The locks pop open. She unhooks the ragtop and pushes it down inside the rear hatch, and slides in behind the wheel. The license plate reads DR CAT.

Sonny guesses her favorite color easily. Green eyes, green car, green clothes, green shoes. Her obsession. He pushes that note back into his mind for later if he ever needs it. If he ever buys her a gift, find the weirdest, wildest, craziest green shade he can and see how she likes them apples. "A green apple," he says softly. His logic pulls up a smile. He climbs in, slams the door, opens it, steps out, climbs in again, and shuts it gently. "Sorry."

Cat notes his obsessive-compulsive action, but says nothing, twists the ignition, shifts into gear, dumps the clutch, chirps the tires. Acceleration pushes Sonny back in his seat, surprising for such a neat little bug.

"Cool!" Sonny says, admiring the smooth leather interior and shining chrome gauges. A black eight-ball tops the shift lever, four on the floor. Cat winds it up, spins it out, and Sonny spouts, "Neat."

Not the 'too sweet' look of a light blue sixty-seven GMC pickup, nor the 'too sweeter' sound of a throaty short-block burble, nor the 'awesome beauty' of a sleek grey metallic sport pickup born the same year as Sonny that he bought six months ago. He grants it the solitary and individual 'cool and neat' of a well-kept and very functional car that sits a few steps below a classic pickup truck on his personal favorites list. One thing for sure, the engines run forever.

Air-cooled system makes it a little tougher in summer though. He wonders if the Volkswagen is a seventy-three, and if so, if Cat bought it to match her birth year too, just like Sonny and K.O. Something in common. Sonny likes something in common, hopes he guessed right figuring the years and ages of people and vehicles. Adds a few points on the friend score he adds onto or subtracts off everyone he meets.

He taps the dash, "What year?"

"Seventy-nine, last year of the original Beetle. So, where can we run around here?"

Nope, not in common, wrong year, only twenty-eight, six years younger than Cat. She looks twenty-eight though, could pass for it easily, and get away with it, but Sonny grins at the odd woman that offers a challenge every minute since he met her. She stops at a tee in the road, aims her eyes toward Sonny, humps her shoulders. Sonny points his nose left. The bug chirps its tires and Cat circles left.

"Bike trail across state park got runs staked out. Three miles for wimps, ten if you got the wind, but we can stop anytime you need a rest." Sonny sticks a great big grin on his face and aims it directly at Cat. Right out front Sonny sets his own challenge, the growing up ways of a teenage man-boy hoping it proves him able and normal, but still very mindful of that doctor tag pinned on her coat back at the office.

Cat laughs out loud, "Show me the ten." A big grin brightens her face. She pulls through a gate and into a dirt parking lot, shuts it down, drags up the top, and locks it.

Sonny aims his jog toward a slot in the trees. Cat catches up immediately. He lets Cat set the pace and she sets one a little quicker than he figured, but no problem for his running skills and wind. A ten-mile trail winds through the forest. Three deer, one rabbit, two cats, a stray dog, a pond and two fields, more birds than they count, a few additional test sprints near the end, and an hour and a half later, both runners sit on a park bench catching breath and chatting, casually building a friendship.

Two athletes begin a bonding, sharing the pleasures of physical exertion, working off stress as it emerges through two identical bio-systems but at different levels and with different results in each body. Only Cat understands it. Although instinct and training drive his pace, Sonny always saves wind and sprints toward the finish, but he held back, and matched her pace instead.

The odd reality though, Cat knows it but says nothing.

It blows his aliens off too, at least for the moment. Still happens when he runs hard, just been a little tougher lately, takes a little longer and a faster clip, more miles. The spook comes and goes often, usually hours between events and even a full day occasionally, but it comes back stronger each time.

Both sweating profusely, Doctor Cat almost kept up with him today but he held back a bit toward the end, the last mile when he usually pours it on, he let her believe she can stay with him, let her feel the burn. A nice woman so far, Sonny likes Doctor Cat. She makes him feel good, so he makes her feel good too if he can. She definitely wins a few more points today though, great physical effort.

Sonny shows her his smile and the sweat dripping off his upper lip. She shows hers too, both the smile and the sweat, and impressive run for a female doctor.

"Okay. Let's talk about genes." Cat settles in. Doctor Morgantholavich begins her work.

37

Cat and Willow sit in the café, coffee cups full and hot. Jones Johnson walks in and joins them. Cat offers him her hand. "Good you brought his files; Sonny has lots and lots of history."

Willow includes Johnson in her discussion, brings him up to date, explains the last release meeting, the pushup challenge Sonny pulled on the clinic staff, the illegal Mexicans and the smart gorilla-guerillas, the way Sonny creates an alien culture to explain his mental images, and justifies what Sonny shared during the meeting when the clinic released him a few days ago.

Cat explains some of the behavior surrounding his life and ideas that motivate how he functions. "Sonny makes extreme logical jumps. Say a social worker claims he 'works on Sonny', and the staff nods and agrees. The social worker logs all these hours 'working on him', but without contact. If Sonny sees each person minimally in his life, then his logic tells him the counselors use mental powers on him, read his mind, or transmit orders into his mind in ways that are invisible, at least to him. That explains how a person 'works on him' without Sonny meeting with the social worker."

"He perceives his life differently than we do ours, and differently that we perceive his, so he organizes his internal world to explain what he sees and hears externally. He includes his unreal notions in it, otherwise he can't act in the social events, or activities, can't understand the distortions in his memory and in his conscious mind."

"Remember, as happens with mental illness typically, Sonny thinks in black and white definitions, and interprets words and sayings in literal translations. Even though his brain hears and sees it in real time, distortions in his brain chemistry push the true meaning aside, and the disconnections often interfere with his perceptions as his brain organizes his memories, and direct sensory input, and his thinking process."

Willow says, "When Sonny entered a hearing room a few weeks ago, the judge told him to 'Please take your seat.' Sonny asked the judge, 'Which one is mine and where should I take it?' Everyone laughed, but Sonny was serious. He wanted to obey the judge."

Cat continues, "It makes sense in a weird way, like the way he interprets terms like 'guerrilla' as an ape, and 'illegal alien' out of Mexican immigrants. It becomes a function of language and meaning. The context flies right past Sonny because he may not be present when all this discussion or action occurs, the counseling and discussions between health care workers. He only hears them talk about meetings when they say they 'worked on him' after the fact. It confuses him because he was not there, but they say they worked on him as if he were. So he appraises that as a mental activity - mind-reading - or a mental stimulus wave."

Jones Johnson jumps right in, understands immediately the thrust of her words, he's been here before, in other discussions. "But, what you're saying here happens all over the place and in many types of meetings."

"For example, when you have six social workers sitting around a table drinking coffee, eating muffins, and discussing what Sonny needs or what he does, or how he can be treated, or in some cases controlled. Then we have six hours of counseling time spent working *on* Sonny, and counted, but not one single hour spent *with* him or teaching him or treating him. I wonder how much actual value comes from six counselors in an office talking amongst themselves about one client for an hour."

Cat breaks in. "They shouldn't need that kind of proof at this level, but some find it empowering, particularly the ones that are insecure in the social and psyche fields. They prove to one another they all read it and know it, but it's totally unproductive in the health care world where kids and adults need hands-on training and social skills. The way a health care worker applies that knowledge counts much more than the knowledge itself."

"And why do they do it?" She answers her own rhetorical question. "Because it's more intellectually stimulating when discussing patients among colleagues than spending those hours training or teaching or treating a patient who has difficulty with certain social activities or speech or learning, or controlling anger."

The main cause, biological disconnections, or hormone triggers, or medication side effects, produce mental or physical limitations or distortions. These kids bring less fun to the table, at least in the caseworker minds, and that's the unfortunate part. A beautiful day will dawn when we stop this trauma and bring these kids back to a full and enjoyable lifestyle."

Willow adds, "Now, that's worth talking about."

*

Two days later, after coffee and an egg sandwich each, Jonesy and Sonny walk down to the gym and meet K.O and Willow. Jonesy says, "Derek Morton down-sized out of his job three days ago. According to a notice Director Terri Birch circulated last week, and I quote, '... both Social Worker II positions receive no funding in our annual grant this year.' So he's out the door, gone, and ain't coming back."

Jonesy offers a smile, knowing Terri Birch downsized both level two counselors, Morton and one other cut from the same cloth and just as worthless. "Got some help from someone upstairs, somewhere. Had to, it's not easy to lay-off high seniority employees, pretty tricky what she did, and a little gutsy too."

Birch promoted one excellent Social Worker II to a level three then kept the three employees that now hold the Class III positions, including Jonesy, and whom actually do the best work with young adults. She then cites budget cuts and dismisses both level twos that she wants gone anyway.

Budget reductions hit every organization this year, state and feds, and non-profits sit at the top of the cut lists. Terri manipulated the grant wording and now four existing Social Worker III employees will split the Class II caseloads, and each one gets a small raise, something she wanted to do for a couple years.

Jonesy says, "In addition, the state realigned its districts as well, to help with the budget issue, and we lost ten patients. That means we have four to assist fifty clients instead of six for sixty. It's twelve each plus two, but Terri believes if we take less meeting time and more field time, we can do a better job. She said she misses fieldwork and wants in it again. She assigned two for herself. Cindy and Erik Penrose, it works out for everyone, including the clients."

Janice pops her eyes open wide. Wow, voluntarily taking Erik, she's asking for it, he's a real hand full. Cindy is a real sweetheart and she'll get along great with Terri."

"Morton bitched that his seniority rules over the two employees she kept but his squawk carries little weight, and he's not a level three. He could fight it, but that takes time and he'd probably lose. Guys like Morton usually have no energy for appealing policy or court fights and prefer unemployment anyway."

Pretty slick deal she pulled off, and completely legal. Terri Birch knew Morton performed poorly, and she's been looking for an excuse to fire him for more than two years. Hard to fire poor performers in non-profit health clinics so it leaves many slackers in the industry as well as in government offices and state systems.

"Heard about that a few days ago, talked to Ellie, says she had nothing to do with it. Morton's firing I mean, not the state stuff." K.O. believes her, but knows the more case workers like Morton that leave the system, the better health care the clients will receive.

K.O. knows Judge Archer has little respect for Morton style no-work employees that show up in every business large enough to tolerate it on its workforce, and in many government positions. She claims she did nothing to influence this one.

"Said if she'd thought of it, she would have, but it never occurred to her."

"Yeah," says Cat, grinning, "Don't ask Aaron Clark that question. He won't want to lie about it. The man has juice I had no clue existed. He pushed some issues at the federal budget hearings so the Feds will give more funding at state level for these small rural mental health clinics. Reminds me of the time three Feds came in once, slick suits and new haircuts, and asked him to run for Senator in Massachusetts."

"He laughed for ten minutes and then told them it's like hiring Senator Ted Kennedy to perform heart surgery. Let the politicians run the country and I'll fix its children."

Jonesy holds up a set of papers. "We do have one more problem though. Morton never filed papers on Sonny for assistance and insurance. This should have been done nine months ago, first time he hit the hospital just to start the process. If it's denied later, or if it turns out not as serious as it seems, we can withdraw it."

"At least then it still gets to the approval panel if it turns serious. Sometimes it takes a year for mental illness rulings. It's not as easy to diagnose as a broken arm. Usually takes an appeal, and a ton of paper."

Jonesy lays out the forms, makes sure it's a complete package. "We'll get Sonny in here and fill these out. The only way he'll learn - complete it himself with a little help." He hands Willow the medical sheets. "Can you get Anderson to fill these out and sign, he's the most recent."

Willow folds the document, stuffs it into her back pocket. "Anderson takes forever. He hasn't even sent papers we signed off last month yet."

Cat holds out her hand, "Give me the forms and I'll fill it all out. I already have the pharmacy and clinic reports. It won't take me long and I'll get Carter to consult as lead over in Gatesville and sign off if we need it. Sonny likes him and he's part-time but continuous, instead of in the random rotations."

*

Cat spends three hours a day four days a week for three weeks, a lot of run time and a lot of gym time, and fitness training courtesy of the KNOCKOUT, and flies back to Boston weekends. Sonny learns the basics, the main ideas, fundamental brain biology, and behavior. A very bright student, he gets it quickly, and he read a psychology text from cover to cover months ago in secret, and read all the articles he copied at the library. He lives the symptoms every day, has no problem understanding that part.

He read about activity, counseling, and legal business, not

much biology, too complex, but it gave him the fundamentals so Cat can explain her ideas with some understanding at his end, and so he can explain his emotions and give her what she needs to help him beat his illness. Sonny knows, deep down somewhere in his basic survival biology that something's amiss in his brain and so far he's been successful in over-riding the alien orders and demands. Unable to focus on exactly what fails in his mind, he lifts 'hope' up out of his word basket and applies it to this challenge.

Cat ran with him, worked out at the gym, ate lunch with him, and earned his trust without forcing his acceptance of her as a doctor. Doctors he usually considers as controllers and often aliens in disguise. Cat first became his friend, not something easily accomplished with mental patients. Some never accept it, some pretend to accept it, some never understand what she offers. Sonny finally opens his heart to Cat, shares everything about his mind, and its experiences with aliens.

After the beginning sessions with Sonny, Cat sets up a routine and drives back and forth from Virginia to Boston, rotating her visits between clients in New York, Maryland, Connecticut, and Rhode Island. She selected five patients with the most intensely violent-based symptoms and who use physical exercise to release the stress.

She constantly develops her theory, adds new information, and wants to test this new treatment model on specific cases, so she can monitor and prove its application. She worries about the violence the abundance of hormones provoke when brain biology lacks the proper balance.

A brain presents high emotion levels during stress and release episodes. Cat believes that if a doctor embeds with her patient in the social settings where that patient lives and interacts, she can gain his trust, and the patient will share the complete truth. Once that happens, she can treat that patient with proper medication based on individual reactions at the minute violence releases its anger and the brain calms itself. She wants to evaluate the feelings at that minute, not over a long period that includes up and down emotions, and delayed responses, and inaccurate observations.

She hopes to train others, doctors and nurses, and other caseworkers in the same personal technique and bonding her theory requires. If it works, it works, and well worth it. Everything else today fits in one category - complex attempts that frequently fail.

Her grant committee worries she may injure or kill a patient, or a patient will injure or kill someone else. The tragedy attached to this condition requires researchers to take precautions as well as chances, as long as those chances remain transparent and her patients remain well informed, and well supervised.

Cat won her legal argument and patients now have the right to treatment using her theories if one chooses, she often wonders and questions her underlying motives. The philosophy behind using sick teens to save sick teens bothers her. She predicts great results if she finds success with these kids, and decides it violates no ethical or moral grounds as long as she maintains full disclosure with parents and guardians. It worries her regardless.

Cat needs to know the emotion exactly when the rage breaks, and exactly what the patient senses when the violence disengages, and how that transition takes place in the mind and the brain – at the exact minute the patient feels the rage release. She needs that specific moment, why and how it happens. What joy comes to the brain when it releases anger and the body achieves comfort or bliss instead of rage or violence?

She wants to know if pushing hard physically wears off the defensive chemistry and the body relaxes in its absence, or if the body produces a different hormone that increases the joy and bliss component and overcomes the fright chemistry. Her main objective - understanding how that chemistry and communication act within the brain - will result in greater knowledge about how chemical processing and electronic communication take place inside an abnormal brain.

She believes if the patients trust her enough she can get blood samples that illustrate the chemistry at that exact moment too, which gives her primary data and provides her dosage calculations, and allows individual formulations. She and Aaron founded CAT-RON Technologies three years ago with that goal in mind.

Her theory extends psychiatric and biological boundaries into areas never before examined, and one CAT-RON project explores a shielded mini-coder a surgeon can temporarily embed in a brain. It can send data over a WIFI signal that gives her the exact chemical readings at any moment of stress or relaxing in the brain. Almost like a tiny alien mind reader, and she grins as this thought passes through her brain. Sonny may be more accurate than he knows. Cat wonders at his insight. The parallels Sonny draws often amuse her in an odd sense, the aliens, the guerillas, the illegal Mexicans, and now he's predicted her mind-reading technology.

In one interesting development, Cat evaluated the Stark facility inmates in her original studies, two experienced a softening in violent actions with an individual medications package she and Aaron created, and two became more violent. One remains the same, minimally violent at times, but never explosive like Ferguson or Nickels.

In her field notes, she attributes age as a factor in two failed cases, and deterioration in the brain over the years. Both men approached forty at the beginning of the study, and had been treated medically only occasionally and for brief periods each time over the entire lifetime.

Those two that had reduced violent tendencies and thoughts were under thirty-five, but still advanced enough in the disease that an extreme and uncontrollable urge to commit violence emerged frequently.

She wants the youngest patients possible, late adolescents, because the disease begins exhibiting its symptoms in males at that age. She can begin her chemical intervention prior to the neuron damage that occurs as a person ages. Concerned the meds might not curtail violence even in younger patients, Cat holds out hope that treatment at a younger age affects the results as a definable and positive characteristic when treating the violence that eventually presents in every case she includes in her project.

38

Sonny stands up every few minutes, grunts, breaks a branch, and tosses it on the fire, keeping his physical activity working minimally for now. This evening two aliens hover above the campfire, a large one and a small one hanging in a tree, both more smoke than spook. Not as strong as usual, but float out there, building substance, gaining strength. He just drove in after lifting iron at the gym and weakening the hallucinations, but he needs more and more workouts lately, longer too, with heavier weights, and more often.

Cat steps into the clearing. "I thought you might be here. I stopped by the gym earlier. Did you forget we had a time set?"

"Oops, yes forgot, sorry Cat. Been less organized than usual lately, lots of stuff kicking around in my brain. Sometimes I forget things after taking these meds if I don't write it down." Sonny busts another limb. "Willow bought me a small notebook – helps some, if I can remember first to write in it." He laughs at himself. "Then gotta remember to open it and read it."

This evening the larger alien pushes hard. Even the small misty one speaks in grating voice and both float a dim but mean face, and even after his gym time, the vision remains. Sonny balances burning out the aliens with courtesy toward Cat.

He stands up, busts another limb, another, then sits again. Stands again and circles the campsite several times, then sits once more. Jumps up, runs a set of twenty-five pushups. Sits on his stump. "Sometimes, aliens get the best over my workouts lately."

Sonny increases his trust in her as time together slowly

loosens him up a little and he shares more of his mental issues. Her physical abilities impress him and he admires her pace, not many can run in his league.

Bright, entertaining, and very smart, Cat never speaks down to Sonny, unlike many health care workers at the clinics. She carries patience and hope everywhere she goes and shares it in every conversation. Last meeting or two, he allowed Cat a peek into his brain and how it feels when anger strikes, and how it feels when physical exercise pushes the demons away. Not easy, revealing his soul, hanging it out there on a weak, flimsy stick, unprotected, while each individual brain wave pauses for dissection. Nope, never easy.

Sonny feels lucky he has three people in his life that earned his complete trust. Count Lisa, she makes four, but she moved on. Sonny misses Lisa and leaves the trust friend count at three for the present, one small obsessive-compulsion he recognizes but engages occasionally without meaning it. He counts his trust friends and gives each value points for positive interactions, and subtracts for negatives. He has no control over it, it happens inside his mind, no stopping it.

He files very few under trust friends, and the remaining people in his life fall into simple friends, except a few which he labels no-trust persons. Sonny considers everyone he meets a friend until a person earns the no-trust label – someone like Little Jumbo and his gang boys, and Morton, and Boone, and lately Anderson.

K.O. wins the trust friend contest easily though, nobody catches K.O., but Willow and Cat earned the label as well. Three trust friends, total in his life.

Lisa stands alone as his first physical friend, even though she left the state. She follows her dream and Sonny respects that determination, that dedication. She sticks in his mind, especially when he sleeps alone in his camp. His experience with Lisa stands alone in his life. So completely different, he smiles often at the memories.

She won plenty of points every time she spent a night, and not points just for the sex part. Smart and cute, and funny counts too, and she laughs a lot. Lisa interests his friend side as well as his male side, so that earns his trust. She lost a few points when she rolled off to college, then got all those back immediately when she wrote him an actual snail-mail letter with a photo, Lisa standing in front of Berkeley and the Golden Bear, waving at the camera. He often thinks of her.

He pinned the Lisa photo up on his wall, beside his only photo of K.O. in a boxing ring at age twenty-two, and beside his posters of Marciano, Ali, Holmes and Frazier, believing in that order the skill rankings of his all-time favorites in the boxing game, although in his mind, Rocky and Ali tie for the best ever. Marciano because his great fight skills and tenacious style let him retire undefeated, and Ali for his truly amazing hand speed and fight style and ability in the ring. Despite several losses in his career, Sonny believes other factors affect those losses. If all things political and social dropped off the screen, and all fighters met in the ring at an equal age and health, Sonny believes Ali would defeat the opponents that show a win against him in the record books, and Ali would join Rocky as an undefeated champion. In his dreams, it feels true, and good enough for Sonny.

For a few seconds Sonny wonders who shot the Lisa photo. Then decides, another college girl snapped it because he wants that as truth. His count remains three trust friends for today. He places Lisa all alone in a separate category. One of a kind in his life, at least so far and probably always she will be as he thinks it through. No matter how many times or how hard a person tries, it can never be a first time twice. Sonny grins at that memory and calls it up often.

"Off somewhere else Sonny?" Cat jerks his thoughts back to the present, softly though. The tone in her voice never resonates negative in any way.

"Just thinking about my friends."

"It's nice to have friends, not everyone has friends. I brought some word games today, idea games. Let me peek inside that mind a little more, you still up for that?"

Cat runs Sonny through some word associations and other mental comprehension tests, spends a half an hour, then she lays down a sheet of paper with several words typed in a row on it. "Read these words aloud."

Sonny studies the sheet for a few seconds then says each word once, "Level, rotator, dad, racecar, kayak, mom, radar."

The second he finishes reciting, she grabs the paper, hides the words, and asks, "What did you see or hear that's unique?"

Sonny looks up at the oak tree, stares for a few seconds as if its foliage offers an answer, seems slow to respond, same as many times in the past when she asks a question.

Cat notices the pause, the time he spends thinking it through, has noted before that it occasionally occurs even outside the treatment sessions, but not every time. It depends on the topic and the situation.

Sonny pauses and thinks about his answer before speaking when the question requires a concrete answer, not an opinion. Opinions just stick out there based on experience and gut instinct. Everyone has opinions, and many opinions imply different interpretations of life, but never express a wrong answer.

An opinion exists in the world as perfect. May be a stupid opinion, may be a smart opinion, may be an odd opinion, may be an enlightening opinion, may be an impossible opinion, but all those answers have one thing in common, opinions are never incorrect.

Sonny responds, "You mean besides each word spells the same backward and forward and all use an odd number of letters? Or do you mean two use three letters, three use five letters, and two use seven? Would guess if you carry it out, the next sequence would hold at three use nine letters, unless you include even letters, like noon or deed. Can't use two letters, ain't no word with two letters reads the same forward and back."

"Correct, the backward and forward spelling, and odd letters. How'd you figure that out? You didn't answer right away."

"Knew it soon as you showed the words, but checked with my friends first, before I told you."

"What does that mean, 'checked with your friends,' how'd you do that? Do you read minds, like the aliens? I thought you can't read minds?"

"Can't, not yet, not until I kill an alien, and steal its powers." Sonny drops his eyes, his aliens an unwilling subject at this moment. He looks at Cat again, draws a breath, and lets it out slowly.

"Okay, each person I know lives in a small room in my brain, like a clear box with a person sitting in it, looks like a face card. When someone asks a question like the one you just asked, a solid question not an opinion, I ask my friends. Don't ask anyone if it's an opinion question. Opinions are a collection of individual experiences expressed as truth."

"But if it needs a concrete answer, then I decide on my own answer first, then flip through and see what my friends think, then compare it between them and decide how each one will answer, then pick the one most likely correct. Most times, I choose my own answer, but got to ask everyone first, see if a friend adds something I forgot, or don't think about. Like a courtesy to my friends, don't want to leave them out on something important."

"So, you figure out how K.O. or Willow would answer, and then you decide?"

"No, all my friends."

"All your friends, how many is that?"

"Don't know exactly. Wait, I'll check. He shuts his eyes for a few seconds. "Two hundred eleven today." Never counted them before, no one ever asked. Plus, it changes as I meet new friends worth keeping. Each one just lives there in a box. Got trust friends, like K.O. and Willow, and Lisa, now you. Randy and Jacki will get there too, the trust friends, but too young now for that. Both sit beside my trust friends but not quite equal yet, still above everyone else and when both get older will become trust friends like K.O and Willow. Well, unless either one changes into a nasty alien before."

"But the rest, everyone I meet becomes a friend, sits in a box inside my head. Each person gets a friend card when we first meet, a king, or a queen, always a face card with that person's face on it. I always ask each one for an answer when the question needs a fact answer, and not opinion. Like this one."

"Never ask people like Little Jumbo or Small Sammy anything. Guys in those nasty gangs got nothing but nasty to offer, so no sense paying attention. Automatically, people like that gang fall into the shut box and get a no-trust jack. Once in a while a new friend gets a king or queen but later switches to a jack if it earns it with some kind of nasty trick, or burns one of my friends, or cheats."

"You just went through a couple hundred people and possible answers in about five seconds. How does that happen?"

"It's like flipping through cards, like shuffling a deck with kings and queens in it, king for male friend, queen for female. Each person lives in a clear glass box and owns one card with a face on it, its own real face, and when the deck shuffles I just ask each one as that card flips by, and then compare the answers. Then I pick the right one, or go with my own, usually go with mine, but sometimes get surprised, not often though. Asked myself how my friends answer your question about these words, for example, making sure I figure it out correctly before telling you."

"And the deck of cards, it's everyone you know, in your entire life?"

"Yup, almost, except some people never become friends. Some I keep, some I ignore. Casual people I meet never stay. Little Jumbo's in there but his box stays shut, never ask him anything, all that gang same thing. All shut boxes, all no-trust cards, the jacks. Those kind sit in a back corner too, no light, so I skip over those cards, saves time, just stop asking before I get to the jacks."

"Some friends are smarter too. I always ask the smart ones first then just check in with the rest. The cards flutter past to make sure I see and hear everything. Trust friends sit on top, the rest circle around in a spiral that flows away from the trust friends, like a coil spring winding down and backwards from the light into the darkness where the jacks live. If the answers ride along unanimous at the beginning then just skip the rest, takes less time." He shrugs.

"Each time I meet someone new, the decks shuffles that person into the right spot, depends on how smart or how good a friend, so the order changes, and changes again sometimes once I know that person a little better. My teachers too, from when I went to middle school, up there pretty high as teachers know a lot, but trust friends always sit on top. Not many in that pile, three right now, plus Lisa."

Cat flicks her eyes at Sonny, her lips tip up at the end briefly. He catches her and puts a very serious face on, "See? Read your mind, or else you sent that thought in. Which is it Cat?"

He stares at her a few seconds, grins then laughs. "Gotcha."

Cat joins in and laughs with him once she realizes he was joking, has not known him long enough to read all the signals yet.

"Yeah, you're in there Cat, a trust friend. Pretty quick, don't usually deal a trust card that fast." He pulls up a very serious face, aims it at Cat. "Don't disappoint me."

"I won't."

Cat glances at her paperwork. "Anderson and Morton both state in your records that you think slower than most patients, you always pause after they ask a question. They both think the questions stump you. They have no clue, do they?"

"So, doesn't everyone think like me?"

"No, not everyone, some people use other methods."

Cat holds some concern in her mind that Sonny might draw away if she admits his brain may be abnormal, his thinking patterns differ from others, and he thinks much faster, but she has never heard this kind of thought-processing method defined so acutely in individuals, except in a very few mental patients. The card shuffle pattern, not a completely new concept in mental health, but never appears as powerful and organized or as fast or as complete in other patients she tested.

"Well, they never asked me how it works. Doctor Anderson and Mister Morton never cared, never believed anything I said. Always told me I was making up the aliens, same at the clinic. Staff thought I was making it up to get spike drugs. May be true, well it is true actually, get the drugs for relaxing, but those aliens live in the real world, no doubt about that. Spike drugs help me unwind, so I can rest and keep my strength up, stay ready when called up, when the aliens attack. Otherwise, I'm too stressed out thinking about it, thinking about aliens hunting my friends."

"So, what's this drug you call a spike drug?"

"Anything powder you can shoot up, or snort. Straw or a spike, a needle, just terms we use. Can either lay it out and snort it, or cook it up and shoot the vein."

He fidgets a few seconds, uncomfortable with the subject, so he cycles back to the words and trust friends. "But, it's always been pretty fast, the answers. People I meet join in the pack, so it takes longer now, flipping through the cards. At one time, it was quicker, with just a few friends, but now takes a little extra time. Never ask Mister Morton or Doctor Anderson anything either – both live in shut boxes, and both own no-trust jacks. Pretty worthless guys outside that box too in real life, best I can tell."

Cat notices Sonny returned each man his title of respect. Wonders a bit about that, why it happens when he has little respect for the medical and social interaction between himself and both these men. She examined all clinic and casework notes from the Anderson and Morton evaluations. Both case files state Sonny acts 'slow in thought processing.' Both wrote similar responses – when asked questions requiring a debatable, empirical, or a pragmatic answer, it takes Sonny several seconds to respond and his mind grasps the question less quickly than a normal brain does – according to clinic notes.

Although it also states Sonny eventually brings an acceptable answer to the table, he takes more time than a control subject. Other clinic caseworkers agree, but the health care workers that wrote these notes have no clue about his brain function, nor how uniquely some mental patients individually cope with the abstract world.

Cat realizes this clinic history identifies completely different personality than the Sonny she knows, and different still than K.O. or Willow know. Extremely bright and multifunctional, his brain processes information much faster than most people, and he gets it right. It also contains distorted biological connections and perception factors that create a unique world in his mind and, in some cases, forces his brain into violent responses to a non-threatening situation. That truly makes her sad, and drives the passion in her work.

"Why are Anderson and Morton in shut boxes, they're pretty smart, aren't they?"

"Don't know for sure about smart. Both ask stupid questions and pay no attention to our answers, so that ain't very smart. Both selfish too, read selfish in both those men right away, but they had some use for me at the time, kept busy with appointments, and earned themselves a paycheck. They kept meeting me, checking boxes, taking notes, making no sense. Never ask me about the real me, only ask me what the check box tells them to ask me."

"How'd you read that in a person, the selfish part, the personality?"

"Just watch them, how they look at you, if they look in your eyes. How sincere the body reacts, and the face, and eyes give it away easy, and little twitches, smile, no smile, sincere, you can just tell. If they look out the window when you talk, spin the pen, or read something else on the desk while you answer, means they care less what you say. Already make up their minds, both of them before I even get there."

Cat barely conceals her astonishment. "Give me a few minutes. You just shared some interesting thoughts. I'd like to write it up, if that's okay."

Sonny and Cat agreed early on in this relationship that Cat might want to take notes when he talked about his internal thought processing. He knows she understands his mind better than any other doctor or counselor, and that she truly tries to help him understand himself better.

"Okay, will just take a run." Sonny jumps up and heads down the trail, jogging at first then picking up speed as he curls away from camp. A full moon brightens the trail tonight but Sonny runs it so often he can follow it even in pitch dark. Moonlight flashing through the trees allows as fast a pace as he wants so he picks it up, running down the pathway at nearly full speed, breaking a sweat quickly.

A demon floats out from the bushes into his path, yells at him, orders him. *Go back, rip off her clothes, she wants you. We Need It! We need you to hurt someone. Hurt Cat!*

Sonny accelerates and blows right through the smoke, listens to its voice shrink in the distance behind him as he picks up speed.

Cat finds his story amazing, the interaction between his mind and his illusions and delusions, his alien culture, violent demon demands, his trust-friends and personal card collection. How it focuses his knowledge, and the mind reading. Cat finds what he revealed about his mental activities stunning. She opens her laptop, begins tapping keys.

Sonny reads body language and facial expressions with no formal training, as if it comes intuitively. He appears slow in his thinking because he holds conversations in real time, exactly like everyone else, but his brain works much faster, sorting significantly more information in much less time, at least if what he says is true. Why lie about it?

Can he make up something as complex as that box and card memory? Well, maybe he could invent it all. If we examine that alien culture he describes closely, it emerges complete and dynamic, and he describes it as real. He believes his alien society and violent culture as an absolute truth, populated with alien leaders, and demons and spooks support a violent cultural hierarchy. He shares it with anyone, no secrets. So again, why lie about the boxes and personal cards? No reason, so it must be a truth in his mind as well.

Cat experienced in person a complete awakening during the past few weeks, and especially today. She gained insight into his brain, into the layered thinking processes, and understand exactly how Sonny perceives his friends, and his enemies.

An incredible amount of information passes through his brain in one decision-making flash. In previous psyche studies performed at our lab, his brain works far faster than any other participants we tested. His comprehension rates in the upper tiers and he observes his world in extremely minute detail, giving evidence that his mental filtering mechanisms fail at blocking even minor and unthreatening situations, and that filter failure triggers his fright, his paranoia.
Inaccurate clinic notes misinform specialists that treat him now and those that will treat him later, and the social workers too if all believe the files, which most clinicians accept despite errors and inaccurate information. Once it appears on the record, it becomes a truth forever, even if false. No wonder recovery stalls with many mental health patients and treatment plans. Anderson's right about one thing - it's nothing like mending a broken bone.

Cat finishes typing in her descriptions, the trust cards and people boxes he stores in his memory. Leaves rustle behind her, and rhythmic footsteps hit the trail leading back into the campsite.

Sonny emerges from the bushes, drops down and counts off fifty pushups, then reclaims his stump, breathing heavily. Cat shuts the laptop, picks up the discussion right where she left off.

"How old were you when this card shuffle began?"

Sonny grabs a towel, wipes his face and neck. "Seems like always, don't remember the early years, but stronger since about twelve or thirteen. About the same age as when the demon first started talking softly at me. And, same time, everything seemed louder and sharper."

"What do you mean, louder and sharper?"

"Loud, like all the regular noise around me sounds like people yelling at me. People not even talking to me yell at anyone they talk to, loud, it's like when people talk to one another, well that voice level sounds like they yell at one another, and when a dog yips, it's very loud like it's angry even when it's not. I can't lower the volume."

"And the visions, when I look at things, the smallest detail stands out ... like Melanie always has small cuts on her fingers where she bites her nails, and she has a little heart tattoo between her toes ... all of 'em. Can't hardly see it, but it's there, red with a blue border. And, I see and hear other things, always seem like everyone's loud, a group yelling, even if it's not aimed at me. You ever been in a cafeteria when all the kids at lunch are talking at once? That's every day loudness to me, even in the market, it's that loud. And, a bird, a little tweet seems like a stereo on blast, and it twists its tongue in different shapes to make different sounds. Wasn't like that when I was younger, none of it compares to now."

Cat opens her eyes wide. It takes very sharp eyes to see a bird tongue move, and a sharp mind even to think of looking. His intimacy surprises her, after such a short time together, weeks not a lifetime.

"We all have filtering mechanisms in our brain, Sonny. It filters out sounds and visions that are not dangerous - so, we can ignore those and use our brains for more important life behavior. Your perception seems very high and the filtering mechanism less acute. It does not distinguish between safe or dangerous, and perceives all information it gathers equally. It's difficult for you to make a decision about a threat, isn't it? You take a lot of time to decide, and most often, you think 'threat immediately' and react, unless something convinces you it's safe - or, if that threat disappears before you act. Is that right?"

"Yup, you got it. I see and hear all kinds of things my brain calls dangerous, I don't even think about it, it's just there and stress builds. So I need to concentrate and weed some of it out, otherwise, I'd be fighting or defending my friends or myself all the time. I'd get no rest."

"But the alien faces yelling and screaming started later, about fifteen or so, keeps getting worse, aliens trying to take over my brain. Aliens got here on earth about ten years ago, but only been pushing thoughts in and actions it wants for a year or two. Mostly wants me to hurt people I like. Always demands violence lately, which it didn't before, getting harder to control."

Sonny gets up, circles the campfire a few times, and glances at his rock then back at Cat. Probably a good idea to keep that smoke secret from Cat yet he decides, maybe never. Figures she may not appreciate his recreational habit, though she already knows he uses street drugs often.

Society in general knows about and either accepts or ignores drug use as a part of the counter-culture, even though it remains illegal, and difficult or almost impossible to control. Prosecution becomes too expensive for the small gain. The drug culture hitches a ride on the social settings, and most ignore it in a variety of situations. Individuals that manifest mental health problems use that culture for its benefit and use street drugs to offset the lack of proper medical care. Street people call it 'self-medicating'. Doctors call it 'stupid'. Kids like Sonny call it 'necessary'.

The idea that he might fire up a bud in her presence seems more an insult than sharing, so he chooses not. "Interesting though, aliens always want me to hurt people I care about, never jerks like Morton or the boy gang, Jumbo and those nasty dudes hanging out with him."

He tosses a couple more wood chunks on the fire, drops down and runs a few more pushups, sits back on the stump.

Cat says nothing, watching him move around, sensing his discomfort, unable to guess what suddenly disturbs him, watching and waiting for a manic state. Sitting here alone with a very powerful athlete, she hopes she can gain a little understanding if it emerges, and control it. A small knot of worry forms on her brow.

Sonny stands, circles around the tent, alternately clenching his fists and relaxing, holding his head, and repeating the sequence as he circles the tent again, confusion and conflict written on his face. Finally, he plops back down on the stump.

Suddenly, he jumps up, opens the tent flap, and offers his hand, still a man-boy but now more confident with girls after Lisa and Melanie. "Feel like a little tent sparring, Doctor Cat?"

Firelight flashes in her eyes and Cat lifts a palm, quickly hides her grin, and stifles a laugh, protecting his awkwardness, his odd perception of reality, and the strength of his emotions, but understanding his attempt at a normal man to woman or boy to girl gesture.

"Nope, don't think that's a good idea ... that's not what we're about, you and I."

Sonny drops his hand, quickly sits back on the stump.

"No big deal, been turned down before," he admits, "a few times, course, not *all* the times." He grins, stretching the truth, wondering how to get off this subject safely now, feeling like he caught himself in his own trap.

Both sit silent, staring into the flames for a minute or two, comfortable with it.

"You don't gotta marry me, Cat." Sonny grins and blurts out the words without thinking, supporting his boy-girl innocence once more and illustrating his disconnection with true reality as well. Sitting on the opposite side of a mimic, he reacts to the memory of the first night he spent with Lisa.

Cat giggles this time. Sonny flicks his eyes at her then starts laughing as well, suddenly realizing how naive his comment sounded, and he says, "Was kind a dumb thought, huh? *Doctor Cat.*" He emphasizes the last two words and grins.

Cat giggles again. "Does that line ever work?"

"Yeah, one time, but ain't me that said it." A light red blush hits his cheeks. "I just fell for it." Sonny explains Lisa and cracks up. Suddenly unable to control it, Cat bursts out laughing with him.

One then the other unable to smother a tiny snicker or an eye-to-eye blink, starting it again like happens sometimes when a bit of humor hits two people exactly right. Giggle, stop, giggle, stop, giggle, can't stop and laugh out loud then finally stop together, then giggle some more now and then the rest of the evening but will probably never find it the least bit funny later in life. It sure hits both as extremely hilarious right now though.

"You truly are for someone else, Sonny. You just haven't met her yet." She stands, dusts off the seat of her pants, and kisses him on the cheek. "Good night, Sonny."

Cat heads down the pathway smiling and shaking her head, but she climbed up there on the right friend note and medical track with Sonny so far. She feels the ice melting and total trust emerging.

Sonny watches Cat stroll down the trail and wishes he had a few more years under his belt, but he appreciates her walk regardless. Not every woman walks like a panther, a truth he begins noticing more as he matures, but this Cat absolutely fits her name.

39

Aaron Clark reads the selection list and treatment plan Cat includes in her new research project. "You picked the five most difficult cases."

"Why not? If the most disorganized brains respond well to our treatment, the rest will gain even more benefit. Sonny will be the most helpful because he already understands the physical component, and without a doubt is the brightest. Intuitively he knows how it works, he rejects the delusion and hallucination when it pushes his mind toward violence, 'Just sweat 'em gone', Sonny calls it when describing his technique."

"He's been using it successfully to some degree for several years, like 'Runner's High'.
Increased endorphin production triggered by intense physical exertion. Probably decreases the dopamine effectives, lessening neurotransmitter activity at the fright levels so he can relax."

Aaron Clark nods in agreement, flips through the pages. "All young too. Twenty the oldest, and only one female."

"Annie studies math at Princeton, and started exhibiting symptoms earlier than most women. Extremely bright, but not very physical. Brilliant in fact, almost finished with her doctorate and she's only twenty years old. She combats her demon with mental challenges, she attacks unsolved math problems and it keeps her mind occupied at an intense level. She says she can feel anger and rage emerging, and puts her brain to work until it releases and the demon fades before she responds with violence. It works for her. She figured it out, just like Sonny with his workouts."

"We want to look at those that use physical exertion to decrease the brain dysfunction, but Annie uses intense brain activity, solving math problems in the same way. So, I thought she was worth a look."

"And, late teens, best time, cell damage has not advanced yet. We can still arrest it at that age. By the time we get to men like Ferguson and Nickels, it's too late."

"Seems you connect with Sonny pretty well, he shares a lot with you already."

"But he needs that connection, Aaron. He's been scared to death for years and knows I'm one person that understands his demons, that I believe him and don't insult him about his mind and his beliefs. He needs someone he trusts that actually understands it and accepts him and his mind. Willow and K.O. connect with him as family, even closer maybe, but it's not the same thing. I'm the first outsider that accepts him."

Aaron chuckles, "And tried to get you in the sack already."

Cat grins at him for a few seconds, but then turns more serious.

"You tell him?" Aaron asks.

"No."

"Why not?"

"Why should I, it wouldn't make any difference."

Cat turns away, not exactly understanding why she experiences discomfort with his question, one she believes irrelevant. She keeps one or two secrets about her private life. It's important to her so she ignores it. Her choice. She believes her private life holds no bearing on her professional life, and accepts no supervisorial appeal for her own personal choice on that subject.

Aaron heads out the door. Cat opens her laptop and begins streamlining her notes and observational analysis. She types almost as fast as she thinks and compares data from her memory as often as from her clinic notes, and consolidates her interpretations.

Sonny tops our study list. He's the most physical by far, and probably the brightest, although one woman, Annie Kittredge, attends Princeton on a full ride math scholarship. She

matches his intelligence level easily, might even pass him in that category, but she's a twig of a woman, and pushes her demons out with intellectual challenges instead. Although she uses physical exertion as much as she can, but physical activity helps her to a lesser degree than Sonny and his workouts because she's not an athlete, she pushes her brain instead.

Equate to John Nash here – refer to notes of our meeting with Nash in England 2005 at economics summit. Nash a very enlightened math professional diagnosed with schizophrenia. He claims the symptoms disappeared naturally, as he aged. Based on his behavior and work later in his life, he may be correct.

Annie hits a genius level in mathematics and computer tech, and fights her single individual screaming demon online. When she loses that control, she drops into deep depression then rises to extreme manic heights and finds herself unable to function at all.

She almost starved to death several times. She combines her limited physical abilities with new methods and creative programming when her mind allows it. Her intense concentration drives the demon out for extended periods. She crowds her brain with intellectual processes and leaves no room inside for it.

Seems most patients find some bizarre way to cope. The brain adjusts as best it can, but the damaging chemistry always wins in the end. Check Nash notes again here. Verify accuracy and medication dates.

Sonny already internalized the idea that hard workouts dispel his aliens and calm his rage. Has no clue why it happens, but he knows it happens, and our scientists often apply the term 'Runner's High' to that specific condition. He describes that behavior condition exactly and correctly, but understands none of the science.

The brain often copes with mental illness in odd and unique ways we don't completely understand. The brain and body adapt intuitively, automatically. Sonny simply realized it intellectually after it worked, so he works out and, in a way, temporarily heals himself.

Amazingly adaptive, human bodies and brains react in ways we cannot consciously conceive. It simply happens and a brain responds in a way that creates the best physical and mental environment for its individual survival.

The other four patients use physical activity as well, but no one responds as physically as Sonny, none as mentally focused, and none as bright except Annie, and she scores off the charts.

We know and understand how that neural transmission and chemistry works in the brain, but not how the individual mind feels exactly when that rage releases. The brain adapts itself automatically but we cannot always track that yet with the available technology.

CAT-RON Technologies is currently investigating the potential for a microchip inserted directly into the brain for a set period, long enough to gather the data.

If we can gain that insight, we can recreate that same chemical balance with a medication mix and the brain will maintain itself under our formula.

If genetics builds a brain the same way it builds a fingerprint, same way it builds DNA, so individual in structure it that requires an individual formula in every human, then organic or synthetic ingredients we have available already can combine in a unique

mixture and balance each brain individually.

Aaron returns carrying coffee and bran muffins, sits across the counter. Cat looks up, "Give me a few minutes." She continues typing.

A brain constantly produces hormones that initiate a fright condition and the mind responds. Its body produces adrenaline first and pushes itself hard physically, and if the perceived threat remains – real or unreal – then endorphins act like opiates, offsetting the exertion and reducing pain, so the body can continue extreme activity and calm itself, or protect itself if necessary, and it burns off that stress energy.

If we identify that balance, that chemical complex that turns off the fright, then the body automatically reduces the need for adrenaline and opiate production. In one negative sense, the addictive nature in endorphins mimics addiction to morphine and induces the brain to repeat the actions, continuously striving for that feeling of euphoria as well.

Scientists never experience it, so understanding it completely and describing those emotions becomes difficult for anyone, including professionals that treat this mental condition. We do not live it, so we observe and listen.

If patients and doctors can define that condition, more individually, and spend more time, and gain trust between doctor and patient, then we can create the mix we need based on what victims tell us and that chemistry data, not what we view in a vacuum.

We need individual time with each patient, insert our micro-processor temporarily, and synchronize a computer program that mixes chemicals according to input the doctor receives directly from the patient, even information unavailable from the

patient, what the patient can't verbalize but the chip can read.

The reader-chip removes the guesswork. We can stop feeding patients one-size-fits-all pills, and create a medication that works individually the first time. Imagine all these kids creating a unique chemical balance and living productive lives.

What then emerges as the most important factor, a balanced brain, but it removes the financial drain on our economy as well. The medical cost benefit – both individual expenses and costs to our social environment and culture – becomes a huge secondary benefit. Each treatment will pay for itself in public savings. Less crime, less violence means less cost to the social economic engine as well, to say nothing about enhancing the lives of these kids and young adults, and their families.

Cat shuts her laptop. "Sonny labels his visions and voices 'aliens or spooks' in his own brain, and believes aliens come from another world and infect his brain and infect his friends. He uses spook, demon or space alien somewhat interchangeably, but believes anyone infected by an alien becomes an alien being but reverts to a human intermittently."

"He describes an entire culture, consistent with an American society, actually reminds me more of the Native American cultures Max talks about, and he fits every nuance into some crack in his alien world. He views his world as an organized alien society that advocates violent methods to achieve its goals. The alien simply executes his enemies instead of a holding a trial, but with Sonny, his morals and ethics interfere, so his mind exists in a constant state of turmoil."

"Amazingly enough, in a different world with different rules, like the alien civilization he creates in his mind or similar to pagan cultures humans developed centuries ago, or even today in some African or South American tribes, his peers would label him a hero or a chief, not a misfit. But misfit or not, that unbalanced hormone interaction will continuously damage his brain and, unless we control it medically, the chemistry destroys brain cells and will either turn him into a vegetable, or kill him."

"Unimaginable to most of us, yes, but so complete it's impossible to argue it as untrue. It's like any religious belief, wherein Sonny accepts these alien fundamentals without empirical evidence. Telling Sonny these aliens don't exist is like telling a Christian there's no Christ or a Buddhist there's no Buddha, or a pagan that no wolf god or corn goddess exists."

Cat looks in her calendar. "Matter of fact, we scheduled a phone consult with Max Whitetail next week. You should listen in. We can teleconference with you if you want. Let me know."

Aaron ponders a moment then adds, "Trouble is, unbalanced brain chemistry increases its effect over time, and will eventually absorb or digest his brain cells even if he continues with his extraordinary physical conditioning. He'd have to work out more and more hours, and harder just to keep even, eventually twenty-four hours in a day will not be enough time."

Cat says, "And Sonny can do this himself most of the time now and earlier in his life before the hormones increased its potencies. What if we can teach him, or he can teach us is more like it, how he does it, what happens inside his brain when he physically pushes those demons out, how his brain turns it off. It would be interesting and beneficial to understand its method."

40

Cat, Willow, and K.O. sit in an office Cat rented in Baxter Town Center, speaker on, dialing, and connected into a three-way phone line, Erin McCord and Aaron Clark at the other end. A click breaks the quiet, then a voice three thousand miles away squawks. "Max. Talk."

Silence. Caught in the odd expression for a few seconds, Cat says nothing. All three look at one another, the speaker squawks again.

"Your dime, your words." Humor evident in his tone, Max laughs aloud, an odd chatter but cheery and infectious. Everyone follows his lead, his audience instantly upbeat. "Must be Doctor Cat, right on time as usual, how are you Catherine?" The group can almost sense the grin in his voice.

"Great, you're on speaker. Two friends here, K.O. and Willow, and we have Erin and Aaron on three-way. You got my note and know why we're all here?"

In a voice clear and crisp despite his eighty-one years, Professor Maxwell Whitetail responds, "Yup, glad to assist if I can." Whitetail lectures often, and can explain the medical issues in social terms K.O. and Willow can grasp as well as the scientists he teaches.

A semi-retired but very active anthropology professor and psychiatrist that lectured at Harvard during Cat's training years, the radical-thinking Native American relic occasionally teaches archaeology and religious theory at UCLA, but mostly attends speaking engagements around the country. Whitetail enjoys a great command of history, language, linguistics, and descriptive prose. His off-the-wall doctrine and ideology combines pagan spiritual healing with genetic theory and practical medicine, and he's quite amusing as well. Professor Whitetail gets many calls and the audience always enjoys his lectures. Max always calls them 'fireside chats' even with five or six hundred, sometimes a thousand patrons in the auditorium.

Occasionally, an individual overlooks his humor, turns a discerning ear and adds a bit of focused study then claims an unexpected reward, a bit more truth and substance in what Max Whitetail professes. Others simply show up for wine and cheese, served with a platter of gossip Max denies exposing.

Max operated a psychiatric research clinic in Los Angeles until he finally embraced the religions he teaches and now combines all pagan spiritual theories into one he believes and practices, a spiritual belief that includes advanced biological and genetics theory.

An extremely well read and intelligent individual, Max Whitetail exhibits quite eccentric behavior as well, but everyone that matters overlooks that trait for the benefit of science. Max Whitetail remains a congregation of one. Been like that for years, way too far out there for anyone to join him.

Cat sent Max her medical notes and ideas two weeks ago, and her first theoretical applications. Very familiar with her work, Max contributes information and original data for her research and his own insight into her theoretical development.

Max emailed appropriate background papers last week, made this appointment to follow up verbally, and enlighten K.O. and Willow in nonprofessional terms as best he can.

K.O. and Willow read some of his work. In it, Professor Whitetail explains pagan religions and the embedded manic actions of priests and holy-men. The concept that holy-men or spirit men, and sometimes women, hear voices, see visions. That each one speaks to God and God replies appears as craziness to outsiders. Holy-men embrace these internal and external spirits, pray and ask for guidance, both expecting it and then respecting it when it appears.

"You get a chance to review what I sent? Max pauses for about two seconds then answers himself. "Of course you have.

Your work habits never change, so I'll just ramble through this, and you butt in whenever you want."

"Native American holy-warriors spend time alone with the internal spirit seeking guidance. When asked, the spirit responds, advising each leader about personal and tribal decisions that are often very wise choices. We believe holy-men are very bright individuals, but some may possess dysfunctional brain chemistry. The tribes hold holy-men in high esteem, often elevating one into a chieftain role, or an equally respected position in the tribal hierarchy."

"We believe many of the historical Native American holy men had mental conditions similar to bi-polar and schizophrenic disorders. We compare the speaking spirit soul to the homeless mentally ill patients that either refuse treatment or have no treatment options. Talking at a post, or a tree, and listening to its response appears crazy to us. But it often guides lives in ways that allow them to cope with a dysfunctional brain. Although it may not always be dysfunctional, just different. The brain takes over, the mind listens, and the body survives."

"Fearless on a battlefield and relentless on the hunt, these spirit-warriors prove beyond a doubt that chemically unbalanced brains develop coping mechanisms that overcome obstacles normal or socially civilized persons may not survive if placed within a less tolerant cultural context."

Cat breaks in and hypothesizes part of what he means. "Possibly this rage and torment, this motivation toward intense activity that thrives in the brain drives physical abilities that project anger toward the enemy or the prey and, in some logical manner, remains acceptable, even exciting in a specific pagan culture. In a similar manner that rage drives Sonny in his fitness training, and his biking and running events."

Cat records everything Max says, but everyone scribble notes while Max rattles on, noting questions that emerge as he explains the connection between spirit and mental images that haunt the minds.

Willow fills coffee cups, dumps cream, no sugar in each, and grabs her pen again.

Max continues. "These warriors quench that innate thirst for violence with physical outlets based in territory and family protection, and gain respect. Conversely, any violence that emerges as Fergie or Sonny seeks this same release meets with jail time, and often sedation, in our social organization."

"That an identical behavior in two individuals meets a diametrically opposing response in each culture evokes interest in many philosophers and anthropologists today. Makes sense in pagan cultures but not to the individual enduring the mental pain in this central *civilized* society we live in today." Professor Whitetail emphasizes the term 'civilized' appropriately in his view.

"These warriors gain respect in the tribe because that fierceness succeeds against tribal enemies, and in the hunt. The madness drives them into very aggressive interaction in whatever these holy-men attempt. We think they might chase the same physical adrenalin rush as does Sonny - the endorphin induced mental state he achieves with intense activities."

All three in the lunch room duck as an unexpected thunderclap rumbles above. The clouds open and heavy rain suddenly floods the parking lot. K.O. jumps up cussing himself, runs outside, winds up the windows in his truck and returns. Dark skies began rolling in early this morning but he ignored it. He shakes the water off his shirt, picks up the conversation.

"Most of this remains speculation at present, but I believe that the identical neurotransmitter imbalance floods the neurons with adrenaline and the same defense and fright hormones that motivate Sonny to work out and run so often works the same way in tribal conflicts and challenges."

"Those chemicals that balance the fears that he experiences most of his waking life work the same way, but in his culture, find antagonism and misunderstanding when he acts out violently. The root of this violence eludes our society – and eludes the pagans and heathens as well – but the pagans and heathens treat it differently. Those cultures embrace it as empowering, and that culture differs from a civilized society in a way that allows those behaviors to express themselves. One simply takes his madness into the forest or the desert and either survives or not, but at the same time, challenges the demons with extraordinary physical abilities and pride. A winner claims the tribal accolades, a loser forfeits his life."

K.O. says, "Pretty high stakes."

The listeners almost feel Max nod through the lines. "Yes, exactly right."

Whitetail continues, "Frequently, these warriors often learn the herbal healing arts as well, particularly the women who fight less often in a hunter-gather lifestyle and more often survive, and become a witch woman, a healer. For some inexplicable reason, in both cultures, the women exhibit the symptoms later in life than men. Males exhibit at about sixteen or so, but women often delay it until early or middle twenties. We have no clue why, at least not yet. Probably something related to child-bearing chemistry."

"The holy-men are often very bright, and make great leaders. These spirituals might act a little nutty, but nobody cares or they all embrace it, although sometimes a tribe throws a misfit out if he can't socialize well enough."

"Now, parallel that exclusion with our homeless, the hobos and derelicts living in alleys and parks, holding conversations with a compound self, often sinking into depression and delusion, but manage to survive somehow in a world that misunderstands behavioral and biological factors and simply labels them crazy. Remember, however on the fringe we claim it, the world these outcasts live in exists as true to them as our world exists to us. If the world contained more outcasts than 'normal folk', we'd be the ones sent away on a cloud or a sky cave and the world would take a real tumble. Hmmm, or maybe not?"

The phone sits silent for a minute or so while the professor in him contemplates that dynamic, a better or a worse earth with more bright schizophrenics in it. Which is best?

Cat finally asks, "You still with us Max?" Brings him back from wherever his thoughts took him, a common event in his personal exploration of life.

Max picks up his words again. "We have little written documentation so we can only speculate, but the stories that pass from generation to generation speak volumes about the similarity between Sonny and his alien beliefs, and Native American folklore or African cultures claiming animal spirits possess the minds of chieftains, healers, and holy-men.

"Suspect I should accept PC here and call these individuals 'holy-people' or 'a holy-person,' but I can't wrap myself around that word pairing quite yet, probably never will. That political flavor passed through pretty quickly, like the hyphenated names that became too complicated after one hyphen married another hyphen and couldn't decide which hyphen the kids got as four names with three hyphens didn't fit well on a nametag at kindergarten functions."

Whitetail barks again, the engaging chatter sounds a bit like a laugh. No way to know for certain without facial expressions, but that fails over a hard line despite the technology kids carry around in a pocket today disguised as a cell phone. "Imagine anyone hyphenating our last names Catherine?"

"Think of it Cat, even if you married a Smith and one of our kids married yours, we'd get Morgantholavich-Smith hyphen Whitetail-Simmons if I add my wife. Our grandkids would need a belt not a name tag." A group smile appears, and Max chuckles through the speaker again. "Thirty-eight characters not including a first name. We'd have to initialize everyone."

"Hold on a second." A couple clicks then Eric Clapton and his rocking blues hum through the speaker. Thunder out-notes his guitar a couple times and rain drums on the roof, but no storm outplays a Clapton guitar for long, and all three soon pick up his beat, nodding in tune without thinking.

The music fades, another click, and Max speaks again. "Sorry, my assistant needed a minute, told her no interruptions but she always forgets that soon as I say it. I'd dock her pay but she works on a research fellowship and no charge for her labor. Just wants to learn. Such a smarty, she earns her keep think-tanking about the world and writing it down. The rest of us buy it and she stays busy." His grin nearly works its way through the cables and a chair spring squeaks through the speaker as Max pushes himself upright and continues.

Cat envisions a crooked grin hanging on a face she remembers so well.

Max barks that odd laughter again. "Remember lunch Cat, you come, I'll pay." Max laughs again and clicks off, the dial tone returns. Cat disconnects the speaker. She realizes today how much she misses Max, his astute manner and humorous delivery. Decides she will fly out next week and taste that lunch. She can pick at his brain while he picks at his plate. She dials again and Max opens it on the first ring. "It's a date, Max. Next week, will fax time and flight plan, okay? Any day not good for you?"

"Nope. Send it, I'll pick you up. See you then."

"And, remember, very important. The stronger the emotion, the stronger the memory, and the more often a specific activity repeats, the better the memory too. Both key points." Papers rustle over the speaker again. "Any questions?"

"Probably later Max, we'll listen again, and read through what you send first."

Max disconnects. The phone clicks and opens a dial tone. Typical Max, stops talking and hangs up, no salutation, and no signoff, two of his several quirky habits.

"Quite a character, isn't he?" Cat closes the phone and shuts off her recorder. "A three-thousand-mile flight for lunch, it better cook itself, and taste pretty damn good." Cat lifts her eyes, thinking about her mentor and dearest friend. She has not seen Max in more than three years, although they consult frequently.

Cat comments about Sonny, and his actions, "Remember, Sonny thinks in black and white, if it seems right at the time, he does it, no thought of any consequences later. When he punched Jumbo, he gained immediate gratification. He got his drugs, briefly his peace of mind, and his revenge, never thought for a minute about later, or if he might get arrested for assault. Same thing with Stanton, the guard, even though Stanton pushed first, it might have gotten very nasty legally because Sonny broke Stanton's nose."

Willow hides a grin. "Sonny says Stanton broke his own nose, tripped and hit the wall, and needs ballet lessons if 'he wants to pull off that pushing kids and posing routine', his words exactly." All three find humor in that recollection, grin at one another again, but hold back actual laughter.

K.O. butts in. "Ellie called the attorney Stanton hired. No threats yet, just explained the applicable law. Everything by the book, she told him. If Stanton presses his case, we push assault of a minor and abuse of a prisoner, also a minor. Deputy Mike witnessed it too. He even bent his version slightly, fits very nicely into a counter-suit. Mike likes Sonny a lot, thinks Stanton deserved it. Stanton signed a release and it's on its way."

K.O. curls up his lips at each end, a row of even white teeth appear in the middle of his face. "He needs a pink slip along with that release."

41

Intuitively, Sonny knows he needs help, needs medical care, but his insurance cancelled. The on again off again emotions he recognizes in himself but cannot control get hooks into him often, and spooks encourage his violence almost beyond his ability to deny it. The law says the hospital will not admit him or treat him now unless he hurts someone, or hurts himself, has to be a life threat, a danger to himself or others, then extended treatment becomes mandatory by law, even without insurance. Sonny read it, researched it, making certain he knows the law as it applies to him.

"Guess I better figure out which person hides the worst demon, or turned all the way into an alien, and just become a danger to it. Maybe just kill it, soon as I know for sure," Sonny mutters aloud. He begins rotating through his trust cards, checking all his friends, figuring out which one fits as a traitor, which one he will miss the least.

"Maybe I'll just kill a jack. All those jack card people no use in this world. Thought I'd get the power when Shanty gave it up, but got nothing. Can't read minds, so maybe should have killed Shanty instead of just choking his demon." Sonny talks softly, rambling, making no real sense of it.

A combination of his personal history tumbles through his mind, his counseling, his reading, the doctors, the rage, the anger, the frustration that eats him alive, the words of his friends, but most of all, what K.O. and Willow tell him, and now his newest friend Doctor Cat. A great doctor, always explains, always patient, and always sharing and caring, but forcing him to accept the truth whenever his brain hits a normal rhythm.

*

Cat operates as an external, independent researcher. Her role includes treatment at some point and any time she can help, but for now, she gathers information and develops her medical theory. Aaron and Cat collaborate with four additional scientists at the biotech firm, and she begins putting her theories into practice. Technology develops slowly, and the transition between ideas and actual treatment moves forward in tiny steps, occasionally even backwards.

Officially, she has no authority over Sonny and less say about his treatment plan. She wants to change that eventually, but for now, it is what it is. She holds no license in this state, but works with Doctor Carter at the Gatesville clinic. She applied for a state waiver, but processing it takes weeks, more paperwork, and she has little time to spare. Sonny cycles through his personal universe filled with chaotic and uncontrollable tragedy faster and faster, falling deeper and deeper into depression and fear.

*

Sonny yells into the phone, "No, it's here, it's there, at the gym, after K.O. The war starts today. Two aliens followed me, tried blowing them off today, on the trails. Two of them, both grabbed me when I woke up this morning, tried to get K.O. too, but he left early, gone in town somewhere. Lucky they missed him, two brother aliens, big strong, screamed at me all morning, tougher than all the spooks. I'm heading back now to save K.O. Stay away, Willow, stay away, it'll get you too!"

A scared female voice rips through the speaker, Willow talking him down. He called her and explained his nightmare, one in which the aliens captured K.O. and threw him off a cliff. Hormones drove him harder than ever when he woke up this morning, a major hallucination and delusion grabbed him, sent him raging onto the running trails earlier.

"Sonny, listen to me. Listen to me!" Her voice rising sharply, "You can't protect K.O. He has no aliens in his brain. He does not need protecting. Wait until I get there."

"I'm on my way, tell K.O. I'll be there and protect him."

Sonny resists, rejects her advice and punches the off button, tosses the phone on the seat. He lost it early this morning, freaked out, tired of the fright, tired of worrying about his friend. The aliens chose K.O., told Sonny they will release him, release his brain if he executes K.O. But his mind flips it over, thinks the aliens will get K.O. instead.

His phone dings again. He opens it, listens. Willow begs. "Stay away Sonny. Meet me at Bear Mountain Trailhead. Please stay away from the gym. You'll hurt K.O. or K.O. will hurt you! You can't go there! You can't!"

"No, can't meet you, gotta help K.O." Sonny stares at the phone a minute, snaps it in two, and tosses it out the window.

Willow dials Cat, knows she's in her office near the gym today. Cat picks up. "Get to the gym, I'm on my way too." Willow says, "Sonny's in trouble, he's going after K.O."

*

Confusion and conflict fills his mind, the rage growing by the minute, by the hour. He's been looking for spike juice three days, found nothing, even broke his vow to himself and checked Jumbo's gang. You do what you do in a pinch. Still nothing. The anger rising, no drugs, no running in the storm, no pushing the aliens away, unable to kick the demons loose these past few days, his rage increases exponentially.

Sonny climbs out of his truck and splashes into the gym, kicks off his wet shoes, upset that a hard downpour cut his run short today. Usually, a light drizzle never bothers him much, but today, storm clouds dropped heavy rain in a very short time. Sonny forgot his sweats and hit the trails with only shorts and a tank top. The winds picked up and chilled him out. Sonny blames the wet weather on aliens, and his anger level kicks up higher.

Damn spooks keep banging on him even now, after running all those miles. But the demons gain strength and require longer and longer runs, and today, the aliens want K.O.

Sonny knows he needs to be here and protect his friend. He shakes his head, the confusion remains, the question unanswered. Does he kill K.O. and release him from the demon, or does he kill the demon and release his friend from the haunting.

The aliens hit him harder this morning so he figures he better hit the weights first, clear his head. His mind bounces in and out of delirium, unending choices – kill the spooks, kill K.O, run more, lift weight, protect K.O., protect the aliens, blast the aliens off earth, sure of only one thing, the war begins today. Aliens began taking over our world and recruited demons and spooks as soldiers.

Better get a bite first, he decides, build a little reserve, a little extra energy. Sonny angles into the lunchroom, finds K.O sitting at the table with an alien crouched on his shoulder, another hanging on his chest reaching for his throat. Sonny races across the room, grabs K.O. and spins him out of the chair, the anger and rage explode.

"Get away from him. Get the fuck off him, GET OFF!" Sonny screams the words, shouting at the demons. Paranoia engulfs his brain. The chemistry implodes, forcing his mind into a survival phase, protecting his family and friends. His physical up-charge engages full force, the fight-or-flight instinct, and Sonny chooses the fight, afraid he can't stop the demon before it kills K.O.

"Get off! Get out! Get off him!" Sonny screams again. "K.O., it's crawling up your chest, it's trying to choke you!"

Completely surprised, the first punch catches K.O on his left shoulder, the second punch clips his jaw, and the third, a straight right punch directly to his heart, knocks him off his feet. K.O scrambles under the table, rolls up into a crouch as Sonny circles the room, kicking chairs aside, screaming at the demons attacking his friend. Briefly fooled and confused, K.O grabs Sonny, clinches, spins him in place, and yells, "What the fuck!"

Sonny breaks free and comes back swinging, enraged, out of control, defending his father, his best friend, his mentor. Years of frustration focus his attack, point it finally directly at one. Sonny spins, brings up a knee, an elbow, a left hook, killing the demon.

K.O backs off, defends himself, the fight turns into a gutter knuckle-buster, a back alley brawl, two athletes using the fighting skills each honed and tuned over the years. K.O. calls up his mean-streets scrapping and his years in the ring, his training. Sonny calls upon all his boxing skills, everything this mentor taught him and the alternative martial arts Brian introduced into his boxing style.

Wrestling, rolling around, clinched tightly then both men break free.

Confused, fear and survival automatically bumps K.O into an up-charged state, matching Sonny. Awareness dawns in his mind, as two athletes circle now, extremely well trained and powerful combatants breathe hard and lock eyes.

"Don't worry K.O., I'll kill it for you, gonna save you! Won't let these demons get you."

Sonny fakes his new punch set, the one that fooled K.O. a few months ago. But fakes this routine too, another newer punch set, his speed, his youth, his strength, and hormonal up-charge wins, and Sonny drives a left jab home to the jaw and a straight right to the heart and K.O. drops onto the floor, stunned. "Stay there K.O., hold on, I'm gonna kill both those mother-fuckers!" Sonny shrieks the words.

Wild-eyed, intense, raging, sweat running off his face and neck, soaking his shirt and chest, Sonny jerks open a drawer, grabs a butcher knife, and whips around, moves a step closer and growls, "Gotcha, you nasty son-of-a-bitch," aiming the point directly at the tight muscular underbelly.

Instinct combines with years of training and K.O rolls clear at the last second, but the blade penetrates deep into his right side, slicing neatly through skin and muscle, right to the bone, deflecting off a rib.

"Got him!" The bloods spurts and Sonny grunts his success, rotates his shoulder, arches his back, raises the blade and curls it into a killing grip high above his head and pointed down, set to plunge into and execute the remaining demon still perched on K.O.'s left shoulder.

"Got one K.O., I'll get that other demon bastard too! Don't move! Let me kill it, save your life!"

Losing blood, weakening, K.O. scrambles free and rolls behind the table and pulls a chair between them, bright red blood turning dark and flooding his shirt. Shock begins sapping his strength.

Two arms wrap around Sonny, grabbing him from behind. He jerks free. Willow screams, "No Sonny, Let him alone! Leave him alone!" She begs. "Leave him alone!" Her panic obvious, Willow pulls at Sonny to no avail.

Sonny shoves her clear. Willow bounces off the wall, no match for his strength and rage. Sonny kicks the chair out of his way and stalks K.O. again.

A cool, calm voice behind him speaks. "Stop it Sonny. Drop the knife. Sonny, it's Doctor Cat. Come on, time for a run, let's go, the rain stopped. Bet I can beat you up Stony Ridge." Cat says the words, her voice sharp, penetrating, clear, sure of herself but at the same time hiding her fear.

She repeats the request, louder, closing in, standing right beside Sonny, her words ring softly in his ear, nearly hypnotic. "Stop it Sonny. Drop the knife. Look at me. It's Cat. Come on, you promised you'd run with me today."

Sonny freezes, the knife poised above K.O. Brutality defined. A muscular and statuesque presence, he pauses for an eternity. Five seconds tick off. Sonny blinks, looks up, looks at K.O., looks at the blood, looks at the knife, looks at Cat, looks at Willow, looks back at K.O.

Sonny stares at Cat, recognition emerging, glances once more at K.O. Another five seconds tick off. His eyes fill with tears, he drops his arms, drops the knife, and says, "Look what the demons did."

Cat wraps her arms around Sonny and hugs him tight, putting every ounce of her strength in it, tears streaming down both cheeks. The ERT arrives. Cat leads, and Sheriff Mike marches Sonny out, his footsteps mimic a hop-stepping robot, his eyes glaze over, his mind fogs up. Sheriff Mike assists him up the steps and Sonny drags himself into the van, lies down, and crosses his arms, awaiting the chest straps. He recalls this routine exactly, plenty of emotion, lots of practice, and no holes in it.

*

Four days pass, Sonny spends his days fretting, ashamed, hates the aliens, hates himself, cries every day, blaming himself for hurting his best friend. Sonny sinks deeper into depression. He speaks with no one, remains in his room, hiding beneath his sheets, embracing its safety.

Melanie sits on the edge of his bed. "Not your fault Sonny, weird brain stuff, it's in your mind. We're here because we need it, even when we don't admit it. It's in your brain Sonny, it's not K.O. It's you dreaming it."

Once again, Melanie exhibits remarkable insight for a patient in mental health treatment. Illustrating why new patients think Melanie works here as a clinic nurse, and why doctors should listen to the patients. Melanie hugs her friend, he hugs her back, and tears drip down his cheeks.

*

First shift, Monday morning Nurse Burkhart arrives, "Come on Sonny, you're leaving. We need this bed. You've been here five days, more than you need, more than your normal three days allowance. Can't even take a few days off, the place falls apart," she mutters.

Sonny grabs his bag, tosses his few clothes inside and hugs Melanie, follows Burkhart out and along the corridor as she keys through locked doors into the discharge office. He sits at the table and picks up a few pages, same table, and identical discharge papers.

Nurse Burkhart says, "No insurance Sonny. Three days already. Someone missed it. I gotta do everything myself around here," she grumps.

She pokes the paperwork at him. Sonny examines it quickly, same routine, same check boxes, same pencil and eraser for mistakes. Sonny fills it out, lies about a ride home, checks the correct emotion boxes. He feels no guilt. Paperwork always includes lies. He sees it often. The clinic made a major error this time, more paperwork, filed the wrong admissions, and Sonny keeps it a secret. "Getting out," he mumbles to no one, and will finish the job he began. He will find and destroy those haunting aliens that began attacking earth a week ago, and will start with the one hiding inside K.O.

42

Sonny jogs back alleys, short cuts through the forest, slips between buildings, and arrives at home in less than an hour. His brain chemistry flips and warps his thoughts in a completely different direction. He carries a towel and a sheet of paper into his room. He writes a few phrases quickly on the page, takes out his buck knife, flips it open, cuts his thumb, and embeds a bloody thumbprint into the paper directly beneath his writing.

He slides the note under the lamp. He unrolls a towel on the bed, wraps a rubber tube around his bicep and ties it off, pumps his fist, watches a vein expand, turns an ear toward the driveway, anticipating the rumble of a well-tuned small-block soon. "Better hurry," he mumbles.

He cocks an ear toward the window, nothing outside. He sparks a lighter and burns a spoon, heats the ash-colored liquid, watches it bubble. He sets it down for a minute, picks up a hypodermic the clinic uses to draw blood, or injecting thicker fluids into muscle. Sonny stole it from the clinic, stole a five-pack last time, used three, two remain.

He flicks the barrel, his fingernail ticking on the plastic tube, and pushes the plunger, testing. He stabs his finger a couple times then pushes his fingerprint on the paper, undeniably his signature. Blood proof, no check boxes, no eraser. He forgot he sliced his thumb and bled on the page a few minutes ago.

A rumble breaks the silence outside. Sonny listens and aims his ears toward the front parking lot, opens the curtain and peeks out the window. The light blue GMC bumps over the curbing and parks. Sonny flicks the lighter once more, renewing the bubbles, and slowly draws the creamy opaque liquid up inside the syringe. A truck door shuts gently outside, footsteps crunch across the gravel.

Sonny holds the point up and flicks the tip, bubbles float up in a spiral, he pushes plunger and squirts tiny bubbles out the tip until the flow clears. He lays the needle over his forearm, pumps his fist, pushes the point into his vein, and slowly engages the plunger. It empties quickly, the warm liquid flooding his system.

A silly grin appears on his face. His eyes light up then close then open again, the grin spreads, his eyes droop into a half-shut dream state, the drug working its magic or its damage, depending on the point of view. Suddenly, he blinks twice and wriggles on the bed, twitches, jerks upright and slumps over, lying on one side, the spike still stuck in his vein, his head hangs over the mattress edge. A thin trickle of blood oozes along the left inner elbow, he twitches again, his breath erratic and labored. His body trembles, his leg jumps, his foot tap, tap, taps on the floor, the rhythms of approaching death stalking another drug-induced victim.

K.O. wanders down the hall toward his office, absently peeking through the open door into Sonny's room. His eyes pop wide open, and he covers the space between the door and bed in a single leap, grabs the spike, and tosses it aside. He pulls Sonny upright and rubs the arm, slaps his face, slaps him again, drapes Sonny over his shoulder, forcing him to walk in circles, yelling at him to open his eyes and move his feet.

Sonny slumps, eyes shut, dead weight in K.O.'s arms, his feet dragging beside him. K.O. whips out his phone and speed dials 9-1-1, holds the phone between ear and shoulder while he rotates in the room then muscles Sonny down the hall and into the showers, turns the cold on full-force, sets the phone on the sink with speaker engaged. He carries Sonny in under the spray nozzle, both men soaking wet in seconds. K.O. yells the information to the emergency response operator.

K.O. tunes an ear while he struggles with Sonny. The siren, louder and closer, and finally the ERTs enter. He unloads the dead weight and the techs go to work. Not fast enough in K.O.'s mind, but as quickly as possible, the tech lays Sonny flat on the stretcher and begins pumping his chest, oxygen mask engaged. A second tech examines the hot-shot K.O. hands him.

Tech says, "Looks like heroin." He injects Naloxone into a thigh muscle and wheels Sonny out. The van whips down the driveway and screams its way north. K.O. jumps in his truck and tails the ERT wagon all the way to the hospital. Tracking the bright flashing colors across town, he speed-dials Willow as he drives.

"Sonny just shot up and OD'd, don't know what, he's alive but out cold. Go by Anderson's office and get all the medical information for the intake psyche docs – tech said he needs everything we can get. What meds he's on daily and dosages, and we'll see what's in this needle." K.O. follows the ambulance, the hit-kit lying beside him on the seat.

Willow jumps into her Pathfinder, sticks her flasher on the dash, runs the single traffic signal in town and both stop signs, and races to Anderson's office. She needs his paperwork and his medication details for the hospital emergency doctors. The medical technician advised K.O. that the ER psyche doctors want information from the clinic, the psychiatrist and any other doctors that treat Sonny, describing treatment and medications. Sonny has not engaged a new doctor yet since K.O fired Anderson, but Anderson has the most up-to-date prescriptions and medical files at his office.

*

"Can't give that out, privacy issues. You need Sonny to sign off," Anderson's assistant tells Willow, very sorry but unyielding.

"What about the one we already signed, last month, the release to Doctor Cat?"

"No good, not valid. He turned eighteen, different forms. He signs, you can't."

Willow asks again, "Please, Mary Ellen." She explains again the near overdose, the emergency room, the request for medical information. No luck.

Mary Ellen refuses, claims patient privacy again - the HIPAA laws. Willow cannot sign off anymore. Once Sonny reached eighteen years of age, it classifies him as an adult, legally responsible, regardless of his illness or state of mind. The medical communities fear liability if it discloses information, so the national administration policy develops into a share nothing concept to protect the office often at the expense of its patients. No one shares a stamp, let alone a complete health record. Everything about a patient remains secret even if it kills one or two occasionally.

"Really sorry Willow, but I can't. I'll get in trouble, could get fired. I can't lose my job. Doctor Anderson needs to approve it. He's really, really strict about it."

Afraid to give his location per his orders, Mary Ellen dials his cell phone and holds the unit up so Willow can hear it too. It rings, one beep, and direct to its answer line. Anderson turns it off when he plays golf, Tuesday and Thursday afternoon, most evenings, and all weekends.

Willow begs, in tears. "Please, if he's out of town, just tell me, we'll find some way – get the ER or police to contact him – it's a real emergency. Sonny's in the hospital, unconscious, comatose, he can't sign even if we bring it. We can't help him if we can't treat him."

Mary Ellen likes Sonny a lot, always feels disappointed when the doctor treats him with less respect than his higher paying golf pals who need the 'happy pills' he prescribes for each colleague, and treats Sonny with less respect than his HMO insurance clients as well. The Medicare and state aid patients sit right on the bottom in his mind. She finally relents, takes Willow's hand, torn between her duty and Sonny. Finally, Sonny wins.

"I can't tell you where he is, but he shuts off his cell on golf days." Mary Ellen stares at Willow, assuring herself that Willow gets the hint. Only one major golf course exists within fifty miles. Mary Ellen has three children and four grandchildren, works in the health care field, understands the dilemma, and can truthfully claim she never revealed his location.

Willow smiles through her tears. "Southside. Thanks. You won't regret this." Willow hugs Mary Ellen hard, pulls away quickly, and dials her cell.

"You're closer, K.O. Go get the sign-off. I'll follow up on Sonny."

Nineteen minutes later, K.O. squeals into the parking lot, pops the door, and hops out. He pushes into the Southside Golf Pro

Shop at the country club development. He asks the desk manager, "Anderson on the greens?" Manager shakes his head sideways. "Know where he is?" Manager points a finger at a double archway that opens into the lounge.

K.O. enters the bar, spots Anderson sitting at a small round bar table with three men dressed in up-scale golf clothes, drinks in hand, peanuts in a bowl. Four golf bags stand beside the group. Fuzzy golf socks with cartoon character faces extend above the rims and protect each club. Anderson glances up, recognizes K.O. hurrying towards the table.

The psychiatrist listens. K.O. explains. Anderson refuses to release medical documents unless Sonny signs off. "Besides, his insurance ran out, he's on self-pay. Make an appointment when he gets released, and bring a check." A smirk appears, Anderson getting a little testy, a little cold revenge maybe because last week K.O. dismissed Anderson as consulting psychiatrist as soon as Sonny finds another doctor. Anderson turns back toward his golf pals and lifts his drink, a rude dismissal.

The doctor comes across a little too insolent, uncaring, unprofessional, and K.O. loses what little tolerance remains after Anderson made insulting remarks about Sonny and his treatment last month, and his low insurance payouts. The ignorant and worthless attitude that now endangers Sonny pushes the final button.

K.O. jerks Anderson off the bar stool, right hand twisting his shirt, and the left grips his throat. Anderson coughs, the glass slips out of his hand, spilling ice and bourbon across the table. The glass rolls in a half-circle, bounces onto the hardwood floor, and shatters.

Squeezing the chokehold tighter, K.O. lifts the doctor up on his toes and shoves him back against the wall. The effort pulls at his stitches, sending a ripple of pain along his ribs and up through his shoulder. K.O. grunts but ignores it.

Anderson turns red in the face, out of breath, sweat beading his forehead. The doctor struggles, flaps his arms, unable to wiggle free, his golf club flab no match for a master gym rat, even an injured gym rat.

"See? You scared yet? You feel that fear? You pissing your pants? Now you know how Mister Bones feels every minute he's awake. Aliens and demons in his brain – afraid for his life – and you're supposed to care, supposed to figure it out, not play games while this child suffers. He's still under your medical care until he picks another doctor, that's the law. You forget that on golf days?"

Four feet away, an apple-cheeked sock-puppet with a friar hairdo, a donut middle, and built like a stump pushes his stool back, stands up, and squeaks. "Hey, you can't do that. Put him down and get the hell out before I call security."

K.O. turns his scare-eyes at the stump. "Can't do what?" A glare sparks across the table. Stump sits down, opens his cell. K.O. shakes his head once. Stump looks at the dial and back at K.O., and K.O. shakes his head twice this time. Stump shuts the phone. K.O. turns his attention back to Anderson, still hanging on the wall, afraid to move, unable to move.

"Remember those HIPAA laws?" K.O. tightens his grip. "You can't share this meeting without my signature. Our secret medical conference, get it?" K.O. growls the words directly into Anderson's left ear. His entire body shudders once and the doctor releases his bladder, urine spreads across the crotch of his golf shorts.

K.O. slides Anderson down the wall until his feet touch the floor, removes his hands and brushes his fingertips gently across the shirtfront, straightens the creases.

"Turn on your cell phone. Call your office. Release those medical details right now, today, immediately. No appointment required. FAX it to Baxter General Hospital, Doctor Morgantholavich." His words bite deep and granite hard into the silence.

"HIPAA again, remember it? Repeat one word of this psychiatric discussion we just had and I'll come back personally and enforce that law. Don't go billing this as a half-hour family visit either. You're no longer his doctor." K.O. contradicts the statement he just made but cares nothing about continuous care laws. Furious at the attitude this physician brings to his profession, K.O. leaves Anderson leaning against the wall, coughing, gasping for breath.

K.O. points, asks the stump still holding his phone, "Those golf clubs yours?"

The man nods, swallows, unable to speak. K.O. slides out

one club, examines it carefully, lays it on the floor, steps on it, grabs the end and bends it up into an arc then curls it back into the golf bag. "Just fixing your slice, be perfect now. Try it out tomorrow. Open your phone again before I reach my truck and I'll come back and fix your hook too. Got it?"

Another nod, no words, but the stump slides his phone into his pocket.

K.O. addresses all three men this time. "You three doctors?"

All three men nod in tandem, speechless, frozen in place, unaccustomed to a sudden lack of control. The authority money and title buys in the suit, tie, and white coat world in which these men normally exist falls absent in the presence of the character and caring K.O. carries into the mix. Well, that and a too tight tee shirt with muscle busting out of it.

"Good, thought you all were Mulligans there for a minute. Consider this conference protected by federal privacy laws. Don't share it with anyone unless I sign off first." K.O. tosses a dollar bill on the table. "Here, divide the fee."

Security arrives, a steel gray uniform with a silver badge stuck on its pocket. Tall, stout male very fit and solid eases into the lounge, carries a baton looped through his belt but no firearm. Two Mixed Martial Arts Champion decals stand out on his forearms, one tattooed above each wrist in bright red and blue ink, an MMA decal no one wears unless he wins it – the truest proof of his physical skills. Security man looks at the bartender. Bartender points a pen at K.O.

K.O. crosses the room and approaches the archway. Security man stands in the center of the arch, then steps aside and tips his cap. "Hey K.O., what's up? We all good to go here?"

K.O. nods his head. "Hey, Brian, all set, just finishing up a free medical conference."

Brian and K.O. bump fists. No one at the table says a word. Probably lucky getting away with this kind of action once, K.O. believes, but it works for now. Convenient too, K.O. owns the only gym in a small town, where Lisa's big brother teaches martial arts and self-defense every Tuesday and Thursday evening.

K.O. steps through the arch and approaches the bar, lays four dollars on the dark oak top, grins at the bartender. "Please bring Andy over there a splash of bourbon, some chipped ice, and a new glass. He got in a real hurry to FAX some papers, but stood up too quick and spilled his drink." K.O turns around and glances back at Anderson.

Anderson pushes himself upright and examines his shorts, then looks through the arch at K.O. staring back. The doctor opens his phone, turns it on, and dials his office. "Send the Bones history to Baxter General." He listens. "That's okay, just change the dates, then copy it, then FAX it." Mary Ellen already had everything copied and ready, helping and hoping.

The documents arrive at the hospital before K.O. even climbs in the cab. He hops in his truck and heads back to the gym, no doubt in his mind the doctor will FAX the papers. He wraps an arm tight against his ribs, and groans. "Damn, that hurt."

A little concern beats on him too, about any ramifications for his actions today, but he'd threaten Anderson again under the same conditions without hesitation. Matter of fact, he might threaten him again just because the man deserves it. The consequences may bite him later, no time for worry now.

43

Phone stuck on her ear, Cat rages into the speaker, very upset, extremely angry. "How can that possibly happen? How! Sonny was admitted on a Violent Hold! Judge Archer signed it! How can the clinic possibly let him out?"

Willow explains. "Shift change-over. Burkhart blew it, came back after her three days off, read the 'no insurance admit' instead and sent Sonny home." Willow rips through a stack of documents, shreds each one into a hundred pieces, tosses the remains into the trash can. "Another paperwork fuck-up!"

Cat almost matches Sonny at times, her rage exploding, her fury unbridled. "What do they mean 'no insurance'? Our clinic pays the fee. Harvard pays all treatment costs! Our grant funds everything! Where do they find these fools in finance?"

"Wasn't finance this time, was the charge nurse. She came on shift and released him without reading the custody sheets," Willow says. "Assumed Sonny was on a three-day no insurance consult again, as in the past."

"Okay, am getting on a plane soon as I hang up. Pick me up. I'll text the info soon as I get a flight."

*

K.O. sits on the bed in the room where Sonny lives, begins searching the closet and drawers for drugs and paraphernalia, taking no chances. K.O. opens the desk drawer, finds clumps of pages torn out of a psychology text, finds the book under the bed, opens the cover, and sees a name etched inside – Elliott Ramsey – Randy's older brother finished a term at the community college a few months ago, same time Lisa finished and transferred to Berkeley.

Surprised, K.O. lifts his eyes, scans the pages, reads notes Sonny scrawled in the margins about symptoms, and hallucinations, medications. Finds an article that claims a suicide attempt really means a kid craves attention, or knows he needs treatment and can't get it. He examines other notes about demons, aliens, imaginary voices, holograms, about a lack of knowledge, and underlined in red, 'no known medications cure biological mental disorders'.

He reads more notes about treatment and recovery, no cure but medications stall the brain damage. Finds more pages stapled together, copies, articles about care, lack of care, and problems that arise when insurance pays so little, the conflicts between care and costs. An article discusses federal health law and mandatory medical care for kids or young adults, or anyone with mental conditions who injure themselves, or injure others due to the illness.

He scans passages, summations of case studies underlined in red ink. Different scholars writing about psyche patients who receive medical treatment at state clinics after harming someone, a brother, a friend, a lover, even strangers. Only if an individual becomes a danger to himself or others – that specific sentence appears in numerous articles, and Sonny underlined it twice in red ink each time he read it. Similar versions of the same critical information underlined in ink, or yellow highlights.

He gathers all the paperwork and boxes it up, carries it all out to his truck. He fires up the engine and dials Willow. "Knew Sonny was smart Willow but this is way too far out there. Wait until you see what he's been studying. And, he left a note, with a blood fingerprint signature. Says I get his truck, and we share his bank account. He says share his clothes between Shanty and Allen at the clinic. He asks us to tell Melanie, Brian, and Bailey goodbye for him. Tell Lisa he loves her." Tears flood down K.O.'s cheeks.

*

"I know it K.O., know the dose, know what kills me, what won't. Been doing this drug stuff a while, years, you know it. You yelled at me enough." Lying on the clinic bed, Sonny tosses the copies back at K.O.

"Look, read it. See the rules, I hurt someone else or hurt myself, then I'm dangerous. That's how this health care system works unless you're rich or have insurance. If you're poor you get nothing, but if you're poor and dangerous you get treatment, otherwise, tough luck. Sonny slurs his words slightly, and his eyelids droop as if he just woke up, but his statements make a terrible kind of sense.

"What about that note?"

"Just proves it. Cops never believe it unless you leave a note. Don't tell anyone."

Sonny glances around, as if hiding his words. "Otherwise, I get no state insurance. Have to hurt myself or someone else. If you watch cop shows and lawyer shows, no one believes it without a note. Right? Besides, if I screwed up, want you to have my truck. You're like my dad K.O."

A young man wise beyond his years speaks a truth few people learn in a life, his personal experience, an extremely harsh teacher. No insurance. Health laws state Sonny gets no long-term hospital treatment unless he hurts himself or hurts someone else, a life threat, a danger to himself, or others. Then, the law makes it mandatory. No problem, Sonny simply made it mandatory.

"So, it's me or no one, K.O. Won't hurt my friends, and don't want to live this way. Spooks screaming at me all the time, frying my brain, just can't fight these aliens anymore, getting too strong. Can't run fast enough, can't lift enough weight. Besides, it's safe in here, can't hurt anyone. Almost killed you K.O. How do I live with that?"

Another conflict bites into his brain. No more financial strain on Willow and K.O, Sonny settles for that small reward, at least for the present.

Willow can't bring herself to tell Sonny, and it breaks her heart. CAT-RON pays all treatment fees with a Harvard research grant. He no longer requires insurance. No one told him, and Burkhart made a huge mistake in discharging him. Burkhart never read the Violent Hold order the judge signed. Sonny nearly lost his life because a financial clerk and a clinic nurse fouled up some paperwork. Unforgivable.

44

K.O. and Willow spent three days organizing care and worrying about Sonny. He plans to meet Willow and Cat later, but this morning K.O. sits in his doctor's office while his nurse checks the stitches, changes his bandages. Luckily, his quick reflexes prevented more damage, and probably saved his life, as well as Willow and Cat arriving at the exact minute Sonny attacked.

*

Willow sits across the desk from Cat, points at two empty coffee cups. "Refill?" She lifts the pot off the burner, pours, adds cream to both. "So, sounds like you disagree with Anderson, and Bateman, and Griswold?"

Cat tried signing on as Sonny's doctor immediately after Anderson sent the files and his release as consulting psychiatrist. State laws deny her practice here until she obtains a state license. She knew it but tried anyway and failed so far, paperwork again. She began the processing at least. The clinic psychiatrist assumes that role at present, until Sonny chooses another doctor, or Cat gets her certification. Cat can consult, but can't take the lead and that's good enough for K.O. and Willow. Sonny already asked Cat and signed HIPAA permissions.

Cat contemplates her answer. A few seconds pass. "Doctors often have different opinions, based on education, experience, and dedication, ability to interact with our patients, desire to treat." Diplomatically, she implies Anderson and his colleagues hold views diametric to her own.

Although Cat opposed the treatment methods Anderson presented right from the beginning, Willow recognizes her tactfully stated position. Cat disagrees with almost everything in Anderson's treatment plan, same thoughts about several other doctors that treated Sonny in the past.

Many mental health specialists have paper credentials but base the practice on a thirty-minute consult, and often do not understand the illness in depth, or individual brain chemistry and thought processing works, or how it interacts. They cannot treat patients with brain disease successfully with talk therapy anyway, no matter what they do or what they claim. And they cannot prescribe medications.

Willow tells Cat, "K.O. almost fell out of his truck when one psychoanalyst called and stated she could cure Sonny if he enrolled in her massage therapy and alternate backyard nature sessions, identifying birdsong harmonic patterns during spring courtship dances. She guaranteed his federal and state funded health insurance covered it under mental disorders therapy. She was only half-right, insurance covered it ... K.O. hung up after the bird chirped."

Cat says, "Social training or medication alone cannot treat biological brain malfunction, but more importantly, only the correct chemistry creates a brain environment compatible with social and cultural rehabilitation. Social training needs the proper biological treatment initially. Chemistry balances the brain environment and stops the cell damage first. Then social organization and behavior training might succeed, or at least help a patient."

Willow aims her eyes toward Cat.

Unwilling to condemn all psychiatric colleagues based upon the sins of a few unprofessional doctors, no other clinics in the country take treatment to the level Cat and Aaron take it, some clinics still do a good job and treat patients correctly and accurately. Cutting-edge research and the treatment models Cat develops stand at the top of the list today in the world of psychiatric medicine.

Willow has come to understand it almost as well, the process not the medicine. Her experience over the past years, her recent independent research, and her meetings with Cat bring it out. These mentally unbalanced kids run toward the end of a pier while specialists chit-chat with the patients one time a month, check a few boxes on a chart describing a pre-conceived notion about each, prescribe a pill that slows them down but leaves the drop-off right out there at the same distance, just beyond the sightline. Simply takes a patient longer to get there – but they all eventually get there – and then it ends, often with a needle in a vein or a bullet to the brain.

The brain eats itself away, leaving a patient either a vegetable or so violent and out of control he knocks over a liquor store and shoots the cashier, or robs a sports-bar and beats the manager with a club, or simply punches a friend and breaks his neck. Then the courts lock him up for life with minimal care and no follow-up treatment. A warehouse.

Some obey the voices and really hurt people, commit violent crimes until caught. Some fight back, deny the voice demands, but never discover enjoyment in life. Some accept the voices as friends, invisible companions, listen for and accept advice they will not otherwise give themselves, some of it sound, some of it whacky, some of it allowing survival in a confused but minimally stable lifestyle, but most of it ignored because a brain simply malfunctions and a cure remains unattainable.

"The lucky ones get a hospital for life, the unlucky a jail cell. If neither happens, the victims prowl the streets and alleys with no one to guide them except disembodied voices many believe come from another planet. Not a very positive prognosis, is it Cat?"

Cat looks at the ceiling. Fighting the system and defining treatments plans leaves her breathless and drained, as worn out as her patients. Her words emerge softly, "I just want to fix these kids."

*

The next morning, Cat and Willow meet again at her office. "The admissions psyche doctor takes lead on Sonny now, Doctor Ian Carter. He's still on record until we get my paperwork approved. Anderson had priority but we intervened, more paperwork. Sonny refused Anderson, and signed that release already. He wants me, but that can't happen yet, so he accepted Carter until we get the license situation fixed, but I can still consult with Carter and Sonny. Carter runs the Gatesville clinic, and works well with other doctors. I'll walk that discharge paperwork through tomorrow and Anderson's officially out, even though he's been out unofficially for a month already."

"Wait for paperwork, paperwork, and more paperwork. Someday, maybe in the future, we'll get to treat our patients instead of filling out forms stating we're treating our patients." Cat shakes her head in frustration then grins at Willow. "I heard K.O. gave Anderson a free fitness lesson, left him leaning against a wall needing a change of underwear." Willow acknowledges nothing aloud, but aims a grin at Cat.

K.O. eases into the room and sits, grunts, pain interfering with his range of motion. His ribs stretch and pull skin and stitches every time he moves. "Damn forms again, always seem more important than treatment. Ellie will help if we need her, she heard the custody case, and probably still has jurisdiction even though Sonny reached age of maturity."

"She's still the state law and on board when we need her. She signed the Violent Hold order too, for all the good it did. She laid a big fat ten-thousand dollar fine on the clinic and diverted it to local mental health research. Interestingly enough, Allen and Shanty may get some benefit from it, Sonny too."

Cat got Carter endorsed as lead as soon as she learned how well he works with young adults, and knew they would make a good team. Carter stays very busy because he puts his patients first, and everyone knows it. Judge Archer prepared, signed, and filed legal documents so Cat can get a waiver and lead the treatment team here in Virginia, but it may not matter as much now, as Carter is on board as well. It still takes time though, paperwork before treatment, as usual.

*

"What do we understand now about Sonny and his condition?" Willow asks.

"You want the layman's viewpoint or a medical techie

viewpoint?"

"Got a biology degree, so how about middle ground." Willow settles in.

K.O. injects, "Forget me, I'll follow best I can, got my certificate in hard knocks at Punch and Bruise University, downtown Buffalo."

Cat shifts in her seat, happy to share her theory and application with any person who cares and understands it enough to track her discussion. "Please K.O., jump in, I want you to understand it too. You're like a parent here."

K.O. grins, rubs his stitches, forever his humorous self. "Seems like I'm a patient too." Cat leans over and opens his shirt, fakes checking the wound. "You're healing fine and eligible to listen."

She begins, "In some ways, Sonny's like everyone else, in some ways, he's like nobody else. Everyone develops this disease differently due to genetics, biology, life experience, and unique DNA, and the way each brain inputs and recalls information."

"These kids and young adults are children with an illness, not just some dangerous monster to sedate and warehouse, or medicate and send home until one hurts himself or someone else. Good example with you K.O. Well, maybe a bad example. That could have ended with jail and a record, and no treatment, just punishment, same with Shanty, and even with Stanton earlier."

"But it's like slapping a six-month-old baby when it fills its diaper. The baby acts how it acts and thinks nothing of that behavior until it receives punishment, but the punishment has no sound basis. Normal behavior for a baby, it eliminates waste, so why punish it. If we punish, that baby learns nothing except fear."

"Sonny feels the same way, he responds violently without guilt until the threat releases. An authority figure grabs him off the street for protecting himself from an imaginary danger and slaps him in a cell. Sonny truly believes a danger existed at the time, but he receives punishment. So, again, his mind fills with conflicted thoughts, but his brain and body act exactly as it should."

"Remember the instinct and survival actions in my earlier notes you read about Walter Ferguson, the lemon analogy, and the tribal folklore Max sent?" Willow nods. "Well, here's the way the Sonny's brain works in relation to that instinct and his life experiences."

"Brain chemistry, its response to external and internal stimuli develops uniquely in every individual, as unique as a fingerprint, or a retina scan. No two brains think alike because no two individuals experience the same history from birth, so brain development, including memory, always differs at least to some degree. Each conscious mind makes decisions based on a combination of instinct, individual memory, and direct sensory input at the time it makes a specific decision."

"In a simplified way, the body survives only to protect the brain and to produce offspring that pass on its basic genetic structure. Same thing with Sonny, he responds to what's best for Sonny, even if it forces violence."

"Remember what Max said about Hobbes' theory, that the human nature restrains itself only through social interaction and the fear of retaliation if we break a law or ritual. He believes human culture will degrade into pure paganism or anarchy without some sort of forced cultural restraint in place."

"Sonny thinks in black and white, no middle ground. Defense behavior exhibits first when his body or brain feels threatened, we all respond in that way. At least until we determine the threat is no threat. Sonny has a weak or absent 'threat filter', so he sees everything around him as a threat until he has the time to evaluate it."

"Sonny's very fit and athletic, so his physical responses appear extreme to others less active and less fit. The oddest part, Sonny feels a threat and responds with defense, but he scares the people that threaten him more than any threat scares Sonny. He holds it back because he feels this moral restraint, then his emotions emerge and he feels guilt when he hurts someone and protects himself. Emotionally, Sonny can't elude the guilt."

"His brain chemistry malfunctions, his perception becomes distorted and he believes he's in danger from situations that are in fact not dangerous. He cannot behave in any other way. His brain chemically produces fright so he fears his social environment each time the neural dysfunction unbalances his brain chemistry."

"His brain fills those memory recall holes when he processes his mental videos and his mind probably contains significantly more holes than a normal mind. He hallucinates in the extreme and over-reacts when K.O., or you Willow, appear as if you're in danger. Primary instinct protects the brain, and secondary, protects the genetic line, the family. You and K.O. are like his family. Sonny would literally die protecting you both if a dangerous situation arose, even if he just mistakenly believes it."

"When Sonny punches a hole in the wall, it's as normal as taking a drink of water. Water relieves thirst. The punch relieves stress, but only for a short period, same as water. Sonny thinks nothing about the damage he causes at the exact moment he hits the wall. To him, it releases his frustration. Sometimes, like Fergie, Sonny believes a demon hides inside the wall. He's aiming to kill it, or injure it, or scare it away."

"Guilt pushes itself in after the fact, when his mind interprets the moral or ethical consequence of that action and plugs it into his thought processing. Like when he stabbed K.O. You can't even imagine the guilt Sonny feels for that action whenever his mind achieves a stable state. At the time, he absolutely believed he was protecting you K.O. He absolutely believed those demons were choking you."

"The aliens appear as a group of individuals equally as complicated as a human society, because he needs something or someone to fight and burn up that energy, and allow his body to rest. Sonny needs some kind of cultural organization that explains behavior he can't understand. Morton and Boone say 'we're working on him', but he's not present. So the logical answer for Sonny, he imagines mind-reading or thought-transference."

"A threat releases hormones into the blood, slows non-essential protective actions such as digestion, increases heartbeat and metabolism, uploads sugars and more oxygen, as well as pain relief when the activity runs at full strength for extended periods. Endorphins act like morphine. Kills pain and allows his body to endure extremes in physical activity, or stress in this instance. His protective actions – fight or flight – produce the high-alert state and stop only after the danger passes."

"It's like a phone system in his brain dials nine-one-one thousands of times a second and triggers his alarm system, producing a high-energy action-ready physical condition. His body can't remain up-charged all the time so must release the up-charge chemistry or it will burn out."

"The demons personify his fright. He creates the demon culture so his mind can interpret a world that Sonny understands, one that he can control, or at least interact with it as real. It releases the endorphins and balances adrenaline and fright chemicals and thus calms his brain. It's a method that his mind developed and maintains so he can cope with chemical conflicts in his brain and body. It's an unconscious reaction."

"His ethics and moral character, his sense of caring is so powerful he won't allow himself to hurt anyone, even if he believes it's an alien being. Instead, he runs, lifts, spars, or works hard so the energy that triggers violence in his brain dissipates and he can relax without hurting his friends. Unfortunately, it builds itself into a rage he can't always control, and you K.O., and Shanty, and others paid the price before anyone knew it."

Willow says, "You forgot Jumbo? Sonny punched him too."

"Not the same thing. Sonny bounces in and out of normal. That was a simple boy-boy fight, normal between kids. Jumbo stole from him, and disgraced his friend Bailey. That was just a kid punching a kid, but the powerful kid won, not even a match. That's why it's so difficult to diagnose, normal and abnormal behaviors are often identical actions visually, but different triggers."

K.O and Willow nod, grasping the difference.

"Different too, his interaction with Stanton had no brain dysfunction trigger. He simply responded as any male would when another male stepped on his tail. Sonny read Stanton as a fool, and refused to sit still for Stanton posturing at Sonny's expense."

"Sonny popped out of his rage episode well before that interaction in the cell, and he felt no fear in that case, he read Stanton immediately as weak and insecure. Sonny was almost joking, pointing the absurdity back at Stanton because the man earned it with his own stupidity. Sonny was not violent the psychotic sense at that time. He was playing with Stanton, like a puppy, but bulldog strong."

"He perceives prescribed drugs as a control mechanism and his mental condition refuses that control. Like everyone else, he wants control of his own life, and so aliens push the poison idea and 'fill a hole' in his mind video. He develops fear of poison medications. He claims he acts normal and needs no chemical contamination. And, they 'worked on him' outside of his presence, if you remember that meeting and the additional hours his health care workers logged."

"As doctors, we must gain his trust so he will share the truth with us and we can adjust his medication and dosage based on how he feels right at the exact time his fears disappear, and not by how he acts two or three hours or even days before or after the fact."

"It might take six months or a year, but it means Sonny can function, stay out of jail, stay out of trouble, and become productive during his life and enjoy it – that's my goal here."

Willow says, "Seems worth it to me."

Cat peeks at the clock. "Okay, enough. I'll let you digest this stuff for now and leave these notes and descriptions here. I'm heading back to Boston in an hour, and have stops on the way with other patients. I'll be back here in ten days, after the clinic seminars conclude for that week. Call me if you need me, any time. Keep me in touch with Sonny and his reactions. They keep him pretty sedated now, letting his mind heal as best it can. The fight with you K.O. and the overdose, very traumatic stuff even if a warp in his brain initiated it. Sonny feels scared, guilty, and a huge sadness. We need to change that, and bring happiness back into his life."

45

Sonny bounces in and out of reality, his psychosis active over minutes, hours, or days, depending on the hormones and brain chemistry interaction at any specific time.

Cat reads the clinic notes, a little more complete now that she trained the staff to properly document what she needs. She finishes her talk at a staff meeting in Baxter.

"More importantly, as doctors, we need time to figure out which medication blend works in each patient. Most patients respond uniquely to any chemical compound, we doctors decide which one works once a patient explains how that individual brain and body respond to it, if a patient can explain it accurately. A dysfunctional mind explaining a dysfunctional brain, not the best scenario in the medical world, but it's all we have at the moment. And who better can explain it than those that truly experience the pain."

*

"You taught me K.O, don't harm anyone. Since the beginning, just fight fair, play by the rules. Ethics of life K.O., your ethics, your morals, good ones, never intentionally injure another boxer. If you got him beat, knock him out or stay away, wait for the win, but never hurt him – it's a sport, not a killing spree. Your words K.O. Remember?"

No fright-eyes this time, mostly wild and twitching as his eyes roam around the room, like chasing a fly, but a notion of sadness sneaks out too. "Almost the first thing you taught me, while I was still sweeping floors and washing windows."

"So, all I had to do was hurt someone, or myself. Read it K.O. It's all right there in those pages. I chose myself, not my friend, not a stranger, not even a no-trust jack. This is me, I'm the nut-kid. I hurt you and I need to fix it. Need your help though, you and Doctor Cat, and Willow, my trust friends."

Willow says, "You're not nuts Sonny. It's brain chemistry. Cat will fix it."

K.O. and Willow listen, eyes wet and dripping tears. Both stare at Sonny, bewildered, unable to cure him. Neither says a word, as no words exist to follow that confession. Eight separate eyes spill over, including Sonny when he finishes his story. Even Nurse Burkhart, standing in the doorway holding his meds and his chart, she heard it all too, and her eyes drip as well. The emotional Miss Nasty.

*

Sonny took a chance and shot the dope in a dose high enough that officials believe he attempted suicide, and he left the note. He knew K.O. would walk past his bedroom on the way to his office every time he comes into the gym. Sonny hurt himself rather than another person and took a huge chance. He hates the aliens enough that it was worth it. He read all kinds of articles about suicide, and that fact that psychologists and psychiatrists interpret that act as a cry for help, unconsciously directed in the brain, but consciously chosen by the mind. He also read where anyone that attempts suicide gets help, and automatically gets state medical coverage. Sonny was afraid he would hurt one of his friends, or even a stranger if his rage gained control. He bet his life K.O. would find him in time. Sonny chose freedom or a grave, and flipped a coin. Fifty-fifty. Lucky for Sonny, he called the winner.

*

"Heard that story many times, a great story K.O., your story. You quit the ring, held back punches, never hurt anyone intentionally."

Sonny took it straight into his own heart and was willing to sacrifice his life before hurting K.O. or Willow, or anyone else. Some may believe that proves the patient truly needs medical care on a mandatory level, but regardless who believes which reason or version, Sonny now receives his medical treatment. Tough method he used to achieve a goal. Worked fine though, he got his medical insurance. That's what he believes, anyway. Neither Cat nor Willow has yet told Sonny about Harvard and CAT-RON paying his fees.

"So the alien gives me an order, I don't follow it. Don't hurt Jacki, don't hurt Randy, don't hurt you, or Willow. Can't do it anyway, even if I want. Never happen, K.O. but I lost it, lost the ability to hold it back, and hurt you. Aliens chose you, and then it was too late."

"Great big hole in my heart when mom died, and you guys filled it up then, you fill it up now. You make me happy. Could never hurt you, you're my family. You're all I got."

"But I got to kill those aliens before they make me do something else dangerous, and I got to protect you guys from the demons they plant in you, or they might get to you without me to stop them." Sonny explains his distorted reality again, blaming the aliens, and blaming himself.

"The demons live in your mind Sonny. It's hormones. Brain chemistry makes you see aliens hiding in your brain, and on your friends, but they don't really exist. It's only your imagination." Willow again attempts to win a battle she can never win.

Sonny sees and hears the aliens, feels the demon power in his brain. To him, it's a real as it gets. "Yeah, well, I believe that Willow, I know you won't lie to me, and demons don't exist." He pauses a moment, closes his eyes, thinking. "But what if it gets out and I'm not here to protect you? Then what? Then it's my fault if you get hurt. Got K.O. once already." Tears fill his eyes, spill over. "Couldn't protect you K.O. Alien got you. My fault. Got Shanty too, once."

K.O stands, tears in his eyes as well, the pain obvious, in his side and in his heart. His stitches pull tight, his face contorts, and he wraps his arms around Sonny. "Not your fault Champ, not your fault."

Willow asks, "Before you begin treatment, you need state approval, right?"

Cat butts in. "Nope, I have permission already, Carter keeps lead, but he and Sonny agree our team can talk with him, treat him, and maintain an observation monitor so we can watch his responses long-term. Judge Archer signed a Violent Hold admission, we can keep him as an in-patient now as long as we believe he's dangerous, our choice not his at this point. The court always agrees after a suicide attempt. And, we have Judge Archer on our side."

"Even though we all know he had more control than the evidence suggests, and we're sure he did it for the exact reasons he said. That was no suicide attempt, not after what he told us, but it helps us so we leave it. But, anyone that has a brain incident like that needs help even if he did it intentionally with a different goal in mind."

"We know his demons exist, his wide awake nightmare. We'll keep that information private for now and hold him in a more stable environment while we track his behavior and prepare mixtures we can test. We have all the base chemistry. We've had it for years. We need to create a drug complex that works on his individual brain, a mixture that induces stable brain function in him all the time, not just occasionally. We have the ingredients, we need to refine the mixture and bake that cake."

"Isn't that against his rights, according to what those legal reps said yesterday?" Willow again follows the logical and tactical approach instead of the medical approach, and plans against legal interference. Right or wrong, legal or not, she's more worried about his health than his legal position at this point, but wants a strategy in her plan just in case. Willow knows Cat controls his treatment, and K.O. stands ready to assist on any level he can – he practically owns all the local contacts, all his friends, which helps. Besides, the court ruled two days ago, Ellie ordered temporary guardianship back to Willow and K.O. during a competency hearing.

K.O. responds after a late night chat with Ellie yesterday. "Legal rights, yup, goes against it but no one's fighting it at this time, including Sonny. We bend the rules a little rather than give it up. None of us want Sonny 'legally right but medically dead,' including Sonny, and not even those legal advocates as foolish as they appear on occasion."

46

Sonny says, "My demon was screaming at me to kill his demon. Saw it hanging behind his ear, hiding in his hair, little green one. My demon kept yelling, 'Kill it! Kill it! Kill it! It stole from Allen.' So I choked it and it let Shanty go."

Cat explains again, elevating her treatment level as Sonny shares his soul with her, and all his torment. She tries different chemical compounds, but nothing works well yet. She's been at it three months, but it takes time to evaluate each one correctly. "There's no alien, Sonny. You choked Shanty, not the alien."

"See that proves it. His alien disappeared. Shanty's happy now, got that sucker out of his hair." Sonny puts on a frown, "He still steals though, pisses people off. I probably only got one of his aliens, must have had two, like K.O."

Cat continues, balancing the medications, listening to Sonny, consulting Aaron, testing one chemical combination after another under extremely controlled conditions. Hope fills her heart. She never quits, never fails her clients.

*

Sonny lies on his bed, awaiting sleep. An extremely wispy spook, a vaporous phantom, hovers in his view. A weak voice hints an order, scratchy, barely a whisper. *Kill them all, you make mistakes. Put Cat on the list now, she makes you eat poison.* Sonny raises his middle finger, points it at the spook, and shuts his eyes.

Five minutes later, his eyes pop open. He glances in the

corner without moving his head, barely hears the complaints, a light breeze wiggles one spook, floating, hanging above the window. Sonny ignores its words, chuckles once then shuts his eyes. Powerless, flimsy, the demon scream too soft to matter, it simply emits a low volume gripe. Sonny fades into oblivion.

His fourth alarm clock claimed 'unbreakable' and 'waterproof' on its carton, at least one of those two assertions turned out to be a lie on the first two. Unbreakable claim failed first time two alarm clocks hit the wall last year. The waterproof claim got one test, a swim in the toilet, three months ago. It failed. He sets his new clock on the table each night, still in one piece after three months. A light chime greets the morning sun streaming in through the bars.

Sonny opens his eyes, pushes the off button and peeks at its face, glad it still works. Fourth clock this year, its little red hand points at the five, big red hand covers the one. Big hand ticks once, ticks again then ticks three more times. Sonny watches it move. Five minutes pass. Sonny waits for his demons. Little hand points at the five, big hand covers the two. Nothing. No demons, no aliens, ten minutes pass without a nasty scream.

His spirit brother murmurs, a very quiet voice nudging itself into the foreground. *You can hear me now. I'm back. Pay no attention to violence. It's never good for anyone.*

"Must be too early for it. Lazy today, must be sleeping in." Sonny shuts his eyes, opens one then the other, waiting, patient, less afraid. "Hey! You fooling me spook?" Nothing. No haunting, no demon, Sonny listens with two ears, silence.

His spirit brother agrees. *No aliens today.*

Four weeks had passed without a major episode, just a fading voice, slipping further into the back of his mind, each morning the same result. Only his spirit brother speaks now, advising, helping him choose, no orders, no demands, no screaming for hurt. A soft voice, very passive, reflective, a new and strange power makes it stronger, makes it real and believable, embraceable.

No longer demanding, no longer frightful, still impossible to befriend, the demon voice now hides, silent day and night.

The spirit voice delivers its words. The passion reveals its heart. *We beat this monster together. Cat and Willow and K.O. will always be your family.*

The spell finally breaks, and Sonny believes it. Every day he swallows his meds, peeks into his mind, and cocks his ears, listens carefully to silence in his brain. No alien, no demon, no spook, and no screaming voice, all absent now, no distorted faces. Sonny wins, Doctor Cat wins. His first fight lasted eighty-nine brief seconds, the last one forty-one long months. Today the final bell rings, and Sonny raises his fists, a winner.

*

Almost ten months after Sonny began treatment, Cat prepares his release papers. Sonny remained in the hospital setting two-hundred ninety-six days. After the first ninety days, one day a week, K.O. or Willow escorted him out and let him run, and eat lunch, enjoy the freedom, but Cat maintained strict security.

Two of the five test patients reacted with extreme violence during this clinic group study. She stopped medications, and changed over to standard traditional psychotic chemistry, sent them back to their home doctors, but still monitors each one.

Traditional medications work to some degree, and have been stabilizer drugs for years. Each medication counteracts dysfunction and creates a passive state in the patients, but patients still have multiple social problems and lose memory, and can't read and retain well. It becomes an ongoing battle. If she stops the demons and stops the brain cell damage that occurs when vibrant hormone chemistry destroys neurons and proteins, then she reached one of her goals. She's ready to discharge Sonny, so he can make his own choices, take back his life, and move on with his career.

Sonny responded well after five months, shared everything, and cycled through an assortment of chemical mixes, a month or more at a time, although two produced such intense side-effects – itching, sleeplessness, weird dreams, muscle twitching – she stopped it after only one week, and another after three weeks. Sonny says he's ready, wants to start training again, and wants to feel the sun on his face every day, and no bar on the window when he opens his eyes.

Cat enters his room and asks, "Ready to go tomorrow?"

"Yup, already packed, got a strange feeling. All you doctors and nurses working on me … you look in a brain, you work on it, and you test it. Then you invent a tech-spook that will sit in a brain and send Wi-Fi waves out so you can figure it out. Kinda like mind reading, ain't it, in a way?"

"Good thing you ain't trying to take over our world Cat. You and Aaron, you're good enough, probably win." Sonny laughs out loud. "Could get me a good job as a future-teller, right? Knew all this mind reading was the answer, right from the start." He laughs again, and Cat joins him, as his theory may be true in some odd way of interpreting her work.

CAT-RON Technologies believes its microchip tests safely, and begins trials in less than a week. Sonny volunteered as its first client. Told Cat if she plants her Number 001 Micro-Spook in anyone except him, he'll send his demons after her. Cat and Sonny both cracked up at that idea, the laughter a huge pleasure after all this turmoil.

*

Tanya Porter, a big-hair, heavy-set, laughs-a-lot, jiggle-belly ward nurse Sonny knows well and likes leads him outside, sits him in the recreation space, an area surrounded by walls and containing one large window open to the outside but covered with steel bars. A place Sonny knows well, the exercise yard.

Doctor Cat enters, formally shakes his hand then Sonny folds her into an emotional hug. Cat finally breaks the embrace and signs his papers. "Good luck Sonny, and stay safe. I know Doctor Martin well. She's a great doctor and she'll do right by you, but if you need me, call me. I'll be here for you, anytime, day, or night." Cat hands Sonny a card.

Sonny examines a small green kitten embossed on its cover, opens it, reads her private cell number and private email. "Day or night Sonny, twenty-four-seven, don't hesitate," she says.

Sonny hugs Cat again, wraps his arms around her waist, and swings her in a circle, her feet floating out behind her. She's light as a feather and a captive in his freedom dance.

"Thank you, thank you, thank you Cat, you destroyed the demons."

"You did that yourself Sonny. We all just showed you the way." She pushes him toward the exit, gently. "Go Sonny, go live a good life, you earned it."

"If I call, will you run with me?"

"Absolutely, I'll even let you beat me once in a while." Both enjoy a laugh, doctor and patient, and two athletes locked in an indefinable bond much stronger than friendship.

Sonny holds out his hand. "Come sit with me a minute Cat, something I need to ask." Cat takes his arm and steps through an arch into walled section in the courtyard, finds a bench and they sit side by side.

"How is it you understand me so well Cat, and all us nut-kids? No one else does, very few care and most never even try. People like Morton and Burkhart, Anderson."

Cat looks at the ceiling, looks at the wall, and looks at the floor. She takes his hand in both of hers, and exhales. "Because I see and hear a demon too, Sonny. It emerged in college, but luckily, I was studying with Doctor Clark and Professor Whitetail. We caught it as it began and developed a treatment that works. It took us three years. I know what it does in your mind Sonny, what it feels like when you lose control."

"I've been there too, and faced that demon. It still haunts me occasionally, always will. It's not as strong as yours, never was, and only one haunting vision, but it's never my friend. I take medication every day just like you, and I run and workout. My spirit sister overpowers it, but it never leaves me alone. It constantly pesters me, pushes me toward violence."

Sonny widens his eyes then wraps his arms around her. "Oh no, no, no, Cat, of all the people in this world, you don't deserve that nightmare." A single tear runs down his cheek. Way down deep in the darkest portion of his soul, weak with almost no volume, a scratchy voice croaks. *You're almost out, almost free. She's an alien. She's lying. She feeds you poison.*

Sonny ignores it. His spirit brother speaks softly, but louder than his demon. *Believe in Cat. She will always remain your friend, and your spirit healer. Trust her as long as we live.*

"I'm not clear yet myself. We continuously adjust my medications, six years. Aaron treats me. You and I, we'll be the first Micro-Spook clients."

Sonny snaps his mind clear and cracks up. "Did you really name it that Cat?"

"You thought of it Sonny, why not, and you're our first live tester."

Cat struggles every day, like the people she heals, and wants her treatment for every mentally ill child or young adult in the world, and for Ferguson and Nickels, and others like them. She knows every human forms a genetically unique brain, and that every abnormal brain needs the right chemical mixture to stabilize it and keep the demons at bay.

Her unbounded enthusiasm and consuming passion drives her relentlessly toward that goal. Sonny helps her research every day, sharing his secrets and baring his soul.

*

Nurse Porter leads Sonny to an exit door a security guard unlocks then pushes open. Sonny steps through, Tanya follows and wraps Sonny up in two thick arms, kisses both cheeks, ruffles his hair.

"You be good Sonny, you're a great kid. Just get out and grab hold that life you got out there waiting. Just take it and run with it. Remember, it's your life. No claims on it, not even those demons or spooks can take it back. You beat them all. You own it now. Go have a great life, you're a sweet kid, never let that get away."

A bare rasp now, the mean voice struggles with its words, a grating whisper. *We're free. Come on, let's hurt someone!*

Sonny shakes his head, ignores the words. He achieved adulthood today. A child no longer exists in his body, more like a millennia of human experience packed into twenty years and a few extra months.

"You keep talking like that, I'll be back at sundown to take you out dancing Tanya, big old buffed-out husband you got or not." He looks out the window, and smiles at the sun.

The darklings vanished and Sonny took back his life. Five fights, five wins, he beat the odds and knocked out the demons. His official fight record now reads four and zero, undefeated. His final bout earns no tally in the ring, but K.O marked it on the gym wall yesterday, large silver 'S' shapes overlapped like Olympic rings, a great big Five and Zero.

A gray steel door swings open and Sonny emerges. The door clicks shut behind him, this time locking him out. Sonny won the fight, but a locked-down psyche ward gathers no crowds. This venue rings silent today. No clapping. No cheering. No demons.

Sonny Bones skips six concrete steps two at a time, laughs out loud, climbing up from the darkness. "Weak-ass aliens can't take a punch. Lightweight demons can't fight worth a damn. Who's next? Bring it on!! Give me a haunt to hit!!!"

The haunt hovers in darkness behind the jacks, hiding until Sonny drops his guard again. Patient.

Two quick jabs and an uppercut, two more jabs, and a right cross, Sonny spars with the wind. "Sonny Bones one, space aliens zero. Copy that down somewhere."

*

He climbs into his truck, slams the door then opens it and shuts it gently. "Sorry." He twists the key and its engine rumbles off the gravel.

Sonny heads north eleven miles and pulls into his camp, unrolls and assembles his tent. He sits down on his stump and laughs, begins building a fire. He picks up a dead limb, busts it against the tree trunk, picks up another, busts it, carefully feeds the flames.

Listen. I'm your spirit brother, your guiding voice. I'm here to help, not hurt. No screams, no orders, just advice. You may always choose for yourself.

The spirit purrs, the meek voice he remembers from his childhood, the one he imagines may resemble a sibling if one exists somewhere in the world his birth mother inhabits. Sonny opens his mind, places his spirit brother in a trust box beside Willow, Cat, and K.O, and his only physical trust card, Lisa. He peeks in his mind again and examines another box, a spirit brother he decides with no true evidence to support it.

Undecided for now where Melanie fits. She's a nut-kid like him, and he has no frame of reference for other mental patients and trust yet. He shuffles through the deck, finds Melanie. She wobbles in her box a few seconds then runs up the line and emerges as the first nut-kid trust card. He deals his spirit brother the next face card but a queen shows up, maybe his sister. Puzzled, he examines it carefully, concentrates, but it says nothing.

It always sounded like a brother in the months past when it argued quietly with his demons, a soft voice like the spirit guide he remembers from his childhood. He thinks of it as a brother, and now believes it sounds like a boy but might be a girl, impossible to tell its gender so it could be a sister. He embraces it anyway and begins loving it like family. Sonny peeks at his spirit card again. It transforms itself into an ace, with a genderless face in its center.

Sonny moves its card up to the head of the deck, but the card evaporates and then materializes. The spirit card hovers above his trust cards, neither replacing nor hiding behind his trust friends, it simply appears as vapor, as a vague spirit with no pain, but a wispy smile turns up its lips whenever Sonny sees it. It sits in his mind now constantly and offers no threat.

He likes this spirit brother or sister that finally returned from its hiding tree. He gathers his patience, knowing its encouraging voice will tell him whom it represents when time stops for one day and his personal spirit claims its totem.

Nearly translucent with no face now, a separate vaporous phantom hides deep in a lightless corner of his mind down behind the no-trust jacks, a dark curtain shielding it from sight. Almost too soft to notice, but slowly collecting its meanness, a space demon whispers, its voice a bare echo in his brain. *You don't need the meds. You're healed now. Stop eating the poison.*

Sonny glances up into his mind, "Fuck off spook. You don't scare me anymore. You're nothing but hot air, can see right through you. You're gas! You're empty! You can't hurt anyone. We don't believe what you tell us." Sonny stands, busts two more dead limbs against his tree trunk.

We're stronger than you. We'll be back. The demon voice argues, but its scream and its influence elude it now. Doctor Cat drained its power and stifled its demonic presence.

Pay no attention to the demon. It lost its abilities. Ace squats in his mental video and smiles.

His personal spirit voice gains strength and deepens. Sonny finally concludes it's a brother, as he imagined the first time he heard it. Firelight sparks in his eyes and a smile brightens his face as Sonny bounces up on his toes, dances in a figure-eight and loops around his campfire, raises both fists above his head and claims his reward – a new life without fear.

Leaves crackle behind him. He spins in place, fright-eyes glance back at the trail then relax and exude warmth and a welcome.

A long brown ponytail flips over one shoulder, a silver feather hangs from each ear, and a turquoise necklace sparkles in the firelight. The sweetness of peach and a taste of honey fill two holes in his brain. The scent of violets floats on a light breeze, and a complete absence of rage greets his first physical trust friend.

Lisa smiles and lights up the night. "Hello Sonny Bones."

:: And Linda ::

Joined at the hip thru an emotion impossible to define
but tragic nonetheless - together we grieve our son forever:

Shawn Paul Delorey
(1989 - 2013)

A true champion in every sense of the word and the
inspiration for the character 'Sonny Bones' in the novel
"Shuffle an Impulse".

Excellence in and dedication to athlete competition tempered
his battle with a major mental disorder. In his own words,
Shawn described the symptoms and hallucinations that help
bring this story alive as he struggled for years with street drug
addiction and abuse to release the pain and anguish a brain
chemistry dysfunction brings out in a mind.
Together, we created the character 'Sonny Bones'.

:: Shawn Quote ::

"I want to tell this story, so it will help other kids
understand mental illness."

We all love you, and miss you Shawn ... RIP